Dauntless Summer

Dauntless Summer

HARMONY OF SEASONS
BOOK TWO

EMMALINE STRANGE

For Mr. Strange, always my safe place to land.

One

osmo never lingered in the temple.

Ever.

He didn't linger the first summer he'd woken up after being cursed, and he didn't wish to linger on the four hundredth summer, either. As soon as he felt blood moving in his veins, felt the heat of the sun on his skin, he climbed down from his plinth and fled the temple and its island without so much as looking at the statues of his brothers. He spent his precious time awake deep in the underbelly of Papia City, where it was easy to lose himself among the thousands of other people. None of them knew him, but they welcomed him. They embraced him. They respected him and, over the last several decades, had come to revere him a little bit.

When summer ended, he would return to the temple, only when he had to. Only when the pull in his chest, drawing him back to his cursed resting place, was too painful to ignore. Cosmo had no idea what all his brothers got up to, when they had their turns awake. He could honestly say he'd never given it much thought. He never *allowed* himself to give it much thought. Contemplating his brothers and what had happened between them…what had almost happened to Cosmo himself…It didn't change things. It didn't make anything better to dwell upon the past, so he did his best not to.

For four hundred somewhat happy summers Cosmo had worked, drunk, feasted, and fucked, only resting when he was ready to keel over where he stood. He didn't think about the past, nor the future—except insofar as it affected his duties as the god of summer.

It was a *good* system. It had served Cosmo very well for four hundred years.

Until this year—until he'd woken from his cursed slumber to find his usually crypt-like temple awfully crowded. Crowded with more than the lichen covered statues of his brothers. There were three flesh and blood men here, only one of whom he recognized: Auro, his youngest brother. Sweet, gentle, Auro—who Cosmo had long since accepted he'd never see again.

Cosmo's heart stopped at the sight of him, four hundred years of grief hitting him at once. Like a house falling on top of him, like an avalanche. The three men hadn't noticed him yet—which was all to the good, because it gave Cosmo a moment to get a grip on himself, to decide if what he was seeing even made sense.

It didn't, actually. This should not have been possible. Had Cosmo ever, in all of his cursed months encased in stone, dreamed, he would have assumed he was now. But he never had, so he wasn't now. Even so, Cosmo found the flesh of his own thigh and gave it a hearty pinch. It hurt.

This was real.

Auro seated on the ground before him would have been strange enough, but the peculiar tableau of Auro naked in the arms of two beautiful men didn't make *any* sense—no matter how long he stared. Cosmo swallowed around the lump in his throat, doing his best to fight the impulse to flee before they saw him.

"Can someone please tell me what the fuck is going on?" Cosmo asked them at last.

One of the men on the ground handed Auro his own cloak, and Auro sprang to his feet. He wrapped the deep crimson fabric around his waist, and before Cosmo could say something clever, or anything at all, Auro collided with his chest, wrapping his arms around Cosmo's middle to squeeze the life out of him.

Cosmo allowed himself a five count to enjoy his brother's warm hug before prying Auro's arms off and taking a few steps back. It was all he could manage, before the questions and the prevailing sense of dread began to invade. He ruffled Auro's hair, which Cosmo realized had faded from its natural vibrant pink to something far plainer, far duller, a pale ashy auburn that didn't suit him. Cosmo's pulse raced. What had Auro been saying right before Cosmo had announced his presence? Auro thought his grace was...*gone?* Cosmo did not think *that* was possible, either, but as he held Auro at arm's length, inspecting his familiar face, he thought, *Well, what the fuck do I know?*

"What has happened to you, little brother? All the color has bled out of you."

"I have so much to tell you," said Auro breathlessly. "It's difficult to know where to start."

"Why not start with your two handsome companions," said Cosmo, and at last he seemed able to summon a smile. That was good; it meant he was regaining some sort of sense.

Auro's pale, round face flushed splotchy pink, so at least he hadn't lost all his vigor.

Cosmo cocked his head to the side, squinting. He realized something was different about his brother.

"This...this is—"

"Alexios," finished the younger of the two men, stepping forward to stand at his brother's elbow. He was tall and lanky, with pretty lips and soft doe's eyes. "I'm Alexios."

"Ah," said Cosmo, understanding at once. He turned to Auro. "Well done."

"What?" Alexios asked, looking between them.

"Nothing at all," said Cosmo, but he winked at Auro.

Auro looked mortified.

Cosmo turned his attention to the other man, who was older, and even more striking than the youthful Alexios, despite the fierce scowl that tangled the sharp lines of his face. Cosmo swept his eyes over him from head to toe, from his shining dark hair to his long, slightly bowed legs. "And you are?"

The man didn't answer, but if anything frowned even *harder*. Alexios spoke for him instead. "This is Leofric," he said. "Captain of my personal guard."

Cosmo pulled his glance back to Alexios, surprised. "You're *that* Alexios?"

Auro frowned. "You know him?"

"Not personally," said Cosmo, taking a step toward Alexios. The silent Leofric tightened his stance, but did not move. "But everyone in Papia City knows the crown prince." He gave Alexios a small, graceful bow. "Your Royal Highness."

Auro's frown deepened, too. Cosmo tended to have that effect on people. "You're familiar with the city?"

"Of course," said Cosmo. Puzzled, he asked, "Where do you spend the spring, when you're awake?"

Auro looked down at his feet and mumbled, "Here."

"You mean *here*, here? You stay in the forest? All by yourself?" This couldn't be true—his heart ached at the thought of Auro being so isolated.

Auro nodded. "Where do you spend your time?"

Cosmo buried his concern for his brother's loneliness, for

now, and summoned his most enigmatic smile. "Oh, you know...around."

Cosmo let his gaze flit from face to face, and all at once, he knew they were here to ask something of him. He narrowed his eyes. "Why—*how* are you here, little brother?" Cosmo found it difficult to say Auro's name aloud after so many years.

At first, Cosmo thought Auro wouldn't answer. He was silent so long, like he hadn't planned out what he needed to say. Then, he blurted, "We found a way to break the curse."

"Impossible," said Cosmo at once. With a roll of his eyes, he turned away. He should have known better than to entertain whatever mad notion had Auro waiting here for him. It should not have surprised him, to find Auro changed from the boy Cosmo had known. They'd been separated four hundred years. Cosmo and his brothers had been strangers far longer than they'd ever been a family. Despite the fact that it was only Auro standing here before him, it was as if Cosmo could feel the judgmental gaze of Cedras and Kryos, too, the cold marble statues glaring at him from their plinths. "Even if what you say *is* possible, I'm afraid I must decline."

"What? How could—"

"I'm not interested."

"You're not—Cosmo, be serious. It has to be *all* of us."

Cosmo was already backing away, rocking up onto the balls of his feet. "All of us?" He laughed, while his eyes desperately searched for an escape. "Well, then, I'm afraid your plan is doomed from the start, little brother."

As he turned on his tail to flee the temple, the statues, and Auro's desperate face, a large hand shot out and wrapped its fingers around Cosmo's wrist. He'd almost forgotten about Leofric, who'd stood by as silent and still as if he were a statue himself. Before Cosmo could even open his mouth to protest, his grace burst from him like a comet, searing through his veins to explode out of his skin. He hadn't even meant to summon it—and usually he *couldn't,* not this soon after waking, not that much power. But somehow, it responded so readily to the boorish grab of this presumptuous stranger.

The man cried out, clutching his hand, which smoked and blistered, scorched by Cosmo's fury, and fear. Their eyes met, and the searing disgust reflecting back at him stole his breath. Pulse hammering, Cosmo shaped his face into a scornful mask, winked at Leofric, and left the temple. Seeing the irate, stricken expression on the man's face had felt good. He felt like himself again, thinking of it, as he made his way through, the forest without looking back.

Almost.

The posting was supposed to be a simple one. A soft service with outrageous wages, playing nursemaid to a spoiled, pampered prince. Prowling the grounds of a royal villa and trailing after a princeling could not *be* more different from Leofric's life with the Sokolian army. And that was the point.

Leofric had never known another life, besides the life of a soldier. He and Hamalcar had played at war since they'd been old enough to grip a stick in one hand, and they'd enlisted in the legion of Sokol together on their sixteenth birthday. For fourteen years they'd marched, slept, ate, breathed, and *lived* that life, and they'd done it side by side, as they had done everything since their mother brought them into the world. If you'd asked Leofric then, he would have assumed he and Hamalcar would die one day side by side as well.

But they hadn't.

Hamalcar was gone, and Leofric remained. It had been three years, and still he felt his brother's loss, daily, like someone ripping a rib from his skeleton, only for him to regrow it each night and start the whole thing again the next morning. His guilt, the responsibility for his brother's death, it was all he had left of Hamalcar now. That, and the vow they'd made each other, one drunken night when they'd first enlisted. It felt like a thousand years ago.

Leofric had fought his way to Hamalcar's side when he saw him fall, and held him as he died, the two of them a small calm eye in the center of the storm of the raid upon their army's camp. His brother's face, so like his own, had twisted, grotesque in its agony, until Leofric had promised he remembered the vow they'd made so many years before. He promised Hamalcar he'd honor the oath they'd sworn, and all the tension had melted from his brother's face. He died at peace.

For that, Leofric was grateful. And for the family he now had, because of his vow. The people he'd sworn to protect, and cherish, and care for. Laela, Hamalcar's widow, and Sorex, their son, were his responsibility now.

It was them he thought of, in difficult moments. When his grief threatened to overwhelm him, or when he had to follow the unruly prince Alexios around the villa to head off his many varied escape attempts.

And now.

Because, while he had selected this posting for the promise of its relative safety and high wages, Leofric had already found himself in several life-threatening situations, and he'd only been here in Papia for a single season. It seemed every single day brought some new, unprecedented disruption, from assassination attempts to the discovery that his charge's lover was a literal god.

And that was only the beginning, apparently, because here he stood, witnessing the reunion between Auro, god of spring, and his own brother, god of summer. He couldn't help but feel a surge of envy. Auro had thought, for four hundred years, that his brothers were lost to him. He had grieved their loss, mourned them, resigned himself that he'd never again lay eyes upon their faces. And here, now, beyond all logic, Auro and one of said brothers embraced, reunited.

Leofric hadn't known what to expect from Auro's brothers. Through his time guarding the crown prince, he'd come to know the boy's paramour fairly well. He was gentle, soft spoken, and kind. Perhaps a *bit* dangerous—he was a god, after all—but it was only a deeply protective nature that ever roused his anger.

This brother of his though. This...*Cosmo*, was about as different from Auro as it was possible for two men to be. He was thin and angular where Auro was soft, loud and brazen where Auro was timid. Freckled and tanned where Auro was milk-pale.

Leofric didn't think he'd ever seen a person with quite so many freckles before—it was as if there were more spots than unspotted skin on Cosmo, and so much of that skin was on display. He dressed in a thin linen wrap about the hips and little else, though he bedecked himself in more jewelry than the queen. With his fiery head of hair, every part of him screamed for attention.

Leofric didn't like it. He did not like the way that the freckles and the fiery hair drew his eyes, drew his focus. It was as if he could not look away.

He also didn't like the flippant way Cosmo had dismissed his brother's anguish, his pleas for help ending their shared curse. And, of course, he didn't like how Cosmo had lashed out and attempted to burn off his hand.

"Apologies," said Auro, for the hundredth time.

"It's fine," Leofric gritted out. But it wasn't. His right hand was his sword hand. Without it, how he could he perform his duties? How could he protect his charge, the prince? Leofric trained with his off-hand from time to time, of course, but it was the right hand that thought for him, protected him in battle. He flexed his fingers, pain searing up his arm as the silk bandages scraped against the broken, cooked skin. Leofric exhaled through his nose and did it again. And again. He had to know and expect the pain, in order to be able to fight through it. To work with it, he had to embrace it. By the fourth time he made a fist, he felt better, though the agony had not lessened.

"Stop that," said Auro, watching as the wounds began to weep through the thin fabric. "You need to rest it for it to heal."

Auro might have lost his...magic—his *grace*, he called it—but he was still gifted with healer's hands. He'd slathered Leofric's palm with a thick, cool ointment before wrapping it in silk bandages. "I didn't think he'd do something like that," said Auro, adjusting the bandage. He fussed over Leofric's hand for a few more minutes before tucking the edge of the bandage neatly out of sight.

Leofric shifted his weight a bit on the stool, looking down at his hand "Perhaps I should have thought before I grabbed him."

"Still," said Auro.

His Royal Highness, Prince Alexios, paced back and forth beside them. "Hello?" Said Alexios. "Not to minimize your injury, Leofric, but there are far more peculiar things to discuss."

"Such as?"

Alexios stalked over and gripped Auro's shoulder, giving him a little shake. "How—*how* are you still here?"

Leofric had been curious about this as well. Less than half a year ago, he would have said the entire notion of Gods and curses was pure nonsense. Now, here he sat, curious as to why the prince's pink haired lover had *not* transformed into a marble statue before their very eyes. How things had changed.

To hear Auro tell it, he and his brothers, gods of the four seasons, had been cursed to turn to stone, with only one awake at a time. Each brother only walked free during the season he ruled. Auro and Alexios had been working to break the curse, to free Auro and his brothers their eternal imprisonment.

Alexios had expected to carry on with that mission when Auro turned to stone at spring's end. Both he and Leofric had not planned on seeing Auro again until spring the following year. But here he stood, flesh and blood, before them.

Auro twisted his fingers over each other, studying them intensely—and thereby avoiding looking at Alexios. "I'm not certain. When I was unconscious, I had...well—"

"Had what?"

"A vision, perhaps? A dream? I don't know. I've never felt anything like it."

"A vision of what?"

Auro hesitated. "I think...I *know* it's something I need to talk to Cosmo about, first."

Alexios cupped Auro's cheeks and kissed the tip of his nose. "Then we'd better go find him, right?"

Leofric sighed, staring down at his burned hand, wondering how fast he'd regain the ability to grip a sword.

Two

Cosmo interlocked his fingers, reaching his hands up, up, up, toward the sky. The stretch in his back was divine after nine long months of confinement. For the first time, he allowed himself to wonder how his brothers felt, upon rising each year. Did they feel it? The amount of time that had passed between sleeping and waking?

Cosmo did.

Or, he *felt* like he could feel it. He wasn't certain there was a difference, in the end. But he certainly felt the relief of being able to stretch his limbs, fill his lungs with air, to eat, drink, dance, fuck and *move* again. And to swim. This year, though, the relief was tainted. No matter how hard he tried to banish it, Auro's wan face kept materializing in his mind's eye.

However, a good swim never failed to clear his head, not once in four hundred years. He'd always started his summers this way, even *before*.

He waited in the shadows of a quay, watching the moon make its lazy trek across the sky. Only when he was certain he was alone did he creep from the shadows and leave his garb in a careless pile on the pier. The subligaria, the jewelry, none of it mattered. Cosmo had learned that early on. One year, in a drunken fit of rage and bitterness at summer's end, he'd tossed it all in a fire and walked back to the temple stark naked. Cosmo had then climbed up onto his plinth and adopted a *very* lewd pose while he waited for the curse to take hold and turn him to stone. His last conscious thought was *My brothers can kiss my freckled ass, the shits—*

But he'd woken the following summer, same as ever: dressed and glittering head to heel with the baubles he'd burned, holding the goblet aloft to the heavens that he'd kicked across the temple last year before returning to sleep. He'd learned a hard lesson, that year: nothing would ever change, and nothing he did outside of his sacred duties really mattered. The only piece he took care with was a roughly made golden ring. It was a heavy, clumsy thing, formed in the likeness of three arrows braided together. Now, Cosmo twisted it around the ring finger on his right hand as he prowled naked to the edge of the pier. This particular quay was always quiet this time of night. It was private, where the royal family kept its pleasure vessels. The entire bay formed a bowl in the side of the mountains, and this quay sat on the very far edge, with only a sheer face of rock abutting it on one side.

This was where Cosmo slipped into the water. His eyes had always adjusted swiftly to the dark, and with the moon high above casting beaten silver shadows on the water around him, Cosmo had light aplenty. The first night of summer, the first swim of summer, this was when Cosmo truly felt he knew who he was. It woke him up, it cleansed him, it offered the seductive promise of a fresh new start.

He swam as often as he could each year, of course. Only ever alone, only ever at night, and it was always the way he reclaimed himself a bit, shedding the trappings of his persona. In the water, in the dark, alone, he was no longer a god. He was just a man. Just Cosmo. Nothing could ever match the euphoria he felt as he dove off the pier the first night of a new summer. It had never dulled, that feeling, and for that, Cosmo was grateful. The cool salty water cleansed all of it away—all the things he woke thinking about, past and future both. Or, at least, it usually did.

By the time he climbed out of the bay it was threatening dawn, and Cosmo was frustrated. His lungs burned, his legs felt filled with lead, but the tightness had not left his jaw and the weight remained upon his shoulders. It figured, five minutes' reunion with Auro, and Cosmo's carefully built acceptance of his lot in life came crashing own around his ears. It wasn't just Auro that occupied Cosmo's mind; for whatever reason, he couldn't stop thinking of Leofric, the guard. The sound of his pained cry, the way his face had twisted in anger, it would not leave Cosmo, itching at him like a pebble in his sandal, and he could not for the life of him figure out why. Cold and irritated, he wrapped the subligaria around his waist, donned his jewelry, and made his way up the quay toward Lapis.

Cosmo had been coming to Lapis for almost two hundred summers. In that time, it had known several names, had been held by several different masters, but it had never closed down. It was the sort of business that would thrive in any port city, no matter the political or economic climate: a pleasure hall.

Over the last two hundred years, as the business had changed hands, one thing was certain: Cosmo came with the keys to the place. It amused him, living as an enigmatic open secret. He would arrive each year on the doorstep of Lapis and be welcomed in, and then mysteriously disappear at the end of summer.

It would seem that with each passing year, his mystique and allure grew. And, if he didn't mind saying so, that was good for business. *He* was good for business. Lapis was more like an erotic inn than a true brothel, though of course it was that too. While there were whores aplenty, many of the patrons came with a spouse, or paramour—or paramours, or alone—and never glanced at the delights on offer, let alone took one of the inn's employees upstairs. The atmosphere itself was heavy with lust and want, electrified by the desire of its occupants, and even the staunchest monogamist would enjoy entertaining their lover in one of the club's many private alcoves. There were workers there to entertain guests, of course, traditional for any brothel, but Lapis also boasted shows, masques, parties, good wine and better music. Rich food. Dancing. Naked people. All the things Cosmo loved most.

He kept a room at the very top of the building, removed a bit from the bawdy ruckus down below, but close enough that he could take part whenever he wished. It had a balcony from which he could perform his duties as god of summer, luxurious bedding for entertaining lovers in private, and when his body absolutely demanded it, sleeping. Cosmo's grace allowed him to offer a variety of helpful services to the people of Papia City, and with a bit of clever showmanship, he'd built himself a reputation as something of a fertility priest. People traveled great distances for an audience with him, which ensured that every summer Lapis was full of patrons. Senelle, the current master of the establishment, was truly grateful for Cosmo's presence. He had all the wine he could drink, food he could eat, and his bed was never empty.

Why would he want anything to change? It was a good life. It was a simple life—as simple as the life of a cursed demigod could be, anyway. It was a life Cosmo had carefully built over the course of centuries. He liked this life. Cosmo was not suited to rule, as he'd foolishly thought in his younger days. He was not suited to take on the mantle of a full-blooded god, and the distance of years and this life he'd built helped him see that. In that way, he was almost grateful for the curse, and everything that had led to it.

Auro was mad to think things should change—even if they *could,* which he still doubted. All of them had learned they weren't fit to walk the earth together, and Ozias had paid for that lesson with his life. Why would they want to tread that path again? Cosmo certainly didn't. He was happy with things as they were.

As he approached the door to Lapis, however, he felt a twist of guilt like a knife in his ribs, Auro's pleading face again swimming before him. It took a few goblets of wine, coupled with the sights and sounds of Lapis overwhelming his senses before it dulled to a manageable ache. Cosmo let himself be absorbed by the human tide and slipped silently into the crowd.

Without a prince to guard, Leofric had more spare time than he knew what to do with. He didn't care for it. He and Auro had been staying at the royal family's domus in Papia City for three days, following any and all rumors that might lead them to Auro's errant brother, the elusive Cosmo.

His Royal Highness had ridden into the city with them, and instructed the captain of the city watch and the staff at the domus that Leofric's commands should be regarded as the prince's own, before he returned to the royal villa in the countryside several hours outside the city. He'd also instructed Leofric that guarding Auro was as important as guarding Alexios's own person, and a sacred command from his charge was not to be ignored. When he had sworn his oath before the king of Papia, Leofric had pledged his life to the prince's.

With his honor in the balance, Leofric did not enjoy being parted from Prince Alexios. It left his stomach tight with nerves, and his hackles up at all times. There were plenty of competent guardsmen surrounding His Highness at the villa, but they didn't understand the dangers lurking the way Leofric did. They hadn't seen what he'd seen in Neossós, had not seen what the sorcerer Janus was capable of. But there was nothing for it. Alexios had been adamant, and Leofric could not refuse a direct order. He insisted that Leofric was the only one he could trust to comb the city for Cosmo relatively undetected. His highness would be recognized in any of the inns, taverns and market streets. On the other hand, in plain garb, with his hair left hanging loose to cover his tattoo, Leofric was no different from the thousands of other men walking the cobbled streets.

"More importantly," Alexios had said, "You're the only one I can trust to watch out for Auro."

This much was true. Auro had spent the last four hundred years hiding alone in the forest. He was sweet, kind, and all together far too trusting for the rougher underbelly of Papia City's docks, especially with his godly power dormant. Together, Leofric and Auro had been asking after Cosmo for days, to no avail. Leofric had begun gently suggesting they give up and return to the villa to regroup—he could hardly abandon his post indefinitely, and frankly, he wasn't nearly as concerned with the breaking of ancient curses as he was with fulfilling his own sworn duty as Prince Alexios's guard. Auro's misery at the suggestion was palpable, though, and it filled Leofric with guilt.

He liked Auro, and of course the prince loved him dearly. It was hard to watch him so forlorn and suffering, moping about the domus, so Leofric allowed himself to be talked into following one more lead. Auro suggested they seek out a young man called Gaius Ursus, who was a friend of Prince Alexios. His Highness had appointed Gaius the magister of roads in Papia, and more importantly, he was an unrepentant gossip, who boasted knowledge of everything and everyone in Papia City. "He *must* know something of Cosmo," said Auro desperately. "He must."

Leofric wasn't so sure, but Auro's sad, earnest face was difficult to refuse. They could hardly confess the true nature of their mission, but after some gentle probing and pointed questions, Gaius told them of a rumor he'd heard—a prophet of fertility who only resided in Papia for the summer months, who operated out of a dockside club called Lapis. "My aunt was thought to be barren," he confided. "But one summer she and her husband spent the night with this prophet. This was ten years ago. Now I have six cousins, and my aunt and her husband are more in love with every passing day."

Auro thought this sounded promising; he insisted that, like himself, his brothers lived only to serve others. Leofric had his doubts, but they had exhausted all their other leads. Papia City's markets had been built into the basin of a mountainside, with three wide descending levels. Lapis was situated in the lowest market—dubbed the Salt Market—closest to the water. Despite his centuries upon the earth, there was an innocence to Auro that told Leofric he might be surprised when he discovered what sort of "club" in which his brother now resided, but he kept such thoughts to himself.

As Leofric had suspected, Lapis was a place like a thousand others, full of sultry music and heavy smoke and people groping one another in shadowy corners. It was, perhaps, an echelon above its peers in terms of cleanliness, but otherwise, the hallmarks of the brothel were the same at Lapis as they were anywhere. Leofric swept his gaze over the writhing bodies who drank and fucked and laughed. It had been years since he'd visited a place like this. Three years, to be exact, but he was no stranger to a pillow house. Leofric had learned at an early age that his tastes and proclivities weren't the sort one could openly flaunt and court, especially not in the kingdom of Sokol. While living and bathing and bunking with his brothers in arms had provided its fair share of opportunity, there were times when the efficiency of flesh exchanged for coin had its advantages.

He parted the crowd with his scowl above Auro's head, and despite the heat, he wore gloves to cover the bandage on his sword hand. He could still fight if he had to, though his hand was stiff and painful, but he didn't need a drunken fool thinking he made an easy target. Leofric kept his gloved hands clasped at the small of his back, as he'd been taught. Never, not once, did he let one twitch toward the pommel of his sword.

Never draw your sword unless you mean to use it.

Never touch your sword unless you mean to draw it.

Imperator Hamate had told him that, every day, for two hundred days. It was sound advice for navigating potential threats in a crowd. Being a guard was very different from being a soldier. It was a hundred parts waiting and watching for every one spent fighting, and even then, it was more about avoiding a fight than winning one.

The imperator of the Sokolian army was a hard man, but fair and level headed. After his brother's death, Leofric had approached him and laid out the facts. He would never desert the legion, of course—but equally sacred to him was the vow he'd sworn his brother. He asked the Imperator what he would do, were he in Leofric's place. It took months for them to arrive at a solution, during which Leofric continued his duties marching with the legion, defending Sokol's borders from the same Órnian troops that had killed his brother, fearing that soon he'd join Hamalcar in the afterlife and leave his family vulnerable, his vow unfulfilled. Then, at last, an opportunity presented itself.

You're a good soldier, and a better man, Imperator Hamate had said. *The King of Papia has need of a good man, as it happens.*

Before he'd been appointed imperator, Hamate had served in the Sokolian King's personal guard, so he knew what he was about. For two hundred days the imperator had trained Leofric in the ways of protecting royalty. When Leofric had at last arrived in Papia, King Nelios had welcomed him warmly. He was an old friend of Hamate's, and Sokolian himself—a legend, if Leofric was being honest. He could not deny that he'd been more than a bit dazed to actually meet the hero of a hundred stories Leofric had heard while marching in the legion. King Nelios assured Leofric that guarding his son, Prince Alexios, would be hardly any trouble at all, when compared with the dangerous life of a legionary.

Since that day, Leofric had lost count of the number of times King Nelios had been proven a liar.

A crowd had gathered toward the center of the brothel's rather grand central hall, watching hungrily as three people copulated on a raised dais. Two naked, muscular men turned an enormous crank beside the them, which spun the dais so the watchers could see the three lovers from every angle. On the spinning platform, a gorgeous woman rode a man's face, grinding eagerly against him. With a start, Leofric realized the hands gripping tight to her thighs were completely covered in freckles, and the head between her legs had a familiar striking head of flame-colored hair. Leofric narrowed his eyes, reflecting that Auro had been partially right—his brother *was* servicing others.

He glanced down at Auro, whose green eyes were wide, round as coins, his cheeks as red as his brother's hair. Enough was enough. After scanning the crowd for any imminent threats, Leofric strode through the people to confront the men who spun the crank which turned the dais. He ordered them, in the name of his Royal Highness, to stop. It took a while for the lovers on display to realize they had stopped spinning, so enthralled were they in each other's bodies. The woman astride Cosmo's face reached her climax, face upturned rapturously toward the ceiling. Whatever Cosmo's tongue did between her legs must have been exquisite; it was a wonder he didn't suffocate when her thighs clamped down around his head. The third performer, a man pumping himself between Cosmo's legs, hit his own peak shortly thereafter. They disentangled from one another, panting, as the crowd applauded and cheered their display.

Cosmo sat up, his lips smeared and glistening, and wiped his mouth on the back of a freckled hand. He stretched his arms over his head, arching his back as if he were waking up in the privacy of his own chambers, confident and unabashed—naked except for the golden bangles and chains dangling from his wrists, his thighs, his ankles. A group swarmed up to him, helping Cosmo into an orange robe so sheer and thin it was like he shrugged on a dressing gown of sunlight. Someone offered him a goblet of wine, into which he poured a few droplets from a small glass phial.

Every movement was a seduction, thought Leofric in distaste, watching Cosmo thread his way through the crowd, stopping to trade whispers, touches and even kisses as he went. The robe was so thin it left nothing to the imagination. It couldn't even obscure the pattern of freckles on his bare chest, let alone the shape of his body, or the shadow of his spent cock between his legs. Leofric felt his cheeks heating as he watched lewd display of Cosmo among through the people who stared at him worshipfully, begging with their eyes for the favor of his smile, or a touch of his hand. His bright hazel eyes were heavy lidded as they swept the room, and locked onto Leofric's. They widened, briefly, in surprise, the soft sensual smile slipping from his lips.

But only for a moment. Cosmo approached him, his face flushed, his red hair sweat dampened and curling over his forehead, down around his ears. "Hello," he said, cautious and wary. He hadn't seen Auro yet, and it was like Leofric could see Cosmo's mask as he hitched it back into place, smiling crookedly at him. "I'm surprised to see you again," he said. "I do believe Senelle offers special rates to members of His Highness's guard."

Leofric did his best to keep his face neutral, to ignore Cosmo's attempts to goad him. He slid a step to the side, allowing Auro to come forward. Cosmo balked at once, shedding his seductive airs like a snake shedding its skin. He drew his arms up, wrapping them around his chest as if Auro's presence frightened him.

"Cosmo," said Auro at once, leaning in to be heard over the sounds of music and moaning that weighed heavily on the air. "Please. Come back to the villa with us. I have so much to tell you. I've missed you! Haven't...haven't you missed me at all?"

A shadow crossed over Cosmo's face. "Of *course*, I have," he said, his voice dropping to a whisper, like what he admitted was a shameful secret. "I just...never thought I'd see you again, little brother."

"Nor I you," said Auro earnestly, reaching out to seize Cosmo's wrist. Leofric noted sourly that Auro was not burned for the crime, though in fairness, Cosmo did appear somewhat stricken by his brother's touch. "Please—just let me explain."

"There's nothing to explain" said Cosmo flatly. He twisted out of Auro's grasp. "You figured out some way to stay awake, but you lost whatever remained of your grace in the process. That's not a trade I would ever make."

"Just come back with us tonight," Auro begged. "Just let me explain before you say no."

"And why should I?" Cosmo turned away, preparing to lose himself once again in the crowd of revelry. "I already have everything I could ever want."

Leofric had heard and seen enough. He opened his mouth to tell Auro they should forget this foolishness and return home, but what came out was, "I can have this *establishment* shut down faster than you could spit. And, if you search for another rock to crawl under, I will follow you there. I will follow you around every *single* day until you turn back to stone. And I can do it again next year, and the year after. And the year after that until I perish of old age."

Both Auro and Cosmo startled, blinking at him with expressions so similar he finally saw the brotherly resemblance between them.

Leofric had certainly not meant to say all of that, but it was too late to recall the words, so he crossed his arms over his chest and said, "Or, you can come home with us now, and hear Auro out."

Cosmo, it appeared, knew when he was beaten. He dipped his head, though not without giving Leofric a cocky leer. "Fine," he said at last. "I must freshen up, and gather my things. Sit, have a drink. I'll be down soon."

Leofric herded Auro to a quiet table in the corner of the room, his eyes on Cosmo's back as he disappeared into the crowd.

Auro seemed unwilling to lift his eyes from his lap, an impulse Leofric understood. The sights and sounds of Lapis were overwhelming, to say the least. With his shoulders hunched and his pink hair faded away, Auro looked quite pitiful. Leofric knew he ought to say something, but his tongue felt thick and knotted up in his mouth. He signaled for wine, and a near naked server brought over a flagon and two cups.

After a few sips, Leofric finally said, "Well, we have found him."

"Yes," said Auro, his voice barely audible above the din.

Leofric waited for him to continue, but Auro stared down into his wine as if the higher mysteries of the earth were swirling around in its ruddy depths. "Something on your mind?" He prompted.

Auro looked up at last. "I did not expect him to say yes," he admitted.

Leofric considered this. "Well, he did." He gave Auro what he hoped was an encouraging sort of smile.

"And now I have to determine what to say," said Auro. He stared piteously at Leofric. "What do you say to someone after four hundred years?"

"I wouldn't pretend to know," he said. "But the fact that he so easily..." Leofric trailed away.

"So easily what?"

But Leofric ignored him. Why *had* Cosmo agreed so easily? The fear on his face at confronting Auro had been one of the only real things about him, if Leofric were any judge. "Son of—" Leofric rose and hurried through the club to the exit without bothering to see if Auro followed him.

Once outside, the fresh sea air cleared his head, for which Leofric was grateful. He gave the building's edifice a long look before cutting around the corner to a narrow, winding alley that separated Lapis from its nearest neighbor.

Just as Leofric rounded the corner, a shadowy figure dropped from a window ledge and landed on the cobble-stones. Leofric braced a hand on his hip, watching the figure's silhouette as it straightened itself out. "Lost?"

Cosmo whipped around, startled, and then cursed. "How did you know?"

Leofric shrugged. He'd had plenty of practice, chasing after Alexios when he'd first taken his post.

Cosmo glanced around Leofric, plainly searching for some point of escape, but Leofric planted himself square in his path. A few cautious steps put Cosmo close enough for Leofric to count the freckles on his nose. "You look awful proud of yourself."

Leofric sized up Cosmo, as he had sized up countless opponents over the years. "It's not every day one out-foxes a god."

Cosmo grinned, raising up on tip toe. "Well, you've caught me, Captain. What are you going to do about it?"

Leofric blinked, flustered, trying to think of something clever to say. The smell of Cosmo was *overpowering*. He opened his mouth to stammer a retort but then—

"Leofric?"

Leofric stepped back and turned, keeping Cosmo in his line of sight. He'd nearly forgotten about Auro.

He hurried toward them in the alleyway. "Cosmo? What are you doing out here?"

To Leofric's immense surprise, Cosmo looked ashamed for the first time all evening. Before he could speak Leofric said, "I think your brother is just...eager to get on home, so you two can talk."

Auro *beamed*, and Cosmo looked even more uncomfortable, which gave Leofric a sadistic sort of pleasure. "Shall we adjourn to the domus?" Auro asked.

"No," said Leofric at once. "We return to the royal villa."

"It's late and—"

"We've been too long away," said Leofric. "It's only a few hours' ride."

"Don't you miss your prince, little brother?" Asked Cosmo, who'd plainly already recovered from his momentary guilt. He sidled up to Leofric. "Or perhaps there's someone *you* can't wait to get back to, Captain?"

Leofric ignored Cosmo's prodding and they set off up the street. It was early enough in the season that the night air blew fresh, cool, and crisp off the bay. It billowed around them as they walked, pressing the sheer chiffon fabric of Cosmo's robe against his skin. It clung to every line of his body, showing every dip, and curve. "Perhaps you'd care to actually dress, before we depart," Leofric said.

Cosmo caught his eye, the smirk still playing on his pouty lips. "I am dressed."

Leofric clenched his jaw, turned on his heel and stalked off, leaving the godling brothers to hurry after him. Auro at least seemed just as eager to leave the overwhelming sights of the pleasure hall behind, for which Leofric was grateful. He felt flush, nearly feverish despite the salty breeze. The sooner they were outside the city, back behind the walls of the royal villa, the better.

On their way out of the city, they stopped at the domus to gather their things and collect mounts from the stables. "Do you ride?" Leofric asked Cosmo.

"I do," he allowed. "But what if I have a change of heart halfway back to your villa? I might gallop off into the night—"

"*Cosmo*," Auro said, sounding embarrassed. "Please."

Leofric bowled over Cosmo before he could continue taunting them. "You can ride with me. We must make haste. I mislike being so exposed after dark."

"Funny," said Cosmo, plucking at the neck of his robe. "That's when I most like being exposed." He raked his eyes over Leofric, letting his gaze linger. The smile on his face was like honey, sticky sweet and messy. Cosmo seemed determined to snap Leofric's composure, but Leofric would not give him the satisfaction. Had Cosmo been a mortal prisoner, Leofric might have tied him up and tossed him over his horse's flanks like a sack of barley—but then, Cosmo wasn't *truly* a prisoner, and Leofric didn't understand his powers yet, not entirely. Cosmo's ability to burn on contact would make short work of ropes, at any rate. Come to think of it, he could probably overpower any captor, so why play this game? The only way Cosmo would accompany them would be if he did so willingly, and they all knew it. Leofric took a step away from

Cosmo, who'd been inching closer and closer as they stood in the dark stable discussing the matter. He stank of sex, smoke, and something else, something that Leofric couldn't place underneath the cloud of debauchery and excess that clung to his skin like perfume.

Flustered, Leofric turned away to saddle his horse, Lyra. When he was finished, he faltered again. He'd been about to boost Cosmo up into the saddle for them to ride double back to the villa. Cosmo was small-boned and light, would be easy for Leofric to lift. However, he wasn't certain there was any place on Cosmo that was safe to grab. Firstly, he did not wish to be burned again. His sword hand still throbbed with every movement, and he didn't want to injure it yet again. Secondly, the gauzy robe Cosmo wore provided as much of a barrier to his skin as morning mist. There was nowhere for Leofric to touch that wouldn't seem...untoward. Fortunately, Cosmo seemed to be done playing. He swung himself up into the saddle in a graceful cloud of orange whisps and the musical tinkling of his jewelry.

Auro had mounted up beside them, and without further discussion, they took off. When they reached the villa, Leofric hailed the night watchmen, and they raised the gate, watching from their post as Cosmo, Auro and Leofric passed beneath the curtain wall. The guards' stares lingered on Cosmo in his peculiar, indecent garb, but they held their tongues, for which Leofric was grateful. At this time of night, the stables were empty of staff, so Auro and Leofric put up their own mounts, and the sun was well toward rising by the time they crossed the threshold into the atrium.

Despite the hour, His Highness was still awake when they returned to his apartments. After greeting Auro with a thorough, *thorough* kiss, Alexios said, "Perhaps we should all get a bit of rest, and start fresh tomorrow?"

Leofric privately felt that *resting* was about the last thing

Auro and Alexios would do in bed together after several days apart, but he said, "Agreed."

Auro showed signs of wanting to push through, to begin immediately the process of repairing four centuries of familial hurt, but Alexios gave his arm a squeeze, and he closed his mouth. "Alright," he said finally. "Cosmo, will you please stay here tonight?"

"Hmm," said Cosmo, sidling up beside Leofric once again. "But where shall I lay my weary head?"

Leofric took a deep, steadying breath and let it hiss out slowly through his nose. "Come."

Without waiting to see if Cosmo followed, he strode across the sitting area of Prince Alexios's private apartments, his footsteps ringing across the marble. Opposite from his Highness's bed chambers were a collection of servants' quarters. After an assassin had made an attempt on Alexios's life this spring, Leofric had moved from the guards' barracks on the villa grounds into these modest, but spacious, rooms with beds and even a small bathing chamber. Alexios might be a prince, but he wasn't the kind to need a flock of servants constantly underfoot, so Leofric's bed was the only one in use. As His Highness's valet, technically one of the sleeping alcoves had been designated for Auro. However, Auro favored sharing a bed with Alexios, and often the bath as well, so Leofric had the place to himself.

Until now.

Leofric wasn't one for personal affects. He'd lived so long carrying everything he owned on his back, or in Lyra's saddlebags, that he'd never accumulated much by way of extraneous objects. His weapons hung neatly on a rack upon the wall by his bed, along with his armor and shield. All of his uniforms, and the clothing he'd brought with him to Papia were folded in a wooden chest at the foot of his bed.

Cosmo stood in the center of the room, and despite his

slight build, he took up an inordinate amount of space. His hair, the color of his provocative robes, the freckles covering every inch of skin, the jewelry—the very sight of him was *loud*, and large. Cosmo simply did not fit in the plainly appointed chambers. Cosmo spun on his heel, taking in the austerity of the place, and wrinkled his tiny nose in distaste. As he did, Leofric noted that there was a cluster of freckles above one nostril in the shape of a starburst.

Leofric ignored Cosmo as best he could as he unbuckled his cape and armor, ready to fall to bed, but he noted the bandages on his burned hand were soiled, the wounds re-opened from the night's ride from the city to the villa. His hand gave a painful throb. He'd meant to have Auro rewrap it for him, but Leofric would wager he was already quite occupied in the other room. He sighed, and began to unwrap the bandages himself. His left hand was clumsy and slow, but he got the bandage down to the last layer, where he discovered with dismay that the blood had seeped through the fabric.

"Allow me," said a soft voice.

Leofric jumped. He looked up to see Cosmo staring at him from where he sat cross-legged on the adjacent bed. "Fine."

Cosmo slid off the bed and dropped to his knees before Leofric in one fluid movement. Before Leofric could so much as blink, Cosmo had reached over and taken the dagger from Leofric's belt, cool as you please. With one hand bracing Leofric's wrist, Cosmo hefted the blade and slid its point beneath the crust that had formed through the weave of the fabric. His hands were deft, confident, and purposeful, and Leofric's sharp intake of breath when the blade made contact with the tender, raw skin of his palm made him smirk—but he said nothing, and pried the soiled bandage away with surprising gentleness.

Leofric expected him to balk at the grizzly sight of the

wound. Someone like Cosmo didn't seem the type to allow blood or dirt to touch his silk-soft hands, but he got to his feet without complaint and fetched a bowl of water from the shaving table by the window. "There are cloths in the bathing chamber," said Leofric reluctantly. "And I have a salve in my trunk."

Supplies in hand, Cosmo knelt once again, and from this vantage point he was close enough that Leofric could find more shapes in the galaxies of Cosmo's freckles, and see the true complexity of color in his crimson locks. His hair really was like fire, Leofric thought. Toward the roots it was a deep, bloodred, and toward the tips it was pale blonde, crossing through every color present in a tongue of flame on the way. Depending on how the light from the torches caught it, Leofric could see hints of silvery blue, and even black, like staring deep into the glowing embers of a cook pit. He was so distracted that when the cool ointment touched his palm he flinched.

Cosmo looked up at him through his fiery fringe and smirked, and Leofric scowled, which only on made him smile more as he began working the salve into Leofric's blistered skin. "I am sorry for this," said Cosmo after a while.

"I shouldn't have grabbed you."

"No," said Cosmo, still smirking. Then he said, "Not without asking first, anyway."

Leofric felt the color rise in his cheeks, but said nothing. Cosmo made a tight circle out of his thumb and forefinger, wrapping it around the base of each of Leofric's fingers in turn. He slid it up, and down, the ointment making obscene, slick noises with every jerk of his wrist.

"I think that's plenty," said Leofric, finding his voice at last.

Cosmo smiled wider. "As you wish," he said.

"There are bandages over in—"

"In your trunk, yes. I saw them."

Cosmo floated back across the room and bandaged Leofric's hand, just as neatly as Auro had done. "My thanks," Leofric said stiffly.

Leofric went about the rest of his nightly routine in silence, keeping his back to Cosmo. As he pulled back the linen sheet on his bed, Leofric heard a flutter of fabric, like moth wings, followed by a series of clangs and clatters. He turned to see Cosmo step out of a puddle of sheer orange silk and kick it away. The bangles, rings and chains went next, a veritable fortune in gold and gems that Cosmo tossed aside without a care in the world. Leofric tracked one ring as it bounced and rolled across the marble tiles, tearing his eyes away from it just in time to see Cosmo stark naked, stripped of his indecent finery, pitch himself face first onto the bed opposite.

Cosmo turned his head to the side, and smiled when he saw Leofric watching him. All of this had happened in the span of a few breaths, but Leofric gelt like he'd been caught spying. He reddened, turning away to busy himself with his own blankets.

From his life spent in the army, Leofric was no stranger to nudity—both his own, and that of others. The men lived, ate, slept and bathed together. It wasn't that he and his fellow soldiers were furtive, exactly...it was more that they were efficient. Nakedness was occasionally a necessary step in a list of tasks, no more interesting or worth lingering over than lacing one's sandals.

Even when Leofric had, in his younger days, realized that he was...stirred by men the way most of his comrades were stirred by women, this fact had not changed. Couplings on the road or in the barracks were like arming oneself for battle: practiced, efficient. Necessary, even, from time to time, but no one luxuriated or flaunted being bare, the way Cosmo was doing now. He didn't even bother to cover himself with a blanket, just lay spread eagled on his belly with his freckled ass pointing straight at the ceiling.

Leofric smothered the torches and blew out the candles before climbing under the covers himself. He faced the wall, pulling the blanket tight around himself, despite the mildness of the evening.

His shoulders had finally begun to creep down from where they pressed into his ears when the distinct sounds of fucking began filtering in from the adjacent chamber. Leofric sighed and stuffed his head under the pillow. This was a regular occurrence, one he'd mostly become used to over the last few weeks. However, he had a curious impulse to apologize to Cosmo, as if Leofric were playing gracious host and Cosmo was an invited guest. Ridiculous. Leofric swallowed the urge to speak. Besides, they'd just pulled Cosmo out of a brothel. The sounds of people coupling were probably like a lullaby to him. In fact, yes. The freckled lech was already snoring on the other side of the room.

Leofric slept a few hours, jolting awake to the dawn sun coming in through the narrow windows in the wall. He was relieved, at first, to find himself alone, but that feeling proved short lived. His chambers had been ransacked. Leofric's trunk was open and his things littered the floor. Cosmo's clothing remained in a wrinkled heap where he'd left it the previous night. Seething, Leofric marched around the room, cursing spoiled demigod princelings with every step as he picked up his own clothes, refolded them, and tucked them neatly back into his trunk. He hesitated before balling up the whisp of a robe Cosmo left behind. He shoved it down, deep into the bottom corner of his trunk and slammed the lid shut with a satisfying *thunk*.

Only then did Leofric dress in a fresh uniform, the least wrinkled of the lot, and buckle on his armor. Looking around at his now tidy room, Leofric realized that before fleeing the mess, Cosmo had at least picked up his jewelry—but then, a glint of gold caught his eye. A heavy golden ring had come to rest behind an extra pair of sandals near the doorway. Leofric stooped to pick it up, barely sparing it a glance before stuffing it into the leather pouch on his sword belt.

He wondered where Cosmo had gotten to as he stepped out of the servants' quarters and into His Highness's sitting room. Part of him, a large part, thought it likely that Cosmo had fled the villa.

First, Leofric did a sweep of His Royal Highness's chambers, as he did every morning. Auro and Alexios lay entwined on the massive sleeping couch that dominated the bedchamber, curled up like only in each other's arms were they safe from the night. They slept so soundly, so serenely that it made Leofric ache. Over the last few turns of the moon, Alexios had gone from being a spoiled nuisance to someone of whom Leofric was deeply fond, and Auro was Auro. He was difficult not to love. Leofric liked that they had found such happiness with each other, and he was gladder still that their faith in each other had been rewarded, some strange turn allowing Auro to remain flesh and blood beyond the end of spring.

When Leofric completed his inspection, he went to the door to relieve the night watchmen who stayed just outside His Highness's apartments. Ever since the night an assassin had tried to drown Alexios, the prince had been even more heavily guarded. Leofric was glad for it; the sorcerer Janus had barely escaped, and Leofric was certain the man would return for vengeance. Together, Auro and Alexios had retrieved a god's power from the bowels of his castle, and snatched that power right out from under Janus's nose. The man would return for it, and soon. They must be ready.

Finally, Leofric went out onto the prince's balcony, as was his custom after he'd performed his morning inspection. As he pushed his way out through the curtains, Leofric startled. Cosmo had not fled. At least, not yet. He sat on the stone railing that wrapped around the balcony, his face upturned toward the sun, and his eyes were closed. The wind ruffled his hair, creating the illusion of flames licking around his ears.

Cosmo did not open his eyes, but after a while he said, "Didn't you get a good enough look last night?"

Leofric cursed himself, both at being caught staring *and* because plainly he hadn't been moving as quietly as he'd thought. "I am surprised to find you here," he heard himself say. Leofric moved around to study Cosmo in profile. The sun seemed to linger on his spotted skin, and with a start, Leofric realized Cosmo was wearing one of *his* tunics.

Cosmo swung his legs over the rail to hop down, landing lightly on the floor. "Thought I'd made a mad escape in the dark of night?"

"No," snapped Leofric. *Yes.*

Cosmo's smile widened, like he knew. "The day promises to be a hot one," he said. It was an innocent enough statement, but his hazel eyes glittered. "I had to make certain all was as it should be."

"You were working?"

"Of course," said Cosmo, a frown breaking over his face. He crossed his arms over his chest. "You'd know it if I wasn't."

"I only meant—"

"I know what you meant." In a flash, the taunting smile was back. "My brother prefers to work with his fingers in the mud. I prefer to be closer to the sky."

Leofric had no idea what to do with that, so instead he said, "You stole my clothes."

Cosmo flattened his hands down the front of his pilfered tunic, pressing the fabric against the body beneath it. *The naked body beneath it,* Leofric thought, unbidden. "Well, in your haste, you didn't give me any time to pack."

"I gave you a chance to pack, and you squandered it trying to escape."

"That's so," Cosmo allowed. He looked down at the tunic once again, teasing his fingers along the bottom hem, lifting it up to reveal the skin of his thighs. "Would you like it back?"

"No," Leofric blurted. "Keep it."

Cosmo sighed and released the hem, letting it fall once again to a modest position.

Leofric narrowed his eyes. "You left my chambers a mess," he said, in attempt to shift the subject.

"At least the fabric added a bit of color to the place," Cosmo retorted.

"To the floor, perhaps."

"It's better than nothing," said Cosmo. "That room is like a crypt."

"It's—"

"Cosmo?"

Leofric whirled around to see Auro and Alexios framed by the doorway leading to the balcony. He hadn't even heard them stir, but he recovered himself as quickly as he could, snapping to attention and masking his immense disquiet. People usually had a difficult time getting the drop on him. Leofric took a step back, distancing himself from Cosmo, and refocused himself. He could not afford any distractions with Janus at large. Leofric couldn't allow any distractions, when the cost of such would be someone's life.

Not again.

Three

L eofric was, at least, partially interested in him. Of this Cosmo was certain. The heat in the man's eyes, masked with anger—or, perhaps, laced with it—was undeniable. It had been a long time since Cosmo had sparred verbally with someone like Leofric, someone who didn't bend immediately to Cosmo's wit, or beauty, or the fact that he was a god. There was something about him, something about the stern set to his jaw, his outward imperviousness to Cosmo's advances, that he found alluring.

Cosmo would bed anyone willing, had sampled all manner of partners in his years upon the earth. Though the occasional craving would strike him, he'd never considered one flavor of lovemaking to be head and shoulders above the others—though some were, perhaps, literally. Each had their merits. And right now, Cosmo was contemplating the merits of long dark hair wrapped around his fingers and full scowling lips wrapped around his cock. He eyed Leofric up and down, watching as the man saluted his prince, every muscle poised, drawn taut as a bowstring, and wondered if he'd ever lain with a man before. Unfortunately, these tantalizing mental images were knocked loose by his brother, just as they had been last night.

Cosmo grimaced. He couldn't say he'd *loved* falling asleep to the sound of his brother fucking, but perhaps it was safer that way. It had cooled his ardor, he who had previously thought his ardor uncoolable, and allowed him to get some sleep.

Which was good, because this morning was sure to be painful, and difficult because now, Auro was summoning him to discuss the impossible.

Servants brought them breakfast on trays while Auro sat opposite him, and suddenly Cosmo was back in the lazy summer mornings of his youth, sitting with Auro and Ozias playing tiles or dice, listening to Cedras reading in his soothing voice. He took a stuttering breath, then a longer, steadier one in attempt to get a grip on himself. Sweet memories were lovely, but they held no power to change the future.

Auro had brought a massive book to sit on the floor between them, called *the Sun Queen's Compendium of Tales*. To hear Auro tell it, the book had been written by their mother. "I don't understand," said Cosmo, brushing his fingers over the leather of the cover. Just as Auro said, there was a faint etching in the surface of it, one of her emblems. But anyone could have scratched a few lines into the cover of a book. It didn't prove anything, not really.

"This story says nothing about you staying awake, beyond spring," said Cosmo, after reading the tale for the third time. "How did you manage that?"

"I'm still not entirely sure," Auro admitted, "I returned to the temple, just like always, but instead of turning to stone I— I dreamed."

Cosmo frowned. He obviously had no idea of his brothers' typical experiences, but he never dreamed, between summers. He simply went to sleep at the end of summer, and woke at the start of the next one. For all he knew, his cursed rest could be the span of a blink, or a heartbeat, or a century. From the way Auro spoke, Cosmo imagined his experience had been much the same. "You dreamed? Of what?"

"Of mother," said Auro, his voice small and raw.

Cosmo twisted his fingers in his lap. Long ago, if Auro was hurting, Cosmo wouldn't have hesitated to pull him into a hug, to comfort him. He was so young, and sweet, and soft. Or, he had been. Cosmo had to remind himself he no longer knew Auro. They'd been apart far longer than they'd ever been together as children. Perhaps it would be too familiar, too forward after the distance of four centuries.

Before he could decide, the moment had passed, and Auro had pulled himself together. He sat a bit straighter as he continued the story. "It was like she'd left me a message. An echo, almost. I think she'd expected us to follow her clues long before this—it was like she had...faded, somehow."

"Faded?"

"The form she took. She was like a specter. I couldn't even understand everything she was saying, like the words had been eroded, by time."

"Even so," said Cosmo, thinking. "That is some serious magic."

"Indeed," said Auro. "I hadn't known she knew anything of the arcane arts."

"Nor I," said Cosmo. "But she must have, that's plain. Because here you sit."

"Here I sit," Auro agreed.

Cosmo pulled the book toward himself, his mind racing as the considered the implications of what Auro was saying. "We didn't know her at all," he said at last.

"What?"

"She had this—this skill, this power, and she still let father curse us. She still let..." *She still let Ozias die.* His mother had no love for Ozias, and she'd not gone to any trouble to conceal that fact from the five of them as boys. Even so, how could she have stood aside and let him be killed? How could she have stood aside and let her sons be cursed? Cosmo had never considered the idea that she might have had a choice. Empress Soli had been dead by the time Cosmo had woken that first summer after they'd been cursed, and he had mourned her. Now though...if what Auro said was true, she'd had a choice. Something twisted in his gut, like he was losing his family all over again, grief crashing over him in fresh, violent waves.

"She did all she could," Auro protested.

"Oh please," said Cosmo. "How could you possibly know that?"

"I know her," said Auro. "I know she didn't wish to abandon—"

Cosmo stood, shaking his head. "Nothing has changed in four hundred years," he said angrily. Auro had always been their mother's favorite, he though peevishly, her sweet baby. "Why did she leave clues for you alone? Why not our eldest brother? Or why not—anyone, really? Why *you?*" *Why not me?* He couldn't help but wonder, but he didn't say it aloud.

"I don't know," said Auro. He got to his feet as well. "'it had to be me,' she said, in her echo."

"Naturally," said Cosmo, in harsh, acid tones. He scoffed. "Her precious little Apricot."

"Hey," said Alexios, who had held his tongue for much of this conversation. "Don't—"

"Alexios, please," said Auro, holding up a hand. "This between my brother and myself."

Alexios showed some signs of wanting to argue, and possibly wanting to toss Cosmo out onto his ass as well. Cosmo wouldn't have objected much; this was already proving to be a colossal waste of time, dredging up the past when they'd all moved on. "But—"

"Alexios."

It was to his paramour that Auro spoke, but Cosmo was the one who startled. Auro was different now. Very different. The boy Cosmo had grown up with could have no more chastised a prince than he could have swallowed the sun whole. "You've changed," Cosmo said.

Auro glared at him. Actually *glared.* "Yes," he said, voice hard. "And a good thing. Four hundred years was long enough for us all to act like children, I think."

Abashed, Cosmo returned to the carpet beside the hearth, standing with his arms crossed across his chest. "Alright," he said. "Alright. So—why do we think you're awake?"

"I had a notion," said Auro. "Based upon the tale in the book, it's clear mother wanted us to work together. The lesson in the parable is that the brothers could only stop the curse if they helped each *other*, not themselves."

"And?"

"And..." said Auro, "I...did. I did my part. I retrieved Cedras's power—proving I care more about our family than I do about myself." Here he glared again. "A foreign concept to some—"

It was Cosmo's turn to scowl. "Enough," he snapped. "I'm here, aren't I?"

Auro raised his hands in acquiescence. "My point is that we can hardly collaborate on a solution if we can never speak. So, this—" he gestured at himself "—makes sense."

"I suppose it does," Cosmo allowed. "But why did you lose your grace?"

"I don't think I did," Auro said, pacing. "I think...we all have a finite amount of power, and I have enough to perform my duties in spring time. That's *all* I have, until we break the curse."

Cosmo considered this. "Perhaps," he said. "But what made you search for Cedras's grace?" *Instead of mine,* he didn't say. He and Auro had always been close as boys. To Cosmo, Cedras had always seemed aloof, apart from the rest of them. He was a few years older to be sure, but it was more than that. Cedras always had more time for his studies than he ever had for his brothers.

"I think I had to," said Auro. "We can only free our counterpart."

A cold, slimy weight settled in Cosmo's stomach at Auro's words. *He cannot mean what I think he means.* "Our counterpart?"

"Yes," said Auro, eager now, oblivious to Cosmo's mounting dread. "So, you would have to—"

"No."

"What?"

"Auro, please, forgive me. I cannot do this."

"You said you'd hear me out!"

"I did say that. And now I have." Cosmo fought to keep his body still. His heart pounded in his chest and all his instincts were screaming at him to flee. "And now I am telling you, I cannot do this."

"Why?" Asked Auro. "Why not?"

"My counterpart..."

"Would be Kryos, yes."

"And that would mean I am his, correct? My only chance of being cured rests in his hands?"

"I think so—"

Cosmo lurched past Auro, his nervous energy too much to contain. "No."

"Cosmo, I know it will be difficult to mend fences between us..."

"*Difficult?*" Cosmo spat. "Impossible."

Auro grabbed his arm. "Just *explain*, Cosmo," he said. "What is it?"

"Based upon what you've learned, I have to locate Kryos's

grace, and restore him to full power. And he is the one who has to locate mine?"

"Yes," said Auro. "At least, I think so."

"He won't do it."

"Of course, he will!"

Cosmo shook his head violently. "He won't."

"What makes you so sure?"

Cosmo took a skittering step away, and shook his head. "I am glad to have seen you, little brother. And I hope you'll still be awake next summer, too. But I want no part in this." Cosmo turned and strode for the door, and a wine cup shattered against the wall a handsbreadth from his head.

"How *could* you?" Auro spat.

Cosmo whirled around, shocked at Auro's impassioned outburst, and furious at him in equal measures. "How could I?" he flared. He could feel the sparks of his grace bursting across his skin, and the hearth gave an answering roar, whooshing tongues of flame straight up and out into the room. They singed the rug before retreating back into the fireplace as Cosmo tried to regain his composure. "How could I? How could *you?*"

"What?"

"We were cursed for a *reason*, Auro," said Cosmo. "Ozias—"

"Ozias's death was an accident," said Auro. "Don't you think we've suffered enough? Don't you think—"

"It wasn't."

"It—it what?"

"Ozias's death was *not* an accident." Even all these years later, he felt ill to think of it. The battlefield was frozen, a wasteland of ice and biting wind. Both he and Ozias had been bundled in dark, hooded cloaks. *Don't worry*, Ozias had told him, through chattering teeth. *I'll convince him to see reason.* They'd watched Kryos from afar, his silhouette huge and broad, casting terrible shadows across the place that would become his killing field. Cosmo had crouched in the shadows, like a coward, hoping Ozias and his honey-tongue would save him, hoping he'd not have to face Kryos himself. He'd known, even then, defeating Kryos was impossible. His only hope of victory in their duel would be if Ozias could convince Kryos to go easy on him, so Cosmo had watched, and prayed. *Let it work,* he remembered thinking. *I will surrender, if he lets me.*

Ozias must have grabbed Kryos's arm, or tapped his shoulder, at that distance it had been hard to make out. Kryos turned with a howl of rage and a white light burst so cold and so terrible that it knocked Cosmo off his feet.

When he'd regained them, Cosmo had crept out onto the field, terrified what he would find. "Kryos wanted to kill *me.*" He said to Auro now. "He thought it was me, sneaking up on him, and he turned around—"

Auro shook his head. "No," he said. "There's no way."

"I watched it happen," said Cosmo. "And all that remained of Ozias was a frozen corpse." He recalled how Ozias had looked almost...beautiful. Like his body had been covered head to toe in glittering diamonds. When Cosmo had reached out to touch his outstretched hand, Ozias had shattered, countless pieces of frozen flesh bursting from his bones, with enough force to cover Cosmo's entire face in scratches. Ozias's brittle, frozen skeleton had crumbled to the ground right before Cosmo's eyes.

"When I found him," said Auro, his eyes narrow and his voice suspicious, "His bones appeared burned and bleached. As if by a mighty sun."

The accusation shouldn't have stung after four hundred years, but it still did. In his heart, Cosmo turned away from it. Outside himself, he said, "I couldn't leave him like that." His throat tightened. "So...cold."

Auro's face softened, and he reached for Cosmo's arm. "I didn't—"

"Right, of course," said Cosmo, shaking off his touch. It was just like it was *then*. Nothing had changed. "I tell you what I saw Kryos do with my own two eyes, and you won't believe it. Someone claims I burned Ozias alive and suddenly their word is good as gold."

"Cosmo—"

"*Forget it.*" It was over, done with. Auro wanted them all to forgive each other, but how could they? Forgiveness came from trust, and any they might once have shared had long since burned away. "It doesn't matter what you believe," he said. "What matters is that I know what I saw, and I'll restore Kryos's grace over my dead body. And he'd tell you the same, I'm certain. Only it would be my dead body either way."

Auro puzzled over that for a moment, before shaking his head, like the unpleasant thoughts were flies buzzing about his ears. "Cosmo, wait," he said, after a moment. "What if it truly was an accident?"

Cosmo laughed full in his face. "When did you ever know Kryos to miss what he aimed at?"

"Never," Auro agreed. "Never, don't you see? A blow that would have killed Ozias would not have killed you."

"What?"

"Ozias had godsblood, but he did not have any of our father's grace. He could easily have been killed by a blow that would only have knocked *you* off your feet."

Cosmo frowned. "No, but..." he trailed away, wondering.

Auro latched onto his hesitation. "It could have been an accident," said Auro, the look in his eyes desperate. It was plain he didn't want to think his brothers capable of murder, even after all of these years. "It could have."

"Perhaps," Cosmo allowed.

"I believe it," said Auro softly, but firmly. He took

Cosmo's hand. "Like I believe you. I believe you wouldn't have killed any of us, even Kryos. Never."

"I wouldn't," said Cosmo. His eyes stung, and suddenly he was a boy of twenty again, pleading and begging with their father to believe him, pounding on the locked door of a basement cell. He would never, *ever* have done that. How could he not see?

"I know," said Auro. "I *know.* Just like I know Kryos wouldn't either."

Cosmo jerked his hand away. "Listen—"

"Believe me," said Auro. "Because I believe *you.*"

Cosmo looked into his brother's eyes, clinging to Auro's faith like a drowning man might cling to a lifeline. After so long, someone believed him. Even if it was just Auro, who believed the best in people so easily. For a heartbeat Cosmo felt it might be worth dying, just to have someone look at him like Auro was looking at him now. He wanted to think Auro could be right, but what if he wasn't? It was easy for Auro to have faith. It always had been. Besides, if he were mistaken, Cosmo would be the only one in real danger. Was he willing to take that gamble?

Leofric stared through the gauzy curtains at Cosmo's silhouette. He stood on the balcony, backlit by the afternoon sun, in much the same position Leofric had found him that morning. After his dramatic pronouncement, he'd excused himself for some air.

"Could he be lying?" Alexios asked Auro now, in a low voice.

Auro looked troubled. "I don't think so."

"What do *you* remember?"

"The day of Kryos and Cosmo's duel, the day we..." he

trailed away, lost in some painful memory. "I had sent Ozias to try to stop them. I didn't hear any word from him—or any of them—for three days, so I went to the spot myself. All that remained was a crater of destruction in the clearing, and Ozias's bones. It looked as though he'd been caught between the two of them, but..."

"Even if what Cosmo is saying is true," said Alexios. "It doesn't change anything."

"How can you say that?" Asked Auro.

Alexios touched his arm. "I only meant, Ozias's death was still a tragic accident."

"That's so," Auro allowed, looking out onto the balcony at the shadow of his brother.

Leofric held his tongue. Auro might be willing to believe the best in his brother, but to Leofric it seemed as though he were being naive. He *wanted* to believe, to see the good in Cosmo, but wanting to believe couldn't make something true that wasn't. To him, it was plain that Cosmo was a selfish coward, and Leofric could never trust a coward. He knew all too well how someone so selfish could easily destroy a family, without even meaning to do so. Even if things had played out the way Cosmo said, he'd still sent his vulnerable brother Ozias to confront the god of winter in his stead, he'd still hidden, valuing his own skin over his brother's.

They were interrupted by a knock at the door. With an impatient nod, His Highness instructed Leofric to see who was on the other side. One of the porters had come with a message. "His and Her Grace have summoned His Royal Highness to their audience chamber," she said. "At once."

"I must dress," said Alexios. "Tell my royal parents I will attend them presently."

"Of course, Your Highness." The porter bowed and made her exit.

Auro hurried to the wardrobe to select a toga for Alexios,

and Leofric waited for His Highness to ready himself. When he was dressed, with a crown upon his head, Leofric fell in step behind him and they set off down the airy corridor toward the marble steps leading down to the atrium of the royal villa.

"What do you make of this?" Alexios asked Leofric.

"The summons?"

"No," said Alexios. He looked over his shoulder, as though to be certain they were alone in the hallway. "*Cosmo.*"

"I'm not certain, Your Highness," said Leofric. "I can't say I know the man."

Alexios held out a hand, stopping Leofric in his tracks. "Leofric," he said. "I trust your counsel. Speak."

Leofric sighed. "I don't know him," he repeated, "But what I have seen...I can't say I like it, Your Highness. He is... very different from his brother."

Alexios smiled, as he always did when speaking of Auro. "Indeed," he said. "I hadn't known it was possible for two brothers to be so different."

Leofric knew Alexios was an only child. "Aye," he said. "It can be surprising, but two siblings raised in the same house never have identical experiences. It can be as if they led two entirely different childhoods."

"You speak from experience," said Alexios. It was not a question.

Leofric dipped his head. "Apologies, Your Highness."

"What? Why?"

"I never meant to carry my home life into my work."

"It's alright, Leofric," said Alexios, puzzled. "I like to think we're friends."

"I just..." Leofric trailed away. "I like to keep my private life private, if it please Your Highness."

Alexios nodded. "Alright, Leofric." He sounded tired. "I wonder what my royal parents want today."

"Let us hurry, and find out." Leofric was eager to change

the subject. When he swore his oath of office, he had sworn to put any life outside his duty aside. To allow it to bleed over would be to compromise his focus, and his focus currently felt tenuous enough.

When they arrived at the audience chamber, Leofric bowed to the king and queen and took his place off to the side, scanning the room and its points of egress for any and all threats. A servant tended the fire, and another brought in a tray laden with wine, cups, cheese, and bread. He knew neither of their names, but recognized their faces. One of the first things he'd done upon accepting his position at the royal villa was to familiarize himself with the staff. He made a point to watch every face, and learn any new ones that might be allowed in the royal presence. *You are an excellent soldier,* Imperator Hamate had told him, *but a guard is not a soldier.* He was right. Of course, Leofric's skill at arms was just as necessary in his current position, but this business of standing and watching could not be more different than his life with the army.

He must always be alert, but never intrusive. Poised for battle, but never make those around him worry. He must fade, fade into the background like a vase or a statue, but never allow his mind to wander. He must watch everything, but never *see*. He must hear all, but never *listen*. And he must never allow his skills to go to rust, either. Never grow lax, or soft. Never allow anything to compromise his sworn oath. There was a special, still place inside his mind, deep within himself, a well of endless patience and razor focus that he must always, *always* be able to access.

He drew from that well now, standing still, his face passive, as Alexios conferred with the king and queen. It helped to pick something upon which to focus, a point on the wall or a person's face, a painting. Sometimes a mental image would do it, but for some reason his mind kept filling with sparks, fire, and freckles. Leofric decided instead to focus upon King Nelios. Nelios was of a height with Leofric, though perhaps two decades older. He was broad shouldered, with dark hair that came to a wicked widow's peak between his severe brows. King Nelios hailed from the kingdom of Sokol, just as Leofric did, and it was that connection he had to thank for this posting. Nelios had once been the imperator of the Sokolian army, before he had been dispatched to seal the Papian alliance with his marriage to its queen.

"A rider came with the sunrise," he was saying to his son now. "Her Grace Queen Dafina should be arriving in three days."

"Excellent," said Alexios, and Leofric noted that he sounded somewhat sincere. He and Queen Dafina had grand plans, hoping to combine their two kingdoms into one larger unified territory. Leofric felt a pang for the prince, and Auro too. Like his father did before him, Alexios planned to cement this great alliance with a marriage. His Highness had done his best to forestall the wedding, but time was running out. If they hoped to combine the kingdom of Neossós and the kingdom of Papia, he would have to face the proverbial music soon enough. The Queen's arrival could only mean that day was approaching even faster.

Alexios had walked into the audience with his back straight and his head high, but when he left some half hour later, his shoulders were slumped as if a great weight had been slung across them. "Your Highness…" he said awkwardly. This had never been his strong suit, but he knew Alexios well enough by now to know he needed some comfort.

"We must begin preparations for Her Grace's arrival immediately," said Alexios abruptly.

"Of course, Your Highness," said Leofric. Leofric would have little and less to do with the preparations, but he still said, "How may I be of service?"

Alexios smiled thinly. "Unfortunately, preparations for feasts and frolics fall squarely under my domain, so you can rest easy knowing you won't have to worry about flowers or decorations or musicians."

"And I appreciate that, Your Highness," said Leofric.

When they arrived back at Alexios's apartments, they found them empty. Alexios found a note on his work table, weighed down by a piece of marble. It was a delicately carved nose, broken off a bust. Alexios smiled faintly as he read the note. "Auro and his brother are touring the grounds," said Alexios. "They'll return by evening meal."

"Very good, Your Highness," said Leofric. He swept Alexios's chambers and then decided perhaps the young man would like some privacy, so he took a place to stand guard just outside his door.

Four

" . . . And this is a cattleya orchid," said Auro, gesturing. They'd been walking the royal gardens for almost an hour. Cosmo still hadn't decided whether or not he wanted to be part of Auro's mad plan to free all four of them from their curse, but he knew for sure he'd missed his brother's company. He couldn't help but watch and listen fondly as Auro waxed on about all the growing things in the royal gardens. Auro had not been awake to see the wonders of summer for four hundred years, and all the flowers and fruits that had only just begun to bud had him tripping over himself with delight and excitement. It was infectious, and Cosmo had some knowledge to share with him, as well. By the time summer rolled around, most of the plants were well on their way through their life cycles, so they didn't require as much careful management as they did in spring—but still, Cosmo's grace touched them all, nourished them on their way.

They were in a massive structure Auro called the greenhouse, the likes of which Cosmo had never seen before. It was a building made entirely of glass with iron frames holding the panes together, like a skeleton. The entire place shone like a massive, faceted gemstone when the sun hit it, absolutely enchanting, and inside the air was warm and moist and fragrant. "Alexios's mother collects rare plants," Auro explained. "When we first met, I spent my nights sleeping in here."

There was a lull in Auro's lecture about the plants, so Cosmo put to words something he'd been wondering since Auro had first told him how he'd spent the last four hundred years. "Why did you spend so long alone?"

Auro didn't answer right away. He crouched beside one of the flowers, touching its petals, his eyes fixated on the blossom.

Cosmo sat beside him. "Auro?" He was still getting used to the sound of his brother's name. It felt oddly like summoning a ghost.

"I felt we deserved it," said Auro. His voice was so quiet Cosmo had to lean in to hear. "I felt *I* deserved it."

The notion was so absurd that Cosmo nearly laughed—but the tearing sensation in his chest was far too painful. "How could you think that?"

Auro tossed him a strange look. "It was my fault," he said. "Whatever happened between you, Kryos, and Ozias..." Auro trailed away. "He never would have found you, never would have known the location of your duel, had I not told him."

"Auro," said Cosmo gently, and it seemed easier to say this time. "That's dumb."

That startled a laugh out of Auro, and Cosmo smiled too. That, at least, he still knew how to do. He could always make his brothers laugh, could always cheer them. Sometimes, he felt it was all he was good for.

After Ozias's death, it hadn't even occurred to Cosmo to run. He'd wandered about, as in a fog, with no destination in mind. If Kryos actually *had* wanted his head, he would have found Cosmo easy prey, then—so perhaps Auro was right. It was their father who found him, and that was worse. He had spoken not a word, simply looked upon Cosmo in disgust, with that terrible, stern face of his.

He beckoned, with one crooked finger, and Cosmo had followed mutely behind. The dungeon cell in which he'd been locked had not been a natural one. Cosmo had never known such darkness. He shuddered, recalling the way he'd strained his ears, listening for sounds of life, for any sign that he had not been abandoned.

When his father came for him at last, blade in hand, Cosmo had been almost grateful.

"Perhaps," said Auro, returning Cosmo to the present. He lowered his voice, as if sharing some terrible secret. "I think father was wrong."

His eyes widened and he clapped a hand over his mouth, and even Cosmo couldn't help the way he twisted around, looking for some sign that Auro's blasphemous whisper had been overheard, even if the far off reaches of the untouchable Godsrealm. "What do you mean?"

"Locking us away didn't fix anything, did it?"

Cosmo allowed the grace to flow down from his fingers as he toyed with the calyx of a nearby lily. He could feel the nectar swelling within, and he encouraged its anthers to split, the golden dust of pollen emerging where they did, soft and enticing to any nearby insects. He'd never had Auro's way with plants, but they still responded to his touch, his power. "The earth seems happier, for our imprisonment."

"It does," said Auro. "But I think it would be even happier if we could learn to work in harmony."

Cosmo withdrew his hand. "Maybe," he said, but he was doubtful. The head of the lily followed his hand, turning its face toward him like it might turn toward the sun in hopes of catching more rays. "Can I see it?" he asked abruptly.

"See...what?"

"Him. Cedras." His name in Cosmo's mouth was just as foreign as Auro's, like something in a language he'd known once, but since forgotten. He realized with a jolt he could not remember the last time he'd spoken any of their names aloud.

Auro nodded. "Come," he said, standing. "We'll need to find Alexios."

Cosmo could not help but note the way Auro's cheeks pinked at the mere mention of his princeling. A jest was on his tongue, but it died there before he spoke it. Teasing Auro had been second nature to him, once—but it seemed like yet another thing he'd forgotten how to do, like something from someone else's life.

They found Alexios in his apartments, along with his handsome, scowling shadow. Cosmo tried to offer Leofric a friendly smile, but it curdled when met with an icy stare. Unconsciously, it seemed, Leofric cupped his burned hand in his off one, flexing the fingers and narrowing his eyes. He did not bother to mask his distaste, and for some reason it gave Cosmo a little thrill.

"I'd like to show Cosmo Cedras's grace," Auro was saying to Alexios.

Cosmo pulled his gaze away from the frowning soldier to smile at Auro's paramour. Alexios opened his mouth, but Leofric cut across before he could answer.

"Your Highness, that would be most unwise."

Alexios appeared taken aback. Auro too.

"What makes you say that, Leofric?" Asked Alexios.

With a furtive glance at Cosmo, he said, "I'm certain your royal parents would only wish to admit *trusted* acquaintances to the lower vaults."

Cosmo told himself the mistrust of a stranger meant little and less, and held his tongue. He was pleasantly surprised when Auro spoke for him. "He's my brother," said Auro, stung.

"He's right, Leofric," said Alexios. "This is as much Cosmo's as Auro's. I have no right to keep either of them from it."

"Perhaps," Leofric allowed, "But it resides in the vaults with all of your family's treasures."

"*Please,*" scoffed Cosmo, twirling the golden cuff on his bicep. "Rest assured, Prince Alexios, I have no interest in your trinkets. I have plenty of my own."

"The vaults are well guarded," added Alexios, untroubled. "No one would be permitted entrance without my or my parents' presence, at any rate."

Leofric sighed and nodded, and Cosmo took that for a victory. They made their way through the royal villa, trailing behind Alexios and Auro, with Leofric bringing up the rear of their party. The upper vault was just behind the throne room, where the Papian royal family displayed some of the artifacts they'd collected over the years since the kingdom's founding. Two guardsmen flanked the door. Stern and alert, they bowed to the prince and saluted Leofric as the four of them passed, and took no notice of Auro or Cosmo. Inside the upper vault, toward the back, another door was guarded as well. This time the men crossed their spears, despite the approach of their crown prince and his guard. "Your Highness," said one. "Respectfully, we cannot allow more guests in the lower vault than there are guards on the door. Two of your party must remain."

"By whose decree?"

"Her Grace, the queen," said one of the men. "Some of her most precious valuables have recently been relocated to the lower vault, for security."

"I forgot about her bloody books," said Alexios under his breath. "Some volumes were stolen from her private library, and no treasure is more sacred to her."

"She and Cedras would get along splendidly," quipped Cosmo, surprising even himself.

The guards cast him a curious look, perhaps wondering who this stranger was, who spoke so boldly of their queen.

"No doubt," Auro agreed. To Alexios, he added, "Perhaps Leofric could remain here, to help guard the door."

Leofric opened his mouth to protest, but Alexios silenced him with a look. "That would bring the numbers even," he told the guards. "Shall we pass?"

"Of course, Your Highness." The men bowed deeply and stepped aside, allowing Alexios to escort Auro and Cosmo through a small antechamber. The door was locked of course, but Alexios had the key.

The lower vault of the Papian royals was something of an anticlimax, after all that fuss at the door. It was far smaller than the upper vault, and had the air of a neglected storehouse. Most of the showiest and flashiest items were on display in the chamber above. A bookshelf had been moved in to house the queen's rare volumes, and there were a few odds and ends hung upon the walls, including a familiar tapestry that was older than Auro and Cosmo put together. It had once hung behind their mother's throne. Alexios's forebearers must have looted it from the fallen Mykellian palace.

Cosmo whirled around, and the flaming sconces on the wall spit and hissed as they echoed his ire. "You have no right—"

"*Cosmo,*" said Auro, touching his arm. "It's alright."

"I don't understand," said Alexios, raising his hands. "What have I done?"

"This belonged to our family," Auro explained to him, indicating the tapestry.

It was a map of the continent, woven in exquisite detail. Cosmo had spent a lot of time staring up at that tapestry in his youth. "Why did they make it so big?" he'd asked his mother once, his neck craning up so he could see all of it.

"To remind us the size of our responsibility," Empress Soli had said. "What we owe our people is as vast as the world."

"Why didn't you tell me?" Alexios asked Auro, cupping his cheek. "I wouldn't have—"

"It's alright, Alexios," Auro soothed. He turned to his brother. "Cosmo—"

"It's just an ancient rag," said Cosmo, turning from it, from them, throat tight. The sconces guttered as he crushed his own anger. "The sight of it surprised me, that's all."

In the awkward wake that followed, Alexios led them to a small, spindly table in a shadowy corner of the room, as unremarkable as the rest of the forgotten artifacts in here. It was draped with a stained, grey linen shroud. Auro removed it with a flourish, and Cosmo gasped. Upon the table was a small wooden box, that had perhaps been plain to start, but tree roots had begun to push their way through the cracks where the wood was joined, shoving against the bronze hinges like something inside were trying to fight its way out.

"I had to cover it," said Auro. "I had to try to conceal the magic."

"People don't come in here, much," Alexios added. "I asked my father if I could store something private. The shroud isn't much by way of a shield, I know, but it's something."

"Yes," said Cosmo faintly, eyes transfixed upon the little chest. He reached a trembling hand toward the box, and he could feel the warmth seeping through the wood.

Auro hovered by his elbow, waiting with baited breath as Cosmo gingerly lifted the lid. Within the box, cradled in a nest of autumn leaves, was a phial of glowing crystal. The light it threw was warm and golden, and when Cosmo reached for it, he could feel the strength flowing from the bottle to his hand. He hefted it, watching the amber liquid inside slosh around. Against his palm, the bottle felt like fall sun. It felt like … the hearth in their den, where they'd gather as children. It felt like knowledge, and it felt like round spectacles and the gentle *hoot* of an owl. It felt like candles and old parchment. When the liquid moved it sounded like wind rustling through stalks of wheat as they ripened in some distant field. It had a smell, too, like apples, cinnamon, and the musty scent of leaf litter on the forest floor. It smelled like… "*Cedras.*"

"Yes," said Auro, but Cosmo barely heard him, because he was drowning. Drowning in a memory centuries stale, a memory he didn't even know he still had, of a stormy spring night when Cosmo had been so young and so afraid. There had been a storm, a terrible one. It was before any of them had been burdened with their father's godly grace. Cosmo had wondered where Auro was, Auro, who was always terrified of thunder. He'd crept through the silent halls of the villa like a ghost, but he'd found Auro's chambers empty. Where would Auro go, if afraid? Before Ozias had come to live at court, he would have crept into their mother's bedroom of a night. After though, even Auro had recognized the change in her, young as he was.

Eventually, Cosmo found his way to Cedras's rooms, peeking through the crack in the door to see them bundled in blankets on the floor, beside the great window that led to Cedras's balcony. Cedras had his face in a book, as ever, and Auro sat curled beside him. Unafraid.

They'd made a game of it, Cosmo recalled, of counting between the flashes of lightning and the cracking of thunder. Alone, Cosmo thought the thunder sounded like it was going to crack their home like an egg. Beside his brothers, though, it had transformed a pleasant, distant rumble that made his belly swoop, like he'd missed a step going down the stairs. No longer terrifying, but thrilling.

Cosmo slammed the lid shut on the chest, sudden enough to make Auro startle.

"I will help," he announced. "I'll help you break the curse."

~

Leofric had no idea what happened down inside the lower vault, and he did not ask. It was not his place. When His Highness emerged however, it was with Auro beaming and Cosmo smiling a shy, tentative grin. Prince Alexios had decided to sup with his parents, and as such would be well guarded. This relieved Leofric of his evening duties, so he took his supper in the barracks with the other men, leaving Auro and Cosmo to their own devices.

Technically, Leofric was the captain of Prince Alexios's personal guard, but it was a mostly empty title—he was the only member of the prince's guard. The rest of the men were formed into commands under other officers, tasked with protecting the royal family and the villa at large, or guarding the king and queen specifically. In the aftermath of all that had gone on in the spring, Leofric had been suggesting His Highness might want to expand his guard, but Alexios wouldn't hear of it.

While he'd never been the most talkative sort, Leofric did feel more at home sitting at the long bench tables in the barracks hall, elbow to elbow with the other soldiers, men like him, men like his brother and all the men he'd known in the legion. Simple men, enjoying simple things and each other's company. Guarding a prince was solitary work, at times, and it was nice to recall what it felt like to belong.

The feeling had been difficult to enjoy, after Hamalcar's death. Soldiers reminded Leofric of his brother, almost as much as his own reflection did. Enough time had passed, now, that Leofric could find comfort amongst them once again. He listened to the men jesting and telling tales as they ate, and the food was plain but filling. The sort of food he might have eaten on the march—but elevated versions, brought to them fresh, served with wine.

The days were growing longer, and warmer. The Papian natives griped good naturedly about the heat, but Leofric did not mind. It reminded him of home, of blistering nights in Sokol passing a wineskin back and forth with Hamalcar, sparring in the camp among the other soldiers, and yes, from time to time, sharing a tumble with another man in the shadows of their tents.

One such night, after far too much wine, Leofric had stumbled back to the tent he shared with his brother. Hamalcar had been drinking, too, and the two of them had made a wager. Their mother had always joked she couldn't tell them apart, so Hamalcar had drunkenly declared the loser of their bet would get a tattoo, making it easier on her. Leofric had lost, so he'd submitted to the needle and allowed a camp follower to carve the vines on the side of his head. He'd been horrified upon waking in the morning. Hamalcar had laughed himself stupid at the sight. "Mother will certainly be able to tell who's who, now," he said. "Be grateful the artist didn't let me choose the design."

Leofric had grown his hair out to cover the tattoo, which only made Hamalcar tease him all the more, as it came in bristly and patchy at first, compared to the luxurious hair on the rest of his head. It was only after Hamalcar had died that Leofric had bared the side of his scalp again, taking comfort in seeing it when he had call to look upon his face in a mirror. It was a part of him now, just as his brother had been.

Back in the present, it was still early, so Leofric wandered out of the mess hall toward the armory beside the practice yard, thinking he might find someone with whom to spar. It was critical his skills not be allowed to rust, and the dance of swordplay always helped calm him, helped him feel as though there was some semblance of balance in this peculiar world. Here, he felt understood.

Hours later, sweaty and sore and feeling quite at peace, Leofric paid a visit to the baths in the barracks. He could have returned to Prince Alexios's apartments for the privacy of his own chambers, but he suspected Cosmo would be there. Leofric had fixated on him far more than was wise, and he knew himself well enough to know that keeping his distance from Cosmo would be the wisest course of action.

The baths were below ground, the room carved out of the earth to form something like a grotto around a natural hot spring. In the antechamber where the soldiers could gather towels and clay cups of water or wine, it smelled like sweat and salt and men, a smell that Leofric had always loved, ever since he'd been a green recruit with the Sokolian auxiliary. It like felt a million years ago. There were pegs to hang one's clothing if it could be worn again without washing, and bins to toss it into if not. Leofric stripped out of his soiled uniform and dropped it in the bin.

In the army, if one's uniform needed washing, one had best wear it swimming as the legion forded a river. Time to bathe and soak was a rare luxury, and after only a few months here in Papia, Leofric still hadn't gotten used to handing off his soiled clothing to servants who whisked it away, and delivered it freshly laundered to his chambers. Some of the men passed their armor and weapon off to servants, too, the other high officers of their grace's guard especially, but Leofric did not. He liked to maintain his own weapons, felt that was part of combat practice. Part of being a soldier. Like his skills, Leofric kept his weapons sharp and honed, should they be needed.

Training with his peers had raised more bruises than usual,

as he'd held his sword in his uninjured left hand. Leofric did practice from time to time with his off hand, even when whole. *You will live and die by your sword arm,* Imperator Hamate had told him. Leofric had seen the truth of that, and thought, *Why hinge my life on one arm, when I have two?* But still, he had one dominant hand, the one that seemed to think on its own, to make the right parries and thrusts without his telling it to do so. The left was...passable. But not passable enough to avoid every blow by his sparring partners, not by a long shot. He would go to sleep sore and aching tonight, but it was an ache he relished.

"You'd think with all your training, you'd have learned how to dodge some of those."

Leofric about jumped out of his skin. He whirled toward the voice to see Cosmo standing beside him, leaning casually against the doorway into the baths. "What are you doing here?"

Cosmo raked his eyes up and down Leofric, completely unabashed to be staring. "Admiring."

"Get out," Leofric hissed. "These facilities are for the guards."

Cosmo tugged at the neck of his tunic, the one he'd stolen from Leofric. "I know," he said. He crossed a fist over his chest in a mocking salute. "And here I am, Captain, reporting for duty."

"What on earth are you talking about?"

"I've been asking around," said Cosmo. "The men seem to think it's customary for a captain of the *royal* guard to take on a tribune, to train as his second."

"It is," Leofric allowed. When he'd suggested such himself, His Highness had declared he'd fling himself off the roof if a second solider started following him around.

"Well, here I am."

Leofric scowled. "Why would you wish to join his high-ness's guard?"

"I wouldn't," Cosmo agreed. "But Auro tells me it raises questions for multiple strangers to be hanging around His Highness, and Auro is strange enough for the two of us."

"What are you saying?"

"I am saying that I'm reporting for training, Captain," he said, smiling. Leering, more like. "If you're up to the task, that is. The bruises have me doubting, but I'd be happy to massage them for you."

Leofric flushed and seized a fresh tunic from the stack beside the towels, all thoughts of a refreshing soak forgotten. He yanked it down over his head. "The bruises are your fault," he snapped. "I was fighting with my off hand."

"And your right is the one that's used to ah...*grasping* a hilt. I understand." He smiled again.

Leofric clenched his hands into fists at his sides, and tried to center himself. He called up his training, picking a point at which to stare. Unfortunately, the point he chose was the loathsome cluster of freckles on Cosmo's neck, dark like a bruise, roughly the shape of chalice—but it still allowed him to cool his anger. "A ruse may be necessary," he allowed, his voice even and steady once again, so steady Cosmo looked shocked. That helped. "But I cannot endanger His Royal Highness."

"Am I quite so fearsome?"

"You mistake me," said Leofric, though he privately felt the true answer was yes. "If I were to take a tribune into my service, he would need to have training, discipline. And ... adequacy at swordplay."

"'*Adequacy?*'" Cosmo looked likely to choke on the word, and it took all of Leofric's self-control to contain his own triumphant smile.

He shrugged. "Aye," he said. "Otherwise, what use would he be for protecting His Highness?"

Cosmo positively smoldered, and with how thick and humid the air, it looked as though he were steaming with anger. "Care to bolster those words in the practice yard?"

"Any time."

"How about now?" Cosmo eyed him boldly. "I see a few inches of skin that still has room to bruise."

Leofric knew immediately that accepting this thrown gauntlet would be a mistake. Call it instinct, call it years of training, call it whatever you wish. It would be a mistake. Leofric took a deep breath and got a handle on himself. He would not be goaded. A guard could never allow himself to be so goaded, when his charge's life and his sacred oath were both at stake. Leofric opened his mouth to tell Cosmo to leave, to tell him he was tired, to tell him there was no need, to tell him *no*. Somehow, though, what came out was, "Yes."

Cosmo grinned. "Lead the way."

Five

Tomorrow, Leofric would have to see if the Medicus had any way to test for madness. Surely that was the only probable cause for his current actions. He hefted a few practice swords, checking the balance. They were made of wood, but filled with cores of lead to increase the weight, carved in the shape of a true blade. They wouldn't cut a man's head off, but they could offer one hell of a beating.

He had sparred with His Highness and Auro, so he knew the strength present in the man undressing opposite him. Auro wasn't a martial sort, but he held immense power in those soft hands of his, and Leofric already had a taste of what Cosmo could do. He tried a practice swing with his left hand. It had plenty of strength behind it, but it was still slower, more cumbersome than a similar blow with his right. Even a second or two could mean his life in battle, and while Leofric didn't *think* Cosmo would try to kill him, the risk of injury was great. It wasn't just his pride that would be singed if he lost here. Risking injury sparring with a volatile demigod wouldn't help feed his sister-in-law or her son. The King would surely dismiss him immediately if injured. What good was a maimed man for protecting the prince?

He should *not* be doing this.

The sun was setting, but Leofric's eyes adjusted well to the dark, and Cosmo seemed likewise unaffected. They readied their weapons, facing one another across a circle drawn in the sand floor of the practice yard.

"Ready?" Cosmo asked him.

Leofric nodded, adjusting his grip on his sword. "Come," he said.

Cosmo sauntered around Leofric in a circle. His form was impeccable, Leofric had to admit, as he spun on his heel, tracking the movement of Cosmo's blade. His steps were so languid, so casual that Leofric almost missed the tell. Almost. Cosmo made to continue his sunwise circle, but his eyes gave him away. He pivoted, faster than Leofric expected, but he got his sword up in time to block the blow. The force of it rang through his whole arm; Cosmo was stronger than he looked. Leofric had the reach on him, and at least two stone of weight if he were any judge, but beneath the freckled skin Cosmo was surprisingly sturdy.

"Very good," said Cosmo, his tone light and mocking as he backed off a step. "A bit slow."

Leofric dodged sideways as Cosmo lunged, went to one knee and tangled his practice sword between Cosmo's legs to send him sprawling. "I'm quick enough."

Cosmo spat out a mouthful of sand. "I'll bet."

Leofric watched as Cosmo got to his feet and regained his fighting stance, sword ready. When he charged, this time he was ready for Leofric's dodge and mirrored it, bring his sword up to catch Leofric's blow. Neither stepped back or gave ground, and their swords came together again, and again, and again. Cosmo plainly had exquisite training, and he was quick as a cat—but Leofric could also see he was rusty, like perhaps he hadn't lifted a sword in the last several decades—or centuries. "You're not half bad," he called to Cosmo, when he finally shoved him off a few steps. He pointed at him with his blade, panting. "For someone so old."

The hilt of Cosmo's wooden sword smoked beneath his hand. "You're the one breathing like a sow in labor," Cosmo shot back.

It was true. Leofric had lost track of things, somewhere during their dance. The sun had truly set, and the torches lighting the walkway seemed unusually bright. How long had they been at it? His arms suddenly felt as lead, but unfortunately, Cosmo still bounced lightly on the balls of his bare feet. Cosmo might have been getting more angry, more reckless, but one thing he hadn't gotten more of was tired. Leofric might well have to yield this fight, or risk being seriously hurt. The thought tasted like bile, and he shook the ache from his limbs as best as he could and readied his sword. "Aye," he agreed. "It's my imitation of your mother."

It was a cheap tactic, and hardly an honorable one. Leofric knew that, but fighters were just men, after all. And men were fools. Cosmo flew at him, as Leofric had known he would. Fast, erratic blows rained down upon Leofric like hailstones, but they didn't land as true as the ones Cosmo had used to open the dance. Leofric cursed, half a dozen opportunities coming and going to strike a blow that his right hand could have seized, while it was all his left could do to keep the sword aloft. His plan to goad Cosmo into making a reckless mistake suddenly seemed foolish, foolish and possibly deadly.

And then Leofric was on his back, staring up at a bruise dark sky. Cosmo stood over him, practice sword ready to core the apple of his throat. "Do you yield?"

The wooden hilt beneath Cosmo's fingers had blackened, Leofric saw, with a thrill of fear. He held his tongue.

Cosmo dragged the blunted point down Leofric's chest,

letting it rest on a fresh bruise that had already formed along his ribs. He squatted in the sand, stared into Leofric's face as he eased just a bit of his weight onto the sword, pressing it into the tender flesh of Leofric's side. "*Yield,*" Cosmo hissed.

Leofric pressed his lips together and shook his head. The point of the practice sword pressed into the bruise, and the sweet, delicious ache spread down his side from armpit to hip, and Leofric shivered.

Cosmo startled, his face transforming into one of astonishment.

They stared at each other in silence for a beat, but Cosmo recovered himself first. "Oh," he said softly, his wicked smile returning. "Is that the way of it?"

Leofric's retort was lost on a choked gasp as Cosmo leaned more of his weight onto the sword, pressing it harder and harder into the bruise. The pain was bone deep and exquisite.

Then, all at once, the pain, the weight, the smell of Cosmo's sweat, all of it vanished. Cosmo stood and tossed his sword aside, laughing. "I yield," he said.

Flustered, Leofric scrambled to his feet. "What?"

"I yield," said Cosmo, the torchlight dancing in his hazel eyes. "No victory could be half as sweet as this."

Leofric watched, furious and bewildered, as Cosmo sauntered back up the path toward the barracks.

The royal villa was in an uproar. Preparations for the arrival of Queen Dafina had the place boiling over with activity as every inch of the villa was scrubbed and polished in advance of her approach. The welcome feast for her entourage would be staggering in its extravagance. Cosmo spent a fair amount of his extra time down at the kitchens, sweet-talking the cooks into sharing some of their choicest morsels as they tested recipes and gathered delicacies to please the foreign queen, all at Prince Alexios's behest.

"Doesn't it bother you?" Cosmo asked his brother.

"Does what bother me?" Auro frowned over a pair of ancient, crumbling scrolls spread in front of him. Cosmo was supposed to be helping him search for any clues that might assist them in their quest to break the curse, or understand the nuance of their mother's attempt to break it herself. Auro loved studying about as much as Cosmo did, which is to say, not at all. Cosmo preferred stories with a lot more pictures, especially if the pictures were of naked people. If ever dragged to the library by in his youth, Cosmo would soon peel off and spend the hours searching the books for old works of art that contained breasts or cocks or something else diverting to look at. None of these dusty old histories had illuminations like that, sad to say, so they did little to keep Cosmo's interest.

"Your prince," said Cosmo. "Going to such lengths to impress this girl."

Auro bristled. "It's expected of him," he said primly. "He doesn't enjoy it."

"Hmmm," said Cosmo, flipping idly through a book. "Are you certain?"

"If you're not going to help, please at least stop distracting me," said Auro, refusing to take the bait.

When he looked up from his scrolls though, Cosmo saw that his blows had landed, and he felt guilty. "I'm trying to help," said Cosmo. "I just don't think the answers to our plight will be found in any of these books."

Auro frowned at him. "Well, they certainly won't, if we don't look."

Cosmo rolled his eyes and heaved to his feet, too restless to remain indoors. Perhaps he could convince Leofric to spar again. Cosmo had thought of little else since their bout a few days ago. "I need to stretch my legs."

"While you do, could you try to give some thought as to where Kryos's grace might have been hidden?"

"Me? How should I know?"

"Because," said Auro patiently. "*You* are his counterpart. I'll put my mind to it, as well but..."

"But what?"

"I don't think our counterparts are so arbitrary. When I truly thought about it, I figured out where Cedras's grace was hidden. I am certain you know, deep down, where Kryos's might be."

"There's no way—"

"*Deep,* deep down, perhaps," said Auro.

Cosmo could tell he was being dismissed. He ventured out onto the balcony, letting the sun warm his face and inform him as to what the world might need. It was a meditative task, helped him clear his head. Unfortunately, when his head cleared, his mind showed signs of returning to his sparring session with Leofric. If he were being honest with himself, it hadn't really left his mind at all.

Leofric was an expert fighter, Cosmo had understood that immediately. He would have to be, to have earned his current position, but seeing him in action had been something else entirely. He had been poised, focused, graceful. Every movement was like a dance. Even fighting with his off hand, Leofric had tested Cosmo sorely. Had Leofric been fighting with his dominant hand, there would have been no contest—Cosmo had used all of his self-control to fight as a mortal man, not to allow his temper to release his grace. All of that was well and good, but it wasn't what had kept Cosmo awake the last few nights.

The arousal in Leofric's tightly wound body had been unmistakable. Cosmo could smell it on him, could feel it humming through the air when he'd pressed his practice sword into Leofric's bruise. It had staggered him, the strength of that want, braided inextricably with the pain. Cosmo couldn't shake the notion, not that he tried all that hard. He wondered if Leofric had already known that about himself, the connection between pleasure and plain. He thought not. Leofric was not the sort to idly pursue his own desires. Before that night, Cosmo would have found it easier to believe Leofric didn't even *have* any of his own desires.

Cosmo would be the first to admit that he was a lover, *not* a fighter. There were so many far more pleasurable things one could use one's body for than the swinging of swords or the shooting of arrows. However, he had trained relentlessly as a boy, desperate to be like his older brothers. Desperate to be as strong, as fast, as...he frowned, remembering. It had been Kryos who had trained him, alongside Ozias and occasionally Cedras. Despite his bookish nature, Cedras had been a terror in the practice yard. His enormous reach and sharp mind had lent themselves well to developing martial skill. Auro usually hid whenever they were summoned to spar with one another. And over all of them, Kryos ruled, serving as master at arms, as no mortal had the stomach to train five Godlings, and their father hadn't the patience. The only times Cosmo could ever remember seeing Kryos smile were when one of them performed some stance or step correctly, when one of his lessons had found its mark.

And there was one other time, too, that Kryos had smiled. At least, smiled where Cosmo could see it. The memory was a dim one—it had already begun fading into the annals of lost childhood moments even *before* Cosmo had been cursed, but he tried to chase it now, tried to catch what remained of it. It was important, he felt, though he could not have said why.

Cosmo and his brothers had not fought much, as children —at least, not anything approaching the animosity of their adolescence, or young adulthood. He had idealized Kryos, at that time. He was older, stronger, taller. He was so fierce.

Cosmo couldn't help but admire him. While Auro was like to run to their mother for protection, there had been a long time when Cosmo would have hidden behind Kryos. He'd defended Cosmo from their father's wroth, from scoldings and punishments beyond count.

Kryos had been the first to drink from the chalice of their father's grace. It was his right, as the eldest son. Cosmo had been *beside* himself with jealousy when he'd found out. Anything Kryos did was something Cosmo wanted part of, too. He couldn't have been more than eleven, Kryos around fifteen. Cosmo sat heavily on a stone bench, smiling to think of it. Kryos was scarcely more than a boy, but at the time he'd towered over Cosmo, seeming like a man, not a child. Father had summoned Kryos, told him they were taking a special journey together to mark his ascent into manhood. Cosmo had not seen why he couldn't have gone, too. He'd followed them.

Never in his life had Cosmo gotten in as much trouble as he had then—somehow, he'd nearly forgotten. They'd been on a mountain top. To young Cosmo it had been a frigid and terrible place but to Kryos... "*Auro!*" He leapt to his feet and ran back inside. "Auro, I think I have it!"

Six

The day Her Grace, Queen Dafina of Neossós arrived in Papia was bright and warm, the perfect early summer's morning. Auro was subdued, Leofric did not fail to note. Cosmo tried his best to cheer his brother up, but the attempted jests fell flat. Nothing would truly distract him from the knowledge that this woman was betrothed to Alexios. He might be *Auro's* Alexios in private, but in the shining light of day he belonged to his people, and this young foreign queen. Leofric felt a pang for the young prince and his paramour both as they rode out to meet her party as they approached up the long, exquisite road leading to the Papian Royal villa.

Cosmo posed as Leofric's tribune, so he wore the uniform of the royal guard and on a long ashen pole he carried the Papian signa, a carved mallard's head with green enameled feathers. He rode a spirited dapple-grey filly called Hestia. Leofric only prayed that Cosmo would keep his mouth shut and refrain from humiliating him. As Leofric's tribune, Cosmo was a direct reflection of Leofric, his commander.

The Queen's party was far smaller than one might expect

from a royal retinue, but Neossós was a small kingdom, made smaller by a plague that had claimed a lot of its citizens over the past year. Prince Alexios was now betrothed to their queen, and the two had plans to combine both kingdoms into one. A complicated notion. Papia would take on Neossós' debts and weaknesses, but would gain access to valuable resources. The trade was not necessarily an equal one, but His Highness Prince Alexios had refused to leave an entire kingdom of people floundering and suffering.

Alexios dismounted, a signal the rest of the party should do the same. He bowed deeply and the rest of them took a knee in the road to greet Queen Dafina. "Your Grace," he said. "Papia is yours."

The Queen wore a sheer black veil to cover her face, pinned below a white gold circlet studded with pearls. Her palla and tunic were died heavy black as well, the fabric torn as a mark of mourning. "Your Highness," came her voice from behind the fabric. She was of an age with Alexios, but she sounded weary as an old woman. "The honor is mine."

"Your Grace may recall Leofric, the captain of my household guard?"

"Yes, of course. Well met, Captain."

"You as well, Your Grace," said Leofric with a respectful bow. "You honor all of us with your presence. I trust the roads were safe?"

"Very," she said. Dafina pulled back her cumbersome veil, revealing a pretty face and sad eyes. She turned to Alexios and added, "And so straight, and level."

Alexios beamed at the praise of his beloved roads. "Of course, Your Grace will remember Auro."

"How could I forget the man who saved my life?" She swooped in and kissed Auro's cheek, and unfortunately next turned her gaze to Cosmo. Leofric had somewhat been hoping he would evade notice entirely. "Have we met?"

"May I present Cosmo, my tribune," Leofric said, resisting the urge to preemptively apologize for him. He'd done nothing untoward, Leofric told himself, even as another voice in his head added, *yet*. "He will be assisting me as we find accommodations for your men."

Cosmo bowed gracefully. When he straightened up, Dafina cocked her head, giving Cosmo a long, searching look. Leofric braced himself, wishing that Cosmo would perhaps decline to speak, or even better, evaporate on the spot. The last thing they all needed was for him to make one of his lascivious comments to the future Queen of Papia. "Your Grace," said Cosmo. "I have not yet had the distinct pleasure of basking in your radiance. Certainly, I would recall such an auspicious day."

Dafina laughed, caught off guard. Cosmo had that way about him, Leofric had to admit. When he said the outrageous things he said, they didn't sound false—simply crude in their earnestness. She offered her hand to Cosmo, who kissed her knuckles. "And yet," she said. "I feel as though I know your face."

"Cosmo is my brother," said Auro.

Recognition dawned on her face, and Leofric saw at once a fissure of tension run through Dafina from head to toe. "Oh," she said faintly. "Another one of...goodness."

Cosmo looked puzzled, but he plainly sensed her change in demeanor too. Before Leofric could sidestep the moment, or usher Cosmo out of sight, Cosmo made attempt to smooth things over himself, with all the grace of a boulder rolling off a cliff. "Your Grace," he said. "The captain has the matter of your men well in hand. Despite your fertile glow, you are in a delicate state. If it would please you, I could escort you to your guest apartments within the royal villa."

"Delicate state?" Dafina echoed, her wide eyes casting frantically around the busy yard. Alexios looked *mortified*, and

Auro ready to liquify. This revelation was obviously not the surprise to them that it was to Leofric.

Cosmo ploughed on, oblivious. Plainly he thought he was being ingratiating. "Yes, of course, Your Majesty. It's the future of the kingdom you carry. And besides—*Ouch!*"

Leofric had finally gathered himself enough to elbow Cosmo in the ribs. Hard. "Be *silent.*"

Cosmo's mouth dropped open, and it was as if Leofric could see it dawn on him in real time that he had made a terrible mistake. Before he could continue babbling and make things even worse, Leofric wrapped an arm around the back of his head, covering his mouth with one hand like one might an unruly child.

Dafina regained her composure and smiled a strained smile. "Yes," she said, too loudly. "I am certain one day his Highness and I will have many healthy children. But that day is still very far away. I think I shall find my own way to my apartments."

She swept away with a small tail of ladies, casting a look over her shoulder. Leofric looked around, certain at least some of those gathered here had heard Cosmo's pronouncement. He hadn't known that Dafina was expecting a child. Certainly, it wasn't public knowledge. Or rather, it wasn't until the freckled menace fighting against Leofric's grip had blurted it out for everyone in the yard to hear.

Cosmo squirmed in his hold, and Leofric hissed as Cosmo's teeth clamped on his finger. He jerked back, releasing Cosmo, who flailed his arms to ensure his continued freedom. "What is the matter with you?" Cosmo asked him.

"Me?" Leofric fumed. "What were you thinking, saying that?"

"I was trying to be gracious," said Cosmo. "I didn't know it was a secret!"

"How could it not be a secret?" Alexios hissed at him.

"I don't know," said Cosmo. He scowled. "It was an honest mistake! I shouldn't have said—"

"You didn't need to say *anything*," said Auro. "And now the rumors will be spread around the entire villa by nightfall."

Cosmo at least had the grace to look abashed.

"I must go do what I can to smooth this over," said Alexios. "Dafina will be furious with me, no doubt, thinking I told her private matters to everyone in my household."

"But you didn't!" said Cosmo. "I could—I could just tell. I thought it was obvious, but perhaps…"

Alexios sighed. "I don't think that really matters in the end. Auro, come."

Cosmo watched them go, looking genuinely distraught, which was a nice change.

Leofric massaged his hand. "You bit me."

"Yeah, well," said Cosmo aggressively. "You wouldn't let go."

"I had to stop you talking *somehow*," said Leofric. "And elbowing you didn't seem to be cutting it." Leofric gave himself a mental shake, smoothed the front of his uniform, and straightened his armor that had been knocked off kilter in his brief struggle with Cosmo. He considered that if Cosmo were to remain in his charge, he should start wearing thick gloves. Come to think of it, perhaps he should just be grateful that he was not scorched for his trouble this time.

"Come," said Leofric. "I must continue my work. And a tribune should follow, and observe. *Quietly.*"

Cosmo followed him to the stables, where they supervised the grooms and stable hands finding accommodations for the mounts the queen had brought with her. Leofric assisted where he could, calming nervous animals and guiding the Queen's stablemaster, a youth called Titus, as he drove her massive carriage into the garage, newly erected behind the stables. Titus had a lot of opinions about the mounts they'd brought, and was not ashamed to share them. "*No, no,*" he was saying now. "You can't put Bijoux in with any other mares, she'll bite their ears off."

All went as smoothly as could expected, but Leofric found himself agitated all the same as he catalogued all the strange faces now flooding the villa grounds.

"What is it?" Cosmo asked him during a lull in the bustle of activity.

"I mislike this," he admitted, unnerved. Cosmo was far too observant. Leofric had been certain to keep his face an impassive mask, but something must have alerted Cosmo to the fact that he was distraught. "Any one of these new faces could be an agent of Janus."

Auro had told Cosmo all about the sorcerer who'd killed Dafina's mother, and sent an assassin after Alexios. "Perhaps they should be questioned," he suggested. "Their belongings searched and inspected?"

Leofric glared at him. "It is not for you to give such orders," Leofric snapped.

"I didn't—"

"My charge—and *yours*—is to obey," Leofric said. "I will *ask* His Highness his thoughts upon the matter."

"You don't trust your own instincts?" Cosmo asked. "Do you need His Highness to tell you the sky is blue, also?"

Leofric rounded on him. "How dare—"

Cosmo smiled, and bowed. "As your tribune I live to serve you, *Captain*," he said mockingly. "Pay me no mind. It was merely the foolish notion of one who thinks for himself from time to time."

Before Leofric could form a retort, Cosmo turned and left him there in the stables. Cosmo had been under Leofric's feet, nose, and skin for a week now, and he was already beside himself. He had gone so far as to beg Alexios to find another suitable position for Cosmo somewhere in the villa.

"Leofric," said Alexios tiredly, "Can you please just tolerate him a bit longer?"

And he'd sounded so world weary that Leofric had instantly felt guilty further burdening the young prince. Leofric, it seemed, was on his own. After the night they'd sparred, the spotty nuisance hadn't been far from Leofric's thoughts, so he couldn't even have a moment's peace inside his own skull.

Cosmo was there, at morning meal. There, in the baths. There in the bed chamber they shared in Prince Alexios's apartments. There, in Leofric's dreams, performing unspeakable erotic acts and laughing when Leofric begged for more. Each morning he woke tired as if he hadn't slept, and hard as a table leg.

And Cosmo knew. *He knew.* Leofric didn't know how he knew—perhaps he'd begun muttering in his sleep—but when he woke each morning, it was to Cosmo smirking at him from his bed opposite Leofric's. He'd stopped his brazen flirting, for the most part, but his new modes of torment were even worse. The smile hovered close to one of pity, like Cosmo knew Leofric's inner needs and felt truly sorry that he lay there in bed alone each night, woefully unfulfilled.

It was almost more than he could stand, especially when so much depended upon Leofric keeping his wits. With Cosmo gone, Leofric yanked his thoughts back to the present and left the stables. Outside in the yard, ordering men around and supervising Queen Dafina's rear guard as they rode through the gate was a man Leofric had not expected to ever see again.

Leofric had met Kato in the spring, at the festival for the spring equinox. He was broad, bull-strong, with a shock of fine blonde hair and bright blue eyes. The night of the festival, while Leofric had been guarding Prince Alexios, Kato had been guarding the Queen of Neossós—Dafina's late mother. He'd eyed Leofric with enough brazen curiosity that Leofric *almost* considered finding out if his intimate anatomy was of a size with the rest of him. Leofric hadn't had anyone since before his brother's death, not necessarily by intent but by urge. That is to say, lack thereof. Five years ago, he wouldn't have hesitated. But that spring, he had.

And thank goodness, because Kato had assisted Janus in concealing his assassination attempt of Prince Alexios. When they had left Neossós, Kato had been nowhere to be found—it seemed as if he had joined Janus in hiding.

But here he was.

"Captain," said Leofric stiffly, approaching him.

"Captain."

"I did not expect to see you here," said Leofric. He eyed Kato up and down, as if he could see through any possible deceptions the man might be plotting if he stared hard enough. Kato *must* still be working with Janus; Leofric couldn't believe that Dafina had brought him here to Papia.

"I had not expected to be here," Kato said with a rueful smile. He removed his helm and tucked it under one burly arm. "In fact, I did not expect to find myself gainfully employed at all."

"I am just as surprised," said Leofric curtly.

"Captain, apologies, but—"

"Her Grace said nothing of retaining your services, after her erstwhile stepfather fled Neossós."

Kato bristled. "Not to *you*, perhaps," he said. "I believe she discussed it with His Highness, Prince Alexios."

Leofric squinted, trying to determine if Kato were lying or not. He couldn't quite decide, which worried him. With his eyes narrow, his lips pressed into a firm line, Leofric tried his best to hide his uncertainty behind a stern mask, but it didn't seem that Kato was fooled.

"You can ask him, if it please you," said Kato, just the hint of a smug smile playing about his lips.

"Oh, I shall."

Hours later, Leofric prepared himself for the feast in Queen Dafina's honor, seething. Kato had apparently been telling the truth, at least inasmuch as His Highness's knowledge of his presence was concerned.

"I understand that you are loath to trust him," Alexios had said. "And that's all to the good. By no means do I think we should lower our guard entirely—but try to see it from his point of view. He had sworn an oath to guard Her Grace and her family, just as you have sworn a similar vow to me and mine. It could just as easily have been *you* doing evil, under the auspices of following orders."

And, naturally, His Highness delivered his stern words in front of Cosmo, who grinned at Leofric from behind Alexios's back, his mirth at Leofric's expense plain as day.

Leofric had two uniforms saved for special occasions, and he donned one now. The tunic and cape richly died crimson, his breastplate far more ornate than the one he wore day to day. He'd bathed in a hurry, hoping to finish before Cosmo returned to the chambers they shared. Most likely the pest would be late. His position was only a disguise, after all, and he plainly did not give committing to the role any weight. Leofric checked the blade on his razor before soaping his skin and using it to scrape away the stubble that had begun to grow in on the side of his skull. The rasp of the blade over the thin skin of his scalp was soothing, in a strange way. A close shave required control and precision, a steady hand. He had done this so many times he barely needed to glance in the mirror above the wash basin. When he finished, he washed the blade and dried it on a towel. With a sigh, he looked at his reflection, turning his head to the side to inspect his tattoo, and thinking of his brother.

"Are you done primping?" Came an irritating voice from the doorway.

Leofric closed his eyes and exhaled slowly, calming himself. He turned to see Cosmo, dressed and ready for the feast. The two of them would be posted by the dais during the meal. Prince Alexios had shied away from Leofric's suggestion that they closely question the Queen's entourage, his misgivings about Kato notwithstanding, which had Leofric on edge before the meal had even begun. His Highness claimed that with the political situation so delicate, it would not do to offend the queen and her people by submitting them to such —especially after Cosmo's gaff in the yard. It was a mistake, Leofric knew, and he hated to think that Cosmo had been correct. He should simply have performed the interviews himself, instead of waiting for Alexios's permission to do so.

Leofric hated that, the impotent indecision he felt. The word "perhaps" had hardly been in his vocabulary before he'd come to Papia. Things had seemed so much clearer to him, before. In the legion, he'd never had to think much. In battle, his sword was part of his arm, the only part that mattered, and it did all his thinking. One day, perhaps, if he'd risen to gain his own command, he would have had to learn more of these twisty ways of diplomatic thinking, but at present, it was foreign.

The feast was in full swing, and Leofric stood the way the Imperator had taught him, eyes alert and wide, searching for any sign of a threat. *Discipline is your strongest armor,* the Imperator had taught him. *You will spend one hundred days standing still for every one day you must act. But you must be ready for that day, whenever it should arrive.* He gave himself exercises to remain alert while he stood for hours, focusing on each table of guests in turn and trying to learn something of each person seated there simply by studying their faces. It was a game that required quiet focus. He watched the servers, the queen's ladies, and even the other royal guardsmen in the hall. He watched Queen Dafina, Prince Alexios, and Auro, who stood behind the table to serve wine to the most honored guests seated at the high table.

Alexios's parents, King Nelios and Queen Clio, had been initially upset about Auro's presence at the feast, but Leofric could tell that Alexios's stubbornness might at last be wearing them down, now that it was clear Auro wasn't going anywhere.

Watching the high table, Leofric could see Alexios and Dafina were becoming fast friends. They leaned toward one another, in almost constant conversation, and Leofric even saw Her Grace smile once or twice. She still dressed in mourning for her mother, but her face was unveiled for the festivities, and though grief still weighed her slim shoulders, Leofric knew she was far more comfortable with His Highness than when the two of them had first met. It seemed to him that the growing trust went both ways, as Alexios relaxed around her more and more as the night wore on.

It was imperative this feast and the subsequent negotiations go well, if Alexios and Dafina hoped to combine their two kingdoms. Hers was limping along on its last legs, and Alexios needed their resources to revitalize the roads in Papia. Long ago, the two kingdoms had been one city state, vassal to a larger empire. Those days were long gone, however, and recombining them would be no small feat.

Of all the faces Leofric spent the feast studying, he took great pains to ignore the man standing beside him. Cosmo would be better suited with almost any other ruse to explain his presence here in the royal villa. He was not cut out for this kind of duty. He fidgeted, shifted his weight, sighed. Scratched his nose, fussed with the pommel of his sword.

"Three quarters of the year I would be the ideal guards-man," he complained under his breath.

"Would that it were any other season," Leofric hissed back. "A statue would be better company."

To his outrage, that only made Cosmo smile. "A statue would be just as useful. Nothing will happen in the hall tonight."

"We cannot know that," said Leofric, struggling to keep the anger from stealing his focus. "Such is the way of a guardsman."

Cosmo huffed.

"Can you not stand still?"

"I can," retorted Cosmo. The feast was in its fourth hour, and he shifted his weight, wincing. "Perhaps I can't."

Leofric couldn't stifle his small smile before Cosmo saw it.

"Oh yes," said Cosmo. "So much pride you take in being as useful as one of these stone columns. Perhaps less so, since the columns hold up the roof. All you hold up is your armor."

Leofric bit down on his tongue, refusing to allow himself to be goaded. "You are a mere tribune," he said coolly. "His Highness is not relying on you to keep him safe. Better for you to excuse yourself than continue distracting those of us with real work to do."

Cosmo turned as red as their cloaks but for once held his tongue, which gave Leofric immense satisfaction. He strode mutely from the hall, and though no one else paid mind to his leave, Leofric followed him with his eyes until he'd left the feast entirely.

Cosmo couldn't believe he'd let Leofric get the last word in. His wits had been wandering for hours as he stood there, watching a spider climb its way up a column to begin weaving its web. He watched the spider as long as he could, otherwise he would surely have fallen asleep on his feet. The life of a guardsmen had to be the dullest life imaginable, Cosmo thought. He would rather be scrubbing the villa's chamber pots daily than do this ever again. At least when cleaning one could *move*. Perhaps His Highness had need of two valets, and he could spend his days with Auro, instead.

That was only part of what had him so upset. Despite what he portrayed, he felt like a complete ass after how he'd behaved in the yard, prattling on inanely while exposing Her Grace's secret. Prince Alexios should have dismissed Cosmo then and there, for inserting his foot so violently into his own mouth in the presence of Queen Dafina.

Auro had been so upset, having to stand by and watch as Alexios played gallant suitor to someone else. All Cosmo had wanted was to cheer Auro up, to cut the awkwardness of the whole affair, and naturally he'd gone and stuffed up the entire thing, making it worse for everyone involved.

Cosmo had been so distraught he hadn't even been diverted by the near constant eye-fucking he'd been getting from one of the nobles at the feast. The man was striking, handsome and broad shouldered, and he plainly had eyes for Cosmo. Normally Cosmo would have found engaging in such games endlessly fun, but not tonight. He stepped out into the garden, and the position of the moon told him four hours had passed, thought it felt more like four years. Embarrassed that Leofric had dismissed him as if he were nothing more than a troublesome gnat, and feeling sorry for himself, Cosmo wondered where he might find a glass of wine, or three.

"Greetings," said a voice behind him.

He startled, and turned to see none other than the nobleman who'd been watching him all evening. He stood, ostensibly gazing out at the magnificent flowers blooming in Queen Clio's gardens, but his eyes trained on Cosmo.

"Greetings," said Cosmo respectfully. He inclined his head. "How may I be of service?"

He grinned wickedly. "I can think of a whole host of ways."

Cosmo weighed the man for a moment. His interest was barely stirred—but stirred a bit all the same. He might be miserable, but Cosmo still had eyes. He still had hot blood pumping through his veins. The man's cocksure proposition was charming, and Cosmo had been dismissed for the evening after all.

All the same, his gut instinct was to refuse. He could appreciate the beauty and strength in the man, the bearing in his posture, but he didn't *want* him. Not the way he was accustomed to wanting. But then, he thought of the way Auro had avoided him all afternoon, furious about what had happened in the yard. He thought of Leofric, who flicked Cosmo away like a speck of dirt on his perfect uniform.

At least *someone* in this bloody villa wanted his company. Cosmo fixed a coy smile on his face. "I had wondered if you noticed my attempt to catch your eye," he said.

"I noticed," said the man. "That and other things."

"You could have approached me in the hall," said Cosmo.

"I would not want to distract one of His Highness's men," he replied, stepping closer. He wasn't unattractive, Cosmo mused. Nothing like the harshly sculpted specimen that was Leofric, but perhaps a dalliance with someone else would help Cosmo take his mind off him.

"Lucky for you, I have been dismissed for the evening," Cosmo said. "And I'm certain his Highness would be pleased if *you* were pleased, Sir."

The man smiled. "You can call me Marcus."

"Alright, Marcus," said Cosmo, taking a step closer. He noted Marcus did not ask *his* name, but that hardly mattered. "What did you have in mind?"

Back inside the atrium of the Papian royal villa, there was an antechamber where dignified supplicants could wait upon the pleasure of the king and queen. There was a fireplace, a table, and several comfortable chairs. At this hour, it was empty, with everyone of note at the feast. No one would be expecting an audience with His or Her Grace tonight. Marcus wasted no time, helping himself to the flagon of wine that stood perpetually at the ready upon the sideboard. He drained one cup and poured himself another. "Come here," he said, and his voice was gruff, and far braver in the privacy of the chamber. More demanding. Cosmo sauntered over, but when he leaned in to offer Marcus a kiss, the man fisted a hand in Cosmo's hair and gave it a commanding yank.

Cosmo winced even as he smiled at the sting in his scalp. "Is that the way of things?" he asked playfully, just as he'd asked Leofric in the practice yard.

"*Quiet*," Marcus hissed. "And hurry."

Cosmo sighed. He'd had couplings like this beyond counting, and he couldn't deny that from time to time he enjoyed being handled roughly, nor could he deny that the fear of discovery could spice such ventures—but for some reason, tonight, any desire withered and died within him as he went to his knees before Marcus. He slipped his hands up Marcus's thighs, feeling for a subligaria beneath his toga and finding none. Cosmo hiked the draping fabric up to get an eyeful of Marcus's turgid manhood, but before he could close his lips around the head, someone gave a shriek. "*Marcus!*"

Cosmo jerked away, letting the noble Marcus cover himself up. "Niella," he gasped in surprise, shoving his way past Cosmo to chase her out the door.

I will most likely pay for this later, Cosmo thought. He got to his feet and helped himself to the rest of Marcus's wine, and waited for the axe to fall.

It fell a scant three hours later. Cosmo, Marcus, and his wife all stood before Prince Alexios and his parents, the king and queen. Cosmo had stepped in shit far more aggressively than he thought. Of all the lusty adulterers no doubt present at the royal banquet, Cosmo had apparently been about to suck the cock of the one who was third in line for the Papian throne. Cosmo could not have picked a worse partner if he'd legitimately tried. Bloody fucking typical.

"You are of course dismissed from your position as Aedile," said King Nelios to Marcus Ajax Velius, who was also his nephew by marriage—because, of *course* he was. "You may remain in Papia City, but you will have no further part in the governance of the territory."

Marcus threw a filthy look at Cosmo, as if it were all his fault. "But Your Grace—"

"Silence," said Queen Clio, her gaze cold. "Be grateful your position in the line of succession is not being questioned as well. You are in violation of the legal contract of marriage, and if you stray again your wife may present her case here before us. If she has further evidence, you will be stripped of all incomes, and properties, which will be given to her to share with her next husband and their children."

"Tribune," said Prince Alexios to Cosmo. He looked terrified to be handing down royal judgements alongside his parents, but his voice was steady as he went on. "You have disgraced the entire Kingdom in front of my betrothed, Queen Dafina of Neossós, which I cannot abide. You are henceforth dismissed from your guard service as well."

Cosmo kept his face a mask and bowed deeply to the prince. "Yes, Your Highness."

They all stared at him for a while, until Alexios added, "Immediately."

"Of course, Your Highness," said Cosmo, a sinking feeling in his stomach. He was only thankful that Auro was not present to bear witness to this sorry display. Cosmo turned on his heel and left the villa. He could feel Leofric's deep scowl on the back of his head as his steps rang out through the marble hall.

A few hours before dawn, Cosmo waited in the shadows

beside the royal villa's curtain wall, waiting for the night watchmen to make their hourly circuit. He had his face hidden in the cowl of a dark robe, as his freckled visage and hair were now well known about the royal villa. When he was certain the coast was clear, he climbed a vining plant up the side of the wall and down the other side, moving swift enough to land on the soft grass before the guards passed this way again. He landed silently, on the balls of his feet, and slipped through the darkened gardens to another vining plant. Both of these ladders had been grown by Auro, Cosmo could tell at once. It was difficult to put a name to the feeling, but when he laid his hands upon them, he felt his brother's power. Auro's grace might have waned, but echoes of it remained in all the things that grew upon the earth.

Cosmo swung up and over the balcony, the balmy summer evening clear and bright with silvery moonglow. The prince separated his bed chambers from the elements with a set of gauzy silken curtains, allowing the fresh air, and Cosmo, to slip in. Once inside, he thought the most difficult part of his infiltration to be complete, but he'd only taken two steps when a colossal weight collided with his side and knocked him to the floor. Cosmo bit his tongue in the struggle, and rolled onto his back to find Leofric kneeling above him, dagger at his throat. "You," he said.

"Me," Cosmo agreed.

Leofric did not move. There was temptation in his eyes, an urge to use the knife in his hand. It was as gone as soon as it appeared, but Cosmo had seen.

"What's going on?"

Cosmo craned his head, twisting his neck to see Auro and Alexios emerging bleary eyed from the bed they shared. "Hi, little brother."

"Cosmo?"

"I thought perhaps I owed an explanation for what

happened at the feast," said Cosmo casually, as if he didn't have a bony kneecap trying to work its way through his breastbone and into his lungs. He coughed.

"Leofric, let him up," said Alexios.

"Your Highness—"

"Auro used to sneak in all the time, anyway," he said, as he shrugged into a bed robe and offered one to Auro.

"Auro used—he what?" Leofric sputtered, rising off Cosmo's chest at last.

Cosmo gulped grateful lungfuls of air as he pulled himself to a seated position.

Once Auro was dressed, he led Cosmo back out onto the balcony so they could speak in private. "You really made a mess of things," said Auro, the moment they were alone.

Cosmo sighed. He had all manner of excuses and explanations ready, but when he saw Auro's disappointment, they withered on his tongue. "I know."

"Alexios had to dismiss you," said Auro. "You know that."

"I do," said Cosmo. It was true. He did not blame Alexios for making a show of Cosmo's discharge from the royal guard. And it wasn't like it were *actually* his job. "I just wanted...I never meant to make things more difficult for you."

"You never do," said Auro, and he did not sound angry. He sounded tired. His voice was resigned, full of pity, and that was worse. Auro *had* to work with Cosmo, if he hoped to break the curse, but he would have been happier to have almost anyone else's help. Something inside of Cosmo cracked at the realization that Auro never really had any faith in him at all.

They didn't speak for several moments, instead standing side by side to stare at the stars. "I still want to... to help. To try," Cosmo said at last, stumbling over the words. "Just because I can't stay here with you any longer doesn't mean I can't search for Kryos's grace."

Auro turned to look at him, a calculating look in his green eyes. "I believe you," he said. And then he smiled.

Cosmo felt a surge of relief, that Auro still trusted him, but it was short lived, because Auro was not done yet.

"But I don't think it wise for you to embark on this quest alone."

Seven

"Your Highness, this is madness."

"Why?"

Leofric stared at Alexios, Auro and Cosmo. The three of them had certainly gone mad; there was no other explanation. There weren't many times he felt like an old man, but standing opposite Alexios, Auro and Cosmo, he did—ironic, considering Auro and Cosmo were older than he by a few centuries. "Janus is still at large. His powers are vast, and we have no idea when or where he next will strike."

"Janus knows precisely where I am," Alexios said. "If he wished to plan an attack, or exact some vengeance, he knows where to find me. Perhaps I would be safer on the road, with only the three of you to know the details of our movement."

"Here you are surrounded by high walls, you have all the strength of the royal family behind you, as well as dozens of well-trained guards. This is the seat of your power, your Highness. It would be as unwise for Janus to attack you here as it would be for you to venture out."

"Janus *has* made attempt on my life here," Alexios pointed

out. "You and Auro thwarted him then, and we have Cosmo with us now, too."

Leofric looked at Cosmo and scowled. He'd sooner entrust someone he cared for to a rabid jackal than to Auro's brother, but something told him that argument would not be heard just now. "Her Grace is here, waiting to negotiate terms of the new kingdom with you. You can hardly leave in the midst of something so important."

Alexios frowned. "That's so."

"You have responsibilities, Alexios," said Auro quietly. Leofric felt a surge of gratitude for him in that moment. "You cannot simply run off."

Alexios, it appeared, knew he was beaten. "Fine," he said. "If I cannot go, who will accompany you?"

"Excuse me," said Cosmo. "I was under the impression this was a quest that only I could undertake."

"Well, part of it, certainly," said Auro. "But I didn't think you'd want to go all by yourself."

"You...you'll come along with me?"

"Of course," said Auro. "And I'm sure Leofric will—"

"No."

"My place is here, guarding you, Your Highness. Not playing nursemaid to ..." he trailed off, embarrassed. Leofric usually kept his tongue well-guarded, but it was the middle of the night and Cosmo had already humiliated him twice today. "I swore an oath."

"I imagine your oath probably mentioned something about following orders, as well," Cosmo put in. "I thought following orders was your favorite thing *about* the bloody oath."

Leofric glowered at him, and the man had the nerve, the *gall*, to wink. He opened his mouth, furious, but Prince Alexios held up a hand to silence him. "Could you two please give us a moment?"

Auro tugged Cosmo back out onto the balcony.

"Your Highness," said Leofric at once. "Even if I did think it was wise to leave your side, I cannot."

"Why not?" Asked Alexios.

"My oath—"

"Leofric, you know as well as I do that your oath should not prevent you from following my commands. Please, tell me what's really on your mind."

Leofric hesitated, wondering how much he should share. He had come to be very fond of Prince Alexios, but Imperator Hamate had stressed to him the importance of maintaining a distance between oneself and one's charge. *You must protect them from every threat, including themselves,* he had said. *That becomes challenging when you think of them as a friend.* He had to tread carefully here, he knew, but it would not help to keep his secrets if it meant Alexios dispatching him on a quest that would not only be dangerous, but had potential to end with him being relieved of his post.

"The first thing you must understand Your Highness," Leofric began, "is that Sokol is a hard and unforgiving place. It's quite different from Papia."

"Different how?"

"The border wars with Órnio have shaped our people since the kingdom's founding. Over the years, many have tried to forge a peace between our two kingdoms, but they never lasted longer than a few years, and even during those small periods of peace, each side sharpened their knives and watched as the other side did the same."

"My father has told me some of this," Alexios said. "He carries the old grudges of Sokol with him still."

"As well he would. He led the legions of Sokol as Imperator for almost ten years, and served since he came of age."

"Did you know my father?" Alexios asked, startled.

"I am not so much older than you, Your Highness," said

Leofric. "But every man my age grew up being told tales of his prowess and ferocity in battle. The king of Sokol showered him with laurels, and as you know, his renown was such that he was able to wed a Queen, and become a King himself. When His Grace left Sokol to wed your mother, a new Imperator took his place."

"Imperator Hamate," Alexios supplied. "My father mentioned him to me, when you first took your post here."

"You are correct, Your Highness. Imperator Hamate was my superior officer. He trained me for my current post, and it is to him I owe all of what I now have."

"But, you no longer fight for Sokol. You fight for Papia. For me."

"With regrets, Your Highness, no."

Alexios frowned. "No?"

"Well, yes, but...it's complicated."

"Leofric, please, speak plain."

"Apologies, Your Highness, this is difficult for me."

"I know that," said Alexios. "Please, come sit. Have a glass of wine to steady yourself."

He must have hesitated, because the prince let out an aggrieved sigh, stomped over to his sideboard, and poured two full goblets of deep red wine. He walked back across the room toward his sitting area and slapped one into Leofric's hand. "Sit," he said. "Drink."

Leofric sat and stared down into his cup. He swirled the wine around, watching the sluggish eddies before he raised it to his lips and drank deep. When he lowered his cup at last, he said, "I had a brother."

Alexios sat opposite him, and did not interrupt. He simply clutched his own goblet and waited in silence for Leofric to continue the tale.

"A twin," he amended. His throat was thick; Leofric still

found speaking of him to be difficult. "Hamalcar was his name."

Leofric was silent for a while, still staring into his wine, so Alexios prompted him to go on. "What happened to him?"

"We enlisted together in the Sokolian legion, and fought and marched side by side for years. Then, once, our column was set upon by a much larger force of Órnian raiders. He was killed in the skirmish."

"Leofric, I'm so sorry," said Prince Alexios.

"Thank you, Your Highness. It was three years ago, but to me the grief is still quite fresh."

Alexios nodded, his dark brows knit together. It had only been three and a half months but Leofric could read the young royal like a book, and in this moment, he was wondering what on earth Hamalcar had to do with Leofric's refusal to accompany Cosmo on his quest.

"Many years ago, when we had first joined the legion, Hamalcar and I made a pact. Should one of us fall in battle, the other would see to it his family was well provided for."

"And Hamalcar had...a family?"

"Yes," said Leofric. "They are...my family now. My responsibility. After Hamalcar's death, I approached my imperator and asked his counsel. He told me that the day-to-day life of a guardsmen was often times far safer than that of a soldier, and that Papia was a safer kingdom than Sokol. Imperator Hamate was once the royal guard of our king, so he knew the way of it. For the next two hundred days he trained me personally, took me under his wing and helped me learn the ways of protecting royals so that I might earn more coin in order to support my sister-in-law and her son without risking myself in the constant fighting on the border. Laela and Sorex are everything to me. They need me, Your Highness. I cannot risk my posting here by neglecting my duty."

Prince Alexios sat and digested that for a bit. "Perhaps we could meet some sort of compromise," he said.

"What do you mean?" Leofric was skeptical at best.

"I could pay you," said Alexios simply. "I could pay you enough to retire and spend the rest of your life in Sokol with your family."

"Your Highness—"

"You said your family is everything to you," Alexios interrupted. He met Leofric's gaze with an uncharacteristically hard look in his big brown eyes. He lowered his voice and said, "Auro is *everything* to me. It is killing me that I cannot help his brothers in this. Please, Leofric. Help them for me."

"I will consider this offer your Highness. It is very generous," Leofric allowed.

"Consider quickly," said Alexios bluntly. "I will give you half the sum now, and on the way with Cosmo, you can deliver it to your family. The second half I will give you when you return."

Leofric's instinct was to refuse. It felt wrong, somehow. He'd always been paid wages as a soldier, and of course now as a guardsman...but he'd also sworn an oath, both to His Highness and his father, the king of Papia—not to mention that he'd only been sent to Papia because the imperator trusted him to maintain the iron reputation of the Sokolian legion.

But he'd sworn an oath to Hamalcar, too.

Perhaps Leofric could find a way to preserve them both. In fact, the gold Alexios offered him didn't even mean he would have to resign his post. He could still perform his duty with the knowledge that Laela and Sorex would be cared for if something happened to him. Leofric was wary though; this offer seemed too good to be true. He trusted Alexios to keep his word, and even half the sum of a lifetime of his wages would be a goodly amount should something ill befall him on the journey—or if something should happen to His Highness while Leofric was off with Cosmo.

That thought was a sobering one. Janus was still at large, as Leofric had said, and of course, the life of a prince could be fraught with perils, even when excluding vindictive renegade sorcerers. Leofric had come to care very much for the brave young man now staring at him, jaw set, arms crossed over his chest. He didn't want to leave him vulnerable, either. It seemed as though no matter what he did, he was forsaking someone.

Leofric had to choose, now, which oath he had to keep, and which ones he could stand to break, no matter how painful it might be. When he thought of Laela and Sorex, the choice was clear.

"I'll do it."

Cosmo spent the next few days in the royal domus in Papia city. He did his very best to keep a low profile while there, so that his presence wouldn't become known to the king and queen, or anyone else. He paced restlessly around his rooms, unable to settle to anything. He'd wanted to take to the road ever since he'd had the revelation regarding the location of Kryos's grace.

It simply had to be on the mountain. It was the place Kryos had always loved, ever since their father had brought him there to impart his grace for the first time. Mount Hiru, it was called, and it sprang up at the place where three kingdoms joined. He knew the length of the journey because he'd made it before, when he'd been so desperate to follow in his brother's footsteps. It would not be overlong, and he hadn't seen much call to delay, but Auro had insisted they spend time preparing, making ready. He now realized it was because Auro was reluctant to allow Cosmo to undertake such an important journey on his own.

The fact that Auro wanted him to have a nursemaid in attendance on the quest was galling, to say the least. And he found it impossible to believe that Leofric would ever surrender his precious honor and leave the side of the crown prince, yet here Cosmo was, waiting on Leofric to escort him on his journey. The more he thought of it, the madder it seemed. Without Auro's reassuring presence, the questions and doubts infested Cosmo's mind like rats in a granary. Chewing, gnawing, biting.

He'd gone so far as gathering his few belongings and striding toward the servants' exit three times, the decision in his mind firm: he would return to Lapis and the simple life he'd made for himself here in the city. Heroic quests and grand sacrifices were not for the likes of someone such as Cosmo. But each time, with his hand upon the latch of the door, he would sigh, curse and throw down his bag in disgust. Something was keeping him from backing out. As much as Cosmo could tell, that something was spite. He didn't want to give that uptight prig Leofric the satisfaction of being right, didn't want any of them to be right. If the quest failed, or Kryos killed him come winter, well. Cosmo had lived a very long time. At least he could die knowing how wronged he'd been, and that was almost worth it.

Almost.

On the third day, Auro, Leofric, and Prince Alexios arrived with a tail of two dozen guardsmen. Most wore uniforms like Leofric's, but some wore the badge of Queen Dafina of Neossós. The queen had dispatched some of her own men to watch out for her betrothed, to hear a very annoyed Alexios tell it.

"This plan is already falling apart," said Cosmo, hiding in

his chambers from the guards who would surely recognize him.

"It is impossible for Alexios to go anywhere absent a proper tail," said Auro, though he too sounded worried.

"How am I to join you on this quest, if all of these soldiers recognize the man dismissed for lascivious behavior?"

"I don't know," admitted Auro.

"Perhaps you can all go on this grand adventure without my help at all," Cosmo said peevishly. "Perhaps I'm not even needed."

"You are needed," insisted Auro, but Cosmo suspected that Auro had his doubts.

It took them another two days to come up with a plan. Alexios, Leofric, and his guards would travel the distance to the border between Papia and the kingdom of Sokol. Cosmo could travel behind them, keeping pace with the column but staying far out of sight. Once they reached the border, Leofric, Cosmo and Auro would peel off from the main column and continue on their journey to Mount Hiru. Alexios would return to Papia city, claiming he had dispatched his most trusted guard to Sokol with an important political message.

"The men should not question such," said Leofric, and Cosmo rolled his eyes. Most of the men wouldn't question it if the king told them to ride their horses off a cliff, it seemed to him. "But your royal parents might."

"True enough," said Alexios. "Perhaps I could tell my father I sent you in secret to recruit more men for the force of royal guardsmen. I think his pride in his homeland would make him more willing to believe such a tale."

Cosmo felt like a caged beast, unable to leave his chambers for fear of being recognized. It took him all of five minutes to make his own preparations. There were barely any personal affects for him to pack, and he was confident in his ability to forage on the road for sustenance. Cosmo was an excellent hunter and a better cook, and in summer the woods would be teeming with life, both flora and fauna. He still had the tunic he'd stolen from Leofric and a few extras that Auro had been able to smuggle him. His usual garb would hardly be appropriate for such an arduous journey, but he felt strange without his vast array of golden baubles. He'd worn them for so long they felt as though they were a part of him, certainly part of the identity he'd worn for four hundred years. They could be concealed, mostly, beneath his plainer travel clothing. And besides, until they reached the boarder of Sokol, he'd be traveling alone. No one would take note of a few extra trinkets, or so he hoped.

Finally, the night before they were meant to set out arrived. Cosmo paid a call on Auro and Alexios to discuss the plans for departure at sunrise. He was restless, and he could not wait to leave the domus and be free to roam beneath the sky again. Leofric stood at the door, ignoring Cosmo as hard as it was possible to ignore someone, it seemed. Cosmo wondered if the man would even look at him if he were bleeding or his clothing caught fire. The journey to Mount Hiru would certainly be a downright painful one, once Auro was the only buffer between them. It was enough to tempt Cosmo to leave without them.

Leofric would probably enjoy that better, he realized, and with a smile Cosmo thought that alone enough reason to inflict his company upon the man. How easy would it be for Leofric to maintain his composure when well away from his charge? Was he truly this rigid in private? Cosmo had to wonder.

Before he could arrive at a definitive stance on the matter, there came a clamor from the atrium down below; a man shouting urgently, though his words were obscured. Soon enough, there came a brisk knocking at the chamber door where Auro, Cosmo, Alexios and Leofric were gathered.

Cosmo retreated, hiding himself in the adjacent washroom as Leofric spoke to the porter just outside.

When Leofric returned, his expression was even darker than normal.

"What is it?" Asked the prince.

"Your Highness, we have a rider downstairs who's come from the villa in all haste. He comes with urgent words from the Queen. You must return home. At once."

Alexios frowned. "What could—"

"It's your father, Your Highness. Something has happened to the king."

Eight

L eofric followed Alexios back to the villa, and spent two days as his silent shadow. Auro had remained at the Domus with his brother, and Leofric could already see his absence weighing on the prince.

The King of Papia was in dire straits. He was bedridden, barely able to open his eyes for more than a few minutes at a time, and was lucid for even less. His condition didn't seem to worsen, but certainly did not improve over the two days they spent without leaving the side of his sickbed. Leofric immediately suspected Kato, or one of the other strangers that had arrived in Queen Dafina's entourage, but Alexios wouldn't hear of it. "What have they to gain?" His Highness asked a dozen times.

Leofric was the first to admit he didn't truly know—especially considering His Grace did not appear to be dying. And, if he did perish, it would do nothing to diminish Alexios's power—it would augment it.

In one of his rare lucid moments, His Grace seemed certain that the assailant hailed from Órnio. "We are Sokol's allies," he said. "And with our power spread thin to assist Neossós, they move to weaken us further."

Leofric did see the wisdom in that, despite King Nelios's fever. In the next breath, he demanded they remove his hands and feet because they had transformed into fish. They did not remove His Grace's appendages, but they did dispatch spies to Órnio.

"Even if you are correct, Leofric, it would be unwise to only pursue one lead, when two present themselves."

"So, you are going to pursue the other?"

Alexios narrowed his eyes. "Of course, I am," he snapped. "I am not the innocent fool everyone thinks I am."

Leofric winced. He knew then he'd gone too far, and he must pull back his familiarity with His Highness, lest he overstep and ruin his chance to care for Hamalcar's family entirely.

Of one thing Leofric was certain: there was no way that His Highness could leave Papia City at all. He must be there to rule beside his mother, to take on the duties the king could not perform in his current state, and of course, he must be there to bolster the treaty with Neossós and his intended bride. If Órnio truly were making moves against Papia, that alliance was more crucial than ever. It was as if Leofric watched the same realization dawning on Alexios's face as he sat beside his mother, staring as his father muttered feverishly in his sleep.

He wondered what would become of their quest, of the deal he and Alexios had made. It was selfish, perhaps, but he couldn't help it. After a few days, when it became clear that the king was not immediately about to die, Alexios begged his mother's pardon. "I must see Gaius Ursus," he told her. "A matter regarding the roads."

"Yes," said Queen Clio vaguely, and Leofric could tell she barely heard him. Her eyes were only for her husband, as if by the strength of her gaze alone she could return him to health. This troubled Leofric. He'd had dealings with Prince Alexios's parents, and found them a near indominable team. The queen, especially, was steady, level headed, and competent in her governance of Papia. The woman seated before him now was nearly unrecognizable.

Alexios did not speak until they had reached the royal stables. They mounted up and set a hard pace toward the city. "Your Highness," Leofric began, when they were well away.

"Before you ask, I have no idea," said Alexios grimly. "But I must speak with Auro."

Leofric nodded and urged Lyra to run faster. Despite longing for the comfort of Auro's arms, he knew Alexios would not wish to linger away from his father's side. They would most likely make the reverse journey tonight. As they continued along the central road of Papia, Leofric made plans in his head, as he always did when he felt the threat of encroaching unknown. He would most likely leave Lyra there, stabled at the domus, and His Highness would most like do the same with Xanthos. It would not do for them to blow either mount when the journey was of such importance. They could trade out their horses for others housed in the city and return for Lyra and Xanthos later. It was hardly the most thrilling chain of thoughts, but that was the point. Creating plans in advance soothed him greatly, settled his nerves and his worry about the king.

Auro waited for them in the small stable at the Domus, as Leofric had known he would. Alexios wasted no time putting up his horse before striding across the room and pulling Auro into a crushing embrace. Auro wrapped his arms around the prince's middle, giving him a squeeze. Of the freckled nuisance, there was no sign. Leofric found himself wondering if Cosmo had grown bored and fled, or if he were out cavorting at some brothel or other.

To his surprise, Cosmo waited for them in the dining chamber, setting out a platter of baked fish and fresh bread for supper. The four of them sat, and for a while, none spoke. Alexios seemed reluctant to part from Auro's touch, keeping one hand firmly anchored in both of Auro's own while he ate. Auro ate nothing, but watched Alexios through the entire meal, concern on his round face.

"This changes things," said Cosmo bluntly. "No?"

The other three looked at him, and Leofric was privately grateful that he'd broken the oppressive silence, though he'd never admit it.

"Indeed," said Alexios, his voice heavy. He had not slept in days. Leofric knew this because he also had not, keeping his post by Alexios's side and refusing to be relieved by any of the other men. This whole thing could very well be some trap, meant to lure his Highness into some new danger.

"Alexios," said Auro quietly. "You cannot leave Papia City."

"I know," Alexios agreed. "What are we going to do?"

"Excuse me," said Cosmo. "I am unencumbered by any sort of royal obligation. I can continue on with our plan alone."

"Cosmo, no!" said Auro. "It's far too dangerous for you to go alone."

Cosmo narrowed his eyes, for some reason insulted by his brother's concern. "I have done things on my own for four hundred years."

"And that's gone very well for you," Leofric said, before he could stop himself.

"*Leofric.*" Alexios's voice cut like a knife, and Leofric flinched. He should know better than to speak so out of turn, but he was exhausted and frayed.

"So haven't we all," said Auro to his brother, sidestepping the uncomfortable moment. "It was not the way."

"What choice do we have?" Cosmo shot back. "Unless you'd have us give up this mad notion."

"There is no one else we can trust with this," said Auro fearfully. "Janus already knows that we are searching for items of power—he nearly made off with Cedras's grace."

Cosmo wrinkled his nose. "And what could he do with a god's power, mortal that he is?"

"Nothing good," said Alexios flatly.

The three of them turned toward Leofric.

Leofric's gaze flitted to each face in turn. "You can all see how this changes everything," he said, setting down his wine.

"No, it doesn't. This changes nothing," said Alexios. "The three of you must still go."

"What? Your Highness—"

Alexios held up a hand. "I promised Auro I would help him in any way I could," he said. "Unfortunately, I won't be able to attend you on the mission, but I can send Leofric."

"Highness, no," said Leofric. "This whole thing could be a ruse, meant to leave you vulnerable."

"Maybe," said Alexios, "Or maybe not. Janus is not the only enemy of Papia. Part of my goal in remaining here is to discover the truth of that. We cannot defend against a threat we do not know."

"Alexios," said Auro. "I fear your mother the queen would find it highly suspect if you sent Leofric away during this time."

"We might wait until next year," Leofric said suddenly.

The other three turned toward him once again. "Pardon?" Said Alexios.

"Auro is awake," he said. "He will remain awake, to my understanding. In the autumn, he will be able to restore..."

"...Cedras—"

"Cedras, yes. He will be able to restore Cedras to power, and it is my understanding that Cedras will restore Auro's own, yes?"

"I believe so," said Auro.

"Then we simply wait. Cosmo will return to sleep, and by next summer we will be more strongly placed to attempt the quest, and we need to not risk such a venture now, when things are not settled."

Alexios and Auro shared a look, and Leofric took pains to avoid Cosmo's gaze. His plan was sound, logical, and the safer course, but still he felt a surge of guilt.

"You all dragged me out of my life to do this, if you recall," Cosmo said irritably. "If we were going to end here, I would rather have been left alone."

"Cosmo—" said Auro, the pain evident in his voice.

"There is another way," Cosmo interrupted him. He took a long, deep sip from his goblet. Leofric watched, annoyed, as the apple of his throat bobbed. It was plain he was extending the pause to heighten its dramatic affect.

"And what is that?" Alexios prompted.

"Well," said Cosmo, and Leofric could sense a trap closing in around him. "If we wish to break the curse this year, and you *obviously* don't trust me to carry out my mission alone—"

"Cosmo, that's not—"

"And there's *no one* else we can trust," he went on, loudly, and at his next words, Leofric felt the bottom drop out of his stomach. "You could dismiss Leofric from your service."

Cosmo took another sip of his wine to conceal his smile. The outrage on Leofric's face was payment enough for making the suggestion even if eventually dismissed; he was nearly purple with sputtering rage. Cosmo let his suggestion land over the room like a heavy blanket. If they disagreed, he would go alone, Cosmo decided. They would expect him to give up, to return to his life of excess and debauchery, and he derived savage pleasure from doing the opposite of what everyone expected. He would retrieve Kryos's grace, return here triumphant, to spite them all.

Leofric and Alexios left the room to discuss Cosmo's idea, and Cosmo returned to his meal.

"That was unkind of you," Auro chided him.

"What?" Asked Cosmo innocently.

"Taunting poor Leofric like that. He's going to burst a blood vessel."

Cosmo looked up, startled, to see Auro grinning, a gleam of mischief in his eye despite everything. He couldn't help mirroring Auro's smile. "Does the man ever unclench?"

"Not that I've witnessed," said Auro.

"Someone ought to remove the spear from his ass," Cosmo observed.

"Yes," said Auro mildly. "*Someone.*"

Cosmo frowned. "What?"

"Oh, please," said Auro. "I know you."

Cosmo's mirth vanished almost as soon as it had arrived. "Once, perhaps."

Auro's smile soured, too. "Yes," he said. "Once."

They stared at their plates. Cosmo cast around for a change of topic. "Would you join me?" He blurted. "When I go?"

Auro chewed his lip. "I had intended it to be so," he said. "I wanted for us to...well. Things have changed now."

Cosmo tracked Auro's gaze, how it bored into the door separating him from Alexios. He'd never seen such an intense expression on Auro's face. Such fierce longing. It was as if a part of Auro was on the other side of that door. Cosmo looked away, like he was intruding on something very private. Perhaps he was. "You do not wish to leave him."

Auro tore his eyes away from the door to meet Cosmo's. "Have you ever been in love?"

"Many times."

Auro threw a roll at him. "You know what I mean."

"I do." He paused. "No," he said, after some thought. "No, I don't believe I have."

"I wondered," said Auro. "When I first met Alexios. I returned to the temple and looked at all of your faces and wondered if any of you had ever felt this way."

Cosmo weighed the question. The more he saw of this new sort of pain on Auro's face the more certain he became. "Definitely not," he decided. After a short hesitation, he said, "You should stay."

"What?"

"You should stay, with Alexios. He needs you."

"But—"

"I'll be fine with Captain Tight-ass, and unless he strangles me in my sleep, I'll return with Kryos's Grace, the conquering hero!"

Auro gave him a tiny, nervous smile. "Oh, surely."

"Besides, if you remain here with your princeling, perhaps you can do some more searching."

"Searching?"

"In the books, those dreadful scrolls and histories. All we have done so far is guesswork, based on what happened to you. Perhaps you'd be able to find something more concrete in the queen's library."

"That's so," said Auro, considering.

In truth, Cosmo doubted it, but Auro plainly wished to stay. If Cosmo could offer him a plausible reason to do so, Auro would feel less guilty. Before Cosmo could come up with any other reasons to bolster his argument, the door flung open, banging against the stone wall opposite. Both Auro and Cosmo jumped.

Leofric stood framed in the door, scowling something fierce. He pointed a threatening finger at Cosmo. "You'd best be ready to depart at first light."

He stormed through the dining room and out the door opposite without turning back.

"Joy," said Cosmo sardonically.

~

Leofric paced back and forth in the small stable. Lyra stood patiently, saddled and bridled, her tail swishing as she watched him storming about. Leofric's stomach tied in knots, and he fussed with the straps on his saddle, double checked the security of the saddle bags across Lyra's flanks, which contained precious cargo: the gold from Prince Alexios. As he waited for Cosmo, Leofric touched the leather cuff beneath the bracer on his sword-arm. There was concealed inside it a secret pocket, in which a sheet of vellum, signed and sealed by His Highness, Prince Alexios Velius Papinus, crown prince of Papia. The paper was of equal value to the bags of golden coins strapped to his horse. It promised Leofric—under care of Imperator Hamate should Leofric fall during this fool's quest—a staggering sum of gold to be presented to him upon return of the letter to Papia.

It also relieved him of the stain upon his oath. *It was my plan to dispatch Leofric, Captain of my personal guard, on a mission for the crown of vital importance. His dismissal was a ruse, and he as always remained loyal to his sworn oath. Should he return to Papia, he should be restored of his office and titles immediately.* Leofric had read the words so many times last night, tossing and turning in his bed, that he had them memorized. Eventually, he'd given up on sleep, gathered his supplies for the journey, and walked down to the stables. Alexios had insisted the gold he promised we be enough to retire, but Leofric had told him he'd prefer to resume his post. What was he, if not a soldier? Besides, Laela and Sorex had their life, mother and son, a family. He wasn't certain he had a place in that life, despite what he'd sworn to his brother. Leofric touched the saddle bag again, hefting its weight. The coin would be enough, he decided. Hamalcar's shade could rest easy, knowing his wife and son wanted for nothing. Leofric could always retire later, but he'd rather have his position secure for his return, and the mark of a dishonorable discharge stricken from his history.

He wondered if Cosmo would be late. He'd told him first light, but who knew how deep into the night he'd stayed up, drinking and carousing. Leofric assumed he'd have to go hunting for him through the domus. He'd been given a spacious bed chamber, but Leofric didn't fail to note that Cosmo was more likely to fall asleep in the sitting room on a settle or even down beside the oven in the kitchens. It seemed the man couldn't keep to one bed, even to sleep. Leofric had just finished perfecting the tongue lashing he'd give Cosmo for being tardy when he strolled into the stable, dressed, packed and ready to go.

And, right on time. "Good morning, Captain," he said, giving another mocking salute.

Leofric snorted, stymied. With Cosmo showing up on time, he could not let fly his diatribe. It was as if Cosmo anticipated this, and showed up in a timely manner simply to throw Leofric off his axis. He seemed to live to disrupt, to disturb plans and expectations. And now he was Leofric's only companion on a mission of vital importance to His Highness.

He and Cosmo would travel to Hiru City, the metropolis that had sprung up near the base of the mountain, by way of Sokol. As they passed through Sokol, they would stop briefly at Leofric's home to drop off the gold. It was not the most direct route, but the journey wasn't overlong and they had all summer. Leofric hoped that perhaps he could stay a few days with his family, to ensure they were doing well. He did miss them, Laela and Sorex. Deeply. It would be sweet to see them again. Perhaps he could leave the missive from his Highness there in Laela's care, as well. She would be able to keep it safer than he could on the road, and it would be an excuse to stop by again, on their return journey to Papia. Laela and Leofric may not have chosen one another, but he still loved her dearly, as a sister. And Sorex was the closest thing to a son Leofric was ever likely to have.

"Captain?"

Leofric shook his head, returning his thoughts to the present. "Pardon?"

Cosmo cocked his head to the side. "I said, 'shouldn't we be setting out'?"

"Yes," he snapped, annoyed to realize Cosmo was already ahorse. He sat confidently in the saddle, a natural horseman. *Well, he's had four centuries to practice,* Leofric thought savagely. "Let us ride."

It was going to be a long journey.

Nine

The pace Leofric kept was grueling. Cosmo was comfortable on horseback but even so, the day was long and painful. Summer was waxing, and the day was hot. They took the main road from Papia City and set out west, toward the wilder countryside that separated the kingdoms of Papia and Sokol. Cosmo saw half a dozen places that would have made excellent places to pause and refresh themselves, but he wasn't about to give Leofric the satisfaction of asking for a break.

When at last they did stop for the night, Cosmo got the sense it was more for the benefit of their mounts, but he was grateful for a rest. Leofric wordlessly set up his pack and bedroll, barely sparing so much as a glance at Cosmo. After a day in almost total silence, Cosmo felt like a ghost. It was lonely, out here on the road, even after only a day of travel.

Every summer, when Cosmo woke, he spent as little time alone as possible. It was only when he swam that he occasionally sought solitude. Otherwise, he preferred to bury himself in the company of others. Riding with Leofric was worse than riding alone, Cosmo decided, as he brushed down his horse.

Hestia, the dapple-gray filly Alexios had lent him, was a superb mount, spirited but well trained. Cosmo stroked her flank and thought dismally that she was likely to be his only true companion for this journey. The only good thing to be said of the journey so far was that at Leofric's relentless pace, they would only have to spend the minimum possible time on the road together.

Cosmo stretched his legs, laid out his bedroll, and when he turned around, he saw the clearing deserted. Leofric's horse, Lyra, stood grazing happily, but Leofric himself was nowhere to be seen. Cosmo spun on his heel, wondering where the man had gotten to. In the absence of anything else to do, Cosmo sat on the grass and pulled a heel of bread from his pack. He'd baked it just the day before, stuffing the dough with nuts and dried fruit to make it nice and hearty. With his belly less rumbly, he was feeling a bit more charitable toward his companion. Perhaps Leofric would like to share some of the bread, when he returned from wherever he'd gotten to.

Leofric came back with two fat quails tied at his belt. Apparently, he was as competent with a bow as he was with a sword. He stopped short when he saw Cosmo sitting to eat, and snorted. Before Cosmo could say anything, he tossed the birds to the ground and said, "I suppose I shouldn't have assumed you'd start a fire."

It was the first thing he'd said to Cosmo in hours.

Mouth gaping, Cosmo clutched his bread and stared as Leofric stomped about, gathering supplies for a fire, getting angrier and angrier the more he watched. It seemed Leofric was determined to assume the worst of Cosmo. Well, if he was going to be that way, why would Cosmo share his delicious bread? So, he didn't. He simply sat and watched and chewed, and wondered if Leofric would share his catch with Cosmo at all.

He did, to Cosmo's surprise, but once he had his first

taste, he wished Leofric had kept it to himself. The meat was tough and overcooked, chewy and stringy, with no seasoning whatsoever, not even a pinch of salt. He ate his portion uncomplaining, however, though he felt he might lose a tooth. The outside of the poor bird had been burned black, too. When Cosmo finally swallowed his last, ashy mouthful, he pried open his jaw to thank Leofric, but before Cosmo could get the words out, Leofric said, "I'm going to sleep."

Cosmo glowered back at him from across the fire. "Fine."

And that was it.

Cosmo felt himself relax once Leofric had tucked himself into his bed roll, and spent the first watch of the night looking up at the stars, listening to the needs of the earth, and did his best not to think too hard about his surly companion. His irritation with Leofric kept him awake without much effort on his part.

After a while though, the night and Cosmo's mind quieted. He glanced across the fire, watching Leofric sleep. He *was* handsome, and his looks were only improved in the softness of sleep, his features still sharp and angular, but less... harsh. His nose was long and straight, his brows dark, his jaw sculpted. His hair curved around his head, draping down the side of his neck in a silky, chocolate curtain. That hair would be the envy of women across the continent, Cosmo did not doubt. If he sold it to a wig maker, he could make a bloody fortune.

The fireflies were out, and their twinkling always made Cosmo smile. It made him feel as if the stars had come down from the sky to keep him company, and he felt a little less lonely. He strained his ears to listen to the sounds of the forest where they'd made their camp, and all seemed as it should be. He watched a wolf stalking through the undergrowth, heard an owl hooting softly. It had been a while since Cosmo had spent a night so far removed from the sights and sounds of

Papia city. Those sounds had their own music to them, Cosmo supposed, but it was different out here in the trees.

In the city, he had to search for his next task as god of summer. He had to *ask* the earth what it needed. Out here, it simply...came to him. For the first time he understood why Auro would have remained so long hidden amongst the trees of springtime. The dryads would be well awake by now; that was one of Auro's charges. His awakening served as the proverbial cock's crow to the tree spirits, who stirred and wakened in spring to care for forest. Cosmo's grace touched and guided the dryadae as well, but he couldn't recall the last time he'd laid eyes, the last time he'd spoken to one. He twisted around where he sat, probing into the darkness with his grace like a sightless man might stretch his fingers to feel his way around the world. It was nighttime, and most trees slept when the sun did, so he didn't think it likely to see one now, but he made a mental note to watch for them when they rode tomorrow.

He fell into an uneasy sleep, plagued by dreams of frozen corpses that chased him through the streets of Papia City. The city was abandoned, but in his dream Cosmo checked every door, every window, calling through the silent streets for someone, anyone to answer him.

None did. He lost track of how many times he woke, covered in cold sweat, only to roll over and descend right back into the dream.

"What in the world—?"

Cosmo woke once again with a start, this time to Leofric stomping about the campsite. He sat up and stretched, watching. Leofric had his sword out, and with one hand over his eyes to block the rays of the rising sun he squinted into the misty dawn gloom between the trees. "What is it?"

"Someone has been through our camp," said Leofric without turning around.

The drowsiness drained out of Cosmo like a wave drawing out to sea. "What?"

"Marauders or...a robber perhaps..." Leofric still searched the shadowy trees, presumably for the culprits.

Cosmo got to his feet, his own dagger in hand. "What did they take?" He asked.

"Nothing," said Leofric absently.

"What?"

"*Nothing,*" he repeated. "They disturbed our rations, and left things."

"They left things?"

"*Yes,*" said Leofric. "Now, you take watch and I'll pack our things. We should leave here as soon as possible, if our position has been compromised."

Cosmo still felt as though he'd woken up a million miles behind, or as if Leofric was speaking a foreign tongue that he couldn't quite recognize. What sorts of bandits left things? Cosmo turned his attention to the place by the smoking embers of the cookfire. Then he laughed out loud.

"What are you cackling about?" Leofric snapped.

"You can lower your weapon, Captain," said Cosmo with a grin. "We are not beset by bandits at all."

Leofric strode over to where Cosmo squatted by the fire surveying the bounty that had been left. A mat of closely woven twigs spread upon the ground, heaped with piles of fruit and tiny bundles of dried herbs tied with vines. There were enormous bouquets of flowers and miniscule bowls formed from stone containing what Cosmo suspected were crushed leaves for tea.

"What sort of robbers did you think they were?" Cosmo asked mildly. He held up one of the bundles of herbs and gave it a hearty sniff. "The sort that leave savory seasonings and peaches for their victims?"

With his arms crossed over his chest and his scowl firmly in place, Leofric said, "Well, who else goes skulking through strangers' belongings in the middle of the forest at night?"

"Dryads," said Cosmo. He hefted a peach in one hand, rolled it up his forearm and with a jerk of his elbow bounced it across the clearing to Leofric, who startled, but caught it.

"Who?"

"Tree spirits," said Cosmo. He selected a strawberry that was near as big as his fist and bit into it, the juice sweet and fresh with all the flavors of summer singing on his tongue.

"There were tree spirits wandering through here while we slept?"

"It certainly seems that way, yes."

"How can you be certain?"

Cosmo shrugged. "I can feel them. They're watching us now."

"They're—" Leofric staggered over to a sump and sat heavily upon it.

"Auro awakens them every spring," said Cosmo, finishing the strawberry in a few sharp bites. "And Cedras returns them to rest. I perform most of my work from the city, so I rarely get to see them. Occasionally I'll see them on my way to or from the temple but...I never linger long in the trees."

"So, what's this then?" Asked Leofric, regarding the peach like he thought it might be poisoned.

"A peach."

Leofric scowled.

"As to the reason for the peach, and the rest..." Cosmo thought he knew, but he found it immodest to mention that it was most likely an offering of sorts, for Cosmo, God of Summer. Instead, he shrugged once again. "Perhaps they saw the awful meal you prepared last night, and were terrified I'd starve in your hands."

Leofric's mouth dropped open in fury, but before he

could say anything Cosmo walked up and stuffed another peach between his teeth.

"Breakfast first," said Cosmo. "Then, you can berate me."

Leofric took a bite out of the peach, juice running down his chin. It was like Cosmo could watch the emotions playing out behind his eyes as he tasted the fruit. Anger, frustration, hunger, pleasure. Some of Cosmo's favorite things.

They ate their fruit in silence, and when Cosmo finished, he took the flower bouquets and wound the blooms in the manes of their mounts. Leofric doused the fire and gathered the rest of their things, and Cosmo thought it best to give the man a little space to do so. When he approached his horse, Lyra, for a split-second Cosmo thought he'd pull the flowers from her mane in a storm of grouchiness. Instead, he paid them no mind and mounted up, leaving the flowers where they were.

Cosmo wasn't certain what made him press his luck, but he did. He plucked an orange tiger lily from Hestia's mane and nudged her at a gentle walk over to Leofric. With a grin, he tucked the orange bloom behind Leofric's ear. He turned sharply to Cosmo, who braced himself for retaliation—but Leofric just rolled his eyes and urged his horse to a trot, leaving Cosmo feeling tingly and confused in his wake.

"You're subdued," Leofric said after a few hours' ride.

Yesterday, he'd been braced for Cosmo's endless chatter, and while Cosmo had managed to hold his tongue, Leofric could almost feel the energy vibrating off him, the *desire* to talk as loud as actual conversation. Today, it was as if Cosmo was asleep in the saddle, sluggish and mellow and slow. "I didn't sleep well," said Cosmo around a wide, gaping yawn.

"Why not?"

"Indigestion from that foul fowl you prepared."

Leofric snorted. He knew he was no proper cook, but the bird had been *fine*. It had been edible, at any rate, and more than Cosmo deserved after not lifting a finger to help set up their camp the night before. "Oh, truly?" said Leofric.

"No, not truly," said Cosmo. "In truth, I was staring at your face."

Leofric blinked.

"You looked quite peaceful, sleeping," Cosmo continued. "Much nicer to look at than your current visage."

You looked quite peaceful. The words rattled around Leofric's skull as they rode that day and he tried to discern why Cosmo would have watched him at all. He could have been lying, of course. Cosmo's truths were as absurd as lies, so it was impossible to tell one from the other. If he *had* stayed up all night, he was a fool if he thought flattery would cause Leofric to let them stop early to rest. The way past the country villas of Papia was a series of wide dirt roads that wound through the fertile hills and woodlands, as yet untouched by Alexios and his new magister of roads. They would be able to cover quite a bit of ground the first few days, until the countryside turned truly wild. They would be forced to slow, then, and stop more frequently to ensure neither mount turned an ankle in a ditch, or let some other catastrophe slow their progress.

When he called a halt the second night, he knew they only had another day or two of covering this much ground. Leofric put up Lyra, brushing her coat and hobbling her to graze. The flowers Cosmo tucked in her mane had wilted and fallen out as they road, leaving only a few petals behind. As Leofric picked them out and let them fall, he recalled with a jolt that Cosmo had tucked a flower behind his ear. He flushed, realizing he'd worn it all day long. Flashing back to his attempt to spar verbally with Cosmo, Leofric cursed himself. The wretch must have been laughing at him all along. Leofric tugged the flower from his hair, resting it in his palm, examining it. It was an orange tiger lily, and it showed no signs of wilting, almost as if some supernatural force kept it looking robust and beautiful. Leofric told himself to crush the flower in his fist, but for some reason his hand did not respond. In the end, he tucked the flower in the leather pocket on his belt.

He watched Cosmo with his own mount. Like his brother, Cosmo had a way with beasts. Cosmo smiled softly at his horse, petting the side of her face and talking to her in a low voice. It was a smile Leofric had not seen before, a soft genuine one, not tinged with mockery.

Leofric had always felt the way a man treated the animals in his care was an indicator of his true self. A horse or a dog could sniff out the unworthy. He always put weight on their instincts. You could not lie to an animal. They could smell how rotten and selfish and fearful a man was, Leofric was certain of that. As Cosmo's mount whickered happily and nuzzled against his chest, Leofric considered that this particular horse might just be stupid.

He went off to hunt, as he had the night before. They had rations with them, but while they were making such good time, they'd do better to hunt while they could. It would keep their strength up, and preserve their rations for harder riding. The desert sands began a few leagues before the border between Sokol and Papia, and the hunting there would be scarce, or even non-existent, especially with summer's heat mounting. All the animals would flee to the cool shelters and burrows they'd made beneath the sands. Cosmo and Leofric would have to rely on their rations then, for a certainty.

As Leofric hunted, he wondered how Cosmo would fare in such austere conditions. Everything about the man spoke of being pampered, spoke of excess. It was hard to imagine him going a day where a single whim didn't appear at his fingertips.

Yesterday, he had been sitting on his ass when Leofric returned from hunting, eating a large chunk of bread instead of preserving it. He'd made no effort to make camp, like he was used to things just being done for him, without him lifting a single freckled finger. If he returned to their campsite this evening to the same site, he would be furious. *You looked quite peaceful.* Cosmo's words floated into his mind once again, and he missed his shot. Cursing himself as the goose took wing and his arrow went sailing errantly into the underbrush, Leofric shouldered his bow and went to retrieve it.

What had Cosmo meant by that? *Peaceful?* Did that mean lazy? Or soft? Every word Cosmo had spoken to him since they met had been sharp with mockery. His flirting, his goading, all of it meant to put Leofric on edge. He was certain Cosmo had meant the same when he said what he'd said. *You looked quite peaceful.* Peaceful was not a word anyone had ever used to describe him before. Certain Cosmo meant it as an insult, Leofric forced it from his mind.

When he neared the camp, a heavenly aroma beckoned him closer. It took him a few moments to realize that it was the smell of home. He stopped dead in the clearing and stared incredulously at the sight before him. Cosmo had not only arranged their camp and lit a fire, but he'd begun preparing a meal of sorts. A small iron pot dangled from a spit above the fire, fragrant steam billowing from within. Cosmo stirred the contents of the pot and then removed the spoon. With his pinky, he took a dab of something thick and brown gathered on the spoon, and tasted it. His sharp pink tongue darted out, savoring the drop from the end of his finger, the look on his face intense. After considering a few moments, he took a pinch of something from a tin cannister and added it to the pot. *Cloves* Leofric realized at once, the sharp spicy scent apparent on the evening air.

Leofric took a step forward and a twig snapped beneath

his foot. Cosmo looked up, saw the rabbit, and said, "I can add that to the stew."

"Alright," said Leofric. He sat beside the fire and used his hunting knife to skin and clean the rabbit. Wordlessly, Cosmo pushed a flat stone toward him so that Leofric could cut the meat into cubes.

After Leofric had scraped the meat into the pot, Cosmo stirred it. The smell was divine, far more alluring than things Leofric had consumed on the march before. After a few more stirs, Cosmo said, "If you had just *told* me yesterday that you were going hunting, I could have had the camp ready when you returned."

Leofric stared into the fire, considering. Perhaps he *had* been unfair to Cosmo. Just a tad. He sighed. "You're right."

Cosmo nearly dropped the spoon into the fire. "I'm—I'm what?"

"You're *right*, I said."

"Pardon? Once again? I'm afraid I didn't hear you..."

"Don't push it," said Leofric. But he couldn't help the way the corners of his mouth twitched.

Cosmo, for once, acquiesced, but Leofric did not care for the smug smile he wore while he ladled out the stew. Leofric took the offered spoon and inhaled the vapors rising from the bowl, breathing deep of the spices he had grown up smelling.

"Is something wrong?"

"No," said Leofric. For some reason, he found himself reluctant to taste the meal in front of Cosmo, like eating the food he'd eaten all his life, and enjoying it, was something private. But he was staring now, staring at Leofric over his own bowl.

So, Leofric took a hesitant mouthful of his supper, and a thousand memories exploded across his tongue. He chewed slowly, savoring every nuanced flavor, the flavors of Sokol, the flavors of home. Hot, smoky, loaded with spices that danced together, salty and rich. The meat had been stewed to perfection, tender and juicy. At last, he swallowed.

"Well?" Asked Cosmo.

Leofric realized he'd closed his eyes. Startled, he opened them. Cosmo looked at him expectantly. "It will serve," he said grudgingly.

Cosmo laughed, and dug into his own meal.

"How did you learn to cook Sokolian food?" Leofric offered, when half his bowl was gone.

Cosmo chewed and swallowed his own current mouthful. He cast a wicked look at Leofric and said, "Papia is a busy port. I have known the company of many, *many* travelers."

Leofric's stomach soured. Of course. He rolled his eyes and finished the rest of his meal with difficulty, images of Cosmo's body being bent into knots by half a hundred rough trade nomads invading his brain, putting him off his food. He scraped the remainder of his meal into the fire.

"What is the matter?"

"Nothing."

"You didn't finish your stew," Cosmo said. "Seems wasteful."

Leofric leveled a look at him. "Mental images of you fucking do little to whet my appetite," he lied.

Cosmo watched the scraps sizzle and burn, looking stricken. "Fine," he said. Before Leofric had a chance to feel guilty, Cosmo had summoned his usual mocking grin. "It's funny," he said, "Mental images of *you* fucking make me *ravenous.*"

Cosmo finished his food without another word, but he stared at Leofric the entire time, and when he finished, he licked each finger clean, slowly. Lewdly. Leofric's cheeks flamed, but he refused to break first, refused to yield, and admit it was getting to him, this constant, brazen seduction. It had been...a long time since Leofric had pursued anyone. A very long time. Cosmo might make him furious, but it wasn't as if Leofric was *blind.* He'd seen everything there was to see of Cosmo, who was not shy about his body in the slightest. There had been a time when Leofric would have met Cosmo jest for jest, pulled the smirking menace into his lap and shared his wine and his kisses, but that time was long gone—almost as if it had been lived by a different man.

When they mounted up each morning, Leofric found it harder to summon the will to ice Cosmo out. Out here on the road it was easier to see Cosmo's better qualities, the thoughtful, soft parts of himself he customarily hid beneath layers of mocking smirks and jewelry and inappropriate comments. His mask slipped a bit day by day, especially at night when they sat by the fire, sharing food and pleasant silence, the orange glow of the embers dancing in Cosmo's lively hazel eyes. Something in Leofric rejected this out of hand, shored up his walls and defenses. He could not afford to become distracted for the sake of a pretty face. And besides, he was sure Cosmo would turn this charm on anyone. His choice of Sokolian cuisine could easily have been coincidence—perhaps it was the only thing he could make. Part of him, the tiny, weak part, hoped that it wasn't. The hapless weakling, slave to his shameful urges, that Leofric had done his best to bury, hoped Cosmo had chosen to cook Sokolian food to please him.

It was folly, and Leofric knew it. The rational part of him, the part of him he told himself was *real,* recognized that he was simply the only potential victim in the area. It was a game to Cosmo, like everything else, and Leofric wasn't interested in being anyone's plaything. Certainly, these tricks worked on lonely sailors and other fools, but they would not work on him.

Ten

Traveling with Leofric was worse than Cosmo ever could have anticipated. He scrutinized Cosmo's every move, refused to let even the smallest thing slide, and took deep, personal offense in every slight from Cosmo—real *or* imagined.

Every time he and Leofric mounted up at dawn, Cosmo told himself to give up on the man. Leofric was carved of stone, and Cosmo told himself he had no hot blood pumping beneath the cold exterior. But then, at night, they would sit opposite the fire, eating the food that he had hunted and Cosmo cooked, and the silence between them would be soft and comfortable. Leofric would stare at him over the fire, like Cosmo was a puzzle he was determined to solve. The intensity in Leofric's looks made him shivery and nervous. Cosmo hadn't been nervous in...He frowned. He didn't think anyone had *ever* made him nervous before. Nervous, unsure of himself, hot and jittery. Unfortunately, it never failed that just when he thought he was making progress, some careless remark would have the shutters closing behind Leofric's dark brown eyes, and then he'd be gone, gone deep inside himself where Cosmo could not reach, no matter how hard he tried.

It did not help that he was beautiful, truly and uniquely beautiful, made even more so, somehow, by his complete disdain of Cosmo. Before meeting Leofric, Cosmo would never have said a scowl could be as captivating as a smile, that contempt could have him as hot as desire. Watching him all day was torture. Leofric rode with confidence, legs wrapped around his horse, back straight, dark hair swept into a tight, impeccable braid that shone in the sun. The shorn side of his head, with its twining tattoos, emphasized the sharp line of his jaw, the bitable ears, and the long, elegant column of his neck. No one just had a neck like *that* by accident, Cosmo thought sourly. A neck like that was meant to be stroked, bit, kissed. Grabbed. Cosmo often found himself wondering what that neck would look like with his own freckled fingers wrapped around it, pressing lightly to feel Leofric's pulse hammering against his thumb.

It was *maddening*. This was the longest Cosmo had gone without taking someone to bed since he'd first surrendered his body to a pair of amorous serving girls at the age of five and ten. There wasn't much to do, of a summer, besides work and fuck. He needed little else, or so he had always told himself, but absent one he found it difficult to enjoy the other, and he felt as if he were slowly coming unglued.

He needed to do something to cleanse himself of these urges, the urges that were destined to starve the life out of him. Leofric was as dry and unwelcoming as the scorching sands of Sokol, his homeland. One evening, as Leofric set their camp, measuring the distance between the rocks of their cookfire so they were perfectly equidistant—or whatever the fuck he got up to—Cosmo announced he was going to find a lake in which to bathe. He didn't care if he had to walk all the way back to bloody Papia City to get into the water, he was going for a swim.

Luckily, the wild forest provided, and Cosmo's grace allowed the trees to lead him through a thicket to a small, hidden pool. His shoulders at last came down from around his ears, each footfall that took him from the camp allowed him to breathe deep, and breathe free. The thought of spending even a few moments weightless, clean, and light had his chest expanding fully for the first time all day. The glade was an intimate little oasis, the perfect thing for a humid, sticky summer evening. A pool fed by a small waterfall, water clear and cold, would be just the thing. Cosmo stripped out of his clothes and bangles and slid into the water, gasping at the chill even as he relished in it.

Lazily, Cosmo swam a few laps around the shallow pond before standing beneath the deluge from the waterfall, letting it sluice over his hair, his face, his body.

The rushing of the water was playing tricks on his hears; he heard what sounded like someone clearing their throat. Then again, louder. Cosmo turned to face the clearing and his heart nearly stopped. Leofric stood there, a thin sheet of white linen wrapped around his hips as he stood barefoot in the grass.

"What are you doing here?" Cosmo blurted. "How did you even find me?"

Leofric looked confused. "I thought you invited me."

Cosmo braced his hands on his hips. "What on earth are you talking about?"

The sun had set hours before, but in the moonlight reflected on the water allowed Cosmo to see a deep flush moving up Leofric's chest like a darkening bruise. "The trees..." he glanced over his shoulder into the shadowy expanse of the forest. "There was a path."

It was Cosmo's turn to flush. The forest must have moved itself around his footfalls, feeling the *want* through the soles of his feet and encouraging Leofric to answer what it thought was Cosmo's call. "No there wasn't."

Leofric raised his brows. "No?"

"Not an intentional one," said Cosmo, wondering if the affect was ruined by the tingly heat surely visible in his cheeks, the catch in his throat as he spoke. It was dark enough that Leofric couldn't see any further damning evidence through the water's surface, so Cosmo decided to push his luck. He cocked his head. "Why would I have wanted you to follow me?"

The confusion on Leofric's face vanished, replaced by embarrassment, then irritation. Soon enough, though, he had reschooled his features into an emotionless mask. If Cosmo hadn't been staring, he might have missed it. "How should I know?" Leofric asked.

They stared at each other.

"So," said Cosmo at last. "What are you doing here, then?"

Leofric looked at him like he was being purposely obtuse. "Bathing."

Cosmo sucked in a breath as Leofric shed his linen to stand naked under the silver light of the moon. Of course, with a few sharp twists of his hands, he folded the towel neatly and hung it from a nearby tree branch. Cosmo scowled at the tree, as if it had presented a convenient towel rack for Leofric on purpose. Perhaps it had.

Leofric stretched his arms above his head, shaking out his hands as he stepped into the water. The long lines of his body seemed even longer somehow, when unobstructed by clothing or armor. Impossibly long, his limbs hard with muscle, tanned and scarred from battle and whatever else he got up to.

Cosmo could not help the way his gaze pulled down from Leofric's arms where they stretched toward the heavens, to his upturned face, his jaw, his unbound hair cascading down over his shoulders. He rarely wore it like that, untamed waves of rich brown tumbling freely and curling around his ears. Leofric finished stretching and turned his face to Cosmo, a barely-there smirk softening the corners of his usually stern mouth, and Cosmo realized with a jolt that his own mouth had fallen open, gaping wide as he blinked stupidly at the man before him.

Damn him, Cosmo thought. *He is doing this on purpose.*

It took a lot of Cosmo's self-control not to ogle Leofric's more private parts as he turned away, his pert buttocks catching the glow of the moon in a way that had Cosmo aching to sink his teeth in. When at last he lowered himself into the water, the look in his eyes was a challenge, a challenge that said that Leofric could play Cosmo's own games, and worse—he could win.

Unless Cosmo was mistaken, the temperature of the little glade and the water had risen, such that he found himself hot all over, warm from his scalp to his toes as his blood fizzed and simmered beneath his skin. He turned his back, dunking his head once again beneath the stream of water from the waterfall and tried to gather himself. What did this mean? Leofric may have already put his shields back up, but the fact remained that he had thought Cosmo invited him to the lake. And he had come.

A fissure of eager lust shot through him, but he did his best to tamp it down.

Cosmo would have had an easier time believing Leofric was interested in lifeless hunks of granite. This was simply his own boredom coupled a healthy dollop of wishful thinking. He peeked over his shoulder. Could something happen between them?

He doubted it.

And yet.

Cosmo straightened up, frowning. What was he doing? He was the god of summer, the god of warmth and heat and *want.* There wasn't a mortal on earth who could defeat him in the arena of seduction, of flirtation, of any kind of bed sport. If Leofric wanted to play, Cosmo wasn't about to back down. He shook himself, and ran his fingers through his wet hair. He peeked over his shoulder at Leofric, just in time to catch his eyes before he shifted his gaze, away from Cosmo, where he'd plainly been looking.

Cosmo grinned. Leofric had no idea what sort of duel he'd entered, but he was about to learn.

Leofric had no idea what he was doing. First off, he was furious with himself and humiliated that he'd allowed himself to think Cosmo had invited him to the pool for some kind of —some kind of what, even? A tryst? What he had expected? That they could wash each other's hair, share an impassioned kiss in the moonlight? He shivered. Even as he mocked himself, he couldn't deny the appeal of the mental images currently flooding his brain.

By arriving in the clearing, he'd certainly made himself vulnerable, and it was plain that Cosmo *knew.* Just as he had known before, known the way Leofric reacted to rough handling, the way he'd craved it. He'd shown his weakness, and now his only defense was to pretend he was unaffected. No.

He had to *be* unaffected. Anything else was madness, like trying to chase the sun without being burned. Leofric lowered himself into the water, forcing himself to remain relaxed and calm, still. Cosmo moved around as he cleaned himself, swam in the water, splashed about. Leofric forced himself to pick a spot on the opposite bank of the little lake to focus upon, a reed waving back and forth in the wind.

Cosmo preened like a songbird, stretching and presenting every freckled inch of himself like washing up was a stage performance and he had a full and captive audience. When he lifted one slim leg out of the water to brace against a stone, bending over it to wash non-existent dirt from his skin Leofric audibly gulped.

He tried to cover it with a cough, but something told him Cosmo was not fooled. Leofric shifted to lean back against the gently sloping stone, tipping his head to skyward in what he hoped was a casual movement.

The night was warm and so was he, while the water was cool. There was no denying the sights of Cosmo's flaunting had him aroused, but the water provided a disguise, and the feeling wasn't an unpleasant one. He'd had neither the opportunity nor the inclination to pursue anything of the sort since his brother's death—his life had been a whirlwind. Helping his family, his discharge from the legion, his new position in Papia, chasing after Prince Alexios.

Even knowing he would not act on anything, the feeling was welcome. It had been a long time since Leofric had felt so present in his body, so at home in being a *man*. It reminded him all at once that he was alive. These days, he only felt this way when fighting. When he fought, Leofric knew who he was. This was nice too, though. The water was soothing and the heavy air warm and pleasant. Over the course of his life, Leofric had traveled thousands of leagues without ever taking the time for such luxury, and part of him wondered why. Soldiers needed to wash, just as anyone else did. More so, after hours marching or riding in the sun.

A disturbance nearby set tiny waves smacking against his ribs, but he was too peaceful to care much. That is, until a voice whispered in his ear, "If you thought I was inviting you here, why did you come?"

That was why. A relaxed man was a vulnerable one.

Leofric jerked away from the voice, from the reflected heat from Cosmo's skin, from the question itself. Cosmo leaned into his space, droplets of water clinging to his dark, ruddy lashes as he waited for an answer.

"Morbid curiosity," said Leofric, with as level a voice as he could muster.

Cosmo smiled. "That's fair, I suppose."

Leofric shifted subtly, putting a bit more distance between their bodies, and did his best to force his muscles to relax again. "Besides," he said. "Letting you out of my sight seems unwise. It's always better to know from which direction the storm is coming."

Cosmo laughed, a bright and startled sound, like he didn't expect Leofric capable of anything resembling a joke, and Leofric supposed he could hardly blame the man for that.

Cosmo was still staring at him, still leaning in, far too close. He was waiting for something, something Leofric couldn't quite identify. His expression was hungry, starved actually, and Leofric could see something of the lonely young boy he'd perhaps once been peering out of Cosmo's eyes.

"This is...pleasant," Leofric said, because he felt as though he had to say *something*. His tongue felt thick in his mouth, twisty and unreliable.

Cosmo smiled faintly. "Agreed. You're much nicer when you're relaxed."

Leofric grunted in response, unsure what else to say.

"Maybe we could..." Cosmo trailed off.

"Spar?" Leofric blurted.

Cosmo blinked, startled. "What?"

"We could spar, again," Leofric said. "If you want."

Cosmo looked bewildered. "Now?"

"No, not now," said Leofric. His face grew hot as he scrambled to make the request to bludgeon one another with practice swords seem normal. "I—I'd been thinking, perhaps when we've finished riding for the day. Tomorrow."

"Oh," said Cosmo. His brow furrowed, and he leaned back a bit, the air cooling between them. "If you like."

"Good," Leofric said. He wrapped his arms around himself, and stared resolutely ahead, avoiding Cosmo's searching gaze. "Good."

Eleven

S parring was *almost* as good as fucking.

It was sweaty and physical and intimate, and Cosmo decided it was most likely the best he was going to get out of his beguiling travel companion. It became a new part of their ritual, and Cosmo had to admit there was something comforting about it.

They rode all day, dismounted in the evening to rest and water the horses. Leofric hunted. Cosmo cooked. They ate, and then they stood opposite in a ring drawn in the dirt, each armed with a stick, and hammered at each other until the sun went down. Cosmo went to sleep every night aching and exhausted, and sated in a strange way he couldn't quite explain. Unfortunately, the gap between what they were doing and what Cosmo wished they were doing itched at him. He wasn't so sure how long he could keep pretending he didn't notice Leofric's arousal as they fought every night, how much longer he could resist the urge to make Leofric yield in an entirely different way. To bend Leofric till he shattered, and lose himself in the resulting explosion.

One morning, they consulted a map before mounting up.

"We are only two or three days from the Sokolian border," Leofric told him, pointing.

Cosmo looked down at the map. "There is a village, here," he said eagerly.

"It will add half a day, at least, to the journey," said Leofric. "No."

"From here the country grows meaner," Cosmo reminded him. "A night at an inn would do us both well. We could refresh our rations and set out, better prepared, for the next leg of the journey." *And perhaps the village would have a pair of willing legs for me to find myself between.*

It was as if Leofric could read his thoughts, damn the man. "This journey is not a for your *pleasure.*" He spat the word pleasure like it was the most base and disgusting pursuit.

"Not all of us are content to be forever lonely and miserable," Cosmo said back. "I'd love to look upon a face that isn't yours." That was a lie, but it felt good to say.

"I as well," Leofric agreed. "But still, no."

Though Cosmo had started it, the words still stung. "It will be raining, tomorrow," he said. Early summer was the time for such. The earth needed to drink deeply, to prepare for the rest of the season when Cosmo could only send sparse rains. "A half a day riding in such with a soft bed at the end of it would do us well. We could wait out the storm at an inn and leave when it ends."

Leofric looked at him, his face full of mistrust. "You lie."

Static zipped over Cosmo's skin, the static that preceded a vicious storm, but he was sick unto death of Leofric's scowling mistrust. He shrugged. "Have it your way then, Captain."

As they rode that day, Cosmo was so angry considered making the rain start early. He calmed himself. It wasn't necessary. The storm would come and he would be proven right; Cosmo needn't hasten it along. By midmorning, the sky was a menacing slate grey, and when the first drops of rain plinked off Leofric's armor, Cosmo did his best to contain his smile.

An hour later they were both drenched to the skin, and they could scarcely see. The mud sucked at the hooves of their horses, slowing their pace even further. Cosmo thought of half a dozen barbs, but he held his tongue. The rain was jibe enough, and Leofric was so angry it was a wonder the droplets landing on his skin didn't sizzle and turn at once to steam.

Finally, he called a halt, under a tree whose canopy was thick enough to slow the rain. Well, some of it at least. Cosmo dismounted when he saw Leofric doing the same, and he stood quietly beside his horse, waiting. Leofric shoved a hand into his pack to retrieve the map, and considered it angrily. When he looked up at Cosmo at last, his mouth was a hard line, and his eyes flashed.

"What is it?" Cosmo asked him in his sweetest, most innocent voice.

Leofric's words were so venomous they would have poisoned a well. "You did this on purpose."

"Did what?"

Like *it* was the one who had so surely vexed him, Leofric crushed the map in his large hand and stuffed it back into his bag. "Come," he said. "We make for the town."

"I rather like riding in this weather," said Cosmo, tilting his face up to the sky. He was treading dangerous ground here, he knew, but taunting Leofric proved impossible to resist. "A little wet never bothered me much."

"Oh, it doesn't?"

Cosmo shook his head, grinning, but before he could offer any further wit, Leofric snapped. Faster than Cosmo would have thought, Leofric took a swift step forward and gave him a sharp shove, right in the chest. It startled him far more than it hurt, but it threw him off balance nonetheless. He took a step back, and his heel connected with a log and all at once Cosmo landed on his ass in a gigantic puddle of mud. He hit the ground with a squelch and the mud seemed to cling to his legs as he tried to get up. Leofric smiled, actually smiled, and swung up into the saddle. "I'll meet you at the inn," he said, and put his heels to his horse, leaving Cosmo on the ground.

By the time Cosmo reached the town and its singular inn, he was sodden and filthy, with mud worked into some very uncomfortable places. He approached the inn-keep after leaving Hestia with a stableboy. "Trouble on the road, good sir?"

"You have no idea," said Cosmo under his breath. "I believe my simple-minded man servant has already procured a room for us? A tall man with a shaven head and fearsome scowl, perhaps looking like he has a stick lodged up his backside?"

The inn-keep gave him a peculiar look. "Aye," she said. "He took room two, at the top of the steps there. And please, take care to step upon the mats, you're dripping everywhere."

"My thanks," said Cosmo.

"Send your things down, I'll have the girl wash them and dry them for you."

Cosmo thanked her again and walked carefully up the creaky wooden steps, hoping Leofric had gotten a good laugh out of his little prank. He was cold and wet and annoyed, wanting nothing more than a good bath and a goblet of wine. Or three. Room two indeed was at the top of the steps, and when Cosmo tried the door it was open. Leofric had gotten them a room with two sleeping couches, and if the sounds beyond the curtain opposite were any judge, a private bathing alcove. Leofric's things were on one of the beds, clean clothing laid out just so, as if he were going to be inspected by a superior officer any moment. Cosmo cast a furtive glance over his shoulder, ensuring the sounds from the bath still indicated a person sloshing and soaping about. When he was certain, he quickly stripped out of his wet, muddy things and cast them all over the bed and Leofric's clothing. He used one of Leofric's cloaks to wipe the mud from his hair, and tossed that in the pile as well. Naked and clean enough, he crawled between the blankets on the other bed and promptly fell asleep, a smile on his lips.

~

The inn was a large daub and wattle building in the center of town, the town Cosmo had pointed out on the map. By the time Leofric had reached it, he felt guilty at shoving Cosmo into the mud. He felt guilty as he brushed out Lyra's coat. He felt guilty as he paid the inn keeper. He felt guilty as a clutch of servants carried kettles of steaming water into the room to fill the copper tub in the bathing alcove.

But then, once he'd stripped off his traveling clothes and climbed into the steaming bath, something strange happened. As he scrubbed himself clean, he found himself smiling. The look on Cosmo's face as he'd gone reeling back into the mud had been a treasure beyond price. Leofric snorted as he washed, and the more he thought of it, the more he laughed. Every time he tried to get a grip on himself, a picture would burst behind his eyes of Cosmo on his ass in the mud, a look of disgust, shock and horror on his freckled face—and he'd dissolve again, laughing hysterically as he scrubbed.

Leofric had not laughed like that in a very long time, and he'd certainly *never* laughed all alone in the bath like a madman. It filled him with a strange sense of giddiness. If he'd had his wits about him, he would have made a grab for the bridle of Cosmo's horse, given him a long, wet walk to the town. When the door clicked beyond the curtain at last and Cosmo called out a stiff greeting, Leofric took pains to stifle his laughter, lest Cosmo hear it.

He and Hamalcar had played games like these, along with all the soldiers. It was simply what happened, when young virile men were forced to travel together, sleep together, spend every moment in each other's company. Petty grievances and rivalries, games and japes, all of it made to bind the men closer together. When they faced a foe, all these things were put aside and they joined as one, like fingers closing into a fist.

As Leofric finished his bath, he found himself wondering if Cosmo would retaliate, and when. He didn't seem the sort to take things like that in stride. His temper always simmered just there beneath the surface, masked behind his teasing smiles, as Leofric's burned hand could attest. He realized the adjacent room was silent as a crypt, and suddenly the bathwater seemed very cold.

What was he doing? He was no green stripling on his first mission, and Cosmo certainly was not a comrade in arms—he was a *god,* a proud and angry one. Leofric shivered. Taunting Cosmo, though it gave him immense satisfaction, was foolish.

When he emerged from the bath, he wrapped a linen towel about his hips and pulled back the curtain, wondering what had given Cosmo cause to remain so quiet. He surveyed the darkened room in trepidation. At first, nothing seemed amiss, which only served to make the hair on Leofric's arms stand on end. Then, he saw it. Cosmo had discarded his muddy things all over Leofric's bed, soaking his clean clothes and the blankets below. Cosmo himself was curled up asleep in the bed opposite, snoring. *Smugly,* Leofric thought.

He waited for the anger to swell in his chest, but it didn't. Instead, before he could stop himself, he shook his head and smiled. Turnabout *was* fair play, after all. He considered what he would have done, as a young man, faced with a similar retaliation from a fellow soldier. There was only one thing *to* do. Leofric dropped his towel and prayed that Cosmo was a heavy sleeper.

Twelve

Cosmo woke up in the tub.

It wasn't the first time, but waking in such a state usually followed a night over indulging in wine, and Cosmo hadn't had a drop the day before. Sunlight streamed in through the window of their room at the inn and he had a fearsome crick in his neck. Disoriented, he sat up, searching for Leofric, and found himself alone.

One of the beds had been fully stripped, and Cosmo felt a surge of guilt. He got up and padded across the room to make certain that his muddy things hadn't damaged the stuffed mattress. They hadn't, mercifully. He dressed, wondering where Leofric had gotten to. When he left the room, he clicked the door shut behind him, musing that Leofric should have given him a key. Down in the common room, the other guests at the inn were tucking in to morning meal, and the place already bustled with activity. Cosmo flagged down the inn-keep.

"Ah," she said, a stern look on her face. "Your friend brought down the bed clothes earlier, muddy as if you'd slept outside in the pigsty."

"Apologies," said Cosmo.

She shrugged. "No need. He paid me an extra silver, and he's helping my girl Dorna wash them now, outside."

Cosmo wandered through the common room and out the side door to find that the inn keep had been, at least partially, correct. Leofric was washing the bed clothes and his own soiled uniform in a basin while a young girl—who Cosmo assumed was Dorna—sat in a chair watching him with an appraising eye.

"You are by far the ugliest washerwoman I've ever seen," said Cosmo to Leofric as he approached.

Was he imagining things, or did the severe line of Leofric's mouth soften, just for the span of half a heartbeat? "I felt it unfair to ask Dorna to scrub these," said Leofric.

"Very unfair," Dorna agreed. She reclined back in her seat, and reached to the ground where she'd set a clay cup of steaming tea. "And I certainly don't find him hard to look upon."

Leofric's cheeks flamed and he busied himself with the mangle, squelching muddy water out of the bedclothes before dunking them back in the tub.

"Did you tell her *why* they were so muddied?"

"Aye," said Leofric. He stood and turned to hang a sheet upon the line. The skies had cleared overnight and a pleasant breeze stirred the clothes already drying there. "I told Lady Dorna here that it was because my traveling companion was an insufferable nuisance."

"That's you, I expect," said Dorna idly, examining her fingernails.

"I expect the same," Cosmo admitted. "I am a nuisance."

"An *insufferable* one," confirmed Leofric, peering out from behind the sheet. "Though truth be told, my lady, I shoved him into the mud."

"Well," said Dorna, who must have been all but fourteen. "I've shoved a nuisance or two into the mud in my time."

"We surely deserve it," said Cosmo, grinning now. He couldn't believe his luck. Perhaps sometime in the night, Leofric had gotten up to relieve himself and taken a nasty spill down the stairs. A head injury was the only explanation for his sudden levity, but Cosmo wasn't about to let it pass by. The sun was shining, and despite the ache in his neck, he'd had an excellent night's sleep. Not only that—he hadn't even had to wash out his own laundry—a victory, if ever there was one.

When Leofric had hung all the linens to dry, he and Cosmo walked down the narrow dirt road that served as the town's main street. "What name do they call this place?" Cosmo asked, curious.

"Westfold," said Leofric. "I think it's the last town we'll find before we enter the border lands on the western road to Sokol."

"We should refresh our rations, then," said Cosmo. Some of his spices were running low, too, and if they were going to be eating on the road, he wasn't about to suffer any more of Leofric's cooking.

"Agreed," said Leofric.

Another surprise. Cosmo suddenly began to worry that Leofric was making plans to murder him in his sleep.

"What?" Leofric asked him.

"What, what?" Asked Cosmo.

Leofric smirked. "I've never seen you speechless before," he said. "I like it."

Cosmo would have liked to spend the day wandering the town, learning of its people, perhaps finding a tavern or three, but Leofric was plainly antsy to be away. This fragile peace between them was so hard won that for once Cosmo did not wish to test it.

Unfortunately, someone was determined to.

They returned to the top of the stair to see the door to their room swinging open on its hinges. Leofric rounded on Cosmo. "You did not lock the fucking door?"

Cosmo startled at his sudden ire. "You didn't give me a key!"

"No key is needed to lock it behind you," snapped Leofric.

Cosmo flushed. *Shit.* "That's so," he allowed. "But—"

Leofric snarled and shoved past him into the room. When Cosmo followed in his wake, he saw the place had been ransacked. Their bags had been shaken out all over the floor, clothing torn and tossed carelessly around. Curiously, Cosmo noted several piles of flour spilled all about the place like tiny piles of snow. Leofric fell to his knees, sifting through the flour with his fingers, searching. "*Fuck!*"

"What is it?" Cosmo asked him. "What is this, of the flour?"

Leofric stood, and covered his eyes with a shaking hand. "Gone," he muttered. "All of it, gone."

"*What's* gone?" said Cosmo, still bewildered.

Leofric turned toward him again, fury etched into every line of his face. With the absence of the robber in their midst, Cosmo was the only possible target. "My *coin*," he said. "I had hidden it amongst the flour."

Cosmo knit his brows together, still several steps behind. "What coin?"

"The coin His Highness gave me," he said. "Coin to convince me to spend any stretch of time with *you*."

It should not have hurt. It shouldn't have. Cosmo had known from the beginning that Leofric detested him, looked down upon him. He had known Leofric would never have willingly left his precious charge behind. But something about the knowledge that he'd been *bribed* to accompany Cosmo was more than he could stand. Like any cornered animal, Cosmo lashed out. "This was not my doing," he said.

"No, perhaps not," said Leofric. "But it was your foolishness that caused it."

"*How*?"

"How? *How?*" Leofric was near purple with anger now. "Your storm, your asinine notion of staying here. Your bloody ridiculous *quest*."

"*My* quest?" Cosmo laughed bitterly. "I was perfectly happy, living on my own till you literally dragged me off to begin this little errand."

"Your brothers—"

"My brothers would be happy to have let me rot. It is only because they need my part in this that they even included me at all."

"That's not—"

"It's not true? Did you not even say that we needn't worry about keeping me awake? We needn't worry about my part in this quest? Saving me is urgent to no one, least of all myself. This is not my fucking doing."

Leofric took a few breaths, but the fire in his eyes did not dull. He paced back and forth, searching through the clothing and scraps of fabric that littered the floor. If anything, all he did was make the room even more messy.

"Let us confront the inn keep," Cosmo tried. "Perhaps she saw the villain enter or leave the grounds."

"Gave them our room number and told them to rob us blind, more like," said Leofric.

"Regardless, she might know something."

Cosmo did the talking when they approached her. "My lady," he began politely. "A word?"

She leveled a look at Cosmo. "Just one?"

"*Many,* in fact—"

Cosmo held up a hand to silence Leofric before he could

offend their only lead. "My lady, our rooms have been robbed."

She squinted at them. "You lose your key?"

"No," said Leofric, taking it from his belt.

"You forget to *use* your key?"

Cosmo and Leofric exchanged a glance. "I'm afraid so," said Cosmo. "We simply felt so at home and safe in your establishment—"

"Spare me," she snapped. "You're the third guest to complain of theft—I'll be bankrupt by the time I'm done making amends. What would you have of me?"

"A name, a face, a cardinal direction," said Cosmo. "Anything you could give us."

She pondered for a moment. "A ragged group of men came in, inquiring after rooms. My first thought had been to refuse them. They had the look of outlaws, I thought, but they had the coin."

"Coin stolen from other honest men, no doubt," said Leofric under his breath.

"No doubt," she agreed.

"Three ragged men robbed more than one room?"

"Aye," said the inn-keep. "Unless there were more than one group of brigands."

"We can take care of three broken men," Cosmo assured her. "Did you know perchance where they headed next?"

"Home, was all they said," the innkeeper told them. "Not much help, I know, but the men had something of your look, if you don't mind my saying," she said, with a gesture toward Leofric.

"They were Sokolian?" he asked, surprised.

"I thought so at first, but one had a mark, just here," she touched the side of her neck. "Three—"

"Feathers?"

"Yes, feathers they were," she agreed. "Black ones. One had

three, another had a whole collar of them, all the way 'round his neck."

Cosmo had no idea what that was about, but plainly it meant something to Leofric. He turned on his heel and stormed out of the common room. "My thanks!" Cosmo called over his shoulder to the innkeeper and hastened to follow Leofric's angry stride.

"*Órnians*," he spat, almost to himself. "Fucking Órnians."

"How can you be certain?"

"The tattoos," he said. "The feathers are their mark. Men in their legions get a feather tattooed after five years of service, and then a new one for every year thereafter. A man with an entire collar would have to be an officer."

By then, they reached the stables. "They are far from home, no?"

Leofric nodded. "I mislike this. How did a band of Órnian outlaws came to be this deep into Papian territory?"

"Well, it matters not how they got here. We know where they are headed. The two of us can handle three, easily."

"Perhaps," Leofric allowed, grudgingly. "If we find them."

"Well," said Cosmo, "Let us make haste, then."

That proved easier said than done however. Cosmo's horse was gone, though mercifully Lyra remained in her stall at the very end of the stables. Lyra was a fine horse, but by look not the equal of the dappled grey filly Cosmo had been riding. Leofric saddled her with haste, and offered Cosmo an arm to swing up into the saddle before him. "Come," said Leofric, urging Lyra with his knees.

"Did the inn-keep not say there were but three brigands?" Cosmo sounded concerned. "There has to be a dozen of them."

Leofric and Cosmo crouched in the shadows, a hundred yards from a crude campsite in the woods outside of town. The men had not been difficult to follow; Leofric had to admit Cosmo was of great use in that regard. His grace allowed him to ask questions of the earth, and the earth provided answer. "Whether it is a dozen or three it makes no matter," said Leofric. "I must retrieve what they took. And we cannot ride double the entire way to Sokol."

Cosmo's horse was hobbled amongst the outlaws' own mounts, distinguished even in the dark by her fine tack and bridle. Despite Leofric's own words, he feared Cosmo would be right. Cosmo could fight, he'd proven that, but revealing his inner powers seemed most unwise. They had more than their own safety to consider. If but a single man escaped to bring word to Órnio that Papia had a someone like a sorcerer in its employ, it could go very ill.

He had to think of a plan, something clever that would allow them to get inside the camp and retrieve their things and Cosmo's horse, without drawing attention. And preferably without bloodshed. The more he stared the more it seemed impossible. And the longer he went without speaking, the more he could feel Cosmo's own stare boring into the side of his head. "We could come back tomorrow," Cosmo suggested. "The town must have a force of men charged with keeping the peace."

"They could be long gone by tomorrow," Leofric hissed back. "And besides, a small token force of lawmen wouldn't leave the border of the town so far behind them. It would leave the people vulnerable."

"Well, we could *ask* them," said Cosmo, his voice rising a bit.

"Be quiet," Leofric barked, and then he flushed. He didn't need to turn his head to know Cosmo was grinning at that little irony. "Let me think."

They crouched in the shadows for some time, and Leofric found his head utterly empty, completely devoid of any plan that would allow them to dance into the outlaws' camp and out again with his gold and Cosmo's mount. "*Well?*" Cosmo asked.

"Just shut *up*," Leofric hissed. "I cannot think with you chirping in my ear."

"I don't believe you can *think* much at all."

Leofric turned. "What did you say?"

Cosmo backed away, and stood, moving deeper into the concealment of the trees. He ignored the question. "What do you want to do, then?" He asked.

Leofric stood and followed him. He was not asked such a question very often at all. "What do *I* want to do?"

"Yes," said Cosmo, his tone mocking. "Unless you can't even fathom an answer. Can you even think for yourself?"

If Leofric's jaw clenched any harder, his teeth would shatter, exploding like pieces of pottery. "Say. That. Again."

Cosmo scoffed, crossing his arms over his chest. "You probably can't even *have* an original thought of your own. Without someone to give you orders, you're nothing. A simple soldier, right? And that is *all* you are."

Something switched off in Leofric's brain, rage igniting every cell of his body. He advanced on Cosmo like a wolf stalking a deer, and what he *wanted* in that moment, was to tear out his throat. "You want to know what I want to do?"

"Yes."

"What I want to do, more than anything?"

Cosmo's breath hitched. "Yes."

Leofric stalked closer to him. "I don't care if you are a god," he said. "I don't care if your precious grace can scorch me where I stand."

By now, he was right in Cosmo's space. Cosmo swallowed,

and Leofric tracked the bob of his throat. He backed away another step, but he did not avert his gaze.

Leofric pulled his lips back to snarl, "What I want, is to grab a fistful of that ridiculous hair and knock your head against that tree."

Cosmo let out an audible gulp, his back colliding with said tree as he continued to step away.

"I want to sink my fist into your smirking *face*," Leofric gritted out through his bared teeth.

"Oh?"

"I want to wrap my hands around your throat and *squeeze*." Leofric said, close enough to Cosmo now that he could smell his skin, could feel the heat rolling off his body. Leofric lifted one hand to press against his neck, gently. A whisper, a promise. He could feel Cosmo's pulse hammering under his thumb as he traced tiny circles with it over his windpipe. Their noses were less than an inch apart. "I want to...bite the taunting smile off your lips," he whispered.

"I—wait, what?"

Their noses touched, and Leofric slid one of his thighs between Cosmo's legs. He boxed him in against the tree with his arms, and he could feel Cosmo's cock swelling against his leg, hot and hard. His pouty lips gaped open, wanting. Scarce the width of a finger separated his lips from Cosmo's. All Leofric had to do was close the distance and *take* them.

That realization brought him back to himself, like a bucket of cold water dousing the fire burning in his chest. He stepped back, and Cosmo nearly slumped to the ground with Leofric no longer propping him up against the tree. "But I can't."

Cosmo took a step toward him, to close the distance once again. "Why not?"

Leofric opened his mouth to answer, but something at last clicked into place in his brain. "A dozen men, did you say?"

Cosmo frowned, the hazy look still clouding his eyes, but he tried to bring himself back to sense. "What?"

"A dozen," said Leofric his heart beating even faster now. He dropped a hand to his sword hilt. Too late, far too late. "I only counted ten."

"Your friend was right, I'm afraid," came a voice from the shadows. "Good evening, gentlemen."

Thirteen

Cosmo and Leofric sat bound, back-to-back, stripped of clothing and armor. He could feel the sweat of Leofric's skin, dripping between his own shoulder blades. The outlaws had left them in nothing but their subligaria to keep their modesty whilst they picked over their clothing. Cosmo's jewelry had the men arguing, heated, over which pieces they would keep.

"What sort of man wears this much gold?" One asked, throwing Cosmo a weird look.

"They have some sick shit going on between them, I do not doubt," said another, the one who had found them... arguing.

Leofric seethed where he sat behind Cosmo; he could feel it. The tension in his muscled back vibrating, setting Cosmo's own teeth on edge. Cosmo felt guilty for goading him and elated in equal measures. He had seen it in Leofric's eyes; he'd been about three heartbeats away from spinning Cosmo against the tree and having him then and there.

But of course, their new friends had *had* to interrupt.

Naturally. And why couldn't Leofric...do what he wished? What wasn't Leofric telling him?

Cosmo eyed the outlaws. Perhaps they had more pressing concerns. He wasn't truly *afraid;* he was confident that with the power of his grace he could send them scurrying like mice. But Leofric had not wished to expose what he called Cosmo's "sorcery." Tensions between Papia and Órnio were mounting, to hear Leofric tell it. He'd complained at length about the Órnian king, its armies, and the devious tactics of both. If Leofric were to be believed, the kingdom of Órnio was singularly populated by villains and scoundrels. Cosmo had never been there, and could not verify Leofric's claim, but based upon his current situation he had to admit he was willing to believe it.

One of the men had been most interested in Leofric's armor. "Sokolian, or I'm the bloody queen," he said, eyeing Leofric with suspicion. "What is a Sokolian legionary doing this deep in Papia?"

Leofric did not answer, but Cosmo could feel the tension shifting in his back. He'd summoned that eerie calm he had, the stony demeanor that made it seem as though his body were merely an empty shell.

"No answer, eh?" said one of the others. "Take an ear, he'll tell you then."

Cosmo trembled. He did not wish to see Leofric maimed —but the only way to prevent it would be for Cosmo to unleash his grace to break their bonds, and he'd be maimed then in any case. With so much of their skin touching the resulting burns would be excruciating. Luckily, the man picking over Leofric's armor said, "Not worth dulling your blade," he said, disgusted. "I've known such shits to bite their own tongue off when put to the question, rather then betray any paltry secret they might carry." The man frowned, digging beneath the steel of one of Leofric's bracers. "What's this?"

From within a secret compartment, he drew a folded parchment.

At that, Leofric stirred, twisting against the rough ropes that bound them back-to-back, but he did not speak.

"Give it here," said one of the others—and Cosmo saw he was the man with the ring of black feathers tattooed about his neck like a collar. Perhaps as a sergeant, he was the only one amongst them who could read.

He paced around, out of Cosmo's line of sight, but Cosmo could hear his footsteps circling closer, and Cosmo craned his neck to make attempt to see him.

"This letter," said the sergeant loudly, so all his men could hear, "Says that this man here is about *His Highness's* business. Important mission for the crown, it says."

The mood around the campfire changed instantly. Cosmo felt it, and he was certain Leofric did too. Where before they had been simple travelers, of no consequence to be robbed blind and left to wander naked back to town, now he and Leofric were dangerous. He knew then that these men would not allow them to leave the fireside alive.

"What else does it say?" one of the other men asked.

"A load of nonsense," the sergeant said, scanning the paper. "It makes mention of a deception, a mission beyond Papian borders, and a great sum of gold."

"Beyond Papian borders?"

"Aye," said the sergeant. "That's what it says here."

"That could mean anything," said one of the others, the one who'd first held the paper.

"Or nothing," said yet another. The men began muttering amongst themselves. Cosmo could discern anger, greed, and a bit of fear.

The sergeant drew his dagger and pointed it at Leofric. "Tell us the meaning of this," he said, "And we'll consider letting you live."

Leofric remained mute, so Cosmo took his cue from him and held his tongue as well.

The sergeant scanned the paper again. "It seems this missive holds great value to you," he said. "You would be nothing but a discharged and shamed soldier without it, yes?"

Still, Leofric did not speak.

"You will tell us of your mission," he said, his voice ringing with authority.

Leofric was not moved. He could have been carved of stone, unconcerned, almost bored to look at him. Cosmo could not help but admire his composure.

"Alright," said the man, after staring at Leofric long and hard. "We will get nothing from him. He was trained with the other savage Sokolians. Most like he cannot even read this missive, but is meant to deliver it to better men."

He stood, and held the parchment in one hand, dangling it precariously over the cookfire.

"No!" Leofric cried, startling Cosmo, who truly expected him to remain silent until these men slit his throat.

"No?" the Órnian sergeant lowered the paper, closer and closer to the tongues of flame.

Leofric twisted frantically against the ropes, but it served him nothing except to dig the bindings deep into the muscles of his arms.

Cosmo had to act swiftly. He reached out with his grace toward the kernels of heat at the heart of the fire, and pulled. Fire did not like to travel through the earth, without the air to strengthen it. He pulled again, harder, coaxing it. It bent to his will, as did all things of light and flame, and the fire dimmed.

The sergeant did not notice, so intent on trying to part Leofric from his secrets.

Cosmo pulled again, and again, the fire slowly retreating, diminishing, its heat traveling down into the earth until it was entirely extinguished and the entire campsite thrown into darkness.

"What on earth—"

Three of the men crouched beside the fire, poking amongst the embers that had, to their eyes, suddenly stopped working. Fires did not often dwindle absent cause, so they leaned in closer to have a look. The sergeant looked toward Leofric and Cosmo, a strange look on his face. He tucked the parchment into his belt. "We will bring them to the Imperator," the Sergeant decided. "He will want to question them himself, to learn what mission the kingdom of Papia is perpetrating beyond its own borders. If they are moving with Sokol against us, he will want to know immediately."

Cosmo twisted his head, to see the shadows that meant several of the men still fussed with the dead, smoking remains of their fire. The Sergeant had moved away, barking orders to get it relit, and to prepare the prisoners for transport.

"*Do it*," Leofric muttered.

"Do—do what?"

"You can free us, can you not?"

"With my grace?"

"Yes," said Leofric. "Quickly. We must escape."

Cosmo frowned. "You will be burned."

"And I expect it will hurt a great deal," Leofric agreed, "but we are short of time. *Do it.*"

"I am working another notion," Cosmo said.

"Then *work it*," hissed Leofric. "And see us freed."

Cosmo waited until several of the men had leaned in to inspect the fire, waiting, waiting, and then—the fire burst forth in a terrible conflagration from the dormant embers, and the night air was suddenly filled with screams and the smell of burning flesh. With another surge of his power, Cosmo summoned his grace to the surface of his skin, letting it grow hot enough that the ropes that bound himself and Leofric took flame at once. They struggled against one another, waiting for the ropes to give, and Cosmo could feel the heat against his arms, his chest. His grace was proof against burns, but he understood that Leofric's pain would be terrible.

Finally, the ropes snapped, and Leofric didn't let the burns slow him down. He lurched to his feet and bowled over the sergeant. Cosmo rolled to the side, scrabbling on the ground for a weapon and coming up with a stick. As soon as his hand closed around it, the wood caught fire and he swung it with all his strength into the face of their nearest captor. The man screamed, clawing at his burning face, and Cosmo collided with him, shoving his shoulder into the man's gut to send him sprawling on the ground.

He whirled to see Leofric standing over the gutted Órnian sergeant, a bloodstained blade in one hand and his parchment from Prince Alexios in the other. In the chaos, Cosmo ran to the horse lines, cutting all but his own. The fire, the screaming, the blood, it had the outlaws' horses going mad with fear, and as soon as they realized they were free they took off into the trees. Most of the men still standing ran after their mounts, and Cosmo was able to grab his pack. Leofric joined him, and swiftly they sorted through the Outlaws' stolen goods, searching for Leofric's gold and the rest of their effects. "Cover me," Cosmo said, tossing Leofric the sword he'd only just reclaimed. "I'll find your coin."

Most of the outlaws were injured, dead, or fled, but there were four men still trying to beat the flames off their compatriots. Leofric caught the hilt one handed and charged off without a word, a sword in each hand, and with the men otherwise occupied, Cosmo wasn't worried.

About Leofric, anyway.

Ignoring the sounds of violence behind him, Cosmo dug through the bags until he found several leather bags stuffed fat with coins. One of the outlaw's saddlebags lay open in the pile, so Cosmo filled it as fast as he could, and then mounted Hestia, who mercifully was still saddled. They'd hobbled Lyra half a mile off from where they'd been spying on the camp; hopefully she was still there. Leofric hammered away at one of the last few soldiers, and as Cosmo galloped across to meet him, two of the other men made move to flank him. Cosmo rode one down and Leofric spun and took the sword arm off the other. When Cosmo extended a hand to pull Leofric up into the saddle behind him, he grabbed it without hesitation, his hand warm and slick with blood.

Cosmo gave Hestia his heels and they took off from the outlaws' camp at a wild gallop, charging heedlessly into the night.

When they reached the place they'd tied Lyra's lead, they paused only long enough for Leofric to switch mounts and took off again. Cosmo thought it unlikely that the outlaws would form up and chase after them, but he supposed it didn't hurt to be cautious. They rode through the night, hard and fast, until the pink light of dawn began to bleed through the trees. Now that he could see somewhat, Cosmo found himself staring at Leofric's back as he rode ahead, blistered and burned from its contact with Cosmo's flesh. From here, he could not see the wounds the ropes had left, but he knew they would be ghastly as well.

The sun had well and truly risen before Cosmo found the courage to suggest a halt. The cast to Leofric's face was grim and drawn, and he gave a terse nod. They found a place where a little river fed a pond, a cluster of rocks providing good shelter to the north.

"We need to rest the horses," Leofric agreed, "And examine what we were able to escape with."

"I believe I got all of your coin," said Cosmo. "Unless His Highness drastically overpaid you for the service of escorting me to Mount Hiru."

Leofric looked at him, and for a second Cosmo was afraid Leofric was going to start shouting at him, but instead, he burst out laughing. It was a *wonderful* sound, and despite everything Cosmo found himself matching it. They laughed themselves breathless, and Cosmo nearly fell from the saddle as he tried to dismount. Leofric's laughter guttered out as he swung down from his horse as well, and a grimace ripped across his face, the pain of his wounds finally catching up with him. His chest was awash in horrific blisters, and charred skin the pattern of them continued around his upper arms like toques.

Their bags and belongings were in complete disarray, so Cosmo simply dumped everything out in front of them, searching for something he could use to bind Leofric's wounds. He heard a stifled groan behind him and whipped around to see Leofric attempting to set up a camp, and with every movement blood and pus oozed from the burns on his chest.

"Will you just *sit?*" Cosmo snapped.

Leofric huffed, hesitated, and then—to Cosmo's amazement—sat heavily with a grunt.

Finally, Cosmo found what he was looking for, a salve made from tea tree oil would help stave off infection, and hopefully provide something of a cooling sensation. It would sting, but with that sting would come healing. Accidental burns had been fairly common around Cosmo during his adolescence, and he'd learned of almost every possible cure under the sun.

They waded into the water. In the center of the lake, it came up to Leofric's hips. It was a bit deeper for Cosmo, who was shorter, but still shallow enough that he could stand. They stripped their sooty, bloody subligaria off and tossed them aside. Mutely, Cosmo used a square of clean linen to clean Leofric's back, and the sides of his arms. "I have hurt you yet again," said Cosmo, almost to himself.

"I asked you to," said Leofric. His muscles trembled at even the gentlest touch, but he raised no word of complaint. "You saved us."

"I suppose," said Cosmo. He kept his eyes downcast, avoiding Leofric's gaze as he was forced to step in closer to cleanse the torn skin upon his bare chest.

But Leofric stooped, seizing Cosmo's wrists. "No," he said. "You did. The trick with their cookfire was a clever one, and I wouldn't have been able to defeat so many without your help."

The sincerity in his words, the intensity in his eyes, made Cosmo uncomfortable. "Plainly this pain is making you delirious," he said, trying to make light.

"No," Leofric said again. "You saved that coin. You could have run off. You could have left it."

Cosmo shrugged. "It was important to you," he said.

Leofric studied Cosmo as if seeing him for the very first time. "Your jewels," he said suddenly.

"What?"

"All of your golden trinkets," he said. "You left them all behind."

Cosmo looked down at himself. "I suppose I did," he said. "They didn't really matter to me. Only..."

"Only what?"

"There was one ring, a gift from my brother. It was his, and he gave it to me."

"Auro's?"

Cosmo looked away. "Kryos."

"You kept your bother's ring? The man who tried to kill you?"

"He's still my brother," Cosmo said. "Was. Is. I don't know. Regardless, it held meaning to me. Now hush. Your back is a horror and I need to make sure it heals properly, or I'm certain I'll never hear the end of it."

Leofric smiled softly, and Cosmo had to look away. He suddenly felt aware of how close they were standing, and how naked they were. Very naked. When he tried to push the thought away, washing the blood from Leofric's skin, he recalled something. He let his hands linger on the skin below Leofric's ribs, mercifully unmarred by fire, and said quietly, "Why couldn't you..."

"Why couldn't I what?"

"Do...do what you wanted. Those things you wanted. That you said, before. Before the men attacked. The outlaws. Why—"

"Because...I'm married."

Fourteen

Why Leofric had waited so long to tell Cosmo that he was wed he didn't know, but now that he had, it was as if a strange, icy wall had sprung up between them. He stood naked in the lake, with Cosmo at his back, afraid to turn around and face him.

How could he have let this get so far, how could he have admitted his twisted fantasies, dishonoring himself, his wife... Laela. Thinking of Laela had his guts churning with shame. He loved her, he did. Not in the way that a man would normally wish to love a wife—more as a sister. It was impossible *not* to love the woman who had made his brother so happy. She was Hamalcar's great love, and her face swam before him now as he let Cosmo wash and dress the wounds on his back and arms. He could never allow his temper to get the better of him again, lest he violate their marriage contract and break the sacred oath he'd made to his brother.

Mercifully, Cosmo let Leofric's admission lie. "Oh," he said. A pause, and then, "I didn't know."

They waded back to shore, and Leofric was afraid to turn around. He could picture Cosmo eyeing his backside, but somehow, fending off his flirty barbs had lost its savor. Perhaps for Cosmo too, the admission of his marriage cooling the heat between them. Cosmo was quiet and subdued as he applied some sticky salve to Leofric's burns. He was amassing quite the collection since meeting Cosmo. The salve stung at first, but with the stinging came with a cooling sensation so soothing he groaned out loud. As Cosmo tended Leofric's wounds, he was certain Cosmo could feel the way his heart pounded frantically in his chest, like it was desperate for Cosmo to hear.

And still, Cosmo had not said a word since they'd emerged from the water. For once, it was Leofric who wished the silence would break. It was cowardly, he knew, blaming Laela, using her and their marriage as a shield to keep Cosmo at bay. Leofric *should* have the strength of will to rebuff Cosmo's advances on his own, but his pathetic behavior earlier that day proved he did not—even when his bloody life was at stake. He was the weak wretch he'd always been, such that he needed to use his brother's widow as his shield—instead of the other way around.

By Sokolian law, a widow must remarry if her heir was not of age, and Sorex was only a boy. By marrying Leofric, Laela escaped having to fend off any male suitors who would be sniffing about after her husband's death. It had allowed her to grieve, safe from the advances of other men. It was on Leofric's tongue to explain this to Cosmo, but for some reason, he could not part with the words. Leofric donned a fresh loin cloth as Cosmo lay their bedrolls side by side. After what happened in the outlaws' camp, Leofric knew they should set a watch, but he was just so bloody tired. If the surviving Órnians tracked them to this spot, a few moments warning wouldn't truly prove much difference in the state he was in.

Now that the thrill of the fight had fully left him, the pain was excruciating. Neither his back nor his chest could stand being laid upon, so Leofric lay upon his side, one arm curled up awkwardly under his head. The wounds stung and smarted as the summer breeze danced across his abused flesh, but it felt better for being clean and massaged with Cosmo's ointment.

"I'll bandage you up tomorrow," said Cosmo, his voice oddly flat and formal. "I think it would be best to let the flesh set a bit first, however."

"Gratitude," said Leofric, equally chilly in his response.

The silence went on so long that Leofric thought Cosmo must have fallen asleep. Just when Leofric had almost drifted off himself, Cosmo's quiet voice floated over to rouse him. "The gold is for her."

"Yes, and..." Leofric hesitated once again, but there would be nothing gained by holding back now. Cosmo would make their acquaintance soon enough. "My son."

"Your—"

"Sorex, he is called. A bright boy. A boy any father would be proud of," Leofric said. "His Highness promised me enough coin to retire and see them cared for in perpetuity, if I completed this quest with you."

"That is quite a lot of coin," Cosmo mused. "Why is Prince Alexios so invested in our power being restored?"

Leofric frowned. "For Auro, of course."

Cosmo blinked, startled. "No one has ever loved me like that," he said, and then his face seemed confused, like he hadn't meant to part with the words at all.

Cosmo found the second leg of their journey almost as painful as the first. Instead of sullen, the silence between them now seemed strained. In place of veiled barbs, they traded brittle courtesies, polite and bloodless. Each treated the other as if he were made of spun glass, delicate, prone to shattering.

Cosmo had no idea what to do about it.

He'd bedded with married folk before, of course. In fact, part of what got Leofric into this mess was Cosmo offering to pleasure a married public figure. Usually though, *usually*, married folk came to Cosmo with the full knowledge of their spouse. Occasionally, they even came together to share him. This felt...different. The way Leofric spoke of his marriage was to place his vows firmly between himself and Cosmo. It seemed to Cosmo that Leofric would part with his cock before he would part with his precious honor.

His oaths were just as much a part of him as the vining tattoo, the scowl, and the armor he always wore. Stripped of those, who was he?

It was a relief when they at last reached the border of the Sokolian territory, if only because it meant encountering more people, finally sparing them of each other's undiluted company. The captain on duty in the barracks knew Leofric, and offered them their hospitality for the night. Cosmo offered to put up their horses while Leofric sequestered himself with the captain, warning him of the movement of Órnian troops beyond their borders, Cosmo did not doubt.

He waited anxiously in the room they would share, listening to the winds moving through the slitted windows up near the ceiling. Leofric had told him the barracks here were called the Flute Halls, for the song the wind made, whistling in and out. When at last Leofric returned, it was only to summon Cosmo to share evening meal with the men. He could scarcely meet Cosmo's eye.

The dinner was a lively one, but Cosmo felt well removed. Leofric seemed far more at home here in the company of other soldiers than he had in the villa in Papia. He was known here, that much was plain. Respected, and popular amongst his fellows. Cosmo even caught a smile or two gracing his lips, though they were fleeting. He could not help but thinking of how close he'd come to tasting those lips, and wondered what kissing Leofric would be like. If his impassioned outburst before their capture were to be believed, it would be lively, to say the least. The notion made Cosmo ache with want, far worse than before. Before, it had merely been an amusing diversion. A game. Now it consumed his every waking thought—and the man could barely stand to look at him. Cosmo cursed himself. What a fucking fool he was.

He excused himself from the meal and retired to their room, an uncomfortable knot in his guts as he waited. Normally he would twist and adjust his jewels when so taken with nerves, and without them he felt naked, and not in a way he liked. While he waited, he tried to marshal his courage and steel himself to address this awkwardness between himself and Leofric. Cosmo knew he could not survive the remainder of this journey in such a strained mood.

When Leofric at last returned, Cosmo opened his mouth to blurt some manner of apologies, of denials, of promises to keep his tongue and salacious words well-guarded behind his teeth, but before he could blech forth such words, Leofric held up a hand.

"Apologies, for how I have behaved since..." He trailed away.

"None required," said Cosmo. "I—"

"I believe we both share some of the blame," said Leofric with a wry grin that made Cosmo's knees weak. "I propose we begin anew. A fresh start, leaving behind misunderstandings and awkwardness."

Cosmo smiled gratefully. "I think that a splendid idea."

"To commemorate our new alliance," said Leofric, "I recalled something I found, and wish to return to you."

Cosmo tilted his head to the side. "And what is that?"

Leofric extended a hand, offering something concealed within his palm. Confused, Cosmo held his own hand, palm up, feeling sparks fly across his skin when their fingers brushed. A cool weight landed in Cosmo's hand, and when Leofric drew away, Cosmo gasped. "My ring! How did you come by this?"

"I've actually had it for a while, and I beg forgiveness for forgetting. The first night you came to the villa in Papia, when you discarded your golden trinkets, this rolled off, concealed behind a table leg. I found it the next morning, and forgot I'd had it."

Before he could stop himself, Cosmo launched himself forward, throwing his arms around Leofric in a grateful hug. As he realized what he had done, he made to back away, and apologize for already seeking to shatter this fragile peace between them. However, before he could, Leofric's arms fell about his shoulders, returning the embrace. Just for a moment, but Cosmo felt it eased away the tension between them, far more than words. "Thank you," he whispered, before he drew away.

Things were easier, after that. There still stood a vast chasm of things unspoken between them, but they had built a bridge across it, and Cosmo felt that would serve. For now.

The journey back to Sokol had been so fraught that Leofric had not allowed himself a chance to realize how much he missed it, how much he missed the dry heat of the sun and the spicy food, the sands and the wind billowing all around him. Even the sting of grit in his eyes was welcome. He felt himself again. He looked forward to seeing Laela and Sorex, too. He'd missed them dearly since being dispatched to Papia. Leofric looked beside him as he rode, watching Cosmo taking in the sights of the rolling golden dunes that surrounded the desert pass. He seemed even more beautiful here in the sunbaked world of Leofric's home. Had the sun blessed him with even *more* freckles, somehow? Leofric would not have thought it possible, yet as they rode, he found himself discerning new shapes in the galaxies of spots on Cosmo's sun-pinked skin. Guilt gnawed at him. He should have told Cosmo the truth of his marriage, should have told him it was not a bond of romantic love between himself and his wife, or that Sorex were not truly his son. But Leofric had a better measure of Cosmo now. Despite what Leofric had initially thought, he was a good man, in his way. A bit hapless, a bit self-indulgent, but a good man all the same. A good, kind Cosmo was far more dangerous to Leofric's willpower than a detestable one. The sham of his marriage was a safe shield between them, one he did not think Cosmo would willfully violate.

"Leofric?"

"Apologies," said Leofric. "I find myself well distracted by the familiar sights of home."

Cosmo gave him a curious look, but otherwise let it pass. "I simply inquired how much further we planned to ride today. I find it difficult to estimate distance looking out at all this."

It was true. For one not used to traversing a desert, the sands and the wide expanse played tricks upon the eye. Things far seemed close, things close seemed far. Leofric gestured toward the sky. "Trust in the path of your sun above," said Leofric. "We travel west beside it, for another day and a half."

"My sun?" a hint of his old teasing present in the question, but it felt different now. Familiar, friendly.

Leofric flushed. "You command it, do you not?"

Cosmo considered that. "I suppose, but more like a sailor 'commands' the sea, or the winds. I harness it, I guide it. I am more a shepherd of the season, than master of it."

Leofric smiled.

"What?"

"It's funny," he said. "I thought you and Auro could not be more different, but sometimes the similarity between you strikes me. There is something of his way in you, I think."

Cosmo plainly wasn't sure what to do with that. "I'll take that as a complement," he said after a while, though to Leofric his tone was accented with a touch of sadness. "People cannot help but love Auro."

"And there is some of you in him, too, I think."

That took Cosmo aback, so much so that he could only sputter incoherently in response. Leofric's smile widened, but he offered no further explanation of his words as they rode on.

The following morning, they traveled up a ridge of dunes that looked down upon a distant valley, a pocket of fertile land within the expanse of desert. Leofric pointed out a tiny splotch on the horizon, revealing it to be the home of his wife and son. Cosmo's face grew solemn, and Leofric could tell he grew more unsure of himself with every step they took.

He could feel Cosmo's eyes on the side of his head, like they made attempt to bore into his skull, to peer into his brain to read the thoughts within. Leofric was glad that he couldn't; his thoughts were a tumult of joy and guilt, so scattered that his only relief was that he could keep them private.

"What does your family know, of our quest?" Cosmo asked him, as they neared the walls that surrounded the small villa.

"Nothing," said Leofric. "I haven't been home, since my deployment to Papia."

Cosmo frowned. "No, letters? Nothing?"

"Letters can be intercepted," said Leofric evasively. In truth, he mostly kept his distance, not wanting to force himself into Laela's life. He glanced sidelong at Cosmo, and could tell he was suspicious. "I can tell Laela some of it, of course but..."

"But what?"

"It is … difficult to know what to share, in regards to—"

"—me?" said Cosmo, a hint of humor in his cheeky expression.

Leofric tingled a bit, flushing, but kept his face a mask. "All of this," he said. "Gods, curses. The whole messy lot."

That much was true, at least. Laela was perhaps Leofric's oldest friend in the world. If there was anyone he could trust with his fears and worries, the secrets and the dangers, it was her. But it was a *lot* to burden someone with, so he hadn't yet decided how much to share. There was more Leofric could have said, much more, but he was trying desperately to protect this new camaraderie between them. He would never admit it out loud, but by now he was used to Cosmo. Enjoyed his company, bawdy jests and all. Perhaps Leofric even liked him, indecent lascivious thoughts aside. Their journey was far from over, and it would not do to destroy this peace between them while it was still so fresh and fragile.

The knot in Leofric's stomach loosened slightly as they rode into the yard. Leofric only just caught a glimpse of Sorex working in the stable before he threw down his shovel and turned to run inside the house, shouting, "He's home! He's home!"

Fifteen

Compared to the royal villa in Papia, Leofric's home was a modest one. However, it was spacious and well maintained, on a nice little tract of fertile land. The place was luxurious enough to give Cosmo cause to wonder if Leofric kept even a single coin of his usual wages for himself, or simply sent it all here to his family. Cosmo's stomach twisted as he caught a glimpse of the boy, tall and gangly, before he ran inside the house to fetch his mother. When the lad reemerged, he got a better look. He had to be perhaps twelve, or thirteen, and the resemblance to Leofric was apparent at a glance. The boy ran forward just as Leofric came down off his horse, and for the first time Cosmo saw a truly relaxed smile break over the man's face.

It stung.

"You will be taller than I, when next I return home, I think," he said, as the boy threw skinny arms around his father for a long embrace.

When they broke apart, Sorex noticed Cosmo for the first time. "Who's this then?"

"Mind your manners," said Leofric, but he was *still* smiling. Cosmo had until this very moment thought Leofric maintaining such an expression for this length of time to be impossible. "This is Cosmo, my tribune in His Highness's royal guard."

The lie came smoothly; of course the gossip from Cosmo's dismissal from the guard—or, for that matter, Leofric's—would not have reached Sokol. "Greetings," said Cosmo. "You must stand brother to brave Leofric, here. It is impossible for a young son to be so tall and mighty a warrior."

The boy tilted his head to the side, skeptical of Cosmo's flattery. Then he scowled, and the resemblance to his father became even more pronounced.

"Leofric?" A woman's voice drew Cosmo's attention, and he looked up to lay eyes on Leofric's wife for the first time.

He wasn't certain what he expected, but Laela was petite, curvy, and beautiful. Her hair was inky black, and the crinkles at the corner of her bright blue eyes only served to enhance her welcoming smile. Leofric pulled her into a tight embrace as well, wrapping his long arms around her, while leaving one hand resting upon their son's skull. He kissed her cheek, and then rested his own cheek upon the crown of her head. Tender, familiar, and intimate. Cosmo looked away, hating the envious spike lodged in his chest.

"This is most unexpected," she said when they broke apart, and Cosmo heard the unasked question there, as Leofric surely did.

"I know," Leofric said, touching her cheek. "But there was no time to send word in advance of visit. There is much we should discuss. Sorex, come. Help me put up the horses."

"At once," said Sorex obediently. He held out his hand for Hestia's reins, giving Cosmo a suspicious glance in the meantime.

Cosmo smiled and thanked the boy before turning to the

mother. "He looks just like his father," said Cosmo, meaning to compliment her.

Her face, warm and friendly a split second before, drained of color. "Yes," she said faintly. "He is the spitting image." She turned away. "Come," she said. "I will show you where you can put your things."

Curious, Cosmo followed her into the villa. It was fastidiously clean, which was expected of a place Leofric had lived, but full of personal touches, art and decoration, which was not. Laela led Cosmo down a short corridor. "You may sleep here," she said. She'd plainly gathered herself, and her welcoming smile had returned. "It's not spacious, I'm afraid. It served as nursery to Sorex when he was very small, and I'm afraid since then it's become little more than a storeroom"

The room was small indeed, but far tidier than her demure words implied, with a small sleeping couch beside a window that would be plenty comfort for Cosmo. He set down his bag and observed his surroundings. His gaze fell to the ring Leofric had returned. He twisted it idly on his finger, thinking about Leofric and his beautiful family, and the secret he was keeping from them. Cosmo had known his like before; men who preferred the company of other men, or women who preferred women. Choosing one or the other seemed impossible to Cosmo, but he understood. Places like Papia had changed a lot since Cosmo had been young, and relationships of all sorts had grown more common with every passing summer. Sokol was another land entirely, clinging to older ways and stricter, more austere traditions. And besides, marriage and children were still the only way to carry on one's name, one's bloodline, one's legacy—at least as far as Cosmo knew.

From time to time, men like Leofric frequented Lapis, often with their wives in tow. Cosmo sometimes acted as a conduit between two loving hearts encased in flesh that was, say, less willing. Those were some of his most heated carnal memories, if he were being honest. Brushing up against such deep love and trust was something rare, sharing the couple's bed made Cosmo feel as a translator between two people who spoke foreign tongues, who could unite as one if only they could understand each other. For the briefest of moments, Cosmo allowed himself to wonder if perhaps something would be possible with Leofric and Laela. No. He recoiled from the thought of it, the wrongness of it apparent even in the realm of his fantasies. It would not be the same. It would not be...*right.*

The sun was well and truly set, but they'd not yet had evening meal. As they'd ridden into the yard, he'd been starving but by the time he heard the call to supper, Cosmo's appetite had all but evaporated.

"Had I known Leofric was bringing a guest I would have prepared far more festive fare," said Laela, once the four of them were all seated at the table, which threatened to groan under the weight of the meal.

"This is far more festive than you give yourself credit for," said Cosmo politely. "Upon the road I was at the mercy of your husband's cooking."

Laela's laugh was as warm and genuine as the rest of her, which only served to inflame Cosmo's jealousy. He'd concocted an image of her, in the intervening days of their journey, since learning of her existence. The unflattering picture had comforted him, while the reality made him feel slimy and dirty. When he could have imagined someone frigid or uncaring, he could understand the urge to stray. But why would Leofric be unhappy with such a wife? She was beautiful, fertile, witty, kind, and plainly an excellent mother. And an accomplished cook, he thought, digging in to the meal. The thought only soured his mood further.

Leofric spent the meal quizzing Sorex about the history of Sokol, and the boy answered nearly every question correct.

The pride of his father was something he clearly craved, and Leofric was far more generous with his smiles to young Sorex than with anyone Cosmo had yet seen. That only made his mood even worse—perhaps Cosmo was as selfish as everyone always insisted. How could he begrudge a son the admiration of his father? A wife, the love of her husband?

Faced with the discovery that Cosmo was as despicable and ugly a creature as everyone always said, he excused himself from the table.

Sixteen

"Sextus and Tulius plan to hold contest," Sorex was saying, but Leofric's eyes tracked Cosmo as he excused himself from the table. "We place a beam over a ditch and practice fighting upon it."

Laela sighed. "And practice falling and breaking your necks, I don't doubt," she chided.

"I can go, can't I?"

Leofric still stared at the doorway through which Cosmo had disappeared.

"Leofric?"

He shook himself. "Apologies," he said. "What?"

"Your son is asking if he can go play some ridiculous, dangerous game by moonlight with Sextus and Tulius."

Leofric pulled his attentions back to the table with difficulty. "It is quite late," he said sternly.

"The game is only *fun* by darkness," said Sorex, exasperated, as if this should be apparent to anyone with a half a brain.

Leofric found himself caught between son and mother. It happened frequently, but it always left him feeling discomfited. Laela plainly worried for the boy's safety, and Leofric understood that. Like his true father, Sorex was occasionally wild with mischief, testing the limits of both safety and sanity. On the other hand, he was a boy. Boys must be foolish so that men can grow to be wise, his and Hamalcar's father had always said. "You may go," he said.

Laela sighed in defeat, and Sorex let out a whoop as he jumped up from the table.

"However," said Leofric. "First, you must help clear away the dinner things, and recall that you will still be expected to perform your share of chores, come tomorrow. You may decide for yourself how much sleep you will need to do so— but it will go poorly for you if you are not of a form, come sunrise."

"I will be careful," Sorex promised, as sincere as only a young boy could be. "I will not stay overlong."

When Sorex had cleaned the table to his mother's satisfaction and galloped out the door to meet his friends, Leofric said, "He is just like his father."

Laela rested her hand on the back of Leofric's. "He shares the traits of both of them, I think."

He gave her a weary smile. "Favorable ones, I hope."

"Some," Laela chided. She gave his hand a squeeze. Now that they were alone, her face turned troubled. "Tell me why you are here."

Leofric stared down at their clasped hands. "I would not even know where to begin," he said truthfully.

Laela raised one of her brows. "Begin with your companion, perhaps."

That startled a laugh from Leofric. How could he begin with Cosmo? He was the most vexing part of this equation, to be sure. Laela was his oldest friend, more trusted than a sister, but there were some things he found it difficult to say out loud.

"Leofric, we have been wed for more than two years, and you have never once looked at me the way you look at that man," she said bluntly. "I am not stupid, nor am I blind."

"I know," he said. He squeezed her hands. "But, our marriage…"

"Our marriage cannot be an excuse for you to remain unhappy forever."

"I am not—"

"Unhappy?" Laela sighed. "I am. I have grown so lonely, without a husband's touch to comfort me in the night."

"I am your husband," Leofric protested, hurt. "When I am home, we share a bed—"

"And dreams are all we share within it," said Laela.

"Laela—"

"Leo, I have known you for longer than my son has been alive. Tell me why you are here. All of it."

For a moment, Leofric was at a loss for words. How could he even begin to tell the tale of what had transpired over the last four months? With an aggrieved sigh, Laela stood from the table. "Come," she said.

Leofric followed her, bemused, as she walked down the hallway toward her—*their*—bed chamber. Upon her sideboard sat a small carved chest, and within that a dusty crystal bottle of dark, amber liquor. She poured them each a healthy glassful. "Drink," she said. "Loosen your tongue."

Leofric drank. The liquor burned going down, warming his chest. He had not sampled such in many years, not since he and Hamalcar had been young, foolish men. "It is not possible to begin the tale with Cosmo," he said.

"Then where does it begin?"

"Apparently, the tale began four centuries ago, and I am merely an instrument of its more recent chapters." And then, Leofric told her all of it. All of it he understood, anyhow, and much of it that he had guessed. He told her of Prince Alexios and his escapes from the villa, of his clandestine journeys to the wild forest where he'd fallen in love with a god. He told her of Neossós, and Janus, and the death of the Neossan queen. He told her of Auro, and the curse upon himself and his brothers. And he told her of Cosmo, of the bandits in the forest. All of it. He did not even leave out that he'd lied, lied about the reason for his and Laela's union, lied about Hamalcar and the truth of Sorex's parentage.

Laela listened to all of it, quiet. She did not interrupt, or ask any questions, but her eyes grew wider and her knuckles whiter as the tale continued. At last, Leofric ran out of words. The story was complete, and the silence in its wake rang like a bell between them.

At long last, Laela raised the glass to her lips and swallowed its contents in one. She considered it for a brief moment before crossing the room, and retrieving the bottle. When Laela returned to sit beside him once again on the bed, she set her glass aside and raised the bottle to her lips, drinking directly from it.

Leofric was shocked, but when she passed him the bottle, he did the same.

"You realize how this tale of yours sounds," she said.

Leofric wiped the back of his mouth with his hand. "I do."

"And if you were another man, I'd think you taken with some sort of...mad fancy."

"If we summon Cosmo before us, he could prove the truth of what I say. Parts of it, at least. The man has...power." Leofric had shown her the burns on his chest and back, the scar on his palm.

Laela nodded. "There's a god beneath my roof," she said faintly. And then she burst out laughing.

Leofric could not help but join her, the absurdity of it all was like to overwhelm them both. The passed the bottle back and forth between them, and Leofric's eyes watered with the strength of the liquor as he took gulp after gulp.

"The coin from His Highness is real enough," said Leofric after they'd calmed down. "It is enough to see you and Sorex well cared for, should I fall upon this quest."

Laela glowered at him. "You do not have my permission to fall, upon any quest. Ever."

Leofric smiled. "Alright."

"I think this matter of gods and curses far removed from the matters at hand," she said.

Leofric chuckled. "This matter of gods and curses is not even far removed from this *room*." Cosmo was surely in the small sleeping alcove, separated from them now by only one wall, pacing or shifting restlessly in his bed. He was not a man for easy rest, Leofric had noticed.

"You are thinking of him, right now," said Laela, aghast.

"I am not," said Leofric, turning away from her, embarrassed.

Laela seized his chin in her hand. "Do not lie to me," she said. "I know your face."

"And I yours," said Leofric. He leaned drunkenly toward her, resting their foreheads together.

"Leo," she said, drawing away. "You know that I have loved you. When I met Hamalcar...I knew you were a part of him, and always would be, as he is a part of you."

Leofric didn't answer. He wasn't certain where she was going with this, and drink had slowed his wits.

"I will never forget what you have done for me and my son," she said. "The years since...well. I do not need to tell you they have been difficult. Having another husband forced upon me would have made them far worse, I do not doubt.

"Your love," said Laela, cupping Leofric's face in her hands, "has allowed me time to begin to heal. Sorex too, I think. He misses his father, of course, but he is young. He looks to you and sees a father now, in truth, not simply legal bond. However," and here she took a great, shuddering breath. Laela reached behind his head, and with nimble fingers untied the leather band that held back Leofric's hair. It fell around his face, and she combed it loose until it fell over the tattoo on the side of his skull. "I think it may be time for both of us to learn who we are, without him."

Cosmo could not sleep. He paced restlessly in the guest chambers, listening to the sounds of drunken mirth from the adjacent room. It was more than he could stand. If he were to hear the sounds of husband and wife coupling through the wall, he might perish, so before it could happen, he left.

It was late, very late. He pulled on a tunic and quietly pushed open the door. Outside, the desert air had cooled the world, and without the sun Cosmo felt cold and alone. He wandered around the yard, taking in the sights, gazing at the starry sky above. The desert had its own beauty, Cosmo supposed, but he could have done with a lake or three to swim in.

He watched the stars for a while, until the nearby sound of retching drew him from his thoughts. Cosmo strained his ears, trying to locate the source of the noise. His night eyes were keen, and soon enough he saw a flurry of movement beside a patch of scraggly bushes at the edge of Leofric's land. He approached with caution, unsure what he would find.

It was Leofric's son, hunched over, spewing violently into the roots. "Sorex?"

A groan was the boy's only reply. He stopped heaving for a moment, gasping to catch his breath.

From the sour smell, it did not take much for Cosmo to

guess what happened. "I was around your age the first time I got this drunk," he said mildly.

Another retch, and, a sickening splat. "I'm not drunk," said Sorex thickly.

"Oh," said Cosmo, raising his brows. "My mistake then."

There was a pause. "What did you do? To feel better?"

Cosmo glanced down. "If you're not drunk, why would you need such advice?"

"Hnnuugh." *Splat.*

Cosmo took pity on him. "Getting it all up is a good start, my young friend. Let me fetch you some water."

"Don't tell my—*hicc*—mother," he said weakly. "*Please. Or—*"

"Just sit tight, I'll be right back."

There was a well only a dozen yards away or so. Cosmo drew a bucket and carried a dipper back for Sorex to drink from. By then, it appeared he'd gotten most of the demon out, as Cosmo was wont to say. Cosmo squatted beside him and offered the water. "Small sips," said Cosmo. "Go slowly or it will also come right back up."

Sorex took the cup, drinking slowly as instructed. When he seemed able to gather his feet under himself, Cosmo lead him away from the pile of sour vomit, before the smell made them *both* sick. A patch of soft grass grew in the shadows the small stables, and there they sat.

"Sextus put something in the wine," Sorex admitted after a moment, his voice still thick and slurred.

Cosmo turned his head sharply. "What was it?"

"Something...he'd stolen it from his older brother, I think," said Sorex.

Cosmo turned his back, and conjured a small flame in his palm. He used its glow to peer into Sorex's face. Sure enough, his eyes stood dilated, irises like wet black coins in his face. "We should waken your parents," said Cosmo, troubled. "Opium is not a child's plaything."

Sorex shook his head so violently he toppled over, and he hadn't even noticed Cosmo holding a flame cupped in his bare hand. "You cannot," said Sorex, terrified. "You *cannot.*"

Cosmo did not think that agitating the boy would serve him well, so he agreed. "Fine," he agreed at last. "But I will remain here with you, if that's alright."

"That's fine," said Sorex, slumping against the cool marble of the stable. His eyes fluttered closed. "That's fine."

"I think it best if you remain awake, for the time being."

"*Unnnhhh.*"

"*Hey.*" Cosmo gave his shoulder a little shake. "Stay with me, or I shall have to go fetch your parents."

Sorex's hazy eyes sprang open. "No!"

"Just stay awake a bit longer," Cosmo soothed. "The feeling will pass, I promise."

"I don't think I believe you," Sorex said.

"Well, I will wait it out with you. You'll see."

"Why should I trust you?"

"Don't I seem trustworthy?"

Sorex grunted, to show what he thought of that, and Cosmo was once again struck by his resemblance to Leofric.

Cosmo sat beside him on the ground, resting his head against the stone as well. He allowed the little flame in his hand to gutter out, hoping the boy would not recall it when he regained sense in the morning. He wondered if he ought to wake Leofric anyway, but for now he didn't think Sorex to be in immediate danger.

When Sorex showed signs of drifting off, Cosmo nudged his shoulder. "Just let me rest my eyes," he said.

"Not yet," said Cosmo. He tore a corner from his tunic and dipped it in the water. When he'd wrung the excess from the cloth, he dabbed it on Sorex's forehead.

"*Mmm,*" he said.

Cosmo gently washed the sweat and crust of vomit from his face and then cast the soiled cloth aside. "Don't drift," he cautioned again.

"My eyelids are lead," Sorex complained. "Lead bags with only my lashes to lift them."

"Poetic," said Cosmo, "But alas, your weighted lids must remain *aloft.*"

"Then you should be more interesting," said Sorex.

Cosmo smiled. He sounded very like his father when irritated. "How shall I entertain you?"

"Story," said Sorex, with difficulty.

"Alright," said Cosmo. Memory had been swirling around him since he'd found Sorex retching in the grass, and it was easy to conjure up the tale. "I'd sampled wine before," he began. "The first time my mother allowed me a goblet at a feast, I truly felt a man. My younger brother, Auro, was still deemed too young. He was envious, you see, being treated as a child, when the rest of us were awarded something that seemed like such an honor."

"How many brothers do you have?"

"Four."

"That's nice," said Sorex heavily. "I should have liked to have a brother."

"Yes," said Cosmo. "But sometimes brothers can be cruel. Auro was so jealous of our supposed laurels that one of our other brothers, Ozias, convinced him that there was a special wine, made for children. Perhaps he could have some of that, at table, and not feel so left out."

Sorex wrinkled his nose, as if thinking was very taxing. "There is no such thing as wine for children," he said.

"You are correct in that," said Cosmo, smiling. "Ozias had smuggled a flagon from the cellar and ensured Auro's cup never stood empty. By the time he'd had three glasses, Auro could barely see straight."

"I thought this was the tale of how *you* first became drunk," said Sorex with a frown.

"It is," said Cosmo. "I'm getting there." Even as a young boy, Cosmo had been able to read the darkening expression on his father's face. Terrified his ire would fall on poor Auro, Cosmo had seized cup after cup, he told Sorex, seeking to erase Auro's misstep with his own, drawing their father's eye and ire upon himself. "By the end of evening meal, both Auro and I could barely stand," he said. "We wandered outside, taking it in turns to be sick."

"Don't say *'sick*,'" Sorex complained.

Cosmo smiled to himself. "Apologies," he said. He and Auro had laid upon the grass, after, staring at the sky and watching the stars spin above them. When Cosmo finished the tale, he turned his head to watch Sorex breathe. His breaths seemed steady, and he seemed to come back to himself bit by bit. Luckily, it appeared this little shit, Sextus, had not been too overzealous with the opium he used to lace their wine. Sorex sat with his eyes closed, and Cosmo stayed with him, allowing the boy to rest a bit. He thought he might have drifted off, and leaned in to vouchsafe for his pulse, when Sorex stirred. "Were they terribly angry?"

Cosmo froze. "Who?" He asked, confused.

Sorex turned to him, and with a massive effort opened his eyes. "Your parents."

They were, his father especially, but Cosmo did not think Sorex needed to hear that. "No," he lied. He brushed the sweaty strands of hair back from the boy's forehead. "No. They were upset at first, perhaps, but...in the end just over-joyed that we were home and safe."

Sorex squinted at him, like he didn't quite believe Cosmo, but he wanted to. After a few silent breaths, some of the anxiety leeched from his young face. "I worry about disappointing him," Sorex said.

Him, Cosmo could not fail to note. Not *them.* "Your father?" He prompted.

Sorex nodded. "I don't wish to fail him," he said plaintively.

"You could not," said Cosmo, with certainty. "He seems stern, I know. But I also know he loves you, beyond all others. You and your mother."

Sorex frowned, and turned to face Cosmo. "You do know that Leofric is not my real father."

Cosmo surely must have misheard. "What?"

"Leofric is my uncle," said Sorex.

"He's...he's what?"

Sorex sighed. "My father...he died. Three years ago."

"Oh," said Cosmo, unsure what else to say. "I am very sorry for that, Sorex."

"It wasn't your doing. At least, I don't think. But Uncle Leofric, his brother, married my mother. After. To care for us." He paused, like he needed to explain more. "They were twins."

"Leofric and your father?"

"Yes."

Cosmo's mind, and pulse, raced. So many things clinked into place at Sorex's admission. Leofric's miserable adherence to his marriage vows; Laela's stricken face when Cosmo said her son resembled his father. "It matters not," said Cosmo, out loud. To himself, and to the boy. "You *are* his blood. And he loves you. No simple mistake could see that bond broken."

"Are you certain?" Sorex asked him, sounding all at once even younger than he was.

"I am," said Cosmo, and he was. Leofric might be furious to learn Sorex had engaged in such ill-advised behavior, but

Cosmo knew, he *knew,* it would in no way diminish his love for him. "I promise."

Dawn was a few hours off, and Cosmo knew young Sorex would have a hellish morning before him. He coaxed a few more cups of water down his throat and helped him find his bed. Yawning, Cosmo stumbled through the darkened halls, in search of his own rest. He was so tired he could barely even register the knowledge that Leofric's marriage was not what it had appeared. However, it begged the question, *why had he lied?*

That issue could keep, until the morning. For now, Cosmo felt he would finally be able to fall to slumber. However, he opened the door to his room to find the night's surprises not yet complete.

Leofric sat upon the edge of Cosmo's sleeping couch, twisting his large hands in his lap. When the door opened, he looked up and said, "Where were you?"

"Where—I—what are you doing in here?" Cosmo asked, closing the door behind him.

Leofric heaved himself to his feet, and stumbled.

Cosmo frowned. "Are you drunk?"

"A bit, I think."

"It's the night for it, apparently," said Cosmo under his breath.

"What?"

"Nevermind." Cosmo scrubbed a hand over his face. "*What* are you doing in here?" he asked again.

"I don't...I don't exactly know." He looked around the room, as if seeing it for the first time.

"Do you know where you are?" Cosmo asked hesitantly.

Leofric looked at him with a sharp frown. "I'm not *that* drunk."

"Alright," said Cosmo, holding up his hands. He was tired of fighting. They stood facing one another, and Cosmo knew

Leofric had come in here for something. He'd lied to keep Cosmo at a distance, but now, here he was. Cosmo could honestly not work out if he was angry at the lie, or happy to finally have the truth. "This is not your real family."

A furious twist of Leofric's mouth told Cosmo immediately that he had misspoken. "How *dare* you—"

"No, I meant only—"

"Laela and Sorex are more than my family," said Leofric. "They are my world. My life. And if you cannot see that, then I truly don't know what I'm doing here."

Even tipsy, Leofric was strong, and he made to shoulder past Cosmo and leave the room. Cosmo stumbled off a step, but managed to keep his feet. He grabbed Leofric's wrist.

"Leofric," he said firmly. "Stop. Wait. My words were ill chosen, and obscure my true meaning."

"Choose them more carefully, then."

"I am trying," said Cosmo, exasperated. "You do not make it easy for a man to gather his wits."

"And you make it impossible for a man to keep them."

"What are you—" but he could not get the rest of the words out. Leofric twisted in his grip, and wrapped an arm around the small of Cosmo's back to smash their bodies together. His gaze dropped briefly to Cosmo's lips before he lunged forward and took them with his own.

Cosmo's knees went to water, and he was grateful Leofric was at least sober enough to keep him on his feet. He parted his lips eagerly for Leofric's tongue, nimble and insistent when it plunged into Cosmo's mouth. Leofric kissed forcefully, thoroughly, with purpose, but every muffled sound that escaped him was weak and desperate. Cosmo swallowed each one down, rising upon his toes to meet Leofric there, to show him how badly he had wanted this.

They broke apart, breathless, and Leofric rested his forehead upon Cosmo's own, and when Cosmo stole a glance upward, he saw Leofric's eyes were clear. Clear of drink, of doubt, of fear. Cosmo swallowed, and suddenly he was the one afraid.

Leofric cradled Cosmo's face in hands large, warm, and rough with callus. The strength in those hands was remarkable, yet his touch was tender, as if Cosmo were a baby bird being set back in its nest. He drew him in for another kiss, softer this time, gentle...almost chaste. It left Cosmo just as hungry as the first one did. With a final peck, Leofric drew away, and said, "I believe there are things you and I must discuss."

Cosmo closed his eyes and groaned. Words were the last thing on his mind "...tomorrow, perhaps?"

"I am afraid not," said Leofric.

About the last thing Cosmo would have expected tonight —sharing a kiss with the man before him—had already occurred. He supposed it wasn't so outrageous to experience the *second* to last thing: Leofric insisting they talk. Cosmo could not help first sneaking in to steal another kiss. He could taste the liquor on Leofric's tongue, but he seemed steady enough. Now that he'd started, he did not wish to stop, and his hands crept down the length of Leofric's trunk, but before they could make too much mischief, Leofric grabbed his wrists. "Stop that," he said, a hint of the old bite in his voice. But when Cosmo looked up, he was stricken by the sight of Leofric's soft little smile. He drew Cosmo to sit beside him on the bed, and for a moment they simply stared at one another, flushed and mussed from their kissing, the heat of it cooling awkwardly on their skin.

"I should have been honest with you," Leofric said at last. "About...about my family."

"Yes, you should have," said Cosmo. It was difficult to be truly upset, not with Leofric's sun dark cheeks flushing so prettily by candlelight. "But I understand why you were not."

"Sokol clings to an older tradition, than Papia," Leofric said. "A widow with a son as young as Sorex would be pressed into a new marriage."

"Things were much the same when I was....before I had been cursed."

"In some places, things have changed. If we were Papian, all might have been different. But we are not."

"No, you are not." Cosmo studied the man before him. "So, what has changed?"

Leofric flushed even darker.

"She gave you permission, did she not?" said Cosmo, delighted. He *knew* he liked that woman.

Leofric nodded. "I still feel as though I must explain myself."

Cosmo had little and less interest in Leofric's explanations, but something told him there were things that needed to be said, even if they did not need to be heard, so he waited, as patiently as he was able, for Leofric to continue.

"You like men and women," said Leofric. "Your appetites are vast."

"I would wager yours are vast, as well," Cosmo said, dancing his fingers up Leofric's thigh.

Leofric gave his hand a swat. "Stop that," he said. "I am trying to explain—"

Cosmo withdrew his hands with a pout. "I find demonstration to be the fastest way to learn."

"My *point*," said Leofric loudly, "is that I have never... wanted a woman. Not the same way I—"

"Hungered for a good hard buggering by some strapping gentleman?"

"You are a bloody menace," said Leofric, looking mortified. "Truly."

"So I have been told. By you. Many times."

"Would you just let me finish? Before I change my mind."

Cosmo held up his hands in acquiescence.

"Because of this," Leofric said, "As a husband, I was perhaps the lesser of many possible evils, while Laela was grieving."

"But now, her grief wanes," said Cosmo, understanding at once. "And being wed to you is like being wed to a ghost. It keeps her wounds from healing."

Leofric looked taken aback. "Yes," he said, startled. "That's precisely what she said to me."

Cosmo shrugged. "I am more than just a pretty face, you know."

Leofric snorted, rolling his eyes, but then his voice grew low, and serious. "I have spent the last three years setting aside my own desires entirely," he said. "It is...a difficult thing to return from."

Cosmo understood, and willed himself to stillness. Pushing now would avail him nothing, and he did not want Leofric to come to him only as result of Cosmo's endless badgering. Cosmo wanted him to dance joyfully into his arms. "Patience is not a skill for which I'm known," he admitted.

Leofric smiled again, and something wicked glittered in his eyes. He leaned in, until his lips were close to Cosmo's ear. "Would it surprise you to know that I once stood much the same?" He whispered.

Cosmo sat very still, every muscle vibrating. "Oh?"

Leofric cupped his cheek again, brushing a thumb over Cosmo's bottom lip. "There is something I would share with you tonight, if you are agreeable."

"And what is that?"

When Leofric blushed, it threatened to do Cosmo in, especially when coupled with a smile that was by turns shy and mischievous. "Something I have never done, before."

The blood surged to Cosmo's groin so fast he thought he might faint. He released a small, eager, choking sound.

"No, you unrepentant lech. Not that," said Leofric. "I would share your bed tonight, if you'll have me."

Cosmo's confusion must have shown upon his face.

"I have never known such a luxury," Leofric explained. "To hold someone close, at night. All night. Without fear of discovery, or judgement."

Cosmo realized at once that this was a very important request.

Perhaps far more important than the kisses they'd yet shared. He took Leofric's hand and kissed his knuckles. "I would be honored," he said truthfully, and Leofric's smile melted Cosmo's heart.

Cosmo rose to blow out the candles, plunging the small room into darkness. He peeled off his tunic, and the answering rustle of fabric from across the room told him Leofric had done the same.

He could just make out the shape of Leofric in the darkness, pulling back the blankets and sliding between them. Cosmo joined him, suddenly nervous, aware of every movement. "Come here," Leofric whispered, and his voice had grown husky and thick. He pulled Cosmo to him, finding his lips in the dark. The night was hot and grew hotter still as Leofric's hands roamed Cosmo's body, his touch eager but fearful, like he was afraid of being scolded. Cosmo held his breath, aching to tangle his fingers in Leofric's hair and pull him close, to kiss him breathless and rut against the muscles of Leofric's thigh, the urge so strong he found himself panting into Leofric's kisses. With a smile so wicked Cosmo could feel it in the dark, Leofric pulled away and gently pushed Cosmo onto his side, so Leofric could hold him close against his chest, Cosmo's back to his front.

Cosmo could not help but feel every part of Leofric pressed up behind him, and he shivered, despite the comforting warmth of his naked skin. Leofric slid an arm around Cosmo's waist, pulling him even closer, and Cosmo could feel his breath ghosting on the nape of his neck. They fit together well, Cosmo could not help but note, comfortably entangled on the narrow settle. Dawn was coming, and Cosmo's eyes grew heavy, soothed by the beating of Leofric's heart and the steady rumble of his breathing.

"Thank you," Leofric whispered.

Cosmo did not answer, but a sleepy smile tugged at the corner of his lips. In the following quiet, he could not fail to note that Leofric's hand had begun to wander, featherlight touches teasing his chest and belly, the bone of his hip. His thigh.

"I can't believe you thought I meant I'd never fucked someone before," said Leofric suddenly.

Cosmo really, *really* enjoyed hearing the word *fuck* in Leofric's mouth. It seemed to shut his brain off, temporarily, and he could not form answer straight away. His skin tingled as Leofric's callused fingers caught upon his flesh, ticklish and teasing. "Stranger things have happened," said Cosmo when he found his voice, though it came out as a croak.

He could feel Leofric smiling against his skin. "I think you'll find," said Leofric, and his voice was low and dangerous. "In that arena, I know precisely what I am doing."

His fingertips brushed up Cosmo's front, teasing lightly over his nipples and then whispering down between his legs, not truly touching, but leaving in their heated wake a promise of things to come.

It was going to be a long night.

Seventeen

Leaving Laela and Sorex was bittersweet. Leofric pulled them both into a fierce embrace as Cosmo readied their horses. His mind was a tumult; joy at clearing the air with Cosmo mixed with sadness as he kissed the crown of Laela's head. Something between them was ending, something safe and comfortable. Leofric had not realized how much he'd hidden behind Laela, in the wake of Hamalcar's death. It was time, as she said, for both of them to begin to move past their loss.

"You mind your mother, and help her when she needs it," he told Sorex. "I will return this way, if all goes well upon my mission."

"I will," said Sorex solemnly. He threw his arms around Leofric's middle and gave him a hug, and that was that.

Back upon the road, Leofric had been nervous that things would be strained between himself and Cosmo, after the last few nights they'd shared in Cosmo's bed. Nothing between them had transpired but soft kisses and teasing whispers, but it felt as though something had changed deep within the earth. Leofric no longer knew precisely where he stood.

But that first night, when Leofric settled into his bedroll, Cosmo sat alert beside him, carding a hand through Leofric's hair, stroking his head until Leofric drifted off to sleep. When he woke, Cosmo was plastered against his chest, snoring contentedly. After that, they settled into a routine that felt comfortable as they traveled the path west. Even in summer, the nights in the desert were cold, but with Cosmo's natural heat beside him Leofric found it easy to sleep. It was strange, not since he'd traveled in the legion with his brother at his back had he found sleep so easily.

A few short leagues from the base of Mount Hiru, a small but busy city had sprung up like a mushroom after a good rain. The mountain was at the juncture of three kingdoms, and so it was an advantageous place for trade. It could be a dangerous place; the bad blood between Sokol and Órnio was hard to ignore, even when gold was at stake. Perhaps especially then. However, Leofric had promised to get a message to Prince Alexios when they reached the town, so they stopped at the center of town and hired a rider.

Then, there was nothing to do but climb the bloody thing. Mount Hiru was steep, and unforgiving. Leofric could hardly imagine what the place would be like come winter. The wind whipped around the stones at night, and Leofric was grateful he and Cosmo were united, in preparation for the ascent. When he and Cosmo made camp each night, Leofric felt like Mount Hiru was watching them, drinking in the light of the sun, intruding in his thoughts. It seemed to drink Cosmo's light, too.

By now Leofric had gotten used to falling asleep with Cosmo tucked into his side. It seemed like they'd worked together to pull down the barrier between them, and Leofric felt so well rested each morning he wondered how he could have gone his entire life without this.

Unfortunately, as their journey brought them

through Mount Hiru's foothills, Cosmo withdrew. He stayed awake late into the night, staring into the fire until it died, and only then would seek out his bed, when he was certain Leofric would already be asleep. Sometimes he was, sometimes he wasn't—but it was clear that Cosmo wanted him to be, so he could make his bed with space between them. There were a few nights when Cosmo did not come to bed at all. After several days of this, each morning when Leofric woke, he would brace himself to face an empty campsite, and wonder how successful he'd be at tracking a fleeing demigod through the wilderness.

But Cosmo, to his credit, never fled. He was restless, though, and jumpy. He seemed fragile, brittle, and delicate in a way that Leofric had yet to experience, like if he approached Cosmo too suddenly, he'd shatter into a million pieces.

"What?"

Leofric, now, was the one startled. "Apologies, what?"

"You have been staring at me like that for days," Cosmo snapped.

"Like what?"

"Like—like you think I'm losing my mind, or I'm about to break any second."

Leofric let a breath hiss out through his nose, trying to remain calm. "Well," he said carefully. "Are you?"

The look Cosmo gave him was one of pure loathing. Leofric had seen his vulnerability, and that was unforgiveable. The sun threatened to set, the change in the light sneaking up on them as they stared at each other across the fire. Cosmo set his jaw, the ruddy glow of fading sunlight illuminating his freckled skin. In that moment, Leofric understood something that until now had eluded him. Cosmo might look like a man. He might talk like a man. He might have a man's needs, a man's hungers.

But he was not a man.

He was something else, something wild and unknowable and powerful—even without the lion's share of his grace churning inside him. Staring at Cosmo just then felt like staring at a venomous serpent from the sands of Sokol. If you stumbled across one, it would bob and weave its head. It would flare its hood. It would hiss, showing its fangs.

These displays said, quite plainly, *back off. Now. I mean it.*

However, Leofric hadn't before faced a snake with whom he'd shared a bed. It didn't seem like the usual rules applied. In fact, they never did, with Cosmo. Leofric weighed his options, much as he would have done facing any normal foe. The options here were much the same as they would be then: advance, feint, or retreat.

It calmed Leofric, to view confrontation in those terms. They were a touchstone of familiarity in the uncertain chaos that swirled between himself and Cosmo. After considering his possible choices, Leofric decided upon a feint.

He shrugged. "Forget I said anything," he said in a neutral, airy voice. "Apologies, again, for staring."

Cosmo's animosity flickered and vanished, to be replaced with confusion. Leofric felt a kernel of satisfaction knowing he'd thrown him off.

Then, Leofric made a very stupid mistake. A mistake that could be fatal when confronting a dangerous, cornered, and fearful animal.

He turned his back.

Cosmo would never know what exactly came over him in

that moment. Even decades later, when he looked back upon this night. He had no idea what he hoped to solve, no idea what he was trying to prove.

Whatever the cause, he took three steps forward, palms outstretched. With a wordless grunt of frustration, he snapped his arms and gave Leofric's back a sharp, hard shove. Leofric stumbled, and Cosmo felt a savage pleasure in watching his knee connect with a stone on the forest floor. That pleasure was short lived as Leofric surged back to his feet, pivoting on his heel. His face was a mask of incredulous fury, his hand upon the hilt of his sword, falling there like it was instinct. Cosmo took a step back.

"What on earth is the *matter* with you?" Leofric seethed.

"Oh, what," said Cosmo contemptuously. He knew Leofric would suffer no worse than a bruised knee. "Did you scuff your precious armor?"

"No—it's—you're—" he blustered, speechless with anger. His face reddened and his neatly braided hair threatened to come undone as he gestured wildly.

"What?" Asked Cosmo, goading. He crossed his arms over his chest, adopted a cocksure smile, and waited. "What am I?"

"You are a fucking *child,*" Leofric spat. "I can't believe that the fate of the natural world rests, even a little bit, on you."

And then, all at once, Cosmo *felt* like a child. He was thirteen again, gut punched by a memory he'd tried his best to forget. He was at the foot of this same mountain, covered in scratches and bruises from days of travel through the woods alone, half a league behind his father and Kryos. He'd wanted so desperately to be taken along, not left home with Cedras and Auro. Cedras would be buried in his studies and Auro was so little. He was so *boring.* They both were!

Kryos and father were having an adventure, and Cosmo wasn't about to be left out of something so grand.

Their father had only just begun to share his grace, to give them the power over the seasons. Cosmo still had yet to master it, had yet to even be able to use his grace with any true purpose. But it was dark. He was lost. And it was just *so* cold. The gap between himself and the others widened by the hour.

It hadn't even been a conscious thought. He'd just been so cold that the sun had come bursting through the clouds, high and hot and powerful, warming Cosmo's face even through the canopy of the trees. The problem, unfortunately, was that it was just going on midnight.

Terras, Cosmo's father, had stormed back through the forest to retrieve his errant son, his fury terrible enough to shake the mountain behind them. Kryos had looked on from their father's elbow, and Cosmo had never hated him more than he did in that moment: the smug look, the disdain sauced with pity, and the preening that he was the *good* son. The obedient son. The true heir their father had always wanted.

When Cosmo returned to the present, he lunged across the space between himself and Leofric, absent even the decision to do so, blind with anger and grief. His body made the choice while his mind was lost in a winter's night four hundred years gone. While Cosmo undeniably had the power of the gods on his side, Leofric had training, and poise, and the levelheadedness of a soldier. He also outweighed Cosmo by at least thirty pounds of hard muscle. Before Cosmo's blow could land, Leofric had side-stepped the assault, seized his wrist, and twisted his arm behind his back. Cosmo flapped his other arm, uselessly, trying to reach up behind him, to find some part of Leofric to scratch or hit.

"I'll grant you the first one," Leofric said, and his voice was so calm it only served to make Cosmo even angrier.

"You can use your grace if you like, to hurt me. But you will not get the drop on me again. You will not frighten me."

Cosmo thrashed in Leofric's grip, unwilling to burn him in true anger, but he did finally manage to throw an elbow back into his stomach. It connected with a clang and pain lanced up Cosmo's arm. He cursed himself—he'd completely forgotten the armor that to Leofric was like a second skin.

With a shove that was almost careless, Leofric sent Cosmo sprawling on the ground. He whirled with a snarl, staring up at Leofric who had the fucking *gall* to appear almost bored.

"Are you finished?" Leofric asked him.

Blood pounded in Cosmo's ears as he scrambled to his feet. His grace hummed dangerously below his skin. If he touched Leofric now, he would burn him. And badly. Their tussle had turned them about, and just when Cosmo had decided burning Leofric might be worth it, his eyes landed on the mountain.

His rage curdled, and died. He realized he was losing himself, again. The self he'd rebuilt so carefully in the centuries since he'd been cursed. Their approach to Mount Hiru had torn that down, obliterated it, transforming Cosmo back into the frightened, erratic person he'd been in the months leading up to Ozias's death. He *hated* that person.

But he wasn't certain he actually liked the rebuilt version of himself, either—the person who cared nothing for anyone but himself, and the current night's pleasures and diversions. He'd liked the person he was becoming, since deciding to help Auro break the curse. With a massive effort, he let his anger dissipate in the light of the setting sun. Scowling, furious with himself, he lowered his hands to his sides, clenched tight into fists. Hoping Leofric would understand, because he found himself unable to speak the words. He stomped across the distance between them and let his forehead collide with Leofric's breastplate with a defeated *thunk*. He stayed perfectly still for several seconds. Breathing, waiting.

Sure as the sunrise that would come tomorrow, Leofric's arms wrapped around Cosmo's tense, rigid body. One large hand cupped the back of his skull, protective and steady. "Yes," said Cosmo, his words muffled. "I'm finished."

Leofric rocked them in a soothing rhythm, and after a few moments, Cosmo released a long, shuddering breath, looping his arms around Leofric's waist. He felt a soft kiss connect with the top of his head. "We should get some rest," said Leofric, all gentleness now. "Tomorrow, the mountain."

"Yes," said Cosmo, squirming deeper into Leofric's embrace. "Tomorrow, the mountain."

Eighteen

The spectre of Cosmo's brother loomed over them as they ascended the mountain, and for the first time Leofric truly imagined what must be going on in Cosmo's head as they moved closer and closer to its apex. He had the air of one approaching a gallows, which Leofric supposed he could understand—he couldn't pretend he'd be perfectly brave and stoic if he was marching into the lair of a literal god who'd tried to kill him once before. Even Leofric had to remind himself often that Kryos was safely asleep, imprisoned in a statue back in Papia, and he wasn't going to leap out from behind a tree and freeze them both to death.

It had Leofric worried, fearful that Cosmo would turn from him again, from Auro, that Cosmo would run. But he did not. He was plainly made of sterner stuff than Leofric had thought, which left him feeling guilty at how harshly he'd judged Cosmo in the past. There were no more kisses, but there were also no more shouting matches, and Cosmo returned to his arms at night. That had to be a victory.

It took about two days before they reached a place that gave Cosmo pause. It seemed unremarkable to Leofric's eyes, no different than half a dozen other outcroppings of rock they'd left behind. "Here," said Cosmo, and his voice had gone hoarse and strange. "My brother has been here."

There was a plateau of sorts, a flat swathe of earth of even, packed earth. In the center of that clearing, there sat a slab of stone, grey and worn smooth, a near perfect circle. It was as if someone had carved it, but judging by the edges it had been worn into this shape by centuries of wind and storms. Cosmo rested a trembling hand upon the stone, feeling for something. His eyes were far away, staring at something only he could see. For his part, Leofric took a moment to look out over the hills and valleys and forests, he could see well into the northern deserts of Sokol stretching out before him. From here, the distance seemed small, like he could take a few steps and be home.

"There is a cavern here," Cosmo observed from behind him, and Leofric was relieved to hear his voice had returned to its normal register.

When he turned, he saw Cosmo standing a bit taller, a bit straighter in the spine. It made sense. The fear *before* a battle was the worst sort of fear: the paralysis invoked by the unknown. Once you faced the foe, it was easier. Not *easy*, perhaps, but easier. The way forward was clear, at the very least.

Overall, Leofric approved of the place for a camp. It was easily defensible, sheltered, with access to water. They hobbled the horses in a spot outside, sheltered enough from the wind, with enough room for them to graze. A spring-fed pool would see them well watered while they remained here. When he and Cosmo entered the cavern itself, it was apparent at once that someone had been living there. Not in the last few months, perhaps, but recently enough. By the mouth of the cavern, banked carefully against the wall, stood a circle of stones stacked carefully to make a hearth. The top layer of ashes within could not be more than a year old, if Leofric were any judge. To the side was a makeshift rack, where one could hang one's cloak, or perhaps weapons.

And, near the fire, a hard stone bed, piled high with furs. Leofric set about building a fire in the existing hearth, wondering if he were angering the god of winter by depleting his store of firewood. He'd have to remember to replace it before they left. Then, he found himself wondering why such a man would even *need* firewood. But trying to find reason in the actions of gods was something he didn't think mortals were meant to do.

Cosmo felt a bit more settled now that they'd actually arrived. It was time to *do,* and the anticipation of this quest was something that he could now confidently say felt way worse than actually facing the prospect of completing it.

Leofric seemed to sense something of what went on in Cosmo's head. He was intuitive, to say the least. Now that Cosmo had some time to calm down and gather himself, he was embarrassed at how he'd behaved on their final leg of the journey. As they settled into the cave that so clearly belonged to Kryos, Leofric busied himself with making their camp, giving Cosmo some space, but remaining nearby, should he be needed. Cosmo was grateful for his presence now, even disregarding the heated kisses they'd shared and the nights they spent tangled around each other.

It was late afternoon. Cosmo returned to the little plateau outside the cave, and the peculiar slab of rock that was too perfect to be anything but intentional. He could *feel* Kryos's presence in the stone. The edges had been worn away by the fury of his grace, he knew at a glance. Hundreds, if not thousands, of years of wind had been harnessed to shape it into something like... "a stage," Cosmo thought, curiously. He smiled. That was just like Kryos. He would never do his work under the scrutiny of others, but he would afford it all the grandeur as if he performed for an audience. Cosmo couldn't say what possessed him to climb atop the stone, to sit cross-legged at its center and tilt his face toward the sky.

Some would guess that summer was an easy season to manage. No storms, no cold, hardly any rain. But summer felt easy because Cosmo *made* it easy. The world and the beings that walked it needed a period of ease, to enjoy the sun shining on their faces, to let their crops ripen and bear fruit. To watch their children playing, to find a lover, to begin a family. To be fat and healthy and warm. Summer was for them, and it was for Cosmo to ensure the earth churned on as it should while its inhabitants fed and bred and played. While he sat upon the stage that had so plainly been his brother's, Cosmo wondered how Kryos felt when sitting here to perform his works.

Kryos had always been drawn to places like this. Remote, wild. Untamed, like he was. Cosmo could understand that. He felt close to Kryos, sitting here. Close in a way that was safe. Close in a way that made him believe, even for a moment, that Auro might have been right. That the four of them could heal everything that had happened between them, that they could find a way to grieve for Ozias together, and move past his loss after four hundred years of mourning.

When he'd made certain everything hummed along as it should, Cosmo stood and stretched his limbs, shaking some feeling into them. He hadn't realized how long he'd been sitting there. The sunset before him was *staggering*. Kryos looked at this every day, when he was awake. Just as Cosmo looked at it now.

Inside the cave, he found Leofric plucking the feathers from a goose. "Where did that come from?" He asked.

Leofric smiled. "I walked right past you, to go hunt. And again, to return."

"Apologies," said Cosmo. "I was…"

"Very focused," said Leofric. He hesitated. "It was nice to see."

A peculiar sort of comment, but it made Cosmo tingle head to toe, pleased. "Were you planning on cooking that?"

"Well, I was going to hold off a *bit* longer," he said. "I've grown sick of watching the faces you make when you try to force down something I've made."

"You're sick of my face?" Cosmo teased, with an exaggerated pout.

Leofric didn't look up, but he froze. His cheeks burned and he said, "Never."

Cosmo prepared the bird once Leofric had cleaned it. He crisped it on the fire, basted with honey and dried peppers. A spicy dish to make one's eyes water, but Leofric ate every bite with gusto. It was based on a Sokolian dish, and Cosmo wondered if it made him think of home, of his brother, of his family.

When Cosmo finished his own portion, he said, "Is there anything you can tell me of Auro's own…trial?"

Leofric tossed a wing bone into the fire and considered this. "Not really, I'm afraid," he said. "His Highness and Auro kept most of that between themselves. I was far more occupied with the immediate aftermath."

Cosmo twisted his fingers in his lap, nervous to ask the question that had been weighing so heavily on his mind.

"What is it?" Leofric asked him.

He was far too perceptive, damn the man. Cosmo looked at him, hoping Leofric would understand how afraid he felt, how raw. He didn't want Leofric to think him a coward. But all the same, he had to ask. "Do you think…was it… dangerous?"

Leofric's face softened. He reached across the distance between them and squeezed Cosmo's shoulder, his hand heavy and warm. "I believe it could have been," he said honestly. "But I think it was more like a test of endurance, and fortitude, than it was something that would actually have harmed him."

"I do not do so well with tests," said Cosmo.

"You will with this one," said Leofric.

Cosmo startled. "You think?"

"I *know.*"

"How?"

Leofric gave his shoulder another squeeze. "I have faith."

Cosmo could have made a joke, could have made a thousand, but instead he seized the hand upon his shoulder, brought it to its lips, and kissed it. No more was said. Once they had cleared away the remnants of their dinner, Cosmo stood. "I will begin my search tonight."

Leofric balked a bit at that. "So soon?"

"It is the reason we are here, is it not? Why wait?" Cosmo said. "I can feel the weight of this task upon my shoulders, and I would see it lifted."

Leofric stood as well. "I can accompany you," he said.

Cosmo smiled, stepped in close to offer him a soft kiss. "Unfortunately, I believe this is a path I must tread alone."

Leofric clenched his jaw, and Cosmo could see uncertainty in his eyes, but he nodded. "I will await you," he said. "Right here."

Cosmo turned his back and approached the rear of the cave. He could not say precisely what filled him with urgency, except now that he was actually *upon* the mountain, it was as if he could feel the presence of his brothers. Kryos, yes, of course —but the others too, as if they all lingered with bated breath to watch Cosmo complete his trial. As Cosmo left the light of his and Leofric's fire behind, he felt as though his brothers walked with him.

He let his instinct guide him, or perhaps it was his grace, calling out to theirs. Or theirs to his maybe, he did not know. It grew dark toward the rear of the cavern in which he and Leofric made their camp, but Cosmo's night eyes adjusted swiftly, as they always had. Strangely enough, he was not afraid. He felt around the rear wall of the cavern, and found a cleft of rock that concealed a narrow passage.

Cosmo slipped around it, and through the crevice, revealing another chamber. Behind that, another. On and on and on he went. Had he stood mortal, he might have held concern that he would become lost endlessly within the bowels of the mountain, but he was not. This challenge was meant for him to succeed, that was what Auro had said. Kyros's grace was hidden from mortal eyes, powerfully concealed, but with every step along the path, his certainty that he was meant to walk it solidified.

He passed through so many caverns and chambers that he soon began to wonder if perhaps the journey would lead him entirely through the mountain, only for him to emerge on the other side. The change in temperature came upon him so slowly it took Cosmo a great long wile to realize that he was cold. For the first time in four hundred years, he was *cold*.

The thought shook his confidence, and he stumbled, his sandal coming loose upon the rock. He toed them off and left them behind, to feel the stone with his toes, and move with more care. The cold seeped in through the soles of his feet, but it made no matter. All at once, Cosmo turned a corner, and gasped.

In the next chamber, a vein of sparkling ice blocked the way forward. It was no ordinary frozen stream, Cosmo knew. That would be plain even if it was winter on the mountain. There was no light in this chamber, but the ice gave its own sort of light. A soft, white glow moved within the frozen vein, beckoning him forward.

Cosmo steadied himself and approached. The presence of Kryos was so strong then that Cosmo half expected to turn and find the man himself standing at his back. Yet...it did not frighten him. He regarded the ice, knowing that if Kryos were here, he would say that such a challenge would only serve to make Cosmo stronger. Cosmo twisted the ring on his finger with his thumb, silently asking for the strength he needed.

He placed his hands upon the ice, and could feel his palms sticking to its frozen surface. It took longer than he was accustomed to feel his grace answer when he made attempt to summon it, and that did frighten him. But it answered at last, a spark in his chest that he could draw from. The heat inside traveled up his shoulders and down through his arms, which trembled from the cold, and into his palms upon crystalline structure.

Soon the ice beneath his hands grew slick, and as Cosmo strained, the entire vein melted away to wash around his bare feet in chilly waves. His panting breaths misted the air before him, and the sweat upon his skin soon seemed as cold as the puddle under his toes. He shivered, and stepped through the now open path into the next chamber.

Though the ice had gone, its silvery soft glow remained. Cosmo could not determine its source, but it served to lead him step by careful step into the darkness. Soon, he saw a stair, hewn roughly into the stone, leading down, twisting and turning into the very heart of the mountain.

Every step saw the temperature drop. Cosmo wrapped his arms around himself, and summoned his grace to warm him against the chill, but it seemed harder and harder to hold it close to the surface of his skin. The cold rendered his steps sluggish, and his wits dull, as if his very thoughts had begun to freeze inside his head. When the ground evened out beneath him, he was startled to find a carpet of frost upon the stony floor.

The warmth in his feet melted the frost, leaving behind wet footprints, steaming in his wake. The staircase deposited him into an antechamber so vast, Cosmo imagined it was the entire inside of the mountain, hollowed out like a gourd for the harvest festival. Frost gave way to a dusting of snow, and the heat from his skin no longer stood proof against it.

Cosmo. He stopped, turned. "Who's there?"

It sounded like many voices that answered. *All of us.* It was his brothers. Kryos, Cedras, and Auro...and...it sounded as if he could even hear the faint echo of Ozias with them. This cold had sapped his sanity, he realized. Looking down, Cosmo saw that he'd stopped moving. The snow now reached the middle of his shin. "How does snow fall inside a mountain?" He wondered aloud.

It did not fall, said the voices. *And neither will you.*

Cosmo realized he'd stumbled to his knees upon the ground. He staggered to his feet. Looking up, he saw with dismay that he'd barely moved into the chamber at all. He felt as though he'd been walking through the cold for days. Perhaps he had.

Keep going, the voices said, and one seemed louder than the rest. The snow flurries swirled around him, and it that they floated from the floor of the cavern to its ceiling, flying up instead of down. Cosmo looked to the cavern's roof and saw clouds above his head. Fat grey clouds, soft and thick as steam. *Do not stop.* Cosmo new the voice belonged to Auro. It was impossible, for Auro to be here with him, but he took comfort in it all the same. He could feel Auro's presence at his back, as certain as if he were truly there—but he also knew if he turned the illusion would fail and he would be alone in the dark and the cold again, so he kept his eyes trained forward, and walked on.

"I am doing my best," Cosmo said out loud, the words a cloud of mist.

We know, said the voices, and this time it was Cedras's timbre most prominent among them. *Keep going.*

Cedras and Auro walked with him, at least. He could keep going, as long as he had them. He took another step, and the other side of the chamber came into view, the darkness and the snow playing tricks upon Cosmo's eyes. The opposite wall could have been close enough to touch, or a hundred leagues away. Regardless, his response must be the same: to take another step.

"Did you all come and cheer Auro, on his quest?" His mind was slow. Auro's shade could not have come to cheer on *Auro,* surely. "Did I?"

My own test was different, said Auro behind him.

He needed to walk alone. That voice was Kryos's, Cosmo knew. He stumbled and fell again, and he could have sworn that the hands of his brothers were what got him back to his feet. *But you need to know that we are with you.*

"Are you?" He asked, ashamed of how scared and weak and childlike he sounded.

Yes, they said. *Keep going.*

So, Cosmo did. He wondered if anyone else would be able to see the three shades walking at his back, or what he himself would see if he turned to face them.

The other side of the chamber was dominated by a massive tree, its bark bone white and its branches barren. Snow collected in the crooks of the branches, and fell around it in graceful flurries. It had been a very long time since Cosmo had seen snow.

There is beauty in it, said Kryos. *If you know how to look.*

He was right. Winter had a beauty to it, as fierce and as wild as the beauty of summer. The crystalline frost, the fluffy clouds, the snow. Everything was tense, as if the entire world held its breath.

"You can do this," the fourth voice said, out loud. It didn't seem to have the strange, echoing quality as the others.

"Ozias?" Cosmo said, and his voice came out as a croak. He took a few more steps, and the urge to turn around threatened to overwhelm him. This time, when his knee connected with the hard ground beneath the snow, he bit his tongue.

In the cold, pain felt magnified, everything about Cosmo felt fragile and brittle. He had to look. He *had* to. He had to know his brothers were with him, to keep his courage. He spat a mouthful of blood on the floor, and the snow drank it up. Before Cosmo could turn, he felt hands upon his arm, beneath his elbow. A whisper in his ear. "I will help you."

"I should have helped you," Cosmo told Ozias's shade, as it helped him to his feet. "I should have protected you."

"We protect each other," Ozias said, his voice close to Cosmo's ear. "Now, carry on."

Cosmo could not help it, he whirled around toward the voice, toward the warmth of the hands bracing beneath his elbow. He twisted his head every which way, but there was no trace of Ozias but the lingering warmth of his hands upon Cosmo's arm. The others were likewise gone. He was alone again.

It was alright though. He knew they were out there, somewhere. Looking forward, determined, Cosmo saw that the tree seemed closer now. His traversal of the cavern moved in fits and starts, and now the goal seemed reachable. He took another step toward it.

At last, Cosmo stumbled up to the base of the wintery tree. Its roots plunged deep into the stone, and he wondered if it truly lived, and how it could milk nutrients from the rock below. Nestled in the cradle of its thick roots was a frozen pool. Cosmo knelt beside it, brushed away the falling snow that covered the surface of the ice.

Something down within the pool glowed with a friendly white light, calling him on. Cosmo raised a hand, curling his numb and frozen fingers into a fist. He focused all of his remaining strength there, summoning heat to the center of his palm, grasping it tight and lending it strength. His arm trembled, but he raised it above his head, and sent it crashing down onto the ice. The pain was like to choke him, a cold stabbing sensation that went from the heel of his hand directly to his heart. But he felt the ice yield.

Cosmo did it again, striking the ice with his fist again and again, and each blow was agony, but with each hit the ice cracked further. He could feel it preparing to give. His arm burned from wrist to elbow, but still he repeated the action.

The final blow struck sparks like a blacksmith's hammer upon raw steel, and the ice cracked loud enough to rival a thunder clap. Cosmo did not hesitate. He plunged his hand into the frigid water, gritting his teeth against the cold and the pain, and his fingers closed around something smooth and hard.

When he pulled it out, he saw it was a bottle, much like the one Auro had shown him, containing Cedras's grace. Cosmo laughed, a wild, unhinged, triumphant laugh, and cradled the bottle to his own chest. It was cold, so cold, cold enough to burn.

Nineteen

Leofric paced in the small cavern, pausing occasionally to toss a log on the fire. He could not settle to anything, but he kept telling himself he was being foolish. Auro had passed a similar trial, and returned unharmed. Drained, perhaps, but unharmed.

Cosmo would be fine. He would come bounding up the passageway soon enough to continue what was plainly his true divine purpose: driving Leofric mad.

Leofric honed and polished his sword, oiled the leather of its hilt. Then he saw to his shield, his armor, his dagger. Sorted through their provisions. Shook the fur blankets out, just beyond the entrance to the cavern. Added another log to the fire, though the blaze already threatened to stifle.

With nothing left to do, Leofric sat heavily on the stone bed beside the fire and tried to put a finger on what had him so anxious. When Auro had undertaken his quest, he had been certain it was something he must do alone. It had felt right— Auro was the youngest brother, and timid, prone to hiding from his problems and letting other solve them—it seemed fitting for him to undergo something like this alone.

Cosmo was different.

He certainly wasn't timid, and rather than hide from his problems, he was just as likely to charge in headlong and create more of them. Cosmo had seemed convinced that, like Auro, he needed to do this alone. He'd asked Leofric to remain behind. It had been phrased as a request, but Leofric understood it for what it was. An order. Before they'd left, His Highness had impressed upon him the importance of helping Cosmo succeed in his quest. Cosmo had told him what he needed, which was for Leofric to wait.

So, he waited, seething with worry.

After watching the fire for another hour or so, Leofric stood and stuffed his sword into the scabbard at his hip. This was ridiculous. Nowhere in any of the ancient books Alexios and Auro combed through had it said any foolishness about each brother going through this alone. Leofric couldn't just stand there idly while someone he...while Cosmo suffered, or struggled, and Leofric was well within his power to help them. He might not be a god, but he was a man. And men helped one another.

He lifted a torch from the floor and lit it in the fire, thinking how the crackling flames reminded him so much of Cosmo's hair, and started toward the back of the cavern. This was Kryos's place, he knew. And though the man himself still slumbered back in the temple of Papia, Leofric could feel his influence. The second he stepped beyond the rosy ring of his and Cosmo's hearth fire, the temperature dropped. It kept dropping with every step he took down the narrow, winding passageway until he could see his breath misting before him, and feel the chill leeching up through the leather soles of his sandals.

In winter, Leofric wore sealskin wrappings beneath the straps of his sandals and greaves to protect his legs and feet from cold whilst on the march. Unfortunately, he had not thought to bring them on a journey in the dead of summer, and soon enough his toes were numb and aching.

This was no natural chill. This was a cold that said, "Go away, mortal. You are not welcome here."

Leofric ignored it and carried on, chamber after chamber, until he found himself sloshing through a puddle of icy water that led to the top of a stair, carved right into the stone. He lowered his torch a bit, forcing himself to stare only through the very edge of its halo, in hopes of avoiding fire blindness. It worked a bit, allowing him to see dimly through the gloom, and hold the fire closer to his body besides.

He wondered how far beneath the mountain he was, uncomfortable with all that stone pressing in so close, almost like he could feel the weight of it on his chest. His homeland of Sokol was a vast expanse of gently rolling dunes, open sky, and just the occasional copse of scraggly trees, so different from this dark and claustrophobic press. He found himself thinking desperately of the sun, trying to call the image to his mind's eye, but it kept transforming into a laughing freckled face with wild eyes. Unnerved, Leofric pressed on.

Eventually, he felt the ground beneath his feet leveling out, the slope lessening with every step. The heavy darkness played tricks upon his eyes, and with a jolt, Leofric realized he wasn't in a tunnel any longer, but an enormous cavern, so large he would have thought the mountain could not contain it. Directly opposite was a massive tree, white bark almost silver, casting a soft glow on the stone around him. Snow and ice collected against its trunk and on the floor before him, as if blown there by some storm. The glittering surface reflected the light, which seemed to come from the tree itself. It fell upon a single, slumped figure on the floor, wrapped in crimson.

Leofric nearly dropped his torch, but by some miracle tightened his fingers around the wood before it could slip from grasp. He jogged forward, his breath puffing around his face in steaming clouds.

Skidding on the slightly frozen ground, Leofric went to his knees before Cosmo, who was huddled on the cavern floor, entirely covered in the cloak he'd borrowed from Leofric. It was stiff with frost, and beneath it, Cosmo trembled violently.

He reached beneath the folds. "Cosmo?" he asked gently.

No answer.

Leofric slipped an arm around Cosmo's back, pulling him into a seated position. The skin beneath Cosmo's freckles was pale as death, and he was *cold*. That scared Leofric more than he could say. "Cosmo?" He said again, cupping his cheek, trying to impart some warmth from his own hands.

One of Cosmo's hands moved sluggishly to cover Leofric's own. "I told you not to come down here," he said thickly.

"Yeah, well," said Leofric gruffly. "That was stupid."

Cosmo blinked his eyes open, and they were unfocused, dim. He leaned into Leofric's touch, like he couldn't resist, but still he mumbled, "It's too dangerous."

Leofric looked around the cavern, and he had to admit he didn't feel as though he was in danger of anything but freezing his balls off if they stayed down here any longer than they had to. "Come on," he said, trying for gentleness. "Up you get."

But Cosmo shook him off, feeble and angry, and lurched to his feet on his own. Leofric followed, clenching his fists to keep them from grabbing for Cosmo, who stood like a man with one foot in the grave, swaying and weakened. Cosmo summoned some of his usual fire and shot Leofric a glare, which Leofric found encouraging, so he backed off a step and lowered his hands to his sides.

Unfortunately, Cosmo made it about two steps before he stumbled on numb, cold—*bare?*—feet. Leofric bit his tongue hard enough to taste blood, but when Cosmo's knee connected with the icy cavern floor and he released a startled, choked off gasp of pain, Leofric couldn't help the way he lurched forward.

"*I'm fine,*" Cosmo ground out. He tightened his pilfered cloak around his shoulders, sending a shower of ice crystals down around him as he got clumsily to his feet.

Leofric bit back a retort, and said nothing.

Cosmo made it another couple yards before he stumbled again, and it seemed like any fight remaining bled out of him, strength sapped out by the cold.

Leofric waited, though it cost him to do so.

The look Cosmo shot him was wretched, but Leofric could see he was at last giving in. "Can you help me?" He spat, like the words were poisonous, like saying them hurt more than falling, like maybe he would rather die down here in the cold, alone, than have to admit he needed a hand.

Silently, steadily, as he might approach a skittish horse, Leofric approached and bent down to slide an arm around Cosmo's tiny waist and haul him to his feet. Cosmo leaned into Leofric's side, and like that they took cautious steps across the cavern, retracing the path that Leofric had just made through the snow until the gentle sloping tunnel took them out of the bowels of the mountain. The air around them warmed with every step, and more importantly, *Cosmo* warmed with every step.

Leofric should have expected he'd bounce back swiftly, but seeing Cosmo weakened like that had shaken him to his core. By the time they reached the rear of the cavern, Cosmo had regained his feet enough to shy away from Leofric's touch. Leofric wanted to tell him that it was alright, that leaning on someone wasn't a mark of weakness, that everyone needed a hand from time to time, but for some reason he couldn't part with the words. Cosmo refused to look in Leofric's direction, to even spare him a glance.

Cosmo had been staring at him for weeks, studying him

any chance he got. Leofric could hardly lift a finger without Cosmo's hazel eyes burning into his skin, and he hadn't realized how much he'd come to expect and crave it. Leofric knew he was being punished. Punished for thinking Cosmo needed help—punished for being right. Punished for seeing Cosmo like that, vulnerable and weak and cold and afraid. Something built in his gullet as he stared at Cosmo's profile, resolute and angry, like he was pretending Leofric wasn't there at all.

By the time they reached their camp, Leofric was furious. "You're welcome," he snapped peevishly, turning his back on Cosmo to check the state of their fire. It burned just as brightly as when he left it, and after his trek through the frozen bowels of the mountain he was grateful he'd built it up so high.

Cosmo approached the fire, holding his trembling hands toward the flames. "I didn't ask you to come," said Cosmo at last.

Leofric gaped at him, incredulous. "*What?*"

When Cosmo turned to face him, his eyes were full of hurt, full of loathing. "I didn't need your help finding the mountain, and I didn't need your help down below."

"Better I let you freeze?"

"I was *fine*," Cosmo insisted. Then, he took a few steps closer to the fire. "*Fuck*, I can't get warm," he muttered, almost to himself.

"You—you—"

"What?" Cosmo challenged. The fire at his back set his hair aglow, and it seemed he was regaining himself a bit, which would have filled Leofric with relief if he wasn't so furious. Why did Cosmo have to make everything, *everything*, so bloody difficult? And why couldn't Leofric help but care?

Cosmo pulled something out from within the folds of his cloak. It was a slim crystal bottle with a faceted stopper, the light within so bright it appeared almost blue. "I got the grace, didn't I? That's all anyone needed of me."

Leofric was so incensed he felt ill. "You're fucking *impossible*," he bit out at last.

Cosmo raised his brows. "*I'm* impossible? All you had to do was wait here. All you do is follow orders, and you couldn't do that. Why?"

Leofric's eyes widened. "I don't take orders from *you*."

"No," Cosmo agreed. "Everyone else, certainly. Never me."

Before Leofric could formulate a retort, Cosmo shucked off his clothes and stepped directly into the fire, sighing as the tongues of flames licked around his ankles. It seemed that Cosmo himself fueled the fire—either his body or perhaps his grace causing the embers to glow sun-bright at his feet and the flames swirled up and over his thighs, his hips, as high as his shoulders. When Cosmo lifted his gaze to Leofric's again, it seemed his very eyes were aflame.

Leofric made himself take a step forward, a step closer, threat of burns be damned. It was like arguing with the sun itself. He took a deep, steadying breath, forced himself to turn his face into the blistering heat, to meet Cosmo's fiery fury. "I *couldn't*."

"Couldn't what?"

"Stay." He said, and pulling a tooth from own mouth would have hurt less. He inhaled. "Away." *Say it,* he fumed at himself. *Say it, you bloody coward.* "From you."

Cosmo blinked in surprise. "What?"

"Anything could have been happening to you, down there," he said. Leofric forced himself to step closer, sweat rolling down his forehead from the heat of the fire, or perhaps it came directly from Cosmo.

"You were worried about me?"

"Of course, I was." Leofric's voice was raw and broken,

but the words came out. And that was what counted. Or so he hoped.

Cosmo's face softened, and the blistering heat ebbed to pleasant warmth. "Oh," he said.

"Yes," said Leofric, his tone still clipped. The urge to reach for Cosmo, to pull him into his arms, to crush him hard against his body and feel his warmth return was so strong that Leofric had to cross his arms to keep them still. "Are you certain you're alright?"

"I will be." Cosmo sat right in the hearth, like the fabled salamanders that Leofric had always hoped to find in fires as a boy. He drew his legs up under himself, smiling serenely as he released a sigh that sent sparks swirling all around him. Leofric shielded his face from the heat, watching transfixed as Cosmo sat in the center of the fire, tension visibly falling from his shoulders like the rippling heat mirages on the sands of Leofric's desert home.

He seemed alright, content in his own peculiar world, so Leofric tore his eyes away and set about securing their camp for sleep. Leofric secured Kryos's grace as well, tucked it carefully into a leather pouch and wrapped in a spare tunic. He sat on the edge of the stone bed, staring into the fire at Cosmo, who now seemed quite far away. His hair swirled around his ears, mingling with the flames in such a way that it appeared one with the fire. The embers glowed against his freckled skin, but none of this phased Cosmo, who sat naked and cross-legged in the very center of the hearth. His eyes were wide open, but they stared at something only he could see, and Leofric understood it would be quite a while before he returned from wherever he was. The sight of him in the fire was stirring, frightening, terrible, yet beautiful. It left Leofric feeling as though his chest cracked open, leaving his heart naked and exposed. It was good to feel he had some privacy to put himself back together, even though physically, Cosmo was a scant few yards away.

Leofric was thoroughly exhausted after the trek through the bowels of the mountain, so he stripped down too and slid beneath the fur blankets, rolling over so he could watch Cosmo in the flames until his eyes grew too heavy.

He woke sluggishly from a deep sleep, sometime later, to someone squirming into the blankets beside him, someone with warm skin and bony knees and no qualms about shoving Leofric's body this way and that in order to get more comfortable. Leofric gave answering grunt, flopping over onto his side. He draped his arm around Cosmo's waist, tugging him close and hoping to squash him into lying still.

It didn't work.

Leofric had almost drifted back to sleep anyway when Cosmo made a small, whimpery sound and nuzzled his nose up just under Leofric's ear. Alert at once, he sat up. "What is it? Are you hurt? What's wrong?"

Cosmo lay on his back, one arm draped dramatically over his eyes. "I am still cold."

Concerned, Leofric cupped his cheek, touched his forehead, rested his palm against the column of Cosmo's throat. "Your skin feels warm to me," he said.

Cosmo leaned up on his elbows, tilting his head to peer up at Leofric through his orange fringe. "I don't think it's that sort of cold."

Leofric frowned, uncertain. "What do you mean?"

The look on Cosmo's face now was vulnerable, raw and afraid once again. Things Leofric knew he hated being above all others. Leofric rushing in to help him back from the frozen cave was bad enough—this open neediness was more than someone like Cosmo could bear. He could see the doors already sliding shut behind Cosmo's eyes. If he fumbled things now Leofric was certain he would lose Cosmo.

Rationally, he didn't understand why that would be so terrible, but the primal, animal part of his brain *knew* that it would be. Leofric surged forward, cupped Cosmo's face in his hands, and brought their lips together. He swallowed Cosmo's startled huff, nipped at his plump bottom lip before tracing the bow of it with his tongue.

There was power in being desired.

It was a power Cosmo wielded comfortably, a power he plainly felt wrong footed without. The moan he released was almost…grateful, because Leofric now allowed him to reclaim that power. Cosmo melted into the kiss, allowing Leofric to lay him back on the heap of fur blankets. All the tension left him, soothed away by the knowledge that Leofric understood what he needed.

Despite that, Leofric knew there was no call to be gentle. He scraped his teeth down the slender column of Cosmo's throat, biting and nipping at the clusters of freckles that he'd spent so long examining. The ones he hated. The ones he loved. He sucked marks of his own into the hollow below the apple of Cosmo's throat, adding the shadowy purple bruises to the patterns on his skin. Claiming them as his own.

Cosmo tangled his fingers in Leofric's hair, clawing at the leather tie he used to hold it back in its braid. He wasn't being gentle, either, and Leofric winced at the tingling points of pain on his scalp. When the tie at last came loose, Cosmo pushed against him for the first time until they both sat opposite one another. With trembling hands, Cosmo combed his fingers through Leofric's hair, working the braid loose until all of it tumbled down around his head and shoulders. He pushed it over to the side, tracing the pad of his pinky over the vines of Leofric's tattoos, teasing the shell of his ear. Smiling.

Leofric startled.

This…was a new smile.

By this point, Leofric had seen so many of Cosmo's smiles,

both false and true. He didn't know how one person could have so many smiles. Leofric barely even had *one*. And here was yet another of Cosmo's, soft and shy and sweet, unsure, yet eager.

Innocent. Leofric had to wonder how many people had been privileged enough to catch a glimpse of this particular smile. It frightened him, so he leaned in to obscure it with harsh, claiming kisses. Cosmo's fingers still tangled in his hair, clutching tight and tugging hard on Leofric's scalp, hard enough to make him hiss.

Leofric guided Cosmo back against the blankets, where he reclined with his head pillowed on one arm, crooked at the elbow. He cocked his head, the teasing grin on his lips now a more familiar one. Leofric followed Cosmo down, blanketing his smaller body with his own, burying his face in his throat to inhale the scent of sparks and smoke and ocean air and starlight that clung to Cosmo beneath the perfumed oils he liked so well.

Leofric mapped Cosmo's slim torso with kisses, impatient as he dipped his tongue into Cosmo's navel. Cosmo squirmed, and his gasp was half a laugh.

"Ticklish?"

Cosmo gave the side of his head a playful swat. "Perhaps."

Leofric smiled against the skin of his waist. It was so narrow that Leofric could almost wrap his hands around it. He grabbed it now, holding Cosmo in place as he traced the grooves of his hips with kisses. The men Leofric had tumbled before had always been like him—big, strong. Hard. Scarred. Dirty from the march. He and Cosmo had been on the road for weeks and yet somehow, he was clean as a princess, his skin so soft, so pale beneath the freckles it almost glowed in the firelight. He was small boned, delicate, with soft hands and softer lips.

So different from anyone he had ever known, let alone

anyone he'd had the privilege to bed. Leofric shoved Cosmo's thighs apart, settling between them on the stone bed. He'd seen Cosmo naked enough times now that it shouldn't have been such a novel, arresting sight and yet, it took his breath away all the same to see Cosmo laid out before him, the pattern of freckles on his skin completely unobscured by fabric, or even the jewelry he'd once worn like armor. The hair around his cock was a deep, wiry crimson, with hints of copper and bronze that caught the light like beaten metal. His cockhead was flushed dark red, too, jutting out from the nest of flaming curls like a firebrand.

Cosmo sucked in a sharp breath, and Leofric knew his silence would not last. Soon, as he always did, Cosmo would speak. Before he could open his mouth and ruin the moment, Leofric opened his own and swallowed Cosmo's cock to the root. Cosmo yelped, his hands tightening even further in Leofric's hair. He liked the feel of it, quite a lot, the sting delicious and the tingles that followed even lovelier to savor. Cosmo gripped his hair with the right and confidence of ownership, and Leofric did not mind one bit.

He worked fast, as he had always done. Couplings in the army were swift and efficient. The release of stress and tensions on the march, performed with little privacy and even less intimacy. Some of his partners would have preferred a woman, Leofric did not doubt, but sometimes upon the eve of battle any warm and willing body would serve. There were plenty of soldiers, like Leofric, who preferred the taste and touch of men, but never had he had an opportunity to linger in pleasure.

He could linger now, he supposed, but he was far too eager, and he ground his own cock against the blankets below them both in an attempt to chase any sort of relief. Leofric hollowed his cheeks, swirling his tongue around the head of Cosmo's cock, teasing his glans and sampling precum that beaded freely at its slit. Cosmo bucked into his mouth, gasps and moans and little pleas falling from his parted lips. Leofric held him in place, one arm snaking under his hips to grip his waist and hold him still.

Cosmo released a strangled cry when Leofric took his cock deep into the back of his throat, working the head with the practiced muscles of his throat. Between that, and his fingers moving to press and tease the sensitive spot behind Cosmo's balls, it was not long before Leofric felt Cosmo stiffen and jerk between his lips, pulsing as he emptied himself down Leofric's throat. He swallowed every last drop of divine seed, and cleaned Cosmo's crown with his tongue, savoring the taste of Cosmo's pleasure until not a single trace remained.

He nuzzled and kissed his way back up Cosmo's trunk, resting on his side with his head upon one hand. Cosmo turned toward him, his eyes wide, panting and trembling as he rode the eddies of his receding climax. Leofric nipped the shell of Cosmo's ear, making him shiver. "Told you I knew what I was doing."

Cosmo laughed, still gasping for breath.

When his breathing slowed at last, Cosmo wilted back against the bed, a fine sheen of dewy sweat breaking over his freckled skin. His chest heaved, and when it seemed at last that he'd regained some sense, he said, "That was…"

"Yes?" Leofric prompted, allowing himself a self-satisfied smirk.

Cosmo cut him a look. He rolled onto his side, too, mirroring Leofric's position. "Altogether far, *far* too brief."

Leofric reached out to tuck a sweat-dampened strand of fiery hair behind Cosmo's ear. "Disagree. You seemed to enjoy yourself."

Cosmo reached down between them, running his fingers lightly over Leofric's own hardness. "And you," said Cosmo.

He frowned, his brows knitting together in thought. "But I wonder, have you ever...taken your time with anyone?"

Leofric wasn't sure how to answer, but Cosmo was not done speaking anyway.

He walked his fingers up Leofric's thigh, skating them over his waist, letting them dance across the skin of his ribs. "Has anyone ever...taken their time with you?"

Cosmo knew the answer before the question had left his lips. The look on Leofric's face told all. He was a thorough, experienced, and confident lover—Cosmo's thighs still trembled with the evidence of that—but had he ever probed beneath the surface level pleasures of fucking? Had anyone ever made his entire body quiver, aching with want, blind with need, until he begged for release?

Had Leofric ever...made love?

Alarmed, Cosmo stuffed that question away, into the deep recesses of his mind. When he returned, he caught Leofric gazing at him thoughtfully, his brown eyes piercing the warm air between them. "Where did you go, just now?" He asked Cosmo.

"Nowhere," said Cosmo, unnerved at being so seen. He lowered his voice to a seductive purr—intentional, but not disingenuous. He cupped the sharp jut of Leofric's jaw, brushing a thumb lightly over his bottom lip. With a tug, he had Leofric leaning in for another kiss. Cosmo welcomed Leofric's tongue, first tentative and curious and then aggressive. He pulled back, letting his breath skitter across Leofric's hungry, parted lips. *Slow down,* Cosmo murmured against Leofric's jaw, hard and sharp as iron beneath the tanned, stubbly skin. He nudged Leofric's shoulder, encouraging him onto his back. He could tell immediately that it was not a natural position for Leofric, to show his belly. The muscles of his abdomen tensed beneath Cosmo's hands. Cosmo paid it no mind, except to rub small, soothing circles on the rigid muscles with his thumb. He brought their lips together once more, forcing himself to keep the same slow, meandering pace. It helped that he'd only just quaked, but even so...taking his time proved a challenge. Leofric had a generous, sweet tasting mouth, strong hands that gripped tight to Cosmo's shoulders, and a truly impressive manhood that he could not ignore, shoved as it was against Cosmo's inner thigh.

Each movement of Leofric's was a question, and each time Cosmo answered *not yet*. He could feel the coal of desire rekindling in his groin already, low and gentle, just beginning to grow warm.

Leofric resisted at first, trying to move things along, to race toward his finish as he was plainly accustomed to doing, but Cosmo rebuffed each advance, gentle, but firm. *Not yet*. He didn't want to let the dance progress until Leofric understood how it was going to go. It took a long time, a lot of soft strokes and gentle kisses, but eventually Cosmo felt the exact moment this tightly wound, rigid, brittle, kill-joy of a man surrendered to him. He savored the victory; it was a gift. A sacred gift. For once in his life, Cosmo savored it in silence, knowing that to prod the beast now would have Leofric's defenses back up. And how could he do that, after working so hard to pull them down?

Cosmo tucked the desire to gloat neatly away for later, and for now he just enjoyed the way Leofric had melted soft and pliant beneath him, like his long hard limbs had filled with liquid lead, like every muscle in his body had released its fight.

Boneless. Submissive.

When Cosmo finally wrapped his hand around

Leofric's shaft, he *whined.* He whined and Cosmo could not hold in the laugh it startled out of him, breathless, and giddy. Immediately, he cringed, afraid Leofric would be angry, afraid Leofric would pull away. But Leofric never ceased to surprise. He met Cosmo's eye, let out a huff, and turned his head to the side. Turned up his throat. Another surrender.

Another gift.

Cosmo stroked Leofric between them, hoping to draw out more of those needy little noises, but after he let that first one escape, Leofric seemed determined to keep any more of them to himself. It was alright, though. One was enough.

The smile against Leofric's bared throat was involuntary, and earned Cosmo another grumpy huff from somewhere above him. Instead of replying, he cupped Leofric's cheek, leaning down to whisper in his ear. "*Shhh...*" he soothed, sucking his earlobe between his lips and biting down on it, coupling the soft reassurance with the sharp bite. Pleasure, sauced with pain, the way Cosmo learned Leofric liked it.

Leofric arched into his hand, his hips popping as he chased the pressure and friction offered by Cosmo's fist. Cosmo had no doubt Leofric would happily come just like this, and thanked Cosmo after.

But that was only because he did not know any better.

There was coming, and there was *coming,* Cosmo had always thought. It was plain to him that Leofric was well practiced at hurrying the pursuit of pleasure, chasing release as swiftly and efficiently as possible. Cosmo slowed his hand on every upstroke, loosening his grip each time until his finger pads barely whispered over the heated skin, stretched so tight around Leofric's shaft that the head of his cock was angry and shiny, flushed a red so deep it was near purple. Cosmo eyed it hungrily, eager to feel the same instrument thrusting home deep inside him. He stilled his hand entirely, and he could feel the frustrated grunt against his lips that Leofric tried—and failed—to stifle. He swiped his thumb once over the velvety soft head, catching a pearl of precum on his fingertip. With his other hand, he braced against Leofric's hip bone, Cosmo sat up, straddling the hard thighs beneath him, his own knees canted wide. Cosmo's soft cock twitched against his thigh, and a warm, tingling sensation surged across his skin. He tilted his head, watching Leofric watching him. Their eyes locked, and Cosmo raised his thumb to his mouth, sucking the salty bead of dew from the end of it. Leofric's mouth dropped open, a burnished crimson flush traveling up the trim muscles of his abdomen and the soft thatch of brown curls on his chest, past his neck and to his sharp, high cheeks. Cosmo lingered on the taste knowing one day, and one day soon, he'd drink this man dry.

He dragged his thumb from his mouth, letting the tip of his tongue dart out to tease, before he stroked his hand down his own chest, agonizingly slow as he carelessly perused the flesh of his own body. His spit slick fingers lingered on a nipple, tugging it until it peaked and ached, then switching to the other. Leofric groaned, watching like it caused him physical pain to do so. His hands flew to Cosmo's hips, squeezing tight, his fingers pushing deep into the skin of Cosmo's waist. *Please, let it bruise,* Cosmo thought. If Leofric woke in the morning having come to his senses, he wanted a reminder of this night to remain.

Cosmo lunged sideways off the bed, expecting Leofric to keep him from falling. He did, but not without a startled cry as Cosmo pitched over the edge of the stone cot. Leofric clung tight to his waist. "What are you doing?"

Cosmo ignored the question, shoving his hand down inside his pack, fishing around in the bottom for a bottle of massage oil. He always carried several with him. Leofric sat up, nearly sending Cosmo toppling to the floor, and Cosmo swung his arm, clutching Leofric's shoulder as he continued his search. Frustrated, he seized the bag and upended it, sending his belongings bouncing and skittering across the stone floor.

"For fuck's—what are you—"

"Aha!" said Cosmo, triumphant, fingers clutched tight around the pot of oil. He twisted and turned, swinging back into place astride Leofric's thighs.

Leofric sat up, sliding his hands around Cosmo's back, clutching tight in attempt to keep him still. He peeked over Cosmo's shoulder, looking at the clothes and other sundry items now spread across the floor. "Are you just going to leave all—*hmmf!*"

Cosmo cut off Leofric's lecture with a kiss and drenched his fingers with oil. With his fingers well slicked, Cosmo disentangled himself, and with one parting bite to Leofric's lower lip, he spun, a new torment in mind. Leofric was taut as a bowstring, and Cosmo planned to find at what point he would lose control. This game of lusty torture was an excellent one, and Leofric's limited patience was surely nearing its end, and Cosmo could not wait to see what would happen when Leofric snapped.

He spun to face the foot of the bed, such that it was, arching his back to ensure his ass pointed right at Leofric. Cosmo was very comfortable on display. He'd never been shy about his body, from the innocence of childhood to his decidedly less innocent adulthood, he'd had no qualms about flesh. Now though, he found himself a bit nervous. Leofric had never had the chance to enjoy sex like this. *Neither have you,* said a snide voice in Cosmo's head. He shoved it down.

Suddenly, he felt the urge to look upon Leofric's face, like if he could not see Leofric's eyes adoring him, he'd fracture. He peeked over his shoulder, and there they were, fixated upon Cosmo with awe that bordered upon worship.

Confidence restored, Cosmo grinned and reached back to

caress his own ass cheek, tracing gentle circles on his skin, teasing Leofric beneath him with a visual feast. Leofric's soft, choked, *"Fuck,"* was all he needed to hear. His other hand snaked down his front, between his legs, on a quest of its own. The angle was not ideal for access, to be sure—but it *was* ideal for putting on a show, for leaving the brittle soldier beneath him entirely spellbound.

Cosmo found his own hole with an oily fingertip, caressing himself, touching himself. He circled it, tapped the puckered skin, shivering with anticipation. His cock had begun to recover, plumping sluggishly where it hung between his thighs. Up tall on his knees, Cosmo rocked against his own wrist, sliding his finger past the delicate furl of skin. He must be driving Leofric mad, absolutely wild. Cosmo grinned as he touched himself, rocking back and forth, wondering how long it would be before Leofric lost his mind, before he begged, before he surrendered entirely to—*oh.*

A long, low moan began deep in Cosmo's throat before his brain could even comprehend what had inspired it. Something had joined his fingers. Something wet and hungry and dexterous, lapping the sensitive skin around Cosmo's hole, teasing its tip inside beside Cosmo's fingers, like it *needed* to taste.

Well.

Leofric smiled, and Cosmo could *feel* his indulgent chuckle, the vibration of it against his rim and the moist, panting heat of Leofric's breath. Chasing it, Cosmo circled his hips, arching his back, eager, thoughts of victory and control long forgotten. Leofric shifted his weight, slipped his hands from Cosmo's hips down to his thighs. His fingers were like stone, pushing harshly into Cosmo's legs, keeping them still. Leofric devoured his meal, feasting like a starving man, and Cosmo slipped his fingers out of the way, leaning forward until the muscles of his stomach shook and ached. He used both his hands to keep himself open for Leofric's tongue, an offering of his own.

So much for victory, Cosmo thought, deciding that perhaps he was the sacrifice, and Leofric the hungry, irascible, insatiable god. Leofric had been quick to take the lesson about lingering, about slowing down, taking one's time. Or perhaps it was time that had slowed, stopped entirely. Perhaps Leofric was a master torturer. None of that mattered, actually, to Cosmo. There was only the stubble burning between his legs and the flexing, teasing, lapping of Leofric's tongue, questing to taste every part of him.

Leofric eased back, pulling Cosmo with him, hunkering down on the wadded-up furs that served as a pillow. He needn't have bothered pulling; Cosmo would have followed that mouth anywhere. As Cosmo settled fully over Leofric's face, he wondered if anyone had ever suffocated like this before, breathing their last breath with their face buried in a lover's ass. *What a way to go,* Cosmo thought with a lazy grin, rocking his hips in tight little waves, grinding against Leofric's tongue.

Leofric mumbled something against his hole, which both tickled and sent little shocks up his spine. Then he touched Cosmo's leg, a few urgent swats, and Cosmo sat up, lifting off Leofric's face. He twisted to peer down at him. "Yes?"

Leofric did not answer right away. Instead, he put his palms on Cosmo's ass and shoved. Cosmo lurched froward, disoriented, throwing his hands out before him to break his fall. He needn't have worried though, Leofric moved cat quick, maneuvering a thickly muscled arm around his waist, the opposite hand pressed lightly against his throat. Plastered together now, on their knees, back to front, Leofric bit savagely at the place where Cosmo's neck met his shoulder. "I need to fuck you," he rasped. "*Now.*"

Cosmo shivered, not because it sounded like Leofric had

seized control—but because it was plain he had lost it. His words were not a threat, or a command. They were a plea. The desperate plea of a desperate man. Cosmo's grin widened and he melted backward into Leofric's arms, tilting his head back up against his chest.

He could feel Leofric's cock like an iron bar, jabbing into the small of his back. Leofric rubbed against him eagerly, like a needy, feral animal, who could not help himself. Cosmo reached his hand back and up, caressed the face he'd come to love so well—the furrowed brow, the hawkish nose. The jaw that could crack ice. The plump, dusky lips that *nearly* always twisted in a frown. Leofric's hand snaked down to wrap around Cosmo's shaft, finding it hard and eager.

"Already?" Leofric asked, surprised.

Cosmo only laughed. "I *am* a god," he said. "I recover quickly."

"That sounds like a challenge," Leofric murmured against the valley between Cosmo's shoulder blades. He tightened the hand around Cosmo's throat, and once again, the motion was less a threat and more the frenetic twitch of someone about to snap. Leofric stroked Cosmo slowly, a question. He pressed needy, open-mouthed kisses up the back of Cosmo's neck, sweeping the hair from the nape and kissing up again to his ear. "*Please,*" he whispered.

Cosmo moaned, rocking his hips to fuck into Leofric's fist. "*Yes,*" he answered on a sigh. Leofric's hand vanished from his cock, and he could feel it fumbling between them as he lined himself up with Cosmo's hole. Cosmo could feel the way his cockhead slipped and slid around his entrance, slick with oil and dripping with spit, and he stilled. "But, I need something from you, first."

Leofric stilled, though his hands still thrummed with tension. "*Bastard,*" he hissed. "Anything."

Cosmo swiveled around, and cupped the side of Leofric's face. "Are you certain?"

Leofric slumped forward, his forehead resting against Cosmo's shoulder. "Yes. Anything."

"Say something nice about me," said Cosmo sweetly.

Leofric growled, and lunged forward like he really *was* a wild animal, pinning Cosmo beneath him on his back. Cosmo writhed in his grip, staring up at his captor. Leofric's pupils had blown wide, his hair a tangled curtain of chocolate silk around his face. It was long enough that the ends of tickled Cosmo's cheeks. Cosmo blinked up at him, suddenly afraid. What if Leofric had nothing to say?

"I can feel that," Leofric said, his voice intent and fierce. Cosmo realized his grace had hummed to the surface, heating his blood and sparking along his skin. Leofric lowered his lips to Cosmo's throat, sucking hard. "Do it. I don't care."

"Wh-what?"

"Burn me," said Leofric. "I won't let go. I still want you."

Cosmo could feel the blood in his veins heating, literal warmth flooding from deep inside him and out onto his skin.

"I still *need* you," Leofric said.

Cosmo opened his mouth to say, "*and I you,*" but all that came out was a broken, needy whine.

"Bastard. Bastard. Bas—tard." Leofric grunted against Cosmo's throat, each word ending on a kiss, or a bite.

Cosmo arched against him, hitching one knee up over Leofric's hip. He tangled his fingers in Leofric's hair, pulling harshly on his scalp until Leofric hissed, and surrendered to Cosmo's pulling. "I believe I'm still waiting to hear something nice," said Cosmo, summoning his most cocksure grin, though Leofric's needy words had shaken him, and deeply.

Leofric cursed again, a look of fury searing across his face, pulling his lips into a snarl. He blinked at Cosmo for several long moments in which Cosmo had time to fear perhaps he had pushed him too far at last, when all the fight bled out of Leofric at once. He sighed. "You, Cosmo…" he said, biting off each word like it cost him a great deal, "Are beautiful."

Cosmo startled. Of all the things Leofric could have said, he had not expected that. Color bled into Leofric's cheeks—not the heated flush of the sexually frustrated or the ruddy glow of those overlong in the sun, but a true, honest *blush.* Leofric *blushed,* and looked away—or tried, but Cosmo caught his chin. "Truly?"

"Fucking *truly,* you absolute menace," Leofric growled, and shoved his cock into Cosmo in one sharp, brutal thrust.

Cosmo arched his back and howled, his fingers hopelessly tangled in Leofric's hair as the sharp burn of pleasure-pain ripped through him. And then Leofric was moving, slinging his hips hard and fast as Cosmo clung to him, answering him thrust for thrust. He squeezed, clenching every muscle he possessed as if he could trap Leofric there, keep him there—*there—there—*just there, forever, and Leofric cursed and cried out, panting as he fucked Cosmo with deep, storming fury, that long hard dick of his impaling Cosmo over and over and over. "Beautiful," Leofric repeated. "And brave. And *kind.*"

Cosmo clawed at Leofric's back, desperate to keep him as close as he could, afraid of letting him go, even for the span of one fevered heartbeat. The lean, muscular thighs Cosmo had spent so long admiring flexed and tensed as Leofric took Cosmo harder than anyone had ever dared take him before. "More," Cosmo begged.

"You are a wonderful cook, you're clever. Your freckles are bloody enchanting." The words were nice, and Leofric's thrusts were anything but, the contrast between the two strangely titillating. It was a wonder he could catch his breath to utter the endearments, to keep his breath at all, really. Cosmo felt as though every thrust punched the air from his lungs. All at once, Leofric stilled. He stared deep into Cosmo's eyes, looking like a man possessed. "You make me smile," he whispered, like a secret. "I try to hide it, but you do."

Cosmo blinked, utterly arrested, but it seemed the time for tenderness was done. Leofric started moving again. If Cosmo stood mortal, surely this savagery would rip him in two, and the tightness down between Cosmo's legs had him choking back sobs as Leofric pounded him into the hard, unyielding stone beneath their blankets. Near blind with ecstasy, Cosmo hurtled toward his peak for the second time, and he felt it, the split second where they crested as one, Leofric's deep voice breaking as he came, and with the fitful pulse of Leofric's cock deep within him, Cosmo heard him whisper hoarsely, *"Beautiful."*

This shattered Cosmo, who quaked on a startled, shuddering gasp, spurts of cum splashing across Leofric's taut abdomen. They clutched tightly to one another, rocking against each other like boats on a stormy tide. Eventually, they slowed, and Leofric slumped on top of him, breath coming in gasps, his trembling weight a welcome touchstone. Just when Cosmo thought he'd regained some of his sense, Leofric nipped sharply at his ear, and he shivered, spent cock giving a feeble phantom twitch. Then, Leofric was gone.

Confused, Cosmo rolled onto his side, watching Leofric stomp around the cave, grumbling as he searched the ground for something amid the things Cosmo had tossed carelessly from their bags. Neither spoke. Cosmo watched, smiling lazily, enjoying the way the firelight glowed against Leofric's sweaty skin, his softening cock glistening wetly between his legs. Finally, he'd stowed their errant belongings and found a scrap of cloth, with which he returned to bed.

After they'd cleaned up, Leofric slid back into the furs behind Cosmo, pulling him close, tucking him safely against his chest. Cosmo had never felt so terrified, yet so protected and cherished, all at once. For once in his life, he was speechless.

It took him quite some time to get drowsy, and just when Cosmo had almost drifted to sleep, a small gust of breath stirred the hair on the back of his neck. Leofric spoke to him, so quietly Cosmo thought maybe he was hoping to go unheard.

"I like the way you fit, here."

Cosmo smiled. Tucked with his back to Leofric's chest, he could hide how soft and pleased it made him feel. He wriggled his ass a bit, pressing it against Leofric's spent groin. "I'll bet you do."

"Fucking *menace*," Leofric snapped, yanking his arm back from where it had wrapped around Cosmo's waist. He rolled away, facing the wall of the cavern.

Immediately, Cosmo followed. He pressed up behind Leofric. "But, I'm *your* menace." Cosmo hesitated, and he hated the quaver in his own voice when he added, "...right?"

Leofric didn't answer right away, but he drew Cosmo's knuckles to his lips, pressing a kiss to each. Then, he said, "And don't you fucking forget it."

Cosmo smiled, wriggled in closer, and gave Leofric's fingers a squeeze.

For the first time in as long as he could remember, Leofric woke well after the sun had risen. On his side, he propped himself up onto one elbow, drowsily returning to awareness, sluggish and content. Such luxury Leofric had never expected to know. He'd shared his bedroll with Cosmo on the road, but nothing like this. He'd never fallen asleep in the arms of a lover, after they'd spent the night devouring one another.

And not just any lover.

He had fucked a god, and lived to tell it. The fact alone was staggering, and the truth of the man beside him even more so. Cosmo lay on his stomach, dead to the world, freckled back rising and falling with every sleepy breath. Leofric allowed himself a small smile.

Looking at Cosmo beside him now, Leofric felt his body stir, arousal building slow and lazy in his gut. Cosmo's lithe, freckled body was beautiful in the morning sunlight. He trailed the knuckle of his thumb up and down Cosmo's spine, feeling every dip and curve.

As he touched and explored, Leofric took stock of everything that had occurred the previous day. Cosmo had prevailed, and located his brother's grace. The frosty vial was tucked snug in Leofric's pack even as he lay here. With their mission a success, they could leave the mountain and at last return to Papia, return to real life. Leofric found the idea did not fill him with relief.

He'd dreaded this journey, dreaded spending so much time with this companion. Now he dreaded their inevitable parting. What would happen when they returned to Papia? He could hardly keep a concubine in the guard barracks of the royal villa. Perhaps Cosmo would wish to return to his rooms at Lapis, and the life he'd had before. Leofric frowned, a hollow pit growing in his stomach, threatening to eclipse the sated happy feeling he'd only just begun to savor. The pit left plenty of room for his guilt to burrow deep inside him, cold and slimy. These weren't things he wished to dwell upon, so instead, Leofric focused on tracing the constellations of freckles on Cosmo's back, letting his fingers dip lower and lower.

Cosmo stirred, rolling his head to the side. He hovered somewhere between sleeping and waking, and Leofric watched the deep ruddy fringe of his lashes fluttering. Leofric settled down lower into the furs, so he could kiss Cosmo's sleep-slack mouth. "*Mmm,*" said Cosmo. He opened one eye to peer at Leofric. "I had a terrible dream."

"Oh?" said Leofric, teasing his fingers down into the cleft of Cosmo's ass. "What about?"

"That you teased me and teased me for hours," said Cosmo. He arched his back, pushing up into Leofric's touch.

"That sounds like an excellent dream," said Leofric, kissing the freckly shoulder closest to him.

"Yes, but at the end, you peeled off all my skin and ate it."

Leofric wrinkled his nose, disgusted. "What on earth is wrong with you?"

"Nothing!" said Cosmo, unable to keep the grin from spreading across his face. "Besides, everyone knows dreams are prophecy."

"Is that so?"

"Yes," said Cosmo. He pushed Leofric onto his back and straddled his hips. "So, you'd best not tease me, otherwise it will come true."

In answer, Leofric rolled his hips and slid his hands up into Cosmo's tousled hair, tugging on the strands. He yanked him down for a possessive, hungry kiss, and soon they fumbled together in the blankets, teeth and lips and questing hands, and neither one had the patience for teasing.

After, with Cosmo draped across his chest, sticky and sated once again, Leofric spoke up. "Once we've had a chance to clean up, we could be on the road by midday, heading back to Papia."

Cosmo went rigid in his arms at once, where before he'd been poured across Leofric in the bed, languid as a spoiled cat.

"What?"

"Nothing," said Cosmo, too quickly.

Leofric cupped his cheek and tipped his face up so they looked into each other's eyes. "Tell me."

Something about Cosmo's expression was haunted, shifty. He chewed his lip before responding, and it was like Leofric could watch him weighing every word before he spoke. "I was hoping we could linger," said Cosmo.

Leofric opened his mouth to argue, but Cosmo smothered it with a kiss. They'd only just finished but Leofric had never met anyone who could kiss like Cosmo, and it took him several attempts before he could regain sense enough to stop him.

"Just for a day, or two," Cosmo wheedled.

"Why?" Leofric did not dare think Cosmo wanted to linger just for him, there had to be more to this.

Cosmo had regained his wicked smile, the one that had his nose crinkling up and his eyes glittering with mischief. His hands roamed beneath the fur blankets, seeking to distract Leofric again. "I thought it would be nice to rest here," he said, lowering his lips to kiss Leofric's neck. He teased his tongue along the side of his throat, bit his earlobe and ground against Leofric's thigh. "I have so much more I wish to share with you."

Leofric surrendered with a helpless groan, wrapping Cosmo in his arms and rolling them both. He pinned Cosmo to the blankets, and while he needed some time to gather himself, it was plain Cosmo did not. Leofric forged a path of kisses from Cosmo's bruised lips down his throat and chest, reaching his groin in no time at all. He took Cosmo in his mouth again and soon all talk of leaving that day had fled from either of their minds.

Every night when he fell into sex-soaked sleep, Leofric told himself, *tomorrow.* They could leave tomorrow. Summer was still high, they had time aplenty before the season waned. He allowed himself to be distracted for the first week of this, having never known such sweet luxury, never known such pleasure and peace. But soon, he began to wonder. Each morning, Cosmo would depart their cave, claiming some need or other—forage, hunting, or perhaps some duty as the season's shepherd, and Leofric would not see him for hours. He always returned, but it left Leofric wondering.

He tried to let it go as long as he could, because their fiery golden nights and soft mornings in the cave were the happiest Leofric could ever remember being, but the hours spent in solitude in the during the day left him restless and unsettled. Cosmo would still use all of his considerable whiles to stave off the conversation of their departure—not that Leofric pushed him *too* hard. One night, he asked Cosmo if he could accompany him, the following day, when he went off on his own.

Cosmo did not answer, and Leofric was almost certain he was *feigning* sleep.

The next day, Leofric felt he had no choice but to follow Cosmo, to see what he was getting up to. It left him feeling sly and guilty, and he did not like it, but he also felt something was on Cosmo's mind that mattered to him a great deal. Leofric only wished to share it. Cosmo wound his way through the trees, down the path, searching for something amongst the crevasses and stony outcroppings. Leofric wondered what on earth he could be searching for—some memento from his boyhood, perhaps? More curious than ever, Leofric followed at a distance, wondering how long he could get away with this secrecy.

"I know you are there," said Cosmo suddenly, as if he could read Leofric's mind. "Why don't you come out?"

Leofric sighed, held up his hands and stepped out from behind the copse of scraggy trees he'd thought concealed him. "Apologies."

Cosmo braced one hand upon his hip. "Why are you following me?"

"I worry," said Leofric. "About you."

Cosmo laughed. "You worry about me? A god?"

"I worry you have something weighing upon you," said Leofric. "I would help you carry whatever burden you're trying to bear alone."

Cosmo melted a bit at that, some of the tension rolling from his shoulders. "You are very gallant, Captain," said Cosmo. He danced a few steps closer, and lowered his voice to a throaty purr. "How can I repay such kindness?"

"Stop that," Leofric snapped, seizing Cosmo's wrists before his nimble fingers could make any mischief.

Cosmo flinched.

Leofric softened, brushing his thumbs over the interior of Cosmo's wrists. He stooped to kiss his forehead. "I will toss you over my shoulder and carry you back our cave this instant," said Leofric, "if you can look me in the eye and tell me there is nothing on your mind but simple bed sport."

Cosmo met his gaze at first, but soon enough he broke with a sigh. He tried to pull away, to pull his shields back up, to keep Leofric away, but they had shared too much. Leofric would not be scared off so easily. He pulled Cosmo close and kissed the crown of his head. "Tell me," he whispered into Cosmo's hair.

"You'll laugh," said Cosmo, muffled against Leofric's chest.

He seized Cosmo's face in his hands and kissed him thoroughly. "Never."

Cosmo covered Leofric's hands with his own and let out a shuddery sigh. At first, Leofric thought he *still* wasn't going to answer, but then he said, "I think my brother is alive."

Cosmo let his admission hang in the air between them, wondering what Leofric would say. Would he think Cosmo mad? Would he coddle him? Laugh in his face?

The answer, as it happened, was none of these. Leofric tilted his head to the side, puzzled. "Your...?"

"Ozias," said Cosmo. It had been weighing on him since he'd retrieved Kryos's grace. Ozias had spoken to him—all his brothers had. He had thought it some spell, some peculiar remnant of each that lived within Kryos's grace, captured in the crystal. Of course, he knew that Auro, Cedras, and Kryos lived—and that they had the power of their father coursing through their veins.

Ozias was different. He had godsblood, to be sure. Terras had fathered Ozias on an enchantress from a far-off land, and that was all Cosmo knew of his brother's mother. But Terras had never imparted his grace to Ozias, never given him godly power.

When he'd first crawled into bed with Leofric that night, it was only after Cosmo had sat in the hearth for hours, thinking, while the fire died around him, trying to get warm. It had been Ozias's words that kept him shivering, the presence of his brother that had felt so different from the shades of the other three. It *was* Ozias, in truth. Cosmo couldn't say where the confidence came from, but he knew it in his bones.

"What makes you say that?" Leofric asked, and he peered around Cosmo, squinting into the distance as if Ozias were hiding just behind them.

It wasn't that absurd, Cosmo thought; he'd been searching for him, combing the mountainside for days. "I felt him," said Cosmo. "I heard him."

"When?"

"When I found Kryos's grace, in its enchanted chamber. He was there, I know it."

Leofric furrowed his brow. "Are you certain?"

"Yes," said Cosmo. "While I was crossing the chamber, I had...visions."

"Visions," Leofric repeated, and Cosmo could hear the skepticism in his voice.

"Yes," said Cosmo, flaring up. He shook off Leofric's touch and backed off a few steps to pace restlessly in the clearing. "Is that really so odd?"

"Of course, it isn't," said Leofric. "Well, it is, but not *so* odd compared to..." he gestured vaguely at Cosmo.

"Compared to me? Because I am so odd?"

"Yes," said Leofric. "This of gods and curses is not usual for someone like me."

"You're right," said Cosmo with a sigh. "Apologies. I just... I don't know what to think."

"Let me help," said Leofric, his voice soft and urgent. "Tell me of the visions."

"They weren't true visions per say," said Cosmo, correcting himself. He considered how best to describe the presences he'd felt in the cavern below the mountain. "Auro was there," he said. "Cedras, and even Kryos. It was as if I could feel them, walking at my back. Walking with me."

"And Ozias?" Leofric prompted.

"Him too," said Cosmo. He hesitated here, wondering how much to divulge. Looking into Leofric's eyes, Cosmo decided on the truth—or, what he understood of it, anyway. If Leofric were going to mock him, well, he'd rather know that now than...*when?*

Leofric's severe brows knit together. "Where did you go?" He asked, as he always did when Cosmo made any attempt to conceal his thoughts.

"Apologies," said Cosmo. He stepped close and pressed a kiss to the corner of Leofric's mouth. "I was just choosing my words. It was a very strange feeling, down there, in the cavern."

"Come," said Leofric. "Let's return to our camp. I've gathered some supplies for supper, but I know better than to cook, absent your supervision." And here he gave a fleeting, encouraging smile, soft enough to melt through Cosmo's defenses.

"Alright," Cosmo allowed.

Once returned to their cozy little campsite within the mountain, Cosmo turned a wild turkey on a spit, and gave a stir to a pot of hunter's porridge he'd pulled together from the things Leofric foraged. The man might be a dismal cook, but he knew his business when it came to hunting and gathering. Savory smells filled the cavern, and beyond the glow of their fire, the stars were out, and fireflies dotted the rocky ground that served them like a terrace.

They ate their fill before breaking further words about Cosmo's experience down below, and enough time had passed that Cosmo had almost convinced himself that perhaps he needn't expand further. Leofric was not about to let him get off so easily, however. Once they'd tossed their bones and scraps into the hearth, he said, "I believe you were going to tell me more of why you refuse to leave this mountain."

"Yes," said Cosmo. "As I said, it is...difficult to find the words."

"You were speaking of your brothers," said Leofric. "And some form of their presence lingering with Kryos's grace below."

"Yes," said Cosmo. "They spoke of Auro's trial. I don't believe it was them truly but...a sort of...echo, crafted through enchantment."

"Alright," said Leofric, and Cosmo could tell these things were outside the realm of his experience. He spoke like a man struggling to stay abreast of something he did not truly believe, but made honest attempt to open his mind.

"The shade of Ozias felt different," said Cosmo. "I cannot explain it, not truly but...it seemed as though his presence was an entirely different one from theirs. It felt more..."

"Alive?"

Cosmo looked at him, hating the pity he saw in Leofric's eyes. "Yes," he said, defiantly.

"Cosmo," said Leofric, his tone softer than Cosmo had ever heard it, and Cosmo hated that too, the coddling, placating lilt to his name as Leofric spoke. "I know the pain of a brother's loss. I understand—"

"No, you don't," Cosmo snapped. He stood, leaving Leofric to his small-minded mortal views and exited the cave.

Cosmo climbed up onto the rounded stone dais and sat. He drew his knees up to his chest and rested his chin upon them, staring out into the vast green sea that spilled down the mountainside, pooling around its feet. It was dark, and sounds and sights of summer evenings comforted him. Cosmo had always enjoyed fireflies, liking how they flitted to and fro like little errant stars, like the night sky had fallen over the earth at night, a sparkling blanket, tucking it in to slumber.

"For someone so old, you have less patience than anyone I'd ever met."

Cosmo twisted in his seat, to see Leofric clambering up beside him. He sat cross-legged, his back rigid as a spear, hands resting on his knees. "You have even less, it seems," he replied. Cosmo had only been out here a few minutes.

"What I mean to say," said Leofric, tilting his face up toward the moon, "is that you have seen more of this world than I could ever hope to see in my lifetime."

Cosmo frowned. This was true enough, he supposed, but he could not see what it had to do with the matter at hand.

"This world of curses and enchantments, living statues, and the grace of gods...I knew nothing of it a year ago. Forget a year—I knew nothing of it a season ago."

Cosmo had a feeling Leofric still had not arrived at his point, so he remained silent.

"You have had four centuries to become used to these things; they are as normal to you as the sunrise is to a man like me. Forgive me, a mortal, my skepticism. I am learning as fast as I am able."

Cosmo smiled, and leaned over to press a kiss to Leofric's shoulder. "Perhaps even one as old as I can learn patience."

"I doubt it."

Cosmo shoved him, and Leofric only laughed. "If you're done," said Cosmo, but he couldn't muster any true annoyance. "I will try to explain again."

"Thank you," said Leofric quietly. "I only wish to help."

"I know," said Cosmo. He waited a while, gathering his thoughts. "From what Auro told me, of the vision he received at spring's end, our mother had left an imprint of herself, like a shade, to convey words even though centuries have escaped since she last truly spoke."

"Yes," said Leofric. "The way he spoke of her, it appeared her presence was fading. Losing strength as it were."

"Indeed. The presence of Kryos, Cedras and Auro below felt much the same as he described."

"But Ozias felt different?"

"Yes," said Cosmo.

"Did you lay eyes upon a...form?"

Cosmo looked at the ground, ashamed. "No," he said. "I was afraid. Afraid that if I turned to look at any of them..."

"...they would disappear?"

He nodded. "It was only after, when I was back up here, that I regained sense enough to peel apart what I had seen, and heard, and felt, below the mountain."

"And what you felt was Ozias?"

"Yes." Cosmo turned to face Leofric. "I am not sure how, or what it means, but I am telling you, Ozias lives."

"Well," said Leofric, "in that case, I suppose we'd better find him, and ask him what the fuck he's been doing for four hundred years."

Twenty-One

L eofric still was not certain what to believe, but Cosmo's certainty that Ozias lived was strong enough to convince him, for a time. They spent the next week combing every crevice of Mount Hiru, and found nothing. They even returned to the gaping cavern below, pressing their hands into the stone, digging through the snow, searching for any evidence that might point to where Ozias had gone. It grew harder by the day for Leofric to imagine a world in which Cosmo was right, imagine a world in which his long-lost brother would appear for a moment, only to vanish again without a trace. He tried his best to pretend though, for Cosmo's sake. He imagined what he would do, if he heard Hamalcar's voice in the shadows of the mountain years after his death, and that made it a bit easier for him to indulge Cosmo's search.

But only a bit. After a week, Leofric grew restless. He now felt certain that *if* Ozias lived, then he did not wish to be found. However, he felt he could not say this to Cosmo. How long could they keep this up? They must return to Papia soon. They had no word of His Highness and Auro, no word if the

King had recovered from his illness, or if other threats and shadows had emerged. Leofric felt blind on this mountain top, blind and beyond useless.

"I can hear you thinking," said Cosmo snappishly one morning.

"I'll try to keep it down," Leofric snapped back, harsher than he'd intended.

Cosmo took a deep breath, and it was as if Leofric could see him crushing his temper, crushing his frustration, dousing the fire behind his eyes. "It may be time to abandon this search," said Cosmo, and Leofric could hear the heartache and loss weighing every syllable. "For now."

Leofric did his best to conceal his relief. "If you think it's time," he said evenly.

Cosmo cut him a look, proving that he hadn't been as outwardly patient as he'd hoped. "If Auro's theory proves correct, I can return here to search for him once we've delivered Kryos's grace to Papia. If I no longer have to rest at the end of summer, there's nothing to stop me from pulling up every root and pebble of this fucking mountain until I find him."

He spoke in ringing tones, but Leofric heard the unasked question there: *will you return with me?* It was a question Leofric was afraid to answer. He had not considered what would happen between Cosmo and himself upon their return to Papia, had not *allowed* himself to consider it. The few times the images in his mind's eye threatened to invade, he'd imagined Cosmo resuming is residence at Lapis, fucking and drinking his way through autumn, winter, and spring until he was called upon to perform his duties at the advent of the following summer. Now, there was the image of Cosmo wandering alone in the wild, searching for traces of a brother who may not even be there, wasting away, a wraith of grief.

It was hard to say which was worse, and Leofric was not

ready to examine how he would feel about Cosmo no longer beside him. Cosmo had been an incessant thorn at his side, but one can get used to anything, even thorns. Leofric had hoped to resume his position at the head of His Highness's royal guard when this quest was at its end, but that was before. Before the mountain, before he'd spoken with Laela about their futures, before *Cosmo*. While he had come to resent the aimless lingering on the mountain top, it had allowed him to forestall asking and thereby answering these questions.

"Perhaps His Highness has left us some message in the town below," said Leofric, offering a safe rail to clutch in this dangerous conversation. "A rider, perhaps, to the magistrate's offices."

"Perhaps," Cosmo allowed. "We can stop there, and refresh our supplies for the return journey to Papia."

Leofric gripped his shoulder. Something seemed to be required of him in this moment, but for the life of him he could not determine what it was. However, the simple touch seemed enough, for now. Cosmo covered Leofric's hand with his own, giving his fingers a squeeze.

It did not take them long to reverse the journey down the mountainside, and Leofric watched Cosmo carefully out of the corner of his eye for its duration. He seemed more or less himself, but perhaps a shade grimmer. Leofric understood that, at least, if not the rest of it—Cosmo had fulfilled his quest. He would return home victorious, in a sense. No one could doubt his devotion to their family, once Kryos's grace sat in the vault beside Cedras's. But to Cosmo, it was not enough. He still burned to find Ozias, to bring home not only hope for one brother, but redemption for them all. It was a sweet notion, but sweet notions and daydreams could easily lead a man astray.

If anyone knew that, it was him.

When they reached the city at the base of the mountain,

a few pennies in the right palms saw them to an audience with the city magistrate. Leofric judged the man to be honorable enough, for a politician, at any rate. "You are Leofric?" He asked, when he met with them in the lofty marble office on the second floor of a well-appointed domus.

"You know of me?" Leofric asked.

The magistrate nodded. "Aye," he said. "I received a rider, with an urgent message. You were expected to return through town several days ago, were you not?"

Leofric exchanged a glance with Cosmo. "It was the initial plan, but our business in the mountain took longer than initially anticipated."

"Well," said the Magistrate, "if you don't mind saying, it might have been wiser to adhere to your initial schedule." He waved the note, which showed a broken wax seal.

"The seal is broken," said Leofric, stunned. Then he frowned. "How is it that you have broken it, when the missive was addressed to me?"

The magistrate was not impressed by Leofric's threatening tone. "When you did not return near the appointed time, I exercised my lawful right as Magistrate to ensure the safety of my people. This city pays its due to the King of Órnio. An urgent letter comes from a foreign kingdom, I would be neglecting my sacred oath not to be aware its contents."

"How dare—" Cosmo stepped forward, positively snarling, but Leofric held up a hand. This situation was delicate. Leofric needed the letter, needed to know its contents. Besides, he and Cosmo were two men against a garrison of soldiers of the city watch. To move against them would be an act of political aggression.

"Apologies, Magistrate," said Leofric in icy calm tones. He gave a grudging bow. "I forget myself. I appreciate your holding the message safe, until our belated return to the city."

This seemed to mollify the man, and he handed over the parchment.

"You have my thanks," said Leofric, bowing once again.

Once outside, they returned to the municipal stables, where they'd paid to shelter their horses while they attended their business with the magistrate. "Well?" Cosmo prompted. "What does it say?"

Leofric's blood pounded in his ears, Cosmo's voice fading into a dull, incessant hum in the background. His heartbeat ratcheted up, as if it fought to escape his ribs. He read the letter again. And then, a third time, trying to make the words different. No matter how many times he read them, they remained the same.

"Leofric?" He jerked from Cosmo's timid touch and thrust the letter at him.

L-

Sorex has fallen ill. He may not survive. We need you. Come at once.

-Laela

Leofric's hands shook when he took the parchment back from Cosmo. "Six *days* ago, this arrived," said Leofric. "Six days."

"What?"

"This letter has been sitting in that man's office for a week, while you had me running about chasing ghosts!" Leofric spat the last word out, all the doubts he'd kept carefully guarded exploding out of his mouth.

Cosmo looked as though he'd been slapped. "*Ghosts?*"

"Yes," said Leofric, pacing now. "We both know Ozias is dead and gone."

"I *saw*—"

"You saw what you wanted to see, what would alleviate your guilt," said Leofric, unthinking. "If Ozias lives, you don't have to take ownership of anything you've done in the past."

"That is..." Cosmo said in an oddly flat voice. "Unkind."

"But true!" Leofric hardly even knew what he was saying. He gesticulated wildly with the letter crushed in his fist. "And now my family has paid the price for *your* self-ishness!"

"I care about them, too."

"*Please,*" scoffed Leofric. "You don't even care about your own family, how can I expect you'd care for mine? I can't believe—*anything* could have happened—Sorex could be...he might be..."

Cosmo braced his hands upon his hips. "Leofric, you know I would have postponed the search for Ozias had I known Laela and Sorex were—"

"It matters not," said Leofric, finally getting his wits about him. "I must go at once."

"Of course," said Cosmo, without hesitation. He hurried to the stall where he'd put up Hestia just that morning. "You have Kryos's grace?"

Leofric barely heard him, moving like a man in a dream, and time seemed to skip. All at once, he sat astride Lyra's saddle, his pack slung over his shoulder. Cosmo was a few seconds behind, trying to get one foot into the stirrup of his own mount.

"You'll only slow me down," Leofric heard himself say, answering the question Cosmo had not asked.

Cosmo's face hardened, the twist of his mouth more like a sneer than his usual irreverent grin. "You have my brother's grace."

"Aye," said Leofric. "And after I help my family, I'll return it to Auro."

"Of course," said Cosmo angrily. "Why wouldn't I trust you to hand over part of my brother's soul? You're only taking it, and leaving me behind."

"Unlike you, I can be counted upon to keep a promise."

"Apparently, you can't," Cosmo shot back. "You can't even protect your own family."

The words cut true, cut deep. Cosmo was right, and his accusation was like a knife in Leofric's gut, twisting, stabbing, turning. He couldn't look at Cosmo one more second, so he put his heels to Lyra and urged her to a faster gait. He blew past a startled Cosmo and took the road from Hiru City at a hard gallop, and he refused to look back.

Cosmo stood in the stables, staring forlornly after Leofric with one foot in the stirrups for so long that when Hestia finally snorted and brought him back to the present, he toppled over and landed on his backside in the dirt.

Fitting, he thought as he rolled about like an insect, trying to disentangle himself. At last he freed his foot from the stirrup, if only to guide Hestia back to her stall so she could browse the food on offer. Once he removed her bridle, he looked around himself, at a loss. Leofric had taken with him some undefinable part of Cosmo and left behind a wide, gaping hole. Empty and achy, and it drew his attention and focus like the crater left behind by a missing tooth. He simply could not stop tonguing it.

Cosmo had, after days of searching with no evidence to the contrary, largely given up on the idea that Ozias was actually hiding somewhere on the mountain. Some essence of him must have clung to Cosmo and the others when he'd left this world, preserved by their grace and his own godsblood. It wasn't the most logical explanation, but truly, most of Cosmo's life with his brothers defied logic, so it seemed as good as anything.

Unfortunately, however, it seemed that he'd hitched his wagon to the hope that Ozias had simply been living hidden in a cave for four hundred years in his attempt to save face with Leofric. Frowning, Cosmo considered his options.

First, he could re-saddle Hestia *again* and return to Papia, tail between his legs. No, not entirely—he'd still recovered Kryos's grace. He felt a tiny, weak ember of pride in his chest. He had at least done *that;* his return to Auro wouldn't be entirely fraught with humiliation.

Second, he could return to the mountain and continue his search, cold and alone, and most likely doomed to fail.

To be honest, neither one of those options sounded appealing. He looked again down the dirt lane that led through town, in the direction Leofric had traveled. Cosmo's third option was to trail pathetically after Leofric in hopes of overtaking him on the road, trying to cut through the layers of guilt that had sent Leofric fleeing for his home and his family, hoping to be welcomed, embraced, forgiven. *Loved?* He rejected that out of hand, recoiling from it with a self-flagellating chuckle.

That option was absurd, mad. A child's fancy. What was it Leofric had said? Four hundred years old, and still a child. What a fool Cosmo was. A selfish, childish fool.

As he realized Leofric, his father, and all his brothers had perhaps been right about him all along, Cosmo realized something else. He had a fourth option.

He could leave this stable, walk through the main streets of this city, find a tavern, and get absolutely obliterated with drink.

Hours later, Cosmo was warm, surrounded by laughing

revelers, and well on his way to ensuring he barely remembered this night come morning. It was not the most elegant, nor the most long-term, solution to his problems, but it certainly did the trick in the moment. Musicians played on a small stage erected in the hall, and the people of Hiru City really knew how to put on a party. He liked this city. It wasn't a port, but it reminded him of Papia's salt market all the same. These people were loud, raucous, earthy. *No one here imagines themselves better than anyone else,* Cosmo thought, *that much is certain.* Most of the revelers were travelers and at a glance Cosmo could tell they came from all walks of life, passing through on their way to some place or other. There was an ever-changing flow of people to talk to, people sharing stories, playing cards or dice, buying drinks, or dragging one another into shadowy corners of the hall, or to the rooms upstairs, for play of a more intimate sort.

Normally, Cosmo would have been among them. He'd booked a room upstairs, paying the innkeeper extra to avoid the question of when he'd be checking out. Cosmo could stay here indefinitely, and with his mug full of wine and one of the kingdom's most famed musicians on the stage, crooning and playing his lyre, he thought perhaps he'd never leave.

He'd sent Kryos's grace with...well. He'd sent it on to Auro, anyway. Maybe Hiru City would become Cosmo's new home. It seemed a jolly place, all told. If Auro's theory about breaking the curse was correct, Cosmo never had to return to the temple in Papia. That was a strangely sobering thought. While Cosmo had done his level best to avoid thoughts of his family for four hundred years, he had in actuality been bound to them, never able to *truly* be free.

Now, he was. Cosmo didn't even particularly care if Kryos never restored his full power. He could carry on his duties as the god of summer well enough without the full strength of his grace, and it had only ever caused pain—both his own and that of others. The point was that he never had to lay eyes on his brothers, ever again—their cold, unfeeling statues or the flesh and blood versions. He never had to set foot in the temple that was like waking up each year in a tomb, with only ghosts for company. The pain of the past scourged away, with the passing of years, never to trouble him again. That was what he had wanted wasn't it? Freedom? His own life?

Cosmo drained his mug and signaled to the barman to refill it once again. If someone had asked him, even a few short weeks ago, the answer would have been yes, but since waking up this year, his summer had been an endless churn of guilt and longing, fear and doubt.

Other things, too, said a voice in the back of his mind. He stuffed it away, draining yet another goblet of wine. The more Cosmo drank, the more he thought staying in Hiru City a splendid notion. The music filled the hall, louder and more alluring with every sip, and Cosmo rocked back and forth in his seat, swaying and wishing he had someone to dance with. Leofric would never dance, he thought. He would most likely give Cosmo a searing lecture on how frivolous and worthless music was.

Something bubbled up his gullet at the thought, a tearing sensation deep in Cosmo's chest. He lurched to his feet, knocking his empty cup to the floor. He stumbled, drunker even than he'd thought, and cast his eyes about the crowd, searching for someone, anyone with whom he might be able to spend a few hours forgetting. Preferably someone short, curvy, and blonde, with soft hips and breasts. Someone...*different,* his brain supplied.

As he scanned the crowd, Cosmo had a difficult time pulling faces into focus. The people talked and danced and moved around like multicolored blobs, or perhaps like one large seething mass. Goodness, but he was drunk. Cosmo didn't think he'd been this drunk in decades, which when you thought about it was really saying something.

It almost didn't matter who, he reasoned, staggering off in a direction in which the blobs seemed especially bright and cheerful. He just needed...*someone.* Anyone. Else.

He made it three steps before colliding with something solid, and Cosmo found himself soaked with wine and crashing into a table. The music screeched to a stop, replaced by the cacophony of shattering ceramic, plates of food and an entire tray of full mugs going sailing across the room. Before Cosmo could form the words to slur an apology, several pairs of hands grabbed hold of his arms and yanked him back to his feet. He detached the coin purse from his belt and tried to offer it to whomever he'd so offended. Someone accepted his offering, but he never saw who, and the rough handed men carried him toward the door to the inn.

The crowd cheered, shouting and hissing. Before Cosmo could protest, someone flung wide the door, the ones carrying him gave an almighty heave, and all at once the rutted dirt road was flying up to meet his face.

A pair of sandaled feet crossed into Cosmo's field of vision, and someone squatted down beside him. He spat out a mouthful of dirt and tried to call their face into focus, but what he saw was impossible.

Cosmo must have been even drunker than he'd thought, because right before he lost consciousness, he stared into the face of a ghost.

Twenty–Two

Leofric rode Lyra hard, harder than he'd ever pushed her before. She was gracious, as always, obeying his every command for more speed. He thanked her as they went, knowing it wasn't a speed he could continue for the whole journey, not without killing her. When he thought they both needed a rest he slowed her to a canter, then a walk. After a hard day's riding both he and Lyra were blown; they needed to stop and rest, if only for a little while.

With every step, he grew further and further from Cosmo, and felt worse and worse about doing so. The half a second it would have taken Cosmo to mount up wouldn't have cost him any time, and Cosmo was a master horseman. So why had Leofric not given him half a moment to follow?

He turned their parting words over in his head, but it seemed he'd been so distracted that the conversation replayed in reverse. For the first leg of the journey home, all he could call to mind was Cosmo's accusation, that Leofric wasn't even capable of protecting his brother's family, and rage carried him along for hours, days, as he memorized every line of Cosmo's hateful sneer, every syllable of his words, etching them eternally in his mind so he could hate Cosmo for them properly.

The next leg, it came back to Leofric that he'd hurled at least three insults at Cosmo before Cosmo had retaliated with his own. If you went by the math, it didn't come out even, so Leofric thought perhaps he could forgive Cosmo—except, Leofric had meant none of the hurtful things he'd said. Cosmo could *easily* have meant what he said; it was the truth, after all. Leofric clearly *couldn't* keep his promises. Leofric couldn't work out which was worse—hurting someone with lies, or hurting someone with the truth. And then, he would picture Hamalcar, dying in Leofric's arms with a smile on his face—only soothed by Leofric's promise. Then, his features would transform. Grow younger. And it was Sorex lying dead in his mind's eye—and it was easier, far easier, to think Cosmo's words the cruelest thing anyone could have said, and his anger at him would return. And the cycle would begin again.

It was the way the words sliced him to the quick that filled him with hot, sick, undulating waves of anger. At first the anger was toward Cosmo, but the truth was...it belonged within. Leofric was the true wretch, the one deserving of anger, deserving of being despised. He'd let his desire for a good fuck blind him, entirely, for *days,* while Laela and Sorex were left alone and unsupported. Certainly, Cosmo had *asked* to stay on the mountain, but Leofric had been the one to answer 'yes.' His own base desires had cost him precious days in this mad dash toward rescue, and he could only apologize to Hamalcar's shade with every breath for being so selfish.

Never again.

The miles seemed to pass at a snail's pace after that, and had the days been cloudy, he would have sworn it had taken him thrice the time to cover the same ground he and Cosmo had covered on the way to the mountain. As it stood, the sun gave lie to his fears. He was making excellent time. Excellent time, however, would hardly make up for six *days* lost while he was fucking his way around the mountain top. *How* could he have been so stupid? So selfish. Such a bloody fool, thinking with his cock, just as he used to when he'd been half this age.

He could see the walls of Laela's villa still quite a ways out from it. Though he'd covered the distance in two thirds of the days, that was still plenty of time for his brain to conjure all the horrible things that could have befallen his family while he dallied on the mountain with Cosmo.

The next thing Cosmo knew, he was drowning. Drowning in a frozen lake, choking and sputtering as water filled his lungs. Drowning, and then—no, no. He wasn't drowning, but he *was* blind. He'd opened his eyes and been met with pain akin to someone carving them out with a dull dagger, so he *must* be blind. Eyes couldn't survive that, surely.

Eventually though, things broke through, swam in and out of focus for a minute, a day, or five years, but then he could see again. His mind whipped blank and not a single thought could find its way through the emptiness. Cosmo stared and stared, drinking in the sight of his brother's face, like he hadn't aged a moment in four hundred years, the same mop of inky curls, the same mischievous grin. He rummaged beneath the cloak now tangled about his legs, found the meat of his thigh, and gave it a good hard pinch, just as he had when he'd woken to see Auro awake beyond the end of spring. It hurt, so Cosmo could rule out the notion that he still lingered in a dream.

"Hi, Cos," said Ozias. His smile split his face ear to ear.

Cosmo gave a wordless yelp, of joy, of fear—of confusion perhaps, and threw back the covers. He leapt to his feet and pulled Ozias into a hug, crushing his slender body tight in his arms. "Is it really you?"

"Yes," said Ozias, somewhat muffled, but Cosmo could hear the light laughter in his voice. "It really is me."

And then Cosmo puked all over him.

"Fucking goodness, Cosmo. How much did you drink?" Ozias's face wrinkled in disgust as he waved a hand in front of his face, a worthless attempt to ward off the scent of vomit.

The headache came galloping in on the heels of the explosive retching, and Cosmo collapsed backward to sit upon the edge of the bed. "Enough that I'm only half certain you're really here."

"I assure you, I am. Here, and covered with vomit."

"I can't believe it," said Cosmo. "I can't believe it."

"Believe it," said Ozias, shaking vomit from the edge of his tunic. "Not the heartfelt greeting I expected, after so long, but here we are."

Cosmo laughed, despite the spike plainly working its way into his brain. "And where is that?"

"Your room at the inn," said Ozias, taking in the modest space. "Or I surely hope it is."

Cosmo knuckled his eyes, which made his brain feel like a juiced orange, and said, "I thought they tossed me out."

"They did," Ozias allowed. "But I managed to convince them you were harmless and simple minded."

"Harmless!" Sputtered Cosmo indignantly.

"*And* simple-minded," Ozias replied. And then he grinned.

Cosmo couldn't help but answer his smile. Then he glanced down at himself. "Why am I all wet?"

Ozias suspiciously set down an empty bucket and nudged it behind the bed with his foot. "Why am *I* all covered in vomit? Let's not ask each other these things."

"Fine," said Cosmo.

They stared at each other, grinning awkwardly. Words utterly failed Cosmo, who could not help but feast his eyes on his brother, currently using one of Cosmo's tunics to dab at his own soiled clothing.

"Why is my stuff all over the place?"

Ozias raised his brows. "So many questions, brother. Your things are all over the place because you're an incorrigible slob at the best of times, let alone when you've drunk enough wine to drown a horse."

"A fair point," said Cosmo. He frowned, trying to call the previous night into focus. His room was so thoroughly ransacked, he must have been searching for something. Ah, well. Hopefully, he'd found it. Cosmo returned his focus to his brother. "One more question, if you'll forgive me."

"I sincerely doubt you'll stop at one."

He ignored the jibe, stared Ozias direct in the face and said, "How can this be?"

"The tale is a long one," said Ozias, after a long pause. "And strange."

"It would have to be."

"I know," said Ozias. Another pause. "Forgive me, Cosmo. I can't do this. We both need to wash before we have this conversation, and I need a fresh tunic."

Cosmo laughed out loud, driving the spike even deeper, but it felt good all the same. "I think that is a valid suggestion," he said. "Apologies," he added.

Ozias waved it off. "How many times have we vomited on one another? I feel as though we're even on that score."

Once they'd washed and changed into fresh clothing, Ozias and Cosmo sat opposite each other at a small table in the tavern.

"It is difficult to know where to begin," said Ozias, peeking up at Cosmo through his untidy fringe, his wide dark eyes as youthful and wild as they'd been when they were children. Ozias had always been slight, perhaps taller than Cosmo but his carriage made him appear diminutive. He ducked his head, rounded his shoulders, hid within himself. He was thinner than Cosmo, too, bony and gaunt, but the look served him well, if Cosmo remembered correctly—the two of them would often prowl the streets and docks together in search of intimate companions of a night, and Ozias had never had a lack of willing partners. The only salient difference was that the Ozias before him had grown a beard, and the rakish appearance suited.

It was plain he was uncomfortable, plain he didn't want to dredge up all the ugliness of years gone. Looking at Ozias, Cosmo realized how much he had missed him—how much he had missed having a comrade, a partner. A friend. A brother yes, but Ozias was more than that. He always had been. "I think we should begin with a drink," said Cosmo. "Or a dozen."

Ozias laughed. "You would think that."

"As if you are famed for abstaining."

"Well," said Ozias, "I haven't had much call for frolics in the last few centuries."

"In that case," said Cosmo, signaling for wine. "We have quite a bit to make up for."

"Hear, Hear," said Ozias, with a grin.

Twenty-Three

It was the dead of night when Leofric arrived at the villa. Leofric's throat tightened as he approached the gate. It was barred for the night, and Leofric seriously considered trying to break it down. However, there was a postern door tucked snug in the rear of the grounds, and Leofric had a key. He led Lyra around the back and unlocked the door. Inside, the place was eerily quiet. His heart and pulse hammered as he approached the stables, and Leofric wondered if perhaps Laela had brought Sorex into the city to find some sort of medical aid.

Inside the stable, all of the horses were present and accounted for, including his brother's warhorse. Just looking at the animal had Leofric's guts churning with guilt. The wagon also parked in its spot just outside the stable, under the lean-to that kept it out of the elements. Did that mean they'd arranged other transportation? Or that Sorex was too ill to move? There was nothing to do now but face his family, and find out how serious things were.

In the atrium, Leofric's footfalls echoed thunderously all around him, but he couldn't muster the self-control to slow his steps. As he passed through the darkened dining chamber, Leofric collided with an errant wooden stool and nearly fell over. Cursing, he righted himself and the stool, waiting for his eyes to adjust to the blackness. Then, he heard something from the corridor.

A slim figure with a candle in one hand leapt out from behind the wall, a knife clutched in the other. Leofric threw up his hands, to show he came unarmed. From a dozen paces beyond the candle's glow, a thick, exhausted voice said, "Leo?"

The person holding the candle lowered their knife. "Uncle?"

Leofric surged forward, grabbing Sorex's face in his hands, searching the boy's eyes. Aside from fear and confusion at his uncle's midnight intrusion, Leofric saw nothing amiss in his face. His hair was sleep tousled, but his eyes stood clear as ever, reflecting the light from his candle. "You should be in bed, resting," Leofric told him. He rested the back of his hand across his nephew's forehead, searching for any sign of fever. His skin was cool and dry to touch.

A timid hand landed upon his arm and he about jumped out of his skin. "I think we all should be in bed," said Laela in a hoarse voice. "What on earth are you doing here?"

"You—you wrote to me," said Leofric, but when the words came out, they sounded like a question. How could it not, when both Laela and Sorex stared at him as if he'd lost his wits.

Laela scrubbed a hand over her tired eyes. "What? When?"

"I don't know exactly—but I got the letter and—the boy was ill!"

"What boy?" Asked Laela, looking around.

"Sorex!"

"I haven't been ill," said Sorex.

"Hush," said Leofric. "If your mother says you're ill, you're ill."

"But I didn't say he was ill," said Laela, irritated. "I haven't written since you were here last."

"You haven't—" Leofric trailed off, rummaging in the pouch at his belt. As he searched for the letter, Sorex went around the room and lit a few more candles, and then busied himself with the hearth. By the time Leofric had extricated Laela's letter, the kitchen was bathed in a warm, orange glow. He handed her the parchment, and Laela took it, her brow furrowing deeply.

After a few moments she looked up. "I did not write this."

"You didn't—what?"

She set the parchment down on the table, carefully, as if it were dangerous. "I did not write this," she repeated.

"Then who did?" asked Leofric.

Laela considered the parchment once again. "Sorex," she said abruptly. "Go to bed."

"But—"

"Now," she said, meeting his eyes. Her voice was quiet, but firm. "Please."

Sorex plainly wanted to argue, to stay, to hear what strange and exciting things the adults were about to discuss, but he was a good lad. He nodded, disappointed, and left the room.

Leofric sat opposite Laela, and frowned down at the letter. It was in Laela's hand, bore her signature at the bottom. "Are you certain you are both alright?"

"*Yes*," she said wearily. "We are well, aside from being woken and frightened in the dead of night."

Leofric was exhausted, his mind trying to whir to life as his body groaned in protest. "I don't understand."

"Neither do I," said Laela. "If that helps."

Leofric stared at the parchment again, as if he could will the words to change and explain what on earth was going on.

"Leo," she said. "What is this? What's happening?"

"I don't know." And then, again. "I don't know."

"Alright," said Laela carefully. She looked around, as if suddenly realizing something. "Where's Cosmo?"

Several hours later found Cosmo and Ozias in their third tavern of the evening, drunk and getting drunker. Cosmo had always found the best cure for a hangover was to erase it as swiftly as possible, and he was well on his way to doing so. However, for some reason, the wine-soaked revels didn't have the same flavor to which he was accustomed. He and Ozias still had not discussed anything of substance, but the more they drank the further away such concerns seemed. However, they were still there, lurking in the distance, and Cosmo was having a difficult time forgetting.

"*Cos!*"

Cosmo returned to the present. "Apologies," he said. "What?"

Ozias's face twisted in irritation. "I thought you'd be a bit happier once you were sauced," he said, leaning back in his chair. He took a heavy glug from his own flagon, eyeing Cosmo over the lip of it as he drank.

"I *am*," said Cosmo.

"You don't seem it," said Ozias sullenly.

Cosmo sighed, trying to marshal his thoughts, to summon one of the thousand questions that had been racing around his head since he'd woken up to his brother's face, but they'd been drinking for hours, and his wits were slow. Before he could come up with something, Ozias said abruptly, "Remember when we stole Cedras's spectacles?"

Cosmo grinned. Of course, he remembered it. "How could I forget? He was furious."

Ozias laughed. "Woe betide he who came between Cedras and his books."

They'd been around ten, or perhaps even younger, and they'd climbed in Cedras's bedroom window in the dead of night. Cosmo and Ozias had done everything together at that age, pulling pranks on their brothers, the villa staff, anyone or anything that stood still long enough in their presence was a potential victim of being hoodwinked or tricked. They were terrors, if Cosmo was being honest, but he couldn't help the smile pulling at his lips as he remembered.

Ozias had come to Cosmo one day, saying that there were caves down by the sea that one could only see when the tide was out. All manner of things could be found in there, Ozias insisted. Shells, lost trinkets, driftwood, bits of old ships, anything that might have washed in on the tide. Cosmo had been burning with excitement to go, but his mother had said it was far too dangerous. "Take one of your older brothers," she'd insisted. Ozias was a bit older than Cosmo, but even then, he'd known she hadn't meant *him*. Kryos had only scoffed, and Cedras had been far too busy. "Perhaps when I finish reading," he'd said vaguely, but he always said that. There was always *another* page, another chapter, an endless pile of scrolls and books demanding his attentions.

When Cosmo refused to sneak out on his own, he and Ozias had hatched the plan to swipe the spectacles from Cedras's bedside table. "If he can't read," Ozias had said. "he'll have nothing better to do than accompany us." When they'd snuck in, they hadn't realized how late Cedras stayed up reading, and they had nearly fallen asleep themselves, waiting for him to extinguish the candle on his bedside table.

When he'd done it at last, Cosmo had crept over and stolen the spectacles, folded neatly atop whatever horrid boring book he'd been so engrossed in.

Ozias had lingered by the table, and when Cosmo hissed at him to hurry so they could make their escape, he'd grinned and pulled a near-identical pair of spectacles out of his pocket. "*What are those?*" Cosmo hissed.

But Ozias hadn't explained until they were well away. "He'll think he's lost his eyesight," said Ozias, grinning. "The glass inside isn't the same as the kind he has in his real pair."

It had only taken Cedras all of six hours to uncover the ruse, and for four of those he'd been asleep. Cosmo had been punished fiercely for the crime, because Cedras's real spectacles had been tucked safely in his bed chambers, damning him as the culprit.

Ozias had never spoken up then, either, Cosmo thought sourly, watching as his brother tucked a lock of golden hair behind the ear of a woman who hung upon his every whispered word. Where had she come from? Cosmo startled, realizing that Ozias had conjured up two women, and not solely because Cosmo was drunk enough to be seeing double. Goodness but he worked fast.

Cosmo rolled his eyes, despite seeing many things from his own traditional courting manual present in Ozias's behavior. From his posture to the look on his face, all of it calculated to better ensnare a potential partner—and it seemed he had ensnared one for each of them. Cosmo wondered why the thought didn't thrill him as it historically would have.

The answer was, perhaps, obvious—but Leofric had ridden off and abandoned him, cast him aside, and drove a knife into his heart as he left besides. Cosmo had been jilted before, of course. A dozen times—perhaps more. He'd been at this a good long while, after all. But he'd never been spurned in quite such a violent fashion. All of it was strange, mixed up in his head with concern for Leofric himself and his family as well—it was, after all, the fault of Cosmo that Leofric had even been pulled into this mess, though perhaps Auro and his princeling shared some of the blame on that count.

Nevermind.

Leofric was gone, and Cosmo was here—here with his brother! Ozias! Despite his own determination that Ozias was alive, he still didn't quite believe it.

"Care to adjourn upstairs, brother?" said Ozias, his eyes gleaming.

Cosmo made himself smile. "You seem to have your hands full."

"Oh, I do," said Ozias. "But Lucretia has had her eye upon you all evening, and Celia has plenty to ah, fill my hands."

"*I'm* Lucretia," said one of the women. "*She's* Celia."

Cosmo laughed and stood. "Well, I can imagine he confused you both because he was simply staggered by your beauty."

The women knew he was spinning a line, and laughed with playful disdain. The one called Celia glided forward, graceful and poised as any noble lady, though her garb was plain. Cosmo liked that; he liked a confident woman. He regarded her from head to heel, and she was indeed beautiful, plump and curvy with lively eyes and a charming dimpled smile. Her hair was swept to the side with comb, tumbling over one shoulder in a cascade of shiny auburn curls, and Cosmo could almost imagine filling his fist with those curls and pulling her in for a kiss. It was such a familiar impulse that the immediate revulsion that followed had him recoil and stumble.

He was drunker than he'd thought. "I think I'd better just go to bed," said Cosmo, in a tone that said *alone*.

Ozias made a face. "You've grown so dull in your old age," he said, before immediately turning his attention to his companions. "More for me, then."

Cosmo couldn't help but smile. Ozias truly hadn't changed, and better than that, he was back. How could he be upset? The wine made him warm and lazy. "I hope one of you ladies has a bed to fall to," he declared, "for I am laying claim to our humble chambers upstairs."

"You wouldn't cast me out in the street, would you?" Ozias asked the women, immediately building on Cosmo's jest. That was familiar too, the way they played off each other, read each other. Ozias would be just fine on his own. Cosmo wandered upstairs, taking the flagon with him. He found their room, with two small sleeping couches inside. The room was tiny enough they were almost touching. Cosmo chose one, collapsed upon it, and was asleep instantly.

He woke with an ache behind his brows and a sudden, gripping terror. Something was wrong. He sat up, gasping, turning around the room wildly. It took him a few moments to orient himself, and when he did, his heart began to pound. Ozias was nowhere to be found.

He cast about wildly, as if Ozias were hiding somewhere in the shadows of the miniscule room, and of course he wasn't. *What had happened to him?*

Where had Ozias gone? Had Cosmo lost him, again, already? Or, had he simply not returned after his evening tryst? His anxiety mounted swiftly to panic as the possibilities coursed through him. Why had they gone out carousing last night? They should have *talked*—they should have...there was a reason Ozias had remained hidden for four hundred years. Were people after him? Had they caught up with him last night, when he'd finally, *finally* revealed himself to his brother, who promptly abandoned him?

Fuck. *Fuck.* Fuck! Cosmo grabbed the first tunic he could reach and pulled it on, scarcely waiting till he was covered before pushing his way out the door and into the corridor. The sun had just risen, but the tavern still had a steady trickle of patrons, the hum of voices below had Cosmo's heart beating faster, and faster. When he turned the corner, he froze. Ozias sat at one of the tables, in last night's clothing, looking tired but hale as he had the day before. Across from him, laughing at something he'd just said, were the two women he'd picked up last night.

"*Ozias!*" Cosmo barked, loudly enough that he made himself wince. He had not meant to shout, but suddenly the entire room fell silent, staring at him.

Ozias looked genuinely surprised. "Come join us, brother!" he called.

"No," said Cosmo. "You, with me. Now." Where Cosmo gripped the banister, the wood smoldered. Ozias eyed the tiny whisps of smoke emerging from between Cosmo's fingers, at once wary, and stood. It was as if he cast aside a mask, so sudden was the change in his visage, and carriage. He bid a curt farewell to his female companions and stood, following Cosmo without another word. Cosmo ignored the indignant gasps from the ladies and turned on his heel.

As soon as Cosmo heard the door click shut behind Ozias, he whirled. "Where the *fuck* were you?"

Ozias let out a nervous laugh. "Downstairs? You just found me there."

"You were there all night? You slept there?"

Ozias shrugged. "I never said I *slept*. I haven't been to bed yet, at any rate." He turned toward the sleeping couch he'd eschewed the night before, and added, "I could use a rest now though..."

"Ozias, *stop.*"

"Stop what?"

"You have to—here, come sit down."

Ozias sat. To look at him, you'd think he was entirely bemused at Cosmo's ire. But Cosmo knew better. The confusion did not reach Ozias's eyes, which remained nervous and wary. That was when Cosmo knew, for certain, that there was something his brother wasn't telling him—something he was desperate to keep concealed.

Cosmo narrowed his eyes. "Tell me," he said.

"Tell you what?" Ozias was a silver-tongued trickster, but Cosmo knew all his tells. He was trying to evade this line of questioning.

Last night, it might have worked, but Cosmo was sober, he was afraid, and he was angry. "Tell me what kept you away for four *hundred* years."

"It is a difficult tale to tell," Ozias said.

"I can imagine," said Cosmo, with an encouraging smile. "I will do my best not to interrupt."

Ozias took some time to gather himself, staring down at his hands. "I supposed it began a few months before the day you were supposed to duel with Kryos."

"A few *months?*" Cosmo blurted.

Ozias laughed. "Your vow of silence proves already broken."

"Apologies," said Cosmo, reddening.

"No need," said Ozias. "It is a comfort, to know that some things have not changed."

Here he paused once again, and Cosmo gripped his shoulder. "Carry on," said Cosmo. "I am listening."

"As you know, father had given the four of you part of his grace. The godsblood that allowed you to control the seasons."

Cosmo nodded, not wanting to already interrupt for a second time.

"Though I loved you all, my brothers, there were times I felt invisible in that palace. I could move from place to place unnoticed. I had always heard more than I was meant, something I realized as I grew older. Father spoke with...with the Empress," and here Ozias's voice cracked, bitter. Even after all this time.

Cosmo shifted uncomfortably where he sat. He loved his mother, but he had to admit she had never shown anything but cold, begrudging tolerance to Ozias's presence in her home.

Ozias let the moment pass, and carried on the story. "I was not meant to hear," he said. "I knew as much, instantly. But I could not help but listen. Your mother loved the four of you well, and she was determined to see you all at equal standing. The four shining princes of the realm, the gods of the four seasons. Equals. Partners."

Cosmo couldn't help but scoff. This had been much the sentiment expressed by Auro, and even now, four hundred years gone from the endless fighting between the four of them, Cosmo still could not imagine how their mother had been so naïve as to think the four of them could rule side by side.

"Father disagreed," said Ozias. "He was determined that one of you would be the *true* heir to his power. 'Four quarrelsome sons will bring the world to ruin,' he told her."

A shiver went down Cosmo's spine. His father's presence was gone from the world, but for the moment he felt as though the man were here with them. Tall and stern and unyielding, staring down at Cosmo as if he were still an unruly child.

"The four of you fought so much," said Ozias. "And with such heat—I didn't think that any words would bring the four of you to reason. I feared you'd destroy each other, or father would destroy you all. The only way to save your lives was for one of you to rise to the top of his preference, for one of you to become the heir he wanted. A *peaceful* transition of power."

Cosmo had to bite his tongue to keep from blurting out what he thought of *that*. His brothers had not shared anything peacefully since they were old enough to learn that their father had such expectations of them.

"It seemed impossible to me, too," Ozias admitted, as if he'd read Cosmo's thoughts. "But I had to try, didn't I?"

This seemed a rhetorical question, but Cosmo couldn't help the way he nodded in reply.

"So, I talked to each of you, watched each of you. And I watched father, and the way he looked at you all. As you know," said Ozias, "I came to the conclusion that it had to be you, or Kryos, who took the lead."

"The strangest thing about this tale is that you had me on your short list," Cosmo said, without thinking. How could Ozias have thought Cosmo worthy? He wasn't as strong as Kryos, as wise as Cedras, or as benevolent as Auro. He wasn't much of anything.

"You and Kryos were premier in father's eyes," said Ozias. "He loved you both, for I think he saw in both of you the most of himself."

Cosmo frowned, unsure if he should be insulted or not.

"Winter and Summer seem opposites," said Ozias, "but that's really just on the surface. Just like you and Kryos. Cedras and Auro are not like you two. Their blood does not run hot enough, the desire to rule does not burn inside them the way it does for you."

"I don't know that I have that desire," Cosmo admitted. It was the first time he'd said it out loud. "Perhaps that was the problem. Had I been more willing to yield, to admit I never was cut out for taking our father's place...this could all have been avoided. Had he chosen me—I don't even know what would have happened. To us, or...or the world."

"Perhaps," said Ozias, and his voice had with it now a bite of impatience. "But there is more to tell."

"Of course, go on."

"So, it was you or Kryos, then," said Ozias. "Now, I knew the two of you could never come to terms on your own.

The only way you'd see reason was with some...help. I must admit, it shames me now to say, but I tried to reason with Kryos first."

This brought Cosmo up short; it was the first of Ozias's revelations that truly shocked him. Kryos had never had much time for Ozias, for most of his younger brothers at all really. Ozias had never had much kind to say about Kryos, either, in their youth. Cosmo had always considered Ozias his closest confidant, and he couldn't deny that even after all these years, the admission that he hadn't trusted Cosmo stung. Perhaps more than it should have.

"I know," said Ozias, his voice apologetic. He must have read the hurt on Cosmo's face. "I know, and it is perhaps my biggest regret. But Kryos *was* our elder, and if the path of least resistance was the path to peace between us all, well, I thought it was worth trying to reason with him."

Objectively, Cosmo could see that this notion had its merits. He might have even agreed, had he been hearing the facts presented about a stranger's family. But it still left a bitter taste in his mouth. Even Ozias, the brother he'd been closest to, had known from the very start that Cosmo was the weakest reed among them.

"As you know, Kryos claimed he would only listen to reason if you could best him in combat. I was so caught up in my own plans of helping you that I fell prey to one Kryos had been cooking all along."

It was as if all of the worst, twisted and darkest fears Cosmo had harbored about his brother crashed over him like waves, and soon he would be drowning. He'd been right about Kryos all along—he never meant to have any sort of harmony with the brothers.

"With your grace and his own, he would be twice as powerful as Auro and Cedras," Ozias continued. "They would not be able to stand against him, and he was convinced that with you gone, they would bend to his will. When he realized I knew the truth, he moved to kill me, before I could tell you."

"It *was* on purpose," Cosmo said, aghast. "Auro thought—perhaps a mistake...he thought you were me, and aimed only to wound."

Ozias shook his head sadly. "Auro is too sweet for the burdens of gods," he said. "He always wanted to see the good in us—even if he had to invent that good."

Cosmo nodded. That was exactly how he had felt when he'd first woken to this mess. His head spun, and his first instinct was that he wished things could go back to how they had been, for four hundred years. Cosmo was happy, or *fine,* at least, and the seasons had been in harmony with one another. The people of the continent, the plants, the beasts, all of them had gotten exactly what they needed without any of this dicing with the politics of gods. But no, before he had not known Ozias lived. He had been wracked with his own guilts —Auro too! Cedras had always been more aloof, but certainly he nursed his own feelings of shame regarding what had happened. They had all carried this for so long...Suddenly, Cosmo frowned. "Why did you wait so long?"

Ozias flinched, and looked down in his lap at his hands. The gesture was achingly familiar; all at once a thousand memories crashed through Cosmo's mind's eye. For the first time, Cosmo realized he was angry with Ozias. *Furious.* The last four hundred years of misery, of guilt, of grief and loneliness, all of it had predicated on the fact that Ozias had perished.

But he hadn't. Here he was. He had hidden, allowing his brothers to suffer, cursed, in shame and guilt and mourning for nearly half a millennium. "Cosmo..."

"Why didn't you reveal yourself...to me, or any of us?"

Ozias grew deeply troubled. "I could not," he

said. "Kryos hunted me, every winter. I had no idea if he had communicated with the three of you, if you'd chain me to his statue so I'd be there right when he woke to take my head!"

"For four *hundred* years?" Cosmo asked. He frowned. That did not feel right. As frightening as Kryos might be—he still only woke for three turns of the moon, every year.

"He tried to *kill* me, Cosmo," said Ozias sternly. "His own brother. In cold blood. So that he could kill *you,* too. Imagine Kryos, with that much power. Auro and Cedras would hardly have been safe, either."

It was difficult for Cosmo to truly imagine Kryos was that dangerous—proving only that he was as childishly naïve as Auro, and Ozias had been right not to trust either of them. Cosmo looked at his brother, the way his eyes swam with misery. He reached for Ozias's shoulder, gripping it tight. "You are safe now," said Cosmo. He wasn't certain that was true, so he clarified. "You are safe with me."

Ozias offered him a tremulous smile. "I have missed you."

"And I you," said Cosmo, unable to resist pulling Ozias in for a hug. "I feel as though I have so much to tell you—but all I can think is how amazing it is that you're *here.*"

"We should leave for Papia, at once," said Ozias. "I'm eager to see Auro, too."

Cosmo opened his mouth to agree, but something tugged at him.

Ozias's smile flickered, just for a second. "What is it?"

"Nothing," Cosmo said. He forced another smile. "You're right, we should leave at once."

"Is there a reason we should delay?"

"No, of course not. We *must* return to Papia," said

Cosmo, shaking his head to clear it. "Auro will be thrilled to see you."

"It's such a relief to know the two of you are on my side."

"Of *course,* we are. You'll see. We will get to the bottom of this, I swear it."

They packed up the rest of their things, and headed down to the stables where Cosmo had put up Hestia. It was high time they returned to Papia to see Auro. Cosmo considered trying to send a messenger ahead, but thought better of it. Ozias was so afraid, and the letter could be very dangerous if it fell into the wrong hands—and if, of course, the message thief believed a word of what they read. They sought the stablemaster out, and inquired if she knew of any mounts for sale in the town. With a few coins to fill her palm she was more than happy to inquire around the city to find a suitable mount for sale. While Cosmo spoke with her, Ozias clucked impatiently. He'd thought it more efficient for the two of them to steal him a mount. "Who knows how long it will take her," he said, once she was out of earshot. "We should be upon our way, *now.*"

"A few more hours won't make difference," said Cosmo, troubled. "And I have coin. There's no point in thievery when it can be avoided."

With a lot of grumbling, Ozias finally agreed that half a day would hardly make a world of difference on their return to Papia. They returned to the inn where they'd stayed the night before to await the stablemaster. Over another flagon of wine, Cosmo wondered if Leofric had made it home yet.

Probably not—it had only been a few days. It was hard to know; Cosmo imagined Leofric would push his horse hard in attempt to make it back to Laela and Sorex as swiftly as possible. He wondered what would happen, when they saw each other once again in Papia. The thought turned his stomach a bit—he missed Leofric so fiercely it was like an ache in his chest, a hunger he couldn't abate, but the angry twist to his features had only grown uglier in Cosmo's mind's eye. Even a few days later, Cosmo could not recall if his face had truly looked that hateful, or if it was Cosmo's own misery aiding in its conjuring.

As they waited, Ozias suggested they search for his feminine companions from the night before, now that they had time to spare. Cosmo could only summon a half-hearted, preoccupied grunt in response.

"Alright," said Ozias abruptly. "What is it?"

"What is what?"

"You *must* tell me what has you in such a state," Ozias said. "I have never known you to turn down any sort of willing, intimate company. And of course, there is that look on your face."

"What look?"

"The look of a whipped cur," said Ozias. "At first, I thought it was me—but it's plain something else is weighing on your mind. So, tell me."

Cosmo fidgeted a bit in his seat.

Ozias softened, and reached across the table to pat Cosmo's arm. "We always shared our courtship woes, before."

They had. Ozias and Cosmo had always been there for one another, been each other's stalwart lieutenant in all matters of the heart and body. Perhaps Ozias could help him make sense of this tangle Cosmo found himself in. He began to speak of Leofric, of everything that had transpired between them since their tumultuous first meeting when Cosmo had burned him, all the way through their parting.

The telling of it took a surprisingly long time, considering it had only been two months since they'd met. Ozias listened through the entire thing, his frown deepening with every piece of the tale Cosmo relayed. "He thought I was chasing ghosts," Cosmo finished. "And his family is everything to him."

"It sounds like there's a lot you two haven't said," Ozias said.

Cosmo made a face.

"You are always talking," said Ozias. "Why not speak *to* him?"

"I doubt he'll even want to see me, after the way we left things."

"He'll have to," said Ozias. "He's returning Kryos's Grace to Papia, is he not?"

"Once he ascertains his son's safety, yes," said Cosmo.

Ozias threw back his drink and stood. "Well, then what are we waiting for?"

"What?"

"We're only a few days behind him," Ozias declared. "Let's go."

Twenty-Four

Leofric was on edge. Even more so than usual. After his arrival in Sokol served only to scare Laela and Sorex out of their wits, after he'd made absolutely certain that his son was *fine*, Leofric's mind went back to the letter he'd received. He examined every speck of ink upon the page, and the paper itself, as if the missive would suddenly blurt out the name of whoever had committed the forgery, and why.

Leofric felt most comfortable with *someone* to fight, a vessel for his anger, for his plans of defense or retribution. Thus, the question of *who* occupied the lion's share of his mind. It was possibly the larger mystery of the thing, but unfortunately, the *who* did not frighten him so much as *why*. The only reason someone would forge such a letter would be to ensure Leofric raced home as soon as possible. Looking at the letter now, he regretted his heedless charge more than ever. He hated being played for a fool, and he'd fallen right into this trap. But, also, what *was* the trap? Get him...home?

That couldn't possibly be it. So, then, he had to ponder what someone would hope to achieve by bringing him here.

By the time Laela had made breakfast for the three of them, Leofric had a pounding headache and no answers.

"Have you been sitting here all night?" Laela asked him as she set a plate before Leofric on the table.

Leofric twisted the handle of his dagger, the point of it sticking into the wood. "Yes," he admitted.

"And have you anything to show for it? Besides a gouge in my table?"

"Apologies," he said. "And no. Nothing I can think of."

"Perhaps you'd be better served after getting some rest," Laela coaxed him. "I can't imagine your wits are at their sharpest."

Leofric grumbled, but didn't argue with her. She was correct, of course. However, he felt as though there were something obvious staring him in the face, and he didn't want to succumb to sleep until he'd realized what it was.

"Perhaps you won't sleep because you feel guilty," said Laela.

"Because I—what? Sorex is fine!"

"Aye," said Laela. "But is Cosmo?"

That stung. While Leofric's first duty was indeed to his family, now that he knew he'd been tricked, he felt thrice as guilty for his deranged flight, and the way he'd left Cosmo behind, the way he'd lashed out. Cosmo, who had been so willing to follow him, to put his own mission aside, to delay the return of his brother's... "Oh," said Leofric.

"See?" Said Laela smugly. "I knew—"

"No, Laela, go get Sorex. Now."

"What?"

"Please," he said earnestly, all trace of tiredness vanishing in his mounting fear. "Just go get him. Now."

She knew him well, sensed the change in his tone and demeanor. Laela might not have all the details, but she was sharp enough to know at once that the three of them were in danger. She left the kitchen to find her son, whom she'd allowed to sleep in after Leofric's rude awakening the night before.

When he entered the kitchen with his mother, yawning and stumbling, the lad said, "I'd somewhat thought your return a dream," he said.

"No dream," said Leofric. "Both of you, sit."

They did as they were bid, plainly frightened. Leofric reached across the table and took one of each of their hands in one of his own. He had to weigh his words carefully—how much to tell, how much to shield them from. Sorex was young, but he was smart and strong, and it would only be the three of them here against whatever might be headed their way. It would not be right to hide from them the encroaching threats.

"Listen," he began. "We are in grave, *grave* danger."

They both started to speak at once, but Leofric silenced them with a squeeze of their hands.

"You will have questions, I know, but first, let me explain." He had told Laela the basics of who Cosmo was, and Leofric's mission with him, but he hadn't explained the grim details of what had occurred with Janus, and Sorex knew none of it. Speaking quickly, he told them of the great power Cosmo had trusted him to carry, and that there was someone out there who would do *anything* to get a hold of that power.

Laela's face drained of blood as he spoke, so that by the time he finished, she was pale as a ghost. "We should go," she said. "At once."

Leofric shook his head. "I fear the time for flight has passed," he said. "If they sent this letter, and I received it six days late, there is a chance Janus has men in place, watching the house."

He could have explained about the grotesque clay soldiers that Janus commanded, but he didn't think that information would help them prepare—they had to be ready for an assault, and for that it mattered not if it were men or golems who came at them.

"Then, what are we to do?"

Leofric felt a pang, detecting the fear in Sorex's voice, the tiny waver in the question. He was trying so hard to be brave, but he was still only a boy. He offered his son a grim, but encouraging smile. "We stay. We prepare. And if we must—we *fight.*"

Janus was dangerous, and powerful. Leofric had given Laela and Sorex some tasks to prepare the villa to withstand a basic attack, but Leofric was not certain Janus would come at them with soldiers, or the weapons of men. He might work his dark powers to create some new threat, against which a blade or walls were useless. But he had to try, didn't he? He prowled the walls that surrounded the villa, checking for points of entry or weakness, and bracing the front gate and the postern door with logs. Sorex helped him getting three mounts ready to ride. Leofric felt a pang as he patted the side of Lyra's neck. If they had to make a flight tonight or tomorrow, he would have to leave her behind. She was near blown after Leofric's hasty flight from Mount Hiru, and she'd had no chance yet to recover. He unhooked the latches of the stalls of the other horses to be left behind as well, knowing the fountain and the grass in the yard would sustain them for a while, and if he had chance to send a message to one of his old comrades in arms to collect them once he and his family were well away, he would.

For himself, Leofric had saddled Selene, who had been Hamalcar's warhorse. After his brother's death, Leofric could not bring himself to ride her, the grief far too close. Nor could he bring himself to sell the beast, despite knowing she would fetch a good price, and neither Laela nor Sorex had call for a warhorse on their modest farm. He was grateful they'd kept her, now, though he hoped none of them would have to flee.

Never had Leofric hoped so badly that he was mistaken about what was to come; never had he been so certain he wasn't. There were now, to his knowledge, two vessels containing the power of gods. One was deeply hidden in the villa at Papia, in its vaults, guarded by a dozen loyal men, surrounded by walls and other guards, with Auro and Alexios nearby to remain on alert.

The other was under the pillow in Leofric's bedroom, with only himself, his wife and son to keep it safe. For one wild moment, Leofric wondered what would happen if he simply cracked open the bottle and drank it, but as he hefted it in one hand, feeling the chill seep through the glass and deep into the bones of his hand, he thought better of it. Some things were not for men to trifle with.

At Laela's insistence, Leofric did sleep for a few hours in the afternoon. He knew as well as she did that an exhausted soldier was a worthless soldier, but all the same, he found it difficult to quiet his mind long enough to rest. It was sunset when he woke, and sent Laela and Sorex down into the cellar, in which they'd been stashing food and other supplies all day. "Bar the door. Do not come out, for anyone but me," he said. "This man can create strange illusions, so even if you hear my voice, wait for the password."

"What's the password?" Asked Sorex.

"*Hamalcar.*"

Laela's jaw tightened, but she nodded. Leofric had wanted to choose something personal, something an imposter would most likely not know. As he sat in the villa's modest atrium, his sword upon his lap, Leofric honed the steel and waited. And waited. He had put Kryos's grace safely down below with his family. Leofric wasn't certain how much he truly owed Cosmo, Auro and the rest of them—but regardless, Leofric knew in his heart that a man like Janus should never have access to a god's power. However, he told his family that should he, Leofric, fall defending them, they should use whatever they could to barter for their own safety. Sorex looked grim at that moment, his eyes wide in his young face, real terror bleeding in. He was brave, and obedient, but the way Leofric spoke put fear in him. Good. Boys should be a little afraid, lest they not live long enough to become men.

Leofric let the fires die and the torches gutter to nothing. He lit neither sconce nor candle, simply sat upon his stool, back rigid, and waited some more. His eyes adjusted to the dark, and soon enough Leofric existed in a world made entirely of shadows. It had been silent so long he could almost have dozed again, but he kept himself alert by the meditative task of honing his weapon. He took stock again, in his head, of the villa's defenses. They were few—but then again, Janus had been run out of Neossós with only his skin and presumably no longer had an army behind him. While his own fell power was significant, someone without allies might hesitate to attack a place where the people stood prepared.

A noise caught Leofric's ear. He stopped the movement of the whetstone and strained against the ambient sound of summer nights. A thud, a rustle. What sounded like a muffled curse. Silent as a grave, Leofric stood, sword in hand. *Never touch your sword unless you mean to draw it. Never draw your sword unless you mean to use it.* Well, if someone had designs on harming his family, Leofric meant to use his sword, without hesitation. The familiar sense of calm washed over him as he strode through the darkened villa, the shadows his friends, helping conceal his movements as he listened for more evidence of the intruder, or intruders. This, *this* he knew. The foe. The fight. These were things with which Leofric was comfortable. He moved into the yard, his path cleaving tight to the wall. He saw a pair of small shadows, across the way, shrouded in cloaks. *Two then, for now,* Leofric thought. Prepared, he was confident he could take two—assuming, of course, that neither was a dark sorcerer. Janus's strange powers would certainly even the contest somewhat. Leofric crept up as close to them as he dared, and lunged. He bowled into one of the shadows, sending him sprawling with another muffled curse. Before the man on the ground could right himself, Leofric seized the other by the shoulder and spun him, drawing his sword back to plunge it into the—

"*Cosmo!?*" Leofric nearly dropped his sword in shock.

Beneath the intruder's hood sat a familiar mop of scarlet hair, sheepish grin, and staggering array of freckles. Cosmo winced, staring up at the sword. Leofric did not lower it; this could very well be some trick. The second man was regaining his feet, and Leofric had to act quickly, to decide if this really was Cosmo.

"Would you like to come inside? I can make you some dinner," he said carefully.

Cosmo frowned. "Are you planning to use the sword? Because that's the only way you're convincing me to eat something *you* cooked."

Leofric let out a sigh of relief, and a laugh. He dropped the sword and surprised even himself when he picked Cosmo up in his arms and spun him around.

Cosmo released a shaky laugh too—but his eyes remained wary. "Alright," he said. "What's going on here?"

"I second that question," said a voice behind Leofric. He spun around to see the other intruder peeling back the hood of his cloak to reveal a pale face with a scruffy beard and shoulder-length tangle of dark hair.

He looked familiar to Leofric, but he couldn't quite place it. Then, it hit him like a boulder. Leofric whirled back to Cosmo. "You *found* him?"

Cosmo chewed his bottom lip and nodded. "After—well, right after you left, actually."

"Technically, I found *him*," said the dark-haired young man who could only be Cosmo's dead brother, Ozias.

The silence, sudden and awkward, brought the reality of their parting screaming back. And besides, just because *this* intruder happened to be an ally, it didn't mean the next would be so friendly. "We'd best go inside," he said. "There's much to discuss."

Cosmo winced, looking very like the child caught misbehaving. It stirred something warm and fond in Leofric's chest, but he stifled it. Now was not the time.

Cosmo followed Leofric into the darkened villa, wondering what on earth had him so on edge in the dead of night.

"I told you we should have waited till morning," Ozias hissed as they trailed behind their host.

"You were right," Cosmo ceded, though at the time nothing had seemed more prudent than getting to Leofric as quickly as possible. He hadn't necessarily expected a *warm* welcome, after the way they'd left things, but he hadn't expected Leofric to draw a blade on him, either. Something was going on, something that had very little to do with Cosmo.

"Is Sorex alright?" He asked, forcing himself to break the silence.

"Yes," said Leofric curtly. But he offered no further information. Once inside, Leofric deposited Cosmo and Ozias at the kitchen table and left. He scarcely cast a glance in Cosmo's direction, and Cosmo's heart fell. Ozias stood and began shuffling around the darkened kitchen, lighting a fire. By the time Leofric returned with his family in tow, the kitchen was aglow in orange and gold.

"Cosmo," said Laela, surprised. "Were we expecting you?"

"Only if you're an oracle," said Cosmo. "This is my brother, Ozias."

"Pleasure to meet you, Ozias," said Laela. Her courtesies were polished, coming out of her mouth while she still plainly grappled with the strangeness of the evening.

Cosmo looked to Sorex, who apart from a look of terror on his face, seemed hale and healthy as when Cosmo had last seen him. "The boy looks well," he said, relieved.

"He was never ill," said Leofric harshly.

"Pardon?"

"I think possibly," said Laela loudly, "it would best if we start from the beginning."

"That will take all night," Ozias complained.

An unhinged laugh burbled out of Cosmo's mouth, and everyone turned to stare at him, except Leofric, who seemed singularly focused on memorizing the contour of his own fingernails. "The letter was a forgery," Laela explained to Cosmo. "We were fine, here."

"Why would someone do that?"

"To separate us." Leofric spoke at last, and it seemed he finally had mustered his courage to look Cosmo in the eye.

Cosmo was confused. "Why?" He repeated.

"I'm assuming it has to do with Kryos's grace," said Leofric.

Ozias fidgeted nervously in his seat, like invoking Kryos's name would summon him to Leofric's kitchen. "Is it that sorcerer? That...Janus?"

"I can think of no other," said Leofric. "Though if it's not him, that presents its own unique set of problems."

"You're not wrong," said Cosmo.

Leofric leveled a gaze at Ozias, considering him for a long moment. "You look pretty hale for a dead man."

Ozias laughed, and Cosmo couldn't help but smile too.

The awkwardness settled over the kitchen until Leofric

stood. "You two may not be the attackers I was expecting, but it doesn't mean we're out of danger. Laela—"

She rested her hands on her son's shoulders and gave them a squeeze. "We're going to bed."

"But—"

"*Now.*"

When Laela and Sorex were gone, and it was just Cosmo, Leofric and Ozias at the table, the awkwardness had grown even worse somehow. Ozias looked between them, back and forth, before biting his lip and standing as well. "I believe I too will get some rest," he announced. "I saw a comfortable looking settle just in the sitting room."

And then it was just the two of them. Cosmo tried with all of his might to let Leofric be the one to break the silence, but really, who was he kidding?

"Can we—?"

"Outside?"

"Alright."

Warily, Cosmo followed Leofric into the modest stable within the villa walls. Then, they were still in awkward silence, except it had a backdrop of cicadas and other night creatures to dull it, and the aroma of dung and straw to accent it. They stood for a while, looking up at the ceiling and not at each other.

Finally, Cosmo couldn't take it any longer. He was nervous, but he was angry too. "I'm glad Sorex is alright," he said carefully.

"Me, as well," said Leofric. More silence.

Cosmo opened his mouth and closed it several times, at an utter loss.

Leofric gave a sharp intake of breath and blurted, "Oh, fuck this."

And before Cosmo could blink, Leofric had seized his

shoulder, spun him around and yanked him close. "But—"
And then his mouth was there, his tongue, his lips his teeth.

"I'm sorry," Leofric murmured between kisses. "I'm so sorry."

"It's—I'm—*hnng*," he returned the kisses, eagerly. Ravenously. Cosmo couldn't stop himself from digging his hands into the front of Leofric's tunic, clutching tightly, as if he feared Leofric would change his mind again.

"I missed you," Leofric breathed into Cosmo's hair. "I missed you so much."

"And with a straight face you said that," said Cosmo. He drew back, looking into Leofric's eyes.

They were wild, darting all over, fearful. He took a step in, closing the distance between them once again. His eyes fell to Cosmo's lips and he stooped, trying to capture them in a kiss. Presumably to prevent words from coming out. Cosmo had a lot of them, queued up over the days he'd spent on the road with Ozias, choice things he'd say to Leofric when they came face to face again, but with Leofric's tongue in his mouth, his big hands clutched tight to Cosmo's back, his teeth eating eagerly at Cosmo's lips, all of those words somehow fell away.

Frantic, Cosmo pushed against the hard expanse of Leofric's chest, deepening their kiss. When he needed to catch his breath, he raised his palms to shove Leofric back a step, until he collided with the wall of the stable. He grunted as his head connected, but it did nothing to slow either of them down. Leofric tore at Cosmo's tunic, until the fabric came apart in his hands. He tossed it aside and wasted no time yanking free the knot of Cosmo's subligaria. The night air flowed over Cosmo's bare skin, and he shoved at Leofric's clothing too, until he pulled his own tunic off and cast it to the ground. Naked—excepting their sandals—Cosmo and Leofric rut against one another, grinding dry and rough until they were both hard and panting desperately in the heat of the night.

Cosmo realized he was still furious, still bursting with all the things he wanted to say. All the things he *needed* to say. But instead of saying them, he bit Leofric's bottom lip, hard enough to taste blood. Leofric whined, in pain perhaps, but it was more than that. He pressed himself shamelessly against Cosmo's thigh, his cock a rod of throbbing steel. Tilting his head with a grin, Cosmo let Leofric hump his leg for a moment, allowing Leofric to bury his face in Cosmo's throat to suck desperately at his skin, to nip the tendons of his neck, perhaps just to hide his face while he ground against Cosmo's thigh. They broke apart, gasping. And Leofric spared himself a heartbeat to rake his eyes greedily over Cosmo from head to toe before lunging for him again.

Being wanted *so* badly was a heady thing.

With his hands on Leofric's wrists, Cosmo tugged him toward the ground. As one, without breaking their kiss, they moved first to kneel upon the stable floor. Cosmo tangled a hand in Leofric's hair, wrapping the end of his sleek, oiled braid around his fist. With a yank, he drew Leofric's head back, all while clamping his teeth down on Leofric's lower lip. Hard.

Leofric cried out, but Cosmo knew him well enough by now, knew he liked it to hurt. Liked his pleasure sauced with pain. However, Cosmo had never taken such aggressive liberties with Leofric before, keeping his nips light and the desperate push of his fingertips playful.

Not so, now. Inside Cosmo, something flared white-hot. Leofric thought he could leave *him*? Cosmo wanted to be certain he *never* left him, never forgot him, no matter how long he lived. He ached to leave a real mark upon Leofric's body, like the battle scars he wore from head to heel. Like the tattoos on his skin, telling the story of the life he'd lived.

Cosmo was part of that story now, whether Leofric wanted him to be or not. He had earned the right to leave his mark.

Cosmo rolled them both until he was on top, and pinned Leofric's arms above his head. Leofric was strong but Cosmo was stronger, the weight of the divine on his side as he used his knees to shove Leofric's thighs apart. Leofric submitted entirely, so eager, so desperate. Cosmo lowered his lips and showered kisses on his upturned throat, interspersed with sharp nips and deep suckling against his skin until he had a collar of rosy bruises and lay weak and trembling beneath Cosmo's assault. Leofric chased Cosmo's mouth with his own, murmuring against his lips, equal parts weak pleas and apologies.

I'm sorry. I need you. I'm sorry. Cosmo could only nod in reply, accepting each individual entreaty as the earnest offering it was—but Cosmo was a god, after all.

And gods were greedy.

Mere offerings were not enough. He required devotion. He required *sacrifice*. He kissed his way to the shell of Leofric's ear, and after teasing it with his tongue, he whispered, "Turn over."

Leofric's breath hitched, and he nodded like Cosmo was giving him a precious gift. "Yes."

Scrambling, Leofric maneuvered himself onto his front, and Cosmo blanketed Leofric's body with his own, pressing against his back. It allowed him to grind his cock in the cleft of Leofric's ass, muscular cheeks clenching helplessly around Cosmo's shaft. He kissed his way up the valley of Leofric's broad, tanned shoulders, licking the sweat from his skin. Gently, he brushed Leofric's hair away from the nape of his neck. He leaned down to whisper in his ear again. "I'm going to fuck you now," he growled.

Leofric arched his back. "*Yes.*"

Cosmo smiled, panting. He was so hard he could barely

see straight. They'd fucked before of course, in all manner of positions all over the cave at the top of Mount Hiru, but Cosmo could have sworn it was the first time. He'd seen Leofric without his clothes but he didn't think he'd ever seen him quite *this* naked.

He faltered, just for a moment. He was frightened. He doubted. After being so rudely abandoned, Cosmo didn't quite trust Leofric's offerings. He had to be certain. He had to —Cosmo let the hand on Leofric's hip soften, brushing tiny, delicate circles against the bone with his thumb. He leaned in once more, to whisper again. "*It*...it is going to hurt."

It may not have sounded like it, but it was a question.

And once again, Leofric answered him, without hesitating. "*Yes.*"

Twenty-Five

There was a part of Leofric, a small, feeble part, that considered letting Cosmo mount and fuck him in the stable wasn't the wisest course of action, given that his family was just inside and they all might be attacked by a dark sorcerer at any moment.

But that part of him died as Cosmo seized Leofric's hips and thrust his cock deep. Cosmo didn't have the biggest cock Leofric had ever taken, but he felt every inch of it as Cosmo fucked into him. The spit on Cosmo's fingers—and then again on his shaft—was a far cry from the delicious, sultry slickness of oil, reminding Leofric of some of his earliest adolescent fumbling, desperate and painful and hurried.

Leofric had liked the burn of it, even then. He'd liked the sting. Now, he loved it. Craved it. Needed it. Wave after wave of pleasure-pain shot through Leofric as he canted his hips, bowing his spine to offer himself to Cosmo, to give everything he was, everything he had, allowing him to take what he wanted. He was so glad Cosmo had come that he would deny him nothing. If this were his punishment for the things he'd said, he would take it joyfully, and beg Cosmo for more.

His hardness had waned, slightly, as Cosmo forced him open and invaded, but as they fell into a rhythm together it returned in full force, bobbing rigidly between his thighs. Cosmo's grunts and brutal thrusting pace couldn't have been more different than the slow, exploratory erotic torture he'd exposed Leofric to on the mountain. That had been nothing like any lovemaking Leofric had ever known, and this was different again. He was being fucked with the fury of a god, and as tears stung the corners of his eyes, he used his body to thank Cosmo for this furious and terrible blessing. Like a hurricane, an earthquake, or a great flood. You must thank the gods for that as much as you thanked them for a full harvest, or a sunrise.

The scent of sweat and leather and horses and fucking overpowered Leofric, sending him deeper, deeper into the world Cosmo made for them both. With a firm hand between his shoulder blades, Cosmo pushed him down, closer to the ground. He could tell Cosmo was close, his breaths short and erratic, his thrusts off rhythm, the grip of his fingers frantic.

Leofric wanted so badly to turn around to look at Cosmo. To see the fury on his face, to see the fire burning in his eyes. To see his freckles, and the savage smirk he loved so well. But when he tried to turn, Cosmo tightened his hold on Leofric's hair and gave it a yank. It was a warning, keeping Leofric's head in place, his cheek pressed to the ground. Leofric was reminded of those old stories where the hero's fortitude was tested, where he must perform a feat without looking over his shoulder at whatever might be lurking there.

He was not to look, just now. But he wanted to, more badly than he'd ever wanted to look at something in his life. Like he couldn't believe Cosmo was really there unless he could see with his own two eyes. Leofric struggled a bit; he couldn't help it, bucking and twisting and writhing.

A resounding *slap* filled the heated, moist air around

them, and Leofric was so startled by the sound it took a moment for him to register the pain. Cosmo had wound up and smacked Leofric's ass with an open palm, hard. Very hard. Leofric cried out even as he felt his cock throb with want.

The slap brought him back to himself a bit, desire flowing from the stinging imprint of Cosmo's hand. The slap was an order, and Leofric followed orders. Obediently, he stopped struggling and surrendered himself entirely, not even minding the way the straw on the floor poked into his cheek where it pressed against the ground.

Besides, by now, he knew Cosmo. Knew what he liked. Knew what he needed, and sure as sunrise, soon Cosmo looped a thin, wiry arm around Leofric's chest and pulled him up, and back, pressing his front to Leofric's back to grind deep against his ass. From this angle Cosmo could hit deep and hard, and Leofric let himself fall back, weak in Cosmo's arms. His climax galloped toward him, threatening to overtake him and run him down as Cosmo reached around Leofric's front to take his aching cock in hand. Leofric knew better than to try to touch himself, but he needed to do something with his hands, so he reached one up, and back, cupping Cosmo's skull and the silky softness of his fragrant hair. He did not have to look. He could feel, he could smell. With his mouth open and panting it was like he could taste Cosmo on the air around them. Leofric knew a fissure of alarm as he realized the two of them were heating up. Literally. Cosmo continued to jerk him, hard and fast, and Leofric could almost imagine the smoke from where the friction burned.

Cosmo had one hand braced upon Leofric's shoulder, his palm growing hot as the sweat poured off both of them, their bodies growing slicker and wetter, their skin more fevered.

"Do it," Leofric blurted.

Cosmo faltered, just for a moment. "What?"

"Burn me," he breathed. "Do it. I want you to. *Please.*"

"I—what? Why?"

"Because you want to," said Leofric. "I can feel it."

Cosmo buried his face in Leofric's hair, the thrusting of his hips slowing to something far less brutal, but no less deep. "You will run from me, again."

"No," said Leofric.

"You will," Cosmo insisted, his voice cracking as he said it.

Leofric covered Cosmo's hand with his own, the one that rested on his shoulder, growing warmer and warmer with every passing second. He squeezed Cosmo's fingers. "Please. Let me show you that I won't run from you, ever again."

Cosmo's entire body shook, with fear, or want, or perhaps with the effort of holding back the power that so clearly wanted to burst out of him. He pressed a tender kiss to Leofric's shoulder, soft and sweet, before he unleashed himself. Leofric braced his hands on the ground to push back against Cosmo, meeting him thrust for thrust as Cosmo pounded into him, fucking hard and fast, slinging his hips against Leofric like a rutting beast. One hand slid down to grasp his hip, and the other grabbed his shoulder. It was right, he thought suddenly. Cosmo's hands heated further with every passing second, and it seemed to Leofric that the cock inside him warmed too, though mercifully not quite as much. He had no interest in being cooked from the inside out.

Faster.

Harsher.

Hotter.

Cosmo quaked like a rupturing volcano, and it was like Leofric could see sparks flying all around them as the points of connection between them ignited. He could imagine Cosmo's palms like red hot brands where they gripped his skin, searing the flesh. Oh, how he wished he was granted permission to look.

At first, Leofric barely felt the pain, and he came with his cock untouched, spurting onto the rushes upon the stable floor, waves of ecstasy smothering anything else that threatened to take hold of him. He was not a soldier, nor a husband, then. Not a father, not a brother, nor even a man, any longer. He was Cosmo's, and that was all he was.

His eyes rolled, pleasure and pain now warring as Cosmo's fingers burned into his skin. His cock pulsed fitfully as his climax went on, and on, and on, and each pulse carried in pain, and out pleasure, like waves, sucking him out into a turbulent sea.

Eventually, the waves washed him to shore again, and he came back to himself, lying face down on the stable floor, covered in sweat and straw and cum and bruises. He half expected to find himself covered in soot from Cosmo's fiery heat. Gingerly, he shifted to a kneeling position, searching for Cosmo, who no longer pressed against him. Cosmo had moved off, searching through their torn and discarded clothing for something to put on. Leofric could not keep the grin off his face as he watched Cosmo take Leofric's tunic and pull it on over his tousled hair.

When his face emerged from the neck hole, Cosmo was smiling, but it faltered when he saw Leofric staring at him from the ground. Leofric stood, wiping his face on the back of his hand and crossing the stable in three quick strides to pull Cosmo into his arms. He ignored the mounting pain in his hip and shoulder, and the stickiness between his thighs. Cosmo fell against his chest, melting into the embrace, and Leofric kissed the crown of his head.

"Thank you," he whispered.

Cosmo nodded against his chest. "I think I'm still cross with you," he said.

Leofric chuckled. "You think?"

He felt the smile, Cosmo's teeth scrape against his pec. "Difficult to be certain."

"*Mmm*," Leofric agreed. "Well, keep me apprised."

"Oh, I will," said Cosmo.

"I never doubted."

At once, Cosmo went rigid in his arms. He shook off Leofric's touch and backed away. "You did doubt, though," he said. "*You did.*"

Leofric sighed. He closed the distance between them again and made to kiss Cosmo's frown.

Cosmo cupped his face in both hands. "Stop," he said, firm, gentle. "Please."

Leofric stopped, winded, and shamed. "I don't know what to say," said Leofric. "I *never* know what to say."

"You don't have to always say the right thing," said Cosmo. "But please, I need to know what happened."

"What do you mean?"

Cosmo took another step back. He wrapped his arms around himself. "I am not your enemy."

"No," Leofric agreed. His hands twitched at his sides, wanting to reach out, to pull Cosmo into his arms again. "I know."

Every word was like pulling teeth, and with each second Cosmo's anger mounted. "You *blamed* me, for your son being hurt," he spat. "You left me on a mountain."

Leofric hung his head. "I know."

"You, whose honor is *everything*."

"I know."

"You know," said Cosmo, frustrated. "You know. Well, I suppose that's something."

"Cosmo, please—"

"You know what? Nevermind. It's plain that no matter what you won't—"

"*Cosmo.*" Leofric's voice came out like a croak. "*Please.*"

"Please what?"

"Just—give me a second, please."

Cosmo let his hands fall to his hips. "I'm waiting."

Leofric looked wretched, staring at Cosmo like all the words had fled his mind.

Cosmo waited, and waited, and waited, but Leofric did not break the silence. "Alright," said Cosmo. "It's very late, so."

He turned on his heel and walked back toward the house. He was about halfway there when Leofric could part with the words at last. "It was my fault that Hamalcar died."

Twenty-Six

Cosmo froze. "Your brother?"

"Yes."

When no further explanation seemed forthcoming, Cosmo sighed, and turned back to face Leofric. "Alright," said Cosmo. "Tell me."

Leofric began to pace, and the words came slowly, they came reluctantly, but they came. "We'd been out in the field for months, far afield. Our legion finally arrived to set its camp outside a city on the Órnian border. The night we arrived, the men in my legion drew lots for guard duty, as we always had. I drew the overnight watch that first evening."

Cosmo could not truly see where this was going, but he allowed Leofric time to draw breath, to steady himself. Something about his carriage alerted Cosmo that perhaps these words had never been spoken aloud before.

"My brother offered to trade with me," said Leofric. "He was married, you see—and he took his vows very seriously. Others in our legion were planning to visit the city, for drinks and dice and..." Even in the dark, Cosmo could tell his face was brick red.

"Wenching? Or...in your case...hmm. I'm not certain I know what the man version of wenching is called."

"Yes," said Leofric, embarrassed. "So, I traded watches with Hamalcar, and myself and a dozen others journeyed into the city. We'd been in town for a few hours when one of the men saw smoke rising from westward. We gathered ourselves and returned to the camp as swiftly as we could, and the place was in chaos. An Órnian raiding party had fallen upon the camp—a full two legions of men stole the march on us and it was a bloody rout.

"We threw them back, once everyone had sounded the alarm, but at great cost. A third of our men were dead or dying, and they'd set fire to our baggage lines, burning all of the supplies and rations we brought with us on the march."

Cosmo had found himself drawing closer with every sentence Leofric spoke.

Leofric grunted, like he had to clear his throat. Cosmo could see the way he fought to keep his voice steady. "It was dawn before we had the full casualty report—and I found my brother by the...by his post."

"He was dead?" Cosmo asked gently. He was close enough now to cup Leofric's elbow and give it a squeeze.

"No," said Leofric miserably. "He lived, he lived long enough for me to make certain he knew I'd care for Laela and Sorex. To give my life for them if need be, just as we had planned years before."

Cosmo frowned. "It was not your fault."

"It *was*," Leofric insisted. "If I could have just controlled myself, if I could have—"

"It would have been you slaughtered at your post," said Cosmo flatly. "And Hamalcar might still have been killed in the fight."

Leofric shook his head, as if Cosmo's words were angry flies buzzing about his ears. "No."

"*Yes,*" Cosmo insisted. "A third of your men, you said."

"I did," Leofric admitted. "I wish—"

"Wish, what? That you'd died? Like that would have made everything better, somehow?"

Leofric didn't answer.

"Blaming yourself might be easier," said Cosmo. "Maybe it kept you going all this time. But you can't do this forever."

"I can," said Leofric stubbornly. "It's the least I could do."

"It *is* the least," said Cosmo. "You're willing to die for your family. Are you willing to live for them?"

"I thought so," Leofric said. "*You* made me think so."

"Then what happened?"

"When I saw the letter, it was like losing my brother all over again—like I was making the same mistake."

"Even if the letter hadn't been a forgery, you do not have the power to bring someone back from the brink of death," said Cosmo harshly.

"I could have *been* there," Leofric insisted. "I could have stood by them. I could have…"

Cosmo scoffed. "You need so badly to punish yourself," he said. "Why?"

"I don't know." He hung his head. "I don't know."

"You cling to your regrets like a lifeline," said Cosmo. "You think they'll save you, but they're just dragging you down below. If you don't let go, you'll drown."

"Funny thing for you to say," Leofric said.

"Perhaps it's good advice, for both of us."

"Perhaps," Leofric agreed, grudgingly. "Laela said something similar."

"She is very wise," said Cosmo.

"Indeed. Though it is difficult to admit that *you* are right."

"Oh, shut up."

"Menace."

"Deviant."

Leofric pulled him in, crushing Cosmo against his chest, nuzzling into his hair. "Did I mention how much I missed you?"

"Yes," said Cosmo. "But I could stand to hear it a few more times."

"And how sorry I am?"

Cosmo stood on tip toe to offer Leofric a kiss. "I know. And I am too."

"So," said Leofric. "Your brother?"

Cosmo stilled. "Yes," he said. "I can't believe it."

"Truly? Neither can I."

Cosmo scowled. "Yes, you made that abundantly clear before you *left* me, on a *mountain*."

"I'm never going to hear the end of that, am I?"

"Nope."

"I suppose I deserve it," he admitted. "So, tell me, where did you finally find Ozias?"

"He found me," Cosmo said.

Leofric frowned. "What?"

"It was the very night you left," said Cosmo. "I was..."

"Wenching?"

Cosmo's gaze was hard. "No, actually, I was drinking, alone, because some heartless scoundrel fucked me and then left me alone on a mountain."

An aggrieved sigh escaped Leofric and he frowned. "So, that night, he found you what, drowning in a vat of wine?"

"Close enough," Cosmo admitted.

Leofric's eyes narrowed further, and his frown deepened. "That seems...peculiar."

"How so?"

"Well, if he appeared at your side, he was most likely watching you, correct?"

"Well, that makes good sense. I doubt it was a coincidence."

"If he was watching you, he knew you searched for him. He knew you were trying to find him."

"Yes, and?"

"*And,*" said Leofric, exasperated. "Why did he wait until you were alone? Why did he wait at all?"

"What are you getting at?"

"Just...the timing. It seems...suspicious."

"He was afraid," said Cosmo, dismissive. "He didn't know you. Didn't know who you were or what you might want."

"But, he has been alive *all* this time? And he chooses the moment you're alone to—"

"Leofric," said Cosmo. "What are you saying?"

"You're sure that Ozias is really..."

"Really *what?*"

"Who he says he is." Leofric sighed. "This letter—someone wanted to separate us. And Ozias appeared as soon as we were separated."

"A coincidence," Cosmo snapped, though the same fear had been niggling at him, too. He didn't want to admit it, didn't want to say it out loud.

"Just..." Leofric grabbed Cosmo's upper arms, giving them a squeeze. "Be careful."

Trying to change the subject, Cosmo leaned into the touch. "You worried about me?"

"Yes," said Leofric flatly.

"Well, you worry too much."

"You don't worry enough!"

"Are we fighting again already? Because I believe I need a brief refractory period."

Leofric's laugh slipped out, startled from him. "I thought you had unlimited stamina."

"For some things."

"Not for arguing?"

"Hmm," said Cosmo. "Perhaps my old age is catching up with me."

"That must be it."

~

They talked all night.

Well, that was a lie. They used their mouths all night, at least. But they did talk a lot, more than Leofric had possibly ever talked in his entire life. He was exhausted. Cosmo never stopped talking, even when he drifted off to sleep mid-sentence, muttering and drooling against Leofric's chest. Dawn would be here soon, and Leofric had just arrived the decision that when the sun rose, they would all set off for Papia. Cosmo was good in a fight, and presumably Ozias had lived the long years of his life because he was a survivor, but the fact that they were so isolated out here did not make him feel safe. He feared for his family's safety, and for Cosmo's. He didn't know if that was rational, but it was there, and it was foolish for him to keep pretending otherwise. He cared deeply for this strange, small, freckled man clinging to him fitfully as he slept.

He stood, scooping Cosmo with him. He mumbled a sleepy complaint but otherwise didn't stir. Leofric tightened his arms around Cosmo, just for himself. He was so glad he was back, glad that they were on the way to repairing what happened between them. It had been hard for him to tell the story of what happened the night Hamalcar died—he'd never told anyone how he felt about it before. Who would he tell? Other soldiers lost brothers all the time—whether blood relations or of the 'in arms' variety—and telling the story to Laela would have most likely only served to alleviate Leofric's guilt while causing her *more* pain. He had no interest in that. He felt raw, but lighter. Much lighter.

Inside the darkened villa, Leofric hesitated. The place had three cubiculae: Sorex's chambers, Melia's chambers, and a guest chamber. The family room had two or three settees, so he could bring Cosmo there. Ozias, presumably, would be snoring on one. But he didn't wish to put Cosmo down, to part with him at all. Instead of going into the family room, Leofric went down the narrow corridor toward the guest chamber. Just as he was about to reach for the handle on the door it swung open from within.

Startled, Leofric took a step back, hoisting Cosmo higher and turning his body away. Instinct, like Leofric had to shield him. But it was only Ozias. He saw them and shot Leofric a conspiratorial grin, like he and Leofric were old friends. "Looks like you made up," he said quietly.

"Yes," said Leofric curtly, unsure why the word came out so sharp and impatient.

Ozias's smile didn't fade, but his eyes narrowed a bit, like he was wondering about the bite in Leofric's voice. "He was moping the entire way here," Ozias added. "He's usually...I've never seen him like this before."

"What were you doing in there?" Leofric asked abruptly.

"Apologies," said Ozias. "I didn't know how long you'd be and I couldn't get comfortable out there in the living room."

"Why were you coming back out, then?"

Ozias shrugged. "Couldn't get comfortable in there either."

Leofric stared at him, long and hard. Ozias looked a bit like Cosmo; they shared the same lively hazel eyes, the same slight build. Ozias was pale where Cosmo was freckled, his hair and beard dark where Cosmo's hair was alive with color. His smile didn't quite reach his eyes, though, and there was something about him like a horse about to bolt. He stood on the balls of his feet, poised to run. They stared at each other for a long, long while before Leofric said, "Alright."

Ozias brightened immediately. "I'm going to keep watch," he said. "You might as well get some sleep, if you can."

Leofric nodded. "We leave for Papia at Sunrise."

"Can't wait." Ozias offered one final smile and walked down the corridor.

Leofric watched him go, but the call of bed was far too strong, and the sleepless nights caught up with him all at once. And, despite Cosmo's slight build, Leofric's arms were getting tired. So, he nudged open the door to the bed chamber. The sconce on the wall cast a low glow, and after a quick scan, Leofric saw nothing was out of place in the room, anyway. He plopped Cosmo on the sleeping couch and stripped out of his own things. The spot on the bed beside a sleeping Cosmo was *so* inviting that for once Leofric didn't bother gathering his clothes and hanging them before climbing in beside him. He pulled Cosmo close and was asleep in seconds.

At the dawn Leofric woke alone, and sat up, startled. He heard voices coming from the kitchen, so he pulled a tunic over his head and walked toward them, dragging his fingers through his tangled hair. The pink glow of dawn transformed the villa, it was warm and happy and bustling with life. Cosmo and Ozias were in the kitchen, jesting and shouting back and forth as they cooked. Occasionally, one of them would holler a question off into the corridor and Laela's voice would answer from somewhere else in the house.

"Good morning," said Ozias, handing Leofric a plate.

"Morning," he said. "You two are up and about early."

"You wanted to leave near sunrise, didn't you?" Cosmo asked, a soft smile on his face.

"I did," he allowed. "But I have to talk to—"

"I already told them," said Ozias.

"You already told—what?"

"I was up early, so when Laela woke and asked me if all was

well, I told her you wanted all of us to be ready to leave for Papia as soon as possible."

"You did *what?*"

"Did you...did you want to leave them behind?" Ozias asked.

"No," Leofric admitted, out of sorts. "No, of course not."

"Well, then, there you go!" Ozias handed him a mug of tea as well. "They've already gotten a jump on things."

Leofric frowned down at his plate, wrong footed. He had wanted to discuss things with Laela, to possibly even discuss things with Sorex himself, too. But then, he supposed it didn't matter. They'd have time enough to talk on the road, and the sooner they left, the better Leofric would feel. Then, Cosmo laid a hand on his shoulder, gave it a squeeze, and the strangeness of the morning was forgotten.

Leofric spent the rest of the morning trying to get everyone to move with a bit more urgency, so in the end he was grateful for Ozias for getting a jump on things. While obviously Leofric did not wish for his family to be under siege, he found it very strange that whoever sent the forged letter had not made their move yet. If the point of the letter had been to isolate him from Cosmo—presumably so that he wouldn't have Cosmo's power to defend himself—why had this person now allowed Cosmo and Leofric to reunite? It made no sense. Perhaps their goal was to throw Leofric off his axis, to distract him and allow them to exploit another vulnerability? Either way, he didn't like it.

The sooner they were all away, back in Papia, surrounded by the high walls of the royal villa, the better. The journey presented its own dangers, but Leofric had to hope that whoever had designs on hurting him or his family would hesitate now that he a demigod on his side.

Two, actually.

That brought him up short. Ozias was surely a demigod,

as well—but he had no idea what powers he might have. Cosmo had told him that his father had imparted the brothers with their own powers and gifts, but he'd never mentioned what gifts might have been granted to Ozias. He would have to ask Cosmo about it, so they could be truly prepared for any possible difficulties on the road.

Leofric finished his breakfast and wandered out to the stables to ready the horses. He debated bringing a wagon, knowing that neither Sorex nor Laela had ridden such a long distance before, but decided against it. It would only encourage them all to take longer packing up their things, since the wagon could carry more. He would try to keep a steady but gentle pace for his wife and son's sake, but the wagon was far too slow.

He saddled Lyra for Sorex. She was a reliable and steady horse, and Leofric knew she was the swiftest mount his family owned. If something happened on the road, he could rely on Lyra to carry Sorex to safety. For himself, he saddled Selene, Hamalcar's warhorse. Ozias and Cosmo had their own mounts, and there were three horses remaining. He chose a mount for Laela, and got all of them ready. As soon as they were away, he would write to the magistrate in the nearby city of Antiope, to send someone out to the property and retrieve the other horses.

"Hey," said a voice.

Leofric jumped, but softened immediately when he realized it was only Cosmo. "Hello."

"Are you alright?"

Leofric sighed, pondering how to answer. "This was my brother's horse," he said suddenly, running the knuckles of his hand down the side of Selene's neck.

"Oh," said Cosmo. He didn't seem like he knew what to say.

"I couldn't bring myself to ride her, after..." he trailed

away. "I couldn't bear to sell her either. She hasn't had much to do with herself for three years."

Cosmo joined him at the animal's side. "Well, she has an important mission now." He ran his fingers through Margaret's mane, until he met Leofric's hand. He threaded their hands together and squeezed. Leofric smiled.

Twenty-Seven

Someday, Leofric thought, he would have to make things up to Laela and Sorex. The pace he set was not as swift as he would like, but it was far more than his family was used to. When they reached the royal villa in Papia, he told himself they would be pampered and spoiled by staff, able to rest and bathe and feast upon delicacies. Prince Alexios would never turn them away, or begrudge them anything. For all his brash impetuousness, Alexios was a good prince and a better man.

For his family to receive such rewards though, they had to make it to Papia alive. One more day, Leofric thought as they rode. *Please, just one more day without trouble.*

One more hour, one more minute.

Every moment on the road that passed without incident only served to put Leofric more on edge. When they made camp each night, they broke the night up into four watches, allowing everyone to get rest. Ozias, Leofric, and Cosmo each always took a watch, and Laela and Sorex switched off on the remaining one. Both of them insisted that they could take a watch every night, but Leofric was firm. He already felt guilty enough dragging them from their home, putting them in danger, and everything else. He would have only split the watches between himself and Cosmo—but Ozias was hale and alert and he didn't really have a *reason* not to trust him. Just a feeling.

One night, a few days into their journey, Leofric was sleeping, and woke to a sound of rustling. Alert at once, he sat up to see a dark shape rifling through one of his bags. He waited, watching, until his eyes adjusted and he could see who it was. It was Ozias.

"What are you doing?" Leofric asked quietly.

Ozias jumped. When he turned, he looked very like the little boy caught with his hand in the sweet jar. "Oh, apologies," he said, withdrawing his empty hand. "I didn't mean to wake you."

"That's alright," said Leofric, though it wasn't—it merely wasn't the cause of his trepidation. "What were you looking for? Perhaps I could help you find it."

Ozias's eyes flickered around the camp, to his sleeping brother, as if Cosmo would wake up and cover for him. "I was —I—" he stammered.

Leofric sat up straighter, and shifted his weight so that Ozias couldn't help but see the dagger sheathed at his hip. "Tell me what you were searching for. Now."

Ozias looked terrified. "I was searching for my brother's grace," he admitted.

Leofric narrowed his eyes. "*Why?*"

Ozias shrugged. "It's hard to say," he admitted. "I worry. I wanted to know where it was, make certain it was safe."

"It's safe."

Ozias hesitated a bit before saying softly, "He's my brother."

Guilt surged through Leofric, and he tried to view the situation from Ozias's point of view. "I understand that," said Leofric. "But Cosmo gave it to me, to protect. To see safely back to Papia."

"Why? Why would he give it to you?" Ozias asked.

"He trusts me," said Leofric simply. He touched his chest, where a secret pocket behind his breastplate concealed the bottle of Kryos's grace. It was cold against his heart, but in a bracing, refreshing way. "I keep it on my person at all times."

"Cosmo trusts me, too," said Ozias angrily. "It should be guarded by *family*."

Leofric fought to stay calm, but something about this had his hackles up. "Perhaps," he made himself say, keeping his voice even. "But you'll have to take that up with him. Now, I'm going to get some rest."

"Fine," said Ozias. "I'll talk to Cosmo in the morning."

"You do that." Leofric curled under his cloak, as if he had no concern whatsoever about what Ozias might do, but he did not sleep a wink the rest of the night.

Cosmo was happy, for the most part, to be on the road again. He worried about their little party, and the future, but he was back at Leofric's side, and it was invigorating. They set their bedrolls side by side at night, and though Cosmo would have wished they had been even closer, Leofric insisted on maintaining some propriety around his family. As they traveled, he felt himself settling into a routine, and it was comforting, in a way. Soon, they'd be back in Papia, and reunited with Auro. He couldn't *wait* to see the look on Auro's face when he saw Ozias.

One morning, however, Cosmo sensed something on

Leofric's mind. After a quick breakfast, they were on the road once again, and Cosmo could almost feel the dark storm cloud above Leofric's head.

After several hours of monosyllabic grunts in response to any query, Cosmo was fed up. He slowed Hestia, falling to the back of their little column to ride beside Leofric. "What is wrong?"

"Nothing," Leofric snapped. His eyes followed Ozias, who rode ahead with Sorex. Ozias pointed out something in a tree, and Sorex laughed before saying something back. Their conversation didn't carry all the way back here, but both were smiling.

"Oh, well, yes," said Cosmo, rolling his eyes. "It seems like nothing."

Leofric sighed. "Apologies. You're right, my mind is clouded this morning."

"Perhaps it would help to talk of it," Cosmo suggested. "Perhaps *I* could help."

Leofric considered this, and Cosmo turned in his saddle to watch the muscles going in Leofric's jaw. There was a time he would have pestered him, repeated himself, or ridden off in a huff. He wasn't *entirely* giving up the idea of riding off in a huff, but overall, he knew better now. Leofric was a very deliberate man, and he weighed each word carefully. He needed patience. So Cosmo tried. And eventually Leofric pried open his mouth to speak, though he kept his voice pitched low. "Ozias was digging through my pack last night."

"What?" Asked Cosmo, aghast.

"During his watch. I woke up when I heard something, and saw him rifling through my things."

"Did you say anything?"

"Of course," said Leofric. "He apologized. But he— Cosmo, he told me he was looking for Kryos's grace."

Cosmo frowned. "Why?"

"He claimed he wanted to be certain it was safe," said Leofric.

"Well," said Cosmo. "That's not the maddest notion."

"No, of course not, but..."

"But what?" Asked Cosmo, bristling at once.

"I wonder what would have happened had he found it."

"What are you saying?"

"Cosmo, I know he's your brother but...do you trust him?"

"How can you say that? Of course, I do!"

"Alright," said Leofric gently. "Apologies. I shouldn't have said anything."

Cosmo spent the rest of the day's ride stewing, wondering how Leofric could be so insensitive. So untrusting. After *everything*. Hadn't Cosmo done enough, finally, to earn the benefit of the doubt? Leofric had not wanted him to find Ozias. Had not wanted to wait. Told Cosmo he was chasing ghosts. And now, now that Ozias was here, alive, Leofric didn't trust him. As he and Hestia plodded along, Cosmo stared at the back of Leofric's head, in a foul mood. When they stopped and made camp for the night, Cosmo considered asking Leofric for the grace back. He'd given it to Leofric because he trusted him, implicitly. Now though, with this vendetta against Ozias...Unfortunately, though, Leofric's words had wormed their way inside his head. There had been a few things that were peculiar, now that he thought about it. The night they'd gone out drinking, Cosmo had woken to their room being ransacked. Had he been looking for Kryos's grace then? He supposed he couldn't grudge him that, but, what would he have done had he found it?

Should he confront Ozias?

No. Cosmo was being ridiculous. Leofric was simply a wary and untrusting sort. Once his family was out of danger, once they all were, he would calm down. He hadn't trusted

Cosmo at the start, either. And for Ozias's part, he had spent four hundred years on the run, afraid and alone, and Kryos was on his heels. Hadn't Cosmo been just as afraid of a Kryos returned to full strength? He shook his head to clear it, and put Leofric's suspicions from his mind. His brother was *alive.* He couldn't let anything sour that.

Twenty-Eight

Their party was tired and bedraggled by the time they reached the front gates of the royal villa. The guards recognized Leofric, and while they knew he'd been dismissed from Prince Alexios's service, they dispatched a porter to let him know of their arrival. Cosmo sidled up to Sorex, who turned around the atrium with awe.

"This place is huge, isn't it?" Cosmo asked him.

"Yeah," said Sorex. "Just one family lives here? That's crazy."

"Well," said Cosmo, "They have staff, too. And sometimes extended family."

"And us?"

"Well, I dunno about living here, but yes. Us too."

They stood in silence for a while, until Sorex broke it. "Did you forgive Uncle Leo?"

Cosmo startled. "What?"

"When he got back without you, he was really upset. We thought it was because he left you behind."

Cosmo couldn't help the small smile at Sorex's words.

"But he still seems pretty miserable," said Sorex.

"How can you even tell?" Cosmo blurted.

Sorex laughed. "Yeah, he's kind of..."

"Uptight?"

"That's a word for it, I suppose." He squinted at Cosmo. "So, did you?"

"Forgive him?"

"Yes."

"Sort of," said Cosmo. "I mean—yes, but things are still... weird."

Sorex nodded sagely. "I understand that," he said. "Sometimes it takes some time for how you feel to catch up with what you *know*."

"Cosmo! Leofric! And—" Auro's voice came echoing down the hall, and broke off into a startled cry.

Before Cosmo could formulate a response, Auro collided with him and squashed the breath from his lungs. He laughed, but then his arms were empty once again, and he turned, unsteady, to see Ozias similarly assaulted. Auro had burst into tears, and refused to release Ozias, who looked desperately uncomfortable, but eventually softened, and returned Auro's hug. Cosmo couldn't help it, he joined his brothers, and threw his arms around them both.

It was a simple thing, a hug. He'd been embraced by countless lovers and friends over the years, but a simple embrace amongst brothers was something he'd written off, something Cosmo assumed he'd never feel again, and the aching grief crashed through him all at once, and he found his own eyes prickling as he squashed his brothers close.

"What on earth is going on?" said a voice.

Cosmo turned to see Prince Alexios approach their party, his brown eyes wide and bemused. "They followed us home," Cosmo said, over the top of Auro's head. "Can we keep them?"

It took half the night for Cosmo, Ozias and Leofric to

relay the details of their journey. "Good grief," said Alexios. "You haven't been gone that long."

"It feels like it," Leofric grumbled.

They sat in the sitting room in Prince Alexios's chambers. Servants had brought them wine and supper, and Sorex was now curled up asleep on one of the settees. Cosmo felt he was seconds away from nodding off, too.

"Alright," said Alexios, once everyone had fallen into silence, realizing they had nothing left to say. "I think… perhaps we should retire for the evening, and resume again when we are fresher."

"Agreed," said Cosmo, with a yawn. He rose and pulled a blanket over Sorex.

"My lady," said Alexios graciously to Laela. "I would be honored if you would take my bed for the evening. The blankets are fresh, and there is a curtain for privacy. We can find more suitable accommodations for everyone tomorrow."

Laela dipped her head. "Gratitude, Your Highness." She looked uncertainly to Leofric, but held her tongue. When recounting their tale, Cosmo had skirted around certain parts of his travels with Leofric, and Leofric had taken his lead. Alexios frowned, watching their eyes flit between each other, but he'd said nothing. An awkward moment descended on the room, and then by some mutual agreement it seemed like everyone made their own sleeping arrangements.

Leofric stayed out in the sitting room, stretching his long body out on one of the other sofas. Alexios and Auro took up residence on a pile of fur rugs in front of the fire, and Ozias followed Cosmo into the chamber of servants' quarters that Cosmo and Leofric had once shared.

It felt strange, having Ozias here. Cosmo found himself with the constant urge to turn and stare at him, as if he were afraid Ozias would suddenly vanish in a puff of smoke. He didn't, not yet at any rate. He took the bed beside the window, bade Cosmo goodnight, and was fast asleep in seconds.

Cosmo was far too keyed up to sleep. After tossing and turning restlessly for an hour, he got up and padded across the room to the trunk where Leofric had kept his things. It was full of his extra uniforms, tunics and loincloths, and for a moment Cosmo just closed his eyes an inhaled. The clothing in the trunk was clean, but Cosmo could still detect a hint of Leofric in the folded fabrics. It soothed him immediately, and he reached for one of the undyed, rough spun tunics, lifting it out of the trunk as if it were a sacred shroud.

Leofric was just outside the chamber door, but Cosmo had no belief in his own ability to keep his touches proper and chaste, even in a suite of rooms stuffed to bursting with their families. Instead, he ran his hands over the linen, rubbing the fabric between his fingers, relishing the feel of it. He wished he was relishing of the feeling of it as the sole barrier between his hands and the heated skin of a certain surly soldier, but this would have to do for now. Cosmo usually slept naked, but without the comfort of Leofric at his side, he pulled the tunic on, pressing it close to his flesh to feel the worn fabric and inhale the scent. When he returned to his bed, he had barely placed his head upon the pillow before he was sucked down into sleep.

Leofric woke, startled, to the sound of rapping on the door. Before he'd even opened his eyes he had a blade clutched in his fist, certain the threat they'd avoided on the road was at last closing its jaws around them.

"Your Royal Highness," came the voice from without. "Her Grace, Queen Dafina, awaits."

"A moment," came Alexios's groggy reply from the rug

where he'd spent the night. He looked around, his eyes lighting upon Leofric. "You can lower your blade, captain."

"We'll see," Leofric muttered sourly, massaging the crick in his neck with his off hand.

Dafina swept into the chambers, her face buried in a scroll, not looking where she was going. "Alexios," she said. "Get up. It's midmorning, for goodness' sake."

"Good Morning, Your Grace," said Alexios.

"I've had a notion about your idea for a standing naval force that would allow—" She broke off and looked up at last, frowning, as if she'd realized Alexios's voice had come not from the luxurious sleeping couch but from the sitting area, where Alexios knelt in front of the fire, tucking a thick blanket around Auro, who was still asleep, as he rose.

Dafina swept her eyes over Alexios's chambers, her confusion mounting as they lit upon each sleeping figure. Cosmo and Ozias now emerged from the adjacent chamber at all the ruckus. "Alexios, who are all these people?" She heard a dainty yawn from behind her and turned to Alexios's bed, aghast, to see Laela sitting up and peering at her through the gauzy curtained canopy. "Why is there a *woman* in your bed?"

Alexios grimaced. "My lady—"

Dafina braced a hand upon her hip. "I know there is nothing passionate between us, Alexios," she said angrily, "And Auro is one thing, but I would have thought—"

"Deepest Apologies, Your Grace," said Leofric, sinking to one knee before her. "The circumstances are peculiar—but the lady is actually my wife."

"Your...?"

"My family arrived late last night, and His Highness gallantly offered use of his bed for her to get some rest."

Dafina narrowed her eyes suspiciously, but relented. "I thought you'd had a party without me," she said.

"Never that, Your Grace," said Alexios. "Come, let us, er, adjourn to my terrace and we can discuss your notion."

Dafina cast curious looks over her shoulder as Alexios shooed her out onto the balcony.

Sorex stirred in his sleep, one leg falling of the couch on which he'd slept. Leofric knelt beside him, easing the boy's leg back up onto the cushions, and adjusted the blankets over him. "I can't believe he slept through that," Leofric said.

"I can't believe a *queen* just accused me of being a harlot," said Laela.

"I feel as though she was accusing Alexios of being a harlot," Ozias put in. He lowered his voice with a glance at Auro, who was still sound asleep as well. "She is his betrothed, after all."

Leofric narrowed his eyes. "How did you know that?"

"Know what?"

"That His Highness and the Queen are to be married?"

"Oh," said Ozias. "Cosmo told me. Or I heard it somewhere, on the road."

"Where exactly?"

"Leofric, enough," Cosmo cut across them. "We discussed it at your home, when we explained the tale of Janus to Ozias *and* Laela. You were sitting right there."

Leofric flushed, recalling now that Cosmo was right. "Apologies," he said grudgingly. "I am not yet myself this morning."

Ozias rolled his eyes. "You seem yourself to me," he said, under his breath, but of course loud enough for Leofric to hear.

Cosmo pinched him. "Both of you, enough. We are all here to work together, no? We are all upon the same side."

Logically, Leofric knew that Cosmo was right. It wouldn't help anyone if they all began fighting amongst themselves.

They must be united into a fist of single purpose if they hoped to smash Janus and unmask his allies.

That brought him up short. Last evening, Prince Alexios had said nothing of his father, the king. His Grace King Nelios had been hovering at the door to the afterlife when Leofric had set out on his quest—it seemed a lifetime ago, now, he thought, looking at Cosmo across the room.

Leofric excused himself and went out onto the balcony. Standing a respectful distance away, he cleared his throat to announce his presence. His Highness and Her Grace looked up, and Alexios beckoned Leofric closer with a terse jerk of his head. "A moment, my lady."

"Alexios," said the Queen, and when she drew herself up to her full height, she could look Alexios directly in the eye. "If you 'my lady' me one more time I'm going to push you off this balcony."

Alexios smiled. "As you wish, Dafina."

He followed Leofric back inside, as Dafina called, "Do take your time! I was *so* hoping to be stuck standing outside on your balcony all morning."

"I see you're doing well in wooing Her Grace," Leofric heard himself say.

Alexios startled. "Are you...are you making a joke?"

"Thought I'd give it a try, Your Highness," said Leofric.

Alexios just stared at him, mouth gaping for a moment. Then he laughed. "Well, alright then. Apparently, you've had quite the transformative journey."

Leofric balked, flustered. "Apologies, Your Highness. I didn't mean—"

Alexios smacked a hand over Leofric's mouth, just as Leofric had done to Cosmo, a thousand years ago. "What did you need, Leofric?"

He waited for Alexios to release him. Once freed, Leofric's

tone turned grave. "A serious matter, Your Highness—how fares His Grace, your father?"

Alexios looked genuinely puzzled. "Still fine, of course."

"What do you mean, still?"

"I sent a messenger, twice, while you were away," said Alexios. "Letting you know he had taken a turn for the better."

"I never received any message, Your Highness."

"Odd," said Alexios, but he couldn't help but brighten. "My father has made a full recovery—shortly after you and Cosmo left."

"How? Why? He was on death's door."

Alexios shrugged. "He's a man, despite what he would have all of us believe. Men sicken. Then they heal."

Leofric supposed that was true, and he supposed it should be a relief. Nelios was a fierce commander, and Leofric felt better having him at the helm of any defenses the villa should have to mount against an assault. "I am relieved to hear it, Your Highness," Leofric said, but even to his own ears the words sounded hollow.

The prince gave Leofric a sidelong look. "Kato was actually a large help. He brought Her Grace's medicus to see to father. The man has more experience than any on the continent, after helping Neossós survive its plague."

"I see," said Leofric, though he didn't. None of this felt quite right—though he couldn't place his finger on why. He stared at Alexios, hard, the way he'd learned from Auro to see through a glamour. No matter how hard he looked, he couldn't discern anything amiss with the man standing before him. There was no shimmer, no swoop of vertigo through his stomach. Nothing out of the ordinary.

So why did Leofric feel so afraid?

Twenty-Nine

Cosmo joined Auro and Ozias in the under vault, deep below the royal villa. Alexios and Leofric remained on the other side of the door, granting the three brothers some privacy. It had taken quite a bit of threatening and cajoling before the men on the door allowed them to enter without Prince Alexios, but eventually they'd relented, upon the promise of a thorough search of Auro, Cosmo, and Ozias when they emerged.

"Something to look forward to," said Ozias, with a roll of his eyes, and Cosmo had laughed.

Now though, the three of them were solemn as they stood before the empty pedestal Auro had dragged over to sit beside the spindly table holding Cedras's grace. Auro had found a painted clay vase depicting hunters after elk in the forest, and wrapped the phial in white fox fur, to insulate it within the vase. Ozias placed the stopper in the vase with trembling fingers, and Cosmo poured melted wax around it to seal it in. None of them spoke until the wax had cooled, and Auro covered the vase in a shroud like the one hiding Cedras's grace from prying eyes.

Cosmo wondered if the phial of grace would extend its influence beyond itself, like Cedras's had. He slid one arm around each of his brother's shoulders, and shared a quiet moment of grief.

"Ozias," said Auro quietly, "Are you certain about what happened?"

Ozias went rigid where he stood hip to shoulder with Cosmo. "Yes," he said tersely.

"But how—"

"Auro," said Cosmo, releasing his shoulders and turning to look him in the eye. "You said before that you believed me, that you trust me."

"I did," said Auro. Then, louder, "I *do*."

"Despite everything, despite everything we have all been through, despite how—how I felt about what happened..."

"Yes?" Auro prompted.

"Despite all of that, I also had a hard time believing such cruelty in Kryos." He swallowed, meeting Ozias's gaze. "I understand."

"No, you don't," said Auro despairingly. "Why am I the *only* one who doesn't assume all of us are ruthless killers?"

"Not all of us," said Ozias angrily. "Just—"

"—Kryos, yes, I know." Auro met Ozias's eye, angry too. "But there's still a matter of a missing four centuries of your tale, Ozias."

"I've been—"

"It matters not," said Cosmo loudly. "It matters not where Ozias has been. He is here, *now.*"

"I know that," said Auro.

"And you did not let me finish," said Cosmo. "Neither of you. For now, we are going to wait. We are not going to decide *anything* until each of us has gotten to say his piece, to explain what happened all those years ago."

"That sounds fair," said Auro, sounding surprised.

"Each of us?" Asked Ozias, skeptical. "Even—"

"Even Kryos, yes," said Cosmo. "When he wakes, he will be outnumbered—and have no notion of what has transpired this year. A distinct disadvantage. We can hear him out without leaving ourselves vulnerable—so why not give him a chance?"

"A chance to *what?*" Ozias spat. "Shoot us full of arrows?"

"If he tries," said Cosmo, "Auro *and* Cedras will be restored to their full strength by then. They should be more than a match for Kryos in a cursed state."

Auro was looking at Cosmo in equal parts shock and pride. "You're very serious, all of a sudden, brother," said Auro.

"Tell me about," said Ozias. "He was absolutely *no* fun on the road."

And then somehow, all three of them were laughing.

They left the vault and returned through the royal villa to Alexios's chambers. Cosmo very much wanted to sit and discuss things further with his brothers, but His Royal Highness's chambers had suddenly gotten *quite* crowded.

Prince Alexios returned from court, casting his crown aside with an irritated flourish. Looking around at the gathered people, he said, "I think we need different arrangements."

"Agreed," said Sorex, who sat with his hands covering his eyes so as not to inadvertently spy upon anyone getting dressed or undressed.

"Also agreed," said Cosmo. "I'd very much enjoy a bed again."

"There are my apartments on the floor below," said Queen Dafina. "I had been discussing with His Highness making a move of my own household to the Domus, in Papia City."

"You won't be ready to move for a fortnight," Alexios protested. "In fact, it would take you that long to pack only your collection of face powders."

Dafina threw a grape at him. "Silence, Harlot," she said. She'd taken to calling Alexios that after someone had told her what Ozias had said the day before. "In the meantime, perhaps Leofric and Laela would like to take their son and prepare the residence for my arrival."

Cosmo made a small noise of protest that he disguised with a hasty cough.

"I cannot move so far from His Highness's side," said Leofric, pointedly not looking at Cosmo. "Nor do I wish to be parted from my family."

Dafina considered this. "Well, Prince Harlot has married off most of my lady companions to his Papian noblemen, and I have sorely missed the company of women amongst this herd of stags."

"What are you saying?"

"Laela and her son could move into my apartments," said Dafina. "It has three bed chambers."

"That's settled then," said Ozias.

"What about you?" Cosmo rounded on him.

"What about me?"

"Where will you sleep?"

"I am happy to remain here, on one of these comfortable settles," said Ozias. "Or I can simply take a bed in the servants' quarters, since Leofric and Cosmo will most likely share a bed anyway."

Cosmo nearly choked on his own tongue, and the silence that fell on the room was sharp and sudden as an axe blow.

Ozias frowned, looking from face to face in confusion.

Alexios said, "*What?*" and Auro said, "I knew it!"

Leofric himself simply made a sad choking noise, his face flushing with embarrassment.

"Did I—did I say something wrong?" Ozias asked.

Sorex sighed. "No," he said. "My uncle just thought he was a lot sneakier than he was."

"Wait, uncle? I thought Leofric was your father," said Dafina. She pointed to Laela. "And *your* husband."

"He is," said Laela.

"Technically," added Sorex.

"It's....complicated," said Leofric.

"Good grief," said Dafina. "I'll say." She turned to Alexios. "And I thought *our* relationship was fraught."

Alexios released a weak chuckle. Beside him, Auro vibrated with barely suppressed glee. "Alright," said Alexios at last. "Laela and Sorex can take up residence in Her Grace's apartments, and the rest of you can keep your bloody sleeping arrangements to yourselves."

Leofric immediately began to argue, but Laela stopped him. "Leo, that arrangement sounds *fine*. You don't need us underfoot, and frankly, we could a bit of space."

Sorex agreed. "Besides, we're a lot safer here than we would have been home alone in Sokol."

"That's true," Leofric allowed, but Cosmo could see the tension in his jaw. "I will be just here. If you need *anything.*"

Laela sighed good-naturedly. "Of course, dear," she said.

"Let lightning strike me down," said Leofric under his breath.

Cosmo laughed. He turned to Ozias. "What do you say?"

"I think it would be a delightful cohabitation," said Ozias, bowing to Cosmo.

"Oh, indeed," said Cosmo, bowing back. "Royal bastards often serve their trueborn relatives," he added. "They find great honor and satisfaction in the task."

"Yes, and some of those suffocate their trueborn relatives in their sleep," Ozias said.

They both burst out laughing, and just for a second, Cosmo felt all the walls between him and Ozias crumble to the floor.

Leofric found it comforting to return to the routine of villa life. He liked Papia, liked having a schedule every day. He loved having his family so close, though he still worried for their safety. But, Sorex had cut right to the heart of things: he would have been far more worried had he left them behind all the way in Sokol.

They'd all discussed, at length, the things they might have to fear from Janus, and what to look for to ensure they weren't falling for any of his glamours or illusions. His nights were occupied in part with standing guard over His Royal Highness Prince Alexios and finding any opportunity to be with Cosmo.

And still, there was no sign of Janus, or any of his agents. There had been not a whisper of him since his mad escape in the spring. All of it was suspicious, in Leofric's opinion, but he did not take for granted the time that it offered him to prepare. If Janus was biding his time, Leofric would bide his as well.

He made sure to familiarize himself with all of the guards and villa staff once again, to make certain who had what keys to which doors. To Auro's chagrin, he commanded the ivy be cleared from the wall below Alexios's chambers, and sent people to ascertain the other walls of the villa stood free of ivy, or any other easy points of egress. All in all, it seemed to him that they were well prepared for an attack, should Janus choose to mount one.

"Tell me again how much you missed me when we were apart," said Cosmo one evening. They were in the bath, candles all around them. Cosmo sat between Leofric's splayed thighs, his back against Leofric's chest. They'd adjourned to the baths well after moonrise that night, to wash up and enjoy some quiet conversation while Ozias slept in the other room.

Leofric smiled, trailed his damp fingers down the nape of Cosmo's neck, delighting in the way he shivered at the touch. "I missed you," Leofric murmured, lowering his lips to trace the same path along Cosmo's skin. "So much."

"So much?" Cosmo echoed.

"*Yes,*" Leofric sighed. He loved the taste of Cosmo, the smell of him, the feel of his warm body against Leofric's own.

"Good," said Cosmo. He spun around, resting his knees on either side of Leofric's thighs, and draping his arms around his neck. "Though, I fear it's time for you to return to your post."

Leofric sighed. Despite Cosmo's lewd suggestions on how they could manage their sleeping arrangements, Leofric insisted upon sleeping out in the central sitting area of Alexios's apartments. With everyone he cared for under one roof, bracing for attack, Leofric knew he needed to shelve his carnal desires in order to stay focused and protect them all. Even so, it was on his tongue to ask Cosmo to join him, just for one night, so they could sleep side by side again.

"I wish I could join you," said Cosmo, cupping Leofric's cheek in one soft hand. He clearly had been keeping pace with Leofric's thoughts. He cast a quick look out of the bathing chamber, toward the darkened room where Ozias slept. "I just don't think...he's so afraid to be left alone."

Leofric sighed. This was another part of Leofric's decision to sleep apart from Cosmo—his brother was an ever-present shadow that always had Leofric upon the back foot. But now, he did not wish to talk about Ozias. He didn't trust him, and whenever the topic arose, it seemed to cause bristling between them. He didn't want *anything* between them. Leofric slid his hands down to cup Cosmo's ass below the water. "I wish you could join me, too."

"The more you miss me," said Cosmo, rocking into

Leofric's touch. "The more you can *tell* me how much you missed me."

Leofric pushed Cosmo off his lap, and he slid into the water with a splash. He came up laughing, and sent a retaliating spray toward Leofric. They kissed messily as they emerged from the bath and toweled off, and Leofric hated to disentangle himself from him. Cosmo was so different from anyone he ever knew—in ways that were both glaringly obvious and others that were subtler. He was....fun. It was a difficult thing for Leofric to name, he who hadn't had any fun at all in nearly four years.

He'd forgotten how, or so he would have thought. But Cosmo helped him remember. Leofric leaned in to place a tender kiss upon his freckled cheek. "Goodnight," he said. "Menace."

"Goodnight," Cosmo replied. "Think of me?"

"Always," said Leofric, without thinking.

Cosmo startled. "Oh," he said. "Well. Um. Good."

Leofric turned before he could say something foolish, giving Cosmo a parting smile as he left. Abed, he tossed and turned, unable to sleep for a long time. Usually, Leofric fell to sleep swiftly and soundly. It was a skill he'd learned in the army. A good night's rest could be the difference between life or death in battle, and Leofric always took the opportunity to ensure he was at his best: well rested and sharp of mind. But tonight, he was preoccupied.

Preoccupied with what might happen in the future with himself and Cosmo, preoccupied with worry about his family, preoccupied with fear of an impending attack. It was *hours* of tossing and turning before he finally drifted off.

In his dream, he was back in the cave he and Cosmo had shared on the mountain top. It was warm and sung, the fire in the hearth inviting. When he turned, he found Cosmo waiting for him in the stone bed. Leofric went to him, and as they kissed he realized they weren't in the bed at all. They were sitting amongst the embers of the hearth fire. Cosmo looked robust and healthy, beautiful. Glowing. The fire seeming to only make him more alive, but when Leofric looked down at himself, watching his clothes burn away to crispy ash, he staggered to his feet in horror as the skin on his arms sloughed off. There was no pain, but his flesh melted away, the fire consuming him.

He woke with the scent of smoke in his nose, tangled in his blanket, sweaty and disoriented. A lingering remnant of his grotesque dream, he thought—until the smell did not fade. Drowsiness evaporated, Leofric stood, breathing deep. That certainly was smoke. Leofric pulled on a tunic and buckled on his sword belt, leaving everything else behind, as he rushed toward the terrace. From Alexios's balcony, he saw it—red as sunrise, but rising from the wrong side of the villa, and several hours too early. He strode to Alexios's bed. "Your Highness," he said urgently.

Alexios woke, groggy. "Unhhh."

"*Your Highness. Auro.*"

"What is it, Leofric?" asked Auro thickly.

There was no time to soften the words. "Fire. Bad. The villa is aflame, we must get out. Now."

Leofric could smell the smoke stronger now, and ironically that chilled him to the bone. Auro and Alexios still fumbled for clothing. "Dress *now*," Leofric barked. "And come at once."

He strode across to the servants quarters, throwing the door wide. Leofric frowned. The room was empty, with no sign of Ozias *or* Cosmo. With no time to question it, Leofric barked at Alexios and Auro to hurry.

They obeyed, following Leofric through the door. The smell was stronger here, strong enough to start them coughing, but he could not yet see flames, which was all to the good.

"Down the stairs," he urged. "Quickly."

One turn down the stairs, he paused. It would take him only a minute out of his way to go for Laela and Sorex. A minute was precious, however, and Leofric still had his duty. Torn, he knew he had to decide, and fast. Before he could change his mind, Leofric sent Auro and Alexios on, and scanning the crowd of people evacuating he recognized the king and queen as well. He dashed off down the hallway, and banged on the door the guest apartments in use by Queen Dafina. When there was no answer, he threw open the door. A quick but thorough search confirmed the place was empty, and Leofric hurried out, grateful. They must have smelled the smoke and evacuated already.

Alexios's mother, Queen Clio, was hysterical by the time Leofric met Alexios outside where he stood with his parents, surrounded by guards. He'd never seen her like that before; compared to her husband she was always cool and calm. "The library!" she cried.

"The library is on the north side of the villa, my love," King Nelios soothed her. "The men will sort out these flames well before they reach your books." He turned and sent a glare Leofric's way, as if to say, *or else.*

"Yes, Your Grace," said Leofric. "I will attend the men at once."

It was only then that he scanned the small area where the royal family stood, flanked by a dozen guardsmen, and realized Cosmo and Ozias were not with them, nor could he see Laela and Sorex.

Leofric pulled Auro aside. "Have you seen my family?"

"I saw Laela and Sorex with Her Grace over by the medicus," said Auro, pointing. "I was about to head there myself, to assist with the injured."

Leofric followed Auro's hand and saw, to his dizzying

relief, Laela and Sorex huddled under a blanket, watching the flames.

Auro frowned. "Where are Cosmo and Ozias?"

Leofric turned back to Auro, panic rising once again in his gullet. "You haven't seen them?"

"No," said Auro. "Can you—"

"Of course," said Leofric, without waiting for Auro to finish. He strode quickly to where Paulus stood, barking orders and organizing the guardsmen for different duties: evacuation, assisting the medicus with any burned staff or residents, and putting out the fire. Leofric squinted through the night and the billowing smoke, searching for a flash of red hair, and finding none. Why had Cosmo and Ozias been from their beds? Had they smelled the smoke and... what, left without waking him? That didn't feel like it could be true. So where were they?

Leofric half listened to Paulus, wondering what to do. Of course, he knew immediately what he should do. What he was honor bound to do. What the King himself had just *told* him to do.

Leofric turned back toward the conflagration now visible from within the villa, casting bright orange shadows on the ghostly white marble of the edifice. *Fuck the king,* he thought, surprising even himself. *His wife is out here, safe and sound.* Well, technically of course, so was Leofric's, but he was already running, running back toward the burning villa.

The flames had spread rapidly, even in the short amount of time since Leofric had been outside, and the interior of the atrium was full of thick smoke, and it felt llike stepping foot in an oven. Even the harshest day on the sands of sokol could not compare to this heat, Leofric realized, his stomach contracting in fear. Now that he was back inside, Leofric realized he had no idea what to do, or where to go. Indecision froze him where he stood, and that indecision was terrifying. Never did he have to *think,* to *choose.* But now, he did. And he had only seconds, if the burning in his throat were anything to go by.

Where would Cosmo go? Leofric had no idea. If he hadn't fled the fire, what would he have done? That was easy—he would have gone after those he loved. Auro and...well. But Cosmo had not come to fetch them, and he'd already been gone from his bed. So where would he have gone? Only then did Leofric recall that Cosmo, no matter where he'd gone, wasn't alone. Ozias was with him. Leofric's brain switched gears, whirring along at lightning speed. *Where would Ozias go?*

And he knew.

Without any further hesitation, Leofric turned and hurried off through the smoke. He drew the neck of his tunic up over his nose and mouth, holding it there with his off hand, feeling his way through the smoke with his right. Down and down and downstairs again, though the animal instinct in him screamed against it, Leofric raced through the villa, empty yes, but filled too—filled with the crackle of flames and the billowing smoke oppressive, the heat growing worse and worse with every step.

When Leofric got to the bottom of the stairs, he saw a shadow of someone moving, off at the end of the corridor. *Ozias,* he thought. He hurried after it, furious. A flaming tapestry had him skirting carefully around the corner, chasing after the shadow. Leofric had a long stride, and he was gaining on the shadow swiftly. He knew he should be taking more care, he knew he shouldn't be risking himself to do this, but he had to catch up with the shadow. The smoke was getting to him a little, and he pressed the sweat-soaked fabric of his tunic tighter to his face.

When he got near enough to make out the person's form, Leofric froze in his tracks.

It was not Ozias.

It was Kato.

Leofric was so shocked that he lingered in place a second too long, and faster than he could think *I bloody knew it*—something struck him across the back, something heavy enough to punch the last gasp of choking breath from his lungs and send pain screaming up his neck and into his skull. His vision swam and he collided with something—a burning bench, perhaps. He never knew. After that, it was more burning, the stone walls spinning, smoke, and then feeling of the floor against his cheek. He didn't remember lying down, and his last thought was that despite the fire, the marble tile still felt cold.

Outside, Cosmo helped a burned porter limp to the Medicus, who had already begun setting up a station for the injured people fleeing the fire.

Cosmo had woken sometime earlier to an empty chamber, Ozias nowhere to be found. Something gripped Cosmo hard, some dread he couldn't name, and he'd risen swiftly and dressed in the first clothes he could find. Out in the halls, all had seemed quiet, and Cosmo had no notion of where Ozias might have gone, so he wandered the halls in hopes of being struck by inspiration. He'd been in the western wing of the villa when he'd heard it, a deafening *whoosh* and the smell of smoke.

Cosmo's instinct was to run upstairs, to shake the others awake and get them safely out, but then he'd heard the screaming—and without even thinking he rushed toward the sound. Now, looking around the area of the lawn the Medicus had claimed to help the injured. He'd been helping people evade the flames, and just now realized how much time had passed. Laela and Sorex huddled on a makeshift cot some few yards to his left, and Auro sat with Queen Dafina, his ear pressed against her back so he could listen to her breaths, checking for damage to her lungs.

Cosmo deposited the man he'd been supporting onto a cot and twisted back over his shoulder. He'd yet to lay eyes on Ozias, or Leofric. The flames had grown, shooting out of the windows of the villa, engulfing anything in their path not made of stone. The villa would be like a burned corpse after this, Cosmo thought, all the flesh and life gone, with bleached bone remaining.

Just like Ozias. He staggered with the force of the guilt that surged through him—both for the version of his brother that he couldn't save, and the bitterness and anger at the version that had saved himself. Cosmo stared at the flames, realizing that while he wanted nothing more than to spend his time making certain those he loved had made it out, the heat from the fire called to him. He knew there was no one as well suited to help them all as Cosmo. He jogged to the man organizing the royal guard, looking in vain to see if Leofric stood among them, and asked how he could help. The man immediately deployed his help for searching the second floor of the villa before the flames broke through the floors and rendered any rescue impossible. Cosmo didn't wait to be told twice and entered the villa. To him, the flames felt warm and inviting. Though his power was limited, he had always had an affinity for flames. Cosmo moved toward the stairs, doing what he could to pull the sources of heat and smoke deep into himself. As he walked, embers closest to him dulled and flames shrank. And Cosmo grew hotter with every step.

He made quick work of checking the second floor, and hurried back down and outside, reporting to Paulus, captain of the king and queen's guard, that he'd fully checked the second floor for any survivors or stragglers. And found none.

"Excellent," said Paulus, before turning and conveying the information to his men.

Cosmo twisted his head every which way, still hoping for a glimpse of Leofric and Ozias. He felt he was being pulled in a thousand thousand directions. Auro still assisted the Medicus, and he called to Cosmo for aid, and Cosmo hastened back across the yard.

After that it was a whirlwind of burned and terrified people, and Cosmo could not have said if four minutes or six days had gone by. Finally, he stood, wiped the sweat from his brow and said to Auro, "Have you seen Ozias?"

Auro gave him a strange look. "I had thought you were with him."

"What?" said Cosmo. "Why?"

"Leofric told me he lost track of you and Ozias! That's why he went back in to search for you."

Cosmo cursed loudly enough that several people startled and looked around. "He went back *in?*"

"Yes," said Auro. "I thought he'd found you and was just off doing—"

But Cosmo wasn't listening. He turned and sprinted across the yard, sprinted past the people fleeing the fire and directly into them, but before he could run back in a door burst off its hinges and the room within belched out black smoke, tongues of flame, hot ash, and two staggering sooty figures. Ozias, with Leofric draped over his shoulder, made it about two feet from the door before collapsing. Cosmo moved quickly, shouting for help and Auro came running. The two of them hauled Ozias and Leofric away from the damage, to a safe distance near the others being treated by the medicus. After a moment, Ozias rolled over coughing and retching, but Leofric did not stir. Cosmo dropped down beside him, listening for the beat of his heart. It was there. Faint, but there. He let out a gasp of relief, and almost jumped out of his skin when Auro touched his shoulder. "He lives," said Auro quietly. "I'll watch after him—I think your help is needed elsewhere."

It tore at Cosmo's heart to leave Leofric's side, but Auro was right. He could help the men put out the flames, using his grace to pull the heat until the fire died, piece by piece.

All at once, Cosmo realized it was noon. The cloud of smoke had allowed sunrise to come unnoticed, and unremarked. As everyone adjusted to the feeble light now coming through the smoke, Cosmo hoped none of those around him noticed the way he shook, the way the sweat dripping down his skin steamed, the way the grass burned black beneath his feet with all the heat he was giving off. Between Cosmo siphoning off as much of the fire's power as he could, and the men of the royal guard hauling water from wells and cisterns, and once a path had been made, the pools on the first floor of the villa, the fire was mostly out.

No one was in any further immediate danger. Cosmo had to get out, had to get away, had to discharge this energy somehow, or they'd have another fire to contend with, with his body at the center.

He staggered over the villa grounds and into the forest, searching for a brook a pond—anything. By the time he found one, Cosmo felt as though his very blood was as magma in his veins, he was a hell mountain about to blow. The pond was scarcely the size of a bath, and when Cosmo pitched face first into the tepid depths, it exploded in a searing cloud of steam, leaving Cosmo damp and shaking on the muddy bottom of an empty puddle.

As the captain of his Highness's Guard, Leofric was offered a private tent in the veritable city of them that had sprung up on the villa grounds after the fire.

At first, Leofric thought he'd been brought there to die.

Fitting, he'd thought, each breath like swallowing razors, every movement an unending agony. Fitting he should die in a field tent, just as Hamalcar had, though Leofric had to admit this one smelled better than any legion's Medicus after a battle. It would be alright to die here, he had thought.

Two days passed and Leofric realized possibly he had been a bit dramatic. He hadn't died yet, and if anything, felt a bit better. But he was still alone. "Hello?" He called, his voice like a death rattle. It had been barely louder than a whisper, though Leofric strained enough to shout. No one came. He wilted back into the pillows, exhausted, and slept for half a day.

By the end of the fourth day, Leofric was sitting up in bed, impatient and sick of the sick tent. He had reported what he'd seen in the vaults to anyone who would listen, but unfortunately a man hunt for Kato would have to wait until the security of the royal villa had been restored. No trace of the man had been found, and it was difficult to discern which of the royal family's treasures were truly missing, and which had been destroyed in the fire. Cosmo had assured him that Kryos and Cedras's grace both remained safely guarded.

The Medicus had been in to see him, and his family, and Auro too. All counseled patience, that his lungs were healing, and they just needed time. Cosmo barely left his side, and Leofric woke the morning of the fifth day to Cosmo soaping the side of his head. "What are you doing?" He croaked.

"Shaving you," said Cosmo. "Head to toe. That's what you wanted, right?"

Leofric tried to laugh, but it bloody hurt. "Who in the right mind would give you a razor?"

"It's good to see you feeling better," said Cosmo with a smile, but his eyes were wide with concern, red and sunken in his face like he hadn't slept. "You've been too weak to berate me for days now, and I found I rather missed it."

Leofric smiled and let Cosmo's touches lull him back to sleep again.

"They're moving everyone back into the villa this afternoon," Cosmo told Leofric when he woke the next morning.

"Excellent," said Leofric who'd had nothing but tepid tea and broth for a week. "Perhaps I can get a decent meal once the kitchen is back up and running."

"You can't swallow anything but broth until the Medicus examines you again," said Cosmo. And he shot Leofric a wink. "Believe me, I asked."

Leofric groaned. He felt fine. Mostly. He still got dizzy and winded walking to the chamber pot, but Cosmo didn't need to know that. "This is killing me."

"No," said Cosmo sourly, "You nearly did that yourself."

Before Leofric could respond Cosmo rose from the edge

of the bed and slammed down the bowl of broth he'd brought, spilling half its contents on the ground. "Eat whatever you like, I don't care."

"*Cosmo!*" Leofric tried to yell, but it sounded more like a growl. "Stop."

For a moment he thought Cosmo was going to ignore him, but instead he sat heavily upon the cot once again. "You could have *died,*" he said.

"I know," said Leofric. He still couldn't believe how stupid he'd been. "I was looking for you."

Cosmo shot him a look. "You know I'm a god, right? And impervious to flames?"

"I didn't say it was my most brilliant moment," Leofric said.

"So why, *why* did you run back into the fire?"

Leofric scowled, the words sticking in his maw.

"There is something you're keeping from me," said Cosmo angrily. "*Still.*"

Leofric took the deepest breath that he could manage. "You are right. I was worried for you, yes, but when I saw you weren't in your chambers I thought—"

"Thought what?"

Leofric hung his head. "I thought Ozias might have been after Kryos's grace."

Cosmo didn't answer.

Leofric kept his eyes trained down, waiting for Cosmo to react, but he stayed silent until Leofric looked up. Startled, he saw that Cosmo's face was one of concern, not anger.

"I thought the same," he admitted quietly. "I woke and he was gone, so I went searching for him, and then I heard the fire. I didn't see him again until he carried you out."

"Cosmo, your brother saved my life."

"I know," said Cosmo, taking Leofric's hand and bringing it to his lips to kiss. "And I'm very grateful."

"As am I," said Leofric. "I feel ashamed for being so mistrustful."

"You didn't know him," said Cosmo. "There is much I still feel *I* don't know about him."

"No, and I did not try," said Leofric. "The fault is mine."

"For the love of—will you stop?"

"Stop what?"

"Leofric, I swear, you aren't happy unless you're miserable."

"I don't—" Then Leofric stopped, with a grimace. "You're right."

Cosmo blinked. "The smoke has plainly addled your brain."

"Maybe," said Leofric, sitting up. He cupped Cosmo's cheek, stroking his thumb over one of his favorite clusters of freckles. "Though I think my madness dates earlier than the night of the fire."

Cosmo scoffed, but he couldn't disguise the pleased little smile, the twinkling in his eyes. "Oh?"

Leofric kissed him softly. "Yes." He paused. "Even so...can you forgive me?"

"For this? Certainly. For abandoning me on a mountain top..."

Leofric groaned.

"Pain?"

"Oh yeah," he grumbled, eyeing Cosmo up and down. "A rather large one."

"I was under the impression that you enjoyed pain."

"I do," Leofric allowed. "And you, you bloody menace, are my favorite."

He seized Cosmo by the neck of his tunic and pulled him in for a bruising kiss. His lungs seared when they broke apart, gasping. "Careful," Cosmo murmured. "Easy."

He encouraged Leofric to slide down until he lay fully

supine on the cot, then stood. Leofric thought Cosmo was actually about to leave, to insist Leofric rest. But instead, he looked down at Leofric with a calculating stare, and then whipped his tunic up over his head, casting it aside.

Leofric sputtered, "The medicus!"

Cosmo grabbed the edge of Leofric's blanket and cast it aside, leaving Leofric naked but for the linen bandages wrapped around his chest. "I doubt he'll bother us," said Cosmo as he toed off his sandals and climbed gingerly onto the cot. "He trusts me to tend your needs."

Leofric gulped, his hands already twitching to reach out and grab Cosmo's narrow hips. "Be still," said Cosmo. "Or you can explain to the Medicus why you're coughing blood."

Leofric debated, for a moment, if that might just be worth the risk, but ultimately, knew he would obey whatever Cosmo asked him to do. Nodding, Leofric lifted his hands above his head to grip the wrought iron frame of the field cot. It felt indecent, lying like that, on his back with his legs spread and Cosmo between them, wearing nothing but a band of linen around his midsection. The look in Cosmo's eyes was indecent, too, and Leofric wondered if his damaged lungs would survive what was about to happen.

But then, nothing did. He waited, and waited, his cock hard against his belly, untouched. Cosmo simply sat between his legs and *looked*. After how many times they'd been together since that first night in the cave on the mountain, Leofric had thought Cosmo wouldn't have any surprises left for him.

Fool, fool. Leofric couldn't have said how long Cosmo looked at him, staring, devouring every inch of Leofric with hungry eyes, but it felt like an eternity. His breath had slowed, though, his chest rising and falling steadily under Cosmo's scrutiny. His gaze was soft, and piercing at the same time. Cosmo still had not even touched him, yet Leofric felt flayed wide open. The first place Cosmo touched him was the place above his ear, the shorn patch of Leofric's scalp that revealed his tattoo.

Using the pad of his pinky finger, Cosmo traced the vines until his touch whispered over the shell of Leofric's ear. He shuddered, a full body shiver, and Cosmo immediately backed off. "Easy," he said again. And then his fingertip was back, tracing his ear, dragging over his cheek, down his nose, over his lips.

Slow and soft and measured, three words he never would have used to describe Cosmo's approach to fucking, but Cosmo had surprised him yet again. He lay still and let Cosmo touch. Eventually, he closed his eyes and floated in the darkness, relaxed and light, the warmth pooling in his groin as soothing and pleasant as sliding into a steaming bath.

He didn't think he'd ever been so aroused and yet so relaxed at the same time, melted into the cot under Cosmo's gentle, worshipful touches. Every muscle, every scar, every dip of his body, every bruise. Not one single inch of Leofric was untouched, except for the skin obscured by bandages. Even those, Cosmo brushed his fingertips over the edge of the fabric, tracing their borders to make sure nothing was missed in his perusal. Only one of his nipples was exposed, and it received quite a lot of attention, and soon enough Leofric was panting to the tent's canopy, and he felt a tiny bead of heat leak out of his cock and pool beneath it on his abdomen.

Aside from his wounds, there was one other notable exception—Cosmo had not touched his manhood yet, at all. Not even once. He could feel the air shifting, tiny breezes as Cosmo's hands fluttered around it, but never once did he connect. It twitched and leaked, and went ignored. Cosmo ran his fingers down the crease of Leofric's groin, stroking the inside of his thigh, down to the place behind his knee, his calf. His ankle. When felt Cosmo's lips at last, it was on the arch of his foot and he couldn't help the frustrated noise that slipped out. Cosmo paid the whine no mind, merely traversed the planes of Leofric's leg with tiny kisses, moving upward at the same agonizing pace. Leofric could have wept with relief when he felt Cosmo's breath, hot and warm as it gusted over his balls. *Finally.* But no, still no, and Cosmo nosed his way behind Leofric's sac, gingerly lifting his legs to drape over his own shoulders.

Staying still was more of a challenge after that as Cosmo used his mouth to worship his hole. Leofric was brought back to the night he'd pulled Cosmo out of the brothel, the way the woman on his face had felt about whatever sorcery Cosmo worked between her legs. He couldn't help but laugh, giddily, that Cosmo was *his* now.

Cosmo doubled down, concern for Leofric's frailty seemingly forgotten as he feasted, clutching Leofric's thighs, crunching him in on himself a bit so he could really get at it, and Leofric threw his head back and moaned. Leofric teetered close to the edge, but it seemed Cosmo was unwilling to help him over, at least, not yet. Leofric tried to cant his hips, to encourage Cosmo, to welcome his fiendish tongue, but Cosmo drew his mouth away, with a parting lick. Before he could complain, a warm weight blanketed Leofric's entire body. "Are you alright?" Cosmo asked, him, even as he sucked marks into the side of Leofric's neck. He bit down, hard, and then said, "Am I hurting you?"

Leofric bucked against him. "Fucking *yes*," he said, releasing the frame of the cot and seizing Cosmo's shoulders to roll them. They landed on the ground beside the bed. Leofric's lungs burned but he couldn't stop, didn't want to ever stop. He kissed Cosmo, tasting a hint of himself on Cosmo's tongue, and nearly spent against Cosmo's belly. Cosmo rolled them again, pinning Leofric on his back upon the ground. "You're supposed to be resting," said Cosmo, panting.

"I am resting," said Leofric. "Lying down and everything."

Cosmo nipped his chin. "I don't think this is what the medicus had in mind."

"No?"

Cosmo shook his head.

"Well," said Leofric, "If you don't fuck me, I'll have to fuck you, and I imagine that is far too strenuous for someone in my delicate condition."

"The medicus did say that you should be well enough for *gentle* lovemaking," Cosmo agreed, maneuvering himself between Leofric's thighs.

"He *what?* You didn't, you—*ohhhhhh.*" He broke off on a satisfied groan as Cosmo pushed inside him in one fluid thrust.

"*Fuck,* you're tight," said Cosmo. "Are you certain this is..."

Leofric rolled his hips, trying to get Cosmo even deeper. "*Yes,*" he said. "Fuck, yes."

"You are such a deviant," said Cosmo with something akin to awe in his voice. He drew out and thrust back in. Harder. Deeper. Leofric sighed, pleasure rolling over him in waves as he felt his body go slack. Cosmo gathered him up, held him tight and whispered, "I never expected this. I never expected you."

"Me—ungh—neither," Leofric agreed, wrapping his legs around Cosmo's waist, arching his back. He thought he could feel his bandage slipping, but he ignored it.

There wasn't much talking after that, as Cosmo moved against him, throwing his weight into every thrust, rolling his hips to change the angle of his cock, pounding and pounding and pounding until Leofric saw lights popping before his eyes, and realized he'd been holding his breath. Dizzy, his vision going fuzzy around the edges, heaved a great, gasping breath and came at the same time, with harsh yell and his vision whiting out.

Cosmo released a harsh, broken moan as Leofric's channel clenched around his meat, and he came in a great hot gush like magma burning through Leofric's gut. They collapsed in a delirious, trembling heap on the floor of the tent, and Leofric clasped Cosmo so tightly he feared some sort of rictus had set in.

Pain of the not so pleasant sort began to seep in as they lay in a daze, and Leofric nudged Cosmo off his chest so he could take in some much-needed breath. He sat up and examined the tattered bandage around his middle, which had been covering some ghastly wounds on his back from where the beam had swung down and nearly decapitated him. Cosmo gasped when he saw them, horrified. "Oh, *Fuck*—I didn't—"

"*Shhh,*" said Leofric. "I told you. I am *fine.*"

Cosmo cleaned them both up and rebandaged Leofric's torso, before forcing Leofric to lay back down on his cot. He then fetched him a cup of water and stroked Leofric's forehead. "I can't believe you let me fuck you like that," said Cosmo after a while.

Leofric didn't open his eyes, but he smiled. "Oh, you can too."

"Well yes, in general, but—" Cosmo sighed. "I love you, but for fuck's sake Leofric you are *such* a fool."

It took a moment for his words to penetrate Leofric's exhausted, oxygen deprived, cum drunk brain. He sat up so fast he nearly knocked Cosmo over. "You—you love me?"

Cosmo looked at him defiantly. "Of course, I do," he burst out. "Didn't you know?"

Stunned, Leofric let Cosmo force him back down onto the pillows, tucking the blanket around him. Cosmo seemed unconcerned by Leofric's reaction—or lack thereof—to his pronouncement, which Leofric probably should have suspected. He was talking now about plans to travel into the forest that night with his brothers.

"It's the last day of summer," he reminded Leofric. "We want to meet Cedras when he wakes up."

"Let me come with you."

Cosmo clucked. "If you can stand up without keeling back over, you can come."

Leofric scowled. "If I'm well enough to fuck I'm well enough for a walk through the woods."

"The Medicus disagreed," said Cosmo. "Gentle lovemaking, yes; trek through the wilderness, no."

Leofric eyed him suspiciously. "I suspect you of lying to me. And besides, you're hardly gentle."

Cosmo kissed his nose. "I'll be alright," he promised. "I'll have my brothers with me."

That was, at least in part, what Leofric was afraid of. They were like magnets for calamity, all of them. "Will you...will you come see me, after?"

"Of course." Cosmo stood, pulled on his tunic and turned to leave the tent. Leofric couldn't let him go, not yet.

Say it, you coward.

"I love you," he gritted out. "So, you better come back to me, you bloody menace."

The sun set on the last day of summer, and Cosmo felt strange. It was the first time in four hundred years he hadn't ended the season with a painful pull in his chest, urging him back to the temple. He didn't miss the ache, exactly, but the absence of it was discomfiting.

After leaving Leofric's tent, Cosmo found Ozias in the garden with Auro. Cosmo wanted very much to spin over his talk with Leofric in his mind, to replay his terse confession of love so he could be sure he could keep the memory forever, but he could not.

He had something far more difficult to address with his brothers. It was good that Ozias had saved Leofric's life, of course. It was good that Leofric had decided to trust him. But Cosmo hadn't been able to let go of one, tiny detail of the whole affair, one niggling question that remained:

Why had Ozias been on hand to save Leofric's life?

The answer was blindingly obvious. There was only one reason Ozias would have been down there, and it wasn't to search for Leofric.

Cosmo, Auro, and Ozias walked together across the grounds to the forest's edge. Auro was excited to go collect Cedras from the temple, but Cosmo could not catch his mood. When they were well within the forest, Cosmo summoned his courage. "Brothers," he called. "A moment."

Ozias and Auro turned, bemused, to see why Cosmo called a halt.

"Ozias, I have to ask you something."

"What is it?"

Cosmo took a deep breath. "Did you set that fire?"

Auro gasped, and Ozias went pale. "Of course, I didn't," he spat, his eyes angry. "How can you think that?"

Cosmo did not let himself look at Auro, who appeared beyond hurt at Cosmo's accusation. "If you did not set the fire," said Cosmo evenly, "Why were you down in the vaults?"

Ozias looked like a cornered beast, his eyes flickering from Auro's face to Cosmo's, as if weighing which he could bowl over and escape. Finally, he closed his eyes, covering his face with his hands. "Alright," he said. "Alright."

"Alright what?" Auro asked.

"He went for Kryos's grace," said Cosmo. "Didn't you?"

"Yes," said Ozias, looking ashamed. "I'm sorry. I didn't—I wasn't thinking."

"Weren't thinking?"

"It is hard for me to…" Ozias trailed away, sitting heavily upon a log. "It is hard for me to trust anyone, anymore. I worried about your plan, about your intentions. I thought, perhaps if I could get my hands on Kryos's grace, I could destroy it or—I don't know. Maybe I could be one of you."

Cosmo and Auro exchanged a look. "One of us?"

"Is that so odd?" Ozias asked, voice raw. "Kryos has proven himself a disloyal, unworthy brother. Or at least—that's what I thought. I don't know anymore."

"Ozias, what were you thinking?"

"I wasn't," Ozias repeated. "I just—I've been alone so long. The fire, the villa was in chaos, I thought, *now. Now. Or you'll regret it.*"

"And Leofric caught you?" Cosmo asked, fury rising inside him like a serpent.

"No," said Ozias, aghast. "I found him pinned beneath a burning beam. And I realized I could only choose one—myself, or my brothers."

"And?" Prompted Auro, hands braced upon his hips.

Ozias rolled his eyes. "And I chose you two, obviously."

Cosmo wasn't certain he believed the story entirely, but the sun was setting and they had only a few hours to make it to the temple before Cedras woke. Ozias walked a bit ahead of them, and as he stepped out across the temple's bridge, Cosmo flung out an arm to stop Auro following him straight away, and waited until Ozias was well across the lake. "What make you of this?" he whispered to Auro.

Auro chewed his lip. "I don't know why—"

"*Cosmo! Auro!*" Ozias's voice came from the temple. "*Come quick!*"

"What now?" Cosmo said, jogging through the shin deep water to follow Ozias to the temple. When he entered the single room, staring at the four plinths, he stopped in his tracks, because he did not understand what he was looking at.

The only statue remaining in the temple was that of Kryos, tall and domineering as ever. The other three stood empty. Auro's, of course, and Cosmo's. And...

This can't be, Cosmo thought. It was still summer, for a few more hours. This—this should not have been possible.

Cedras was gone.

Thank you for reading *Dauntless Summer!* **Wondering what happened to Cedras's statue?** Click here to read SAGE FALL, the third book of Harmony of Seasons.

Emmaline Strange is the author of *Mighty Quill*, *Crown of Aster*, and *A Walrus & A Gentleman*. She loves to write and read about smooching. She lives in Boston with her husband, dog, and cat, all of whom she loves to smooch. When not smooching, she can usually be found doting on her plants, baking, or watching far too much television. Ms. Strange is a lover of all things nerdy, from *Dungeons & Dragons*, to *Lord of the Rings*, to the MCU.

She enjoys iced coffee, long walks on the beach, complaining about her feet after long walks on the beach, and long sits on the couch to recover from long walks on the beach.

For updates on upcoming projects, come say hello on instagram (@EmmalineStrange) where she's always talking about writin', readin', and... well, not so much 'rithmetic.